Praise for *Sunrise Highway*

"Peter Blauner has created one of the most memorable psychopaths since Hannibal Lecter." —*The Washington Post*

"And just as Robles notes the empty Bacardi bottles and crushed Capri Sun juice packs littering the beach, so too does Blauner keep a tight focus on his regional setting." —Marilyn Stasio, *The New York Times Book Review*

"First-rate suspense, with a soupçon of horror in the Hannibal Lecter vein . . . You won't be disappointed." —Stephen King

"The prose is economical and precise, the setting well drawn, and the characters real enough to give you a chill the next time you cruise past a police car." —Associated Press

"Blauner excels with strong, realistic characters, believable police work, and smart, propulsive dialogue." —*Kirkus Reviews* (starred review)

"An action-packed and plot twist–laden thriller. Exploring such subjects as police corruption, misogyny, and racism, this is a page-turner of the highest order." —*Publishers Weekly* (starred review)

"The murderer is well developed and a pleasure to root against, evoking genuine anger and frustration from readers, who will find the book difficult to put down. . . . This fast-paced, well-told police procedural and thriller with a serial killer, conspiracies, and police corruption will appeal to fans of Reed Farrel Coleman and John Verdon." —*Library Journal*

"Unforgettable characters in an epic battle of good and evil." —*New York Journal of Books*

"Peter Blauner's bracing, suspenseful *Sunrise Highway* has everything you want in a thriller—a badass female detective, a relentless serial killer, and . . . Long Island accents? (Trust us, you'll be into it all.)" —*POPSUGAR*

"[A] sumptuously elegant tale that's the best dark thriller this side of James Ellroy as channeled through the classic film noir *Chinatown* or HBO's sterling first season of *True Detective* . . . Reminiscent in all the right ways of Roderick Thorp's classic *The Detective, Sunrise Highway* is a crime thriller extraordinaire, its pitch-perfect pacing equaled only by its superb characterizations." —*The Providence Journal*

Praise for *Proving Ground*

"Blauner's characters are complex and his prose is as impressive as his plot. His gritty portrayal of urban crime recalls the work of Richard Price and Dennis Lehane." —*The Washington Post*

"A great thriller . . . I just kept turning those pages." —Nancy Pearl, *Morning Edition*, NPR

"Edgar winner Blauner hasn't lost his touch, as this page-turner demonstrates. . . . Blauner has crafted two strong and complex leads in Natty and Lourdes and given readers an intricate plot that never feels forced." —*Publishers Weekly* (starred review)

"The murder of a liberal lawyer in Brooklyn puts his Iraq War–veteran son and two detectives on a collision course in this complex, character-rich tale. . . . A top-notch crime novel that avoids easy resolutions and is all the better for its unanswered questions." —*Kirkus Reviews* (starred review)

"With *Proving Ground*, Peter Blauner continues to prove why he's one of the most consistently bracing and interesting voices in American crime literature. A beautifully written and relentlessly exciting thriller." —Dennis Lehane

"Over the last twenty-five years Peter Blauner has proven to be a master of the urban dark side, his crime novels suffused with a knowing compassion for the bottom dogs who live in the minotaur's maze that is New York City. *Proving Ground* is one of his finest efforts." —Richard Price

"Peter Blauner's new novel, *Proving Ground*, is an old-school page-turner, as war-damaged army vet Nathaniel 'Natty Dread' Dresden and police

detective Lourdes Robles close in on the killer of Natty's father . . . and, maybe, each other. Taut narration, spot-on dialogue, and sharply etched action sequences make this one a must-read. I couldn't put the sucker down."
—Stephen King

"A new Peter Blauner novel is cause for celebration, and *Proving Ground* justifies the wait. This is a thoughtful, nuanced novel of crime and war and the human heart. Blauner's authentic and powerful writing is worthy of comparison to Richard Price and Dennis Lehane, and his story is coiled with emotional impact. Not to be missed."
—Michael Koryta, *New York Times* bestselling author of *Rise the Dark*

"Peter Blauner's first book in ten years, *Proving Ground,* is a showstopper. A tour de force of smart, gutsy, relentlessly entertaining storytelling that counts as one of the finest novels I've read in the past five years. Blauner has a painter's eye for detail, a playwright's ear for dialogue, and a film director's kinetic narrative vision. All combine to create a turbocharged reading experience. *Proving Ground* is a masterpiece of contemporary fiction."
—Christopher Reich, *New York Times* bestselling author of *Rules of Deception* and *Numbered Account*

"*Proving Ground* is a startlingly powerful tale of lost lives and lost souls with a crackling crime drama at its core. No one understands the NYPD, the backroom politics of New York, or the heart of the city like Blauner. No one."
—Reed Farrel Coleman, *New York Times* bestselling author of *Where It Hurts*

"Like Richard Price, he has a bone-deep feel for New York's neighborhoods, a talent for making his characters fully alive, and the gift of turning descriptions into moments of found poetry on nearly every page. He's pretty handy with plot, too. Blauner is a terrific novelist and *Proving Ground* is proof of it. Is it selfish to ask him to turn off the TV and write nothing but novels in future? We don't want to wait another ten years for a book as elegantly written and engrossing as this one."
—*Reviewing the Evidence*

ALSO BY PETER BLAUNER

Proving Ground

Slipping into Darkness

The Last Good Day

Man of the Hour

The Intruder

Casino Moon

Slow Motion Riot

SUNRISE HIGHWAY

PETER BLAUNER

MINOTAUR BOOKS

NEW YORK

Published in the United States by Minotaur Books, an imprint of St. Martin's Publishing Group

SUNRISE HIGHWAY. Copyright © 2018 by Slow Motion Riot Inc. All rights reserved. Printed in the United States of America. For information, address St. Martin's Publishing Group, 120 Broadway, New York, NY 10271.

www.minotaurbooks.com

Designed by Omar Chapa

The Library of Congress has cataloged the hardcover edition as follows:

Names: Blauner, Peter, author.
Title: Sunrise Highway / Peter Blauner.
Description: First edition. | New York : Minotaur Books, 2018.
Identifiers: LCCN 2018018911 | ISBN 9781250117410 (hardcover) |
    ISBN 9781250117434 (ebook)
Subjects: LCSH: Women detectives—New York (State)—New York—Fiction. |
    Murder—Investigation—Fiction. | BISAC: FICTION / Crime. | FICTION /
    Mystery & Detective / Police Procedural. | GSAFD: Mystery fiction.
Classification: LCC PS3552.L3936 S86 2018 | DDC 813/.54—dc23
LC record available at https://lccn.loc.gov/2018018911

ISBN 978-1-250-11742-7 (trade paperback)

Our books may be purchased in bulk for promotional, educational, or business use. Please contact your local bookseller or the Macmillan Corporate and Premium Sales Department at 1-800-221-7945, extension 5442, or by email at MacmillanSpecialMarkets@macmillan.com.

First Minotaur Books Paperback Edition: August 2019

10 9 8 7 6 5 4 3 2 1

For my mother

No crime if there ain't no law!

—THE DAMNED

PROLOGUE

He liked to have his house in order, which was why he'd never had a family or pets. He liked his routines and there was nothing wrong with that. Every day, in the summer months, he wore his father's old fire department windbreaker, with a blue FDNY polo shirt, khaki shorts, and flip-flops, so he could walk down to the beach without getting a chill from the ocean. When the weather turned, he had a half dozen identical blue sweatshirts that he wore with velour track pants and thick wool socks for going out on the deck that faced the Atlantic on one side and Jamaica Bay on the other. Fortunately, he only had to go out once a week for groceries at C-Town, because the settlement he got from the city after the accident let him stay home and mind his business. So naturally he wasn't going to open a door to a stranger in the middle of a hurricane.

The doorbell started ringing just after the first commercial break for the *Cheers* rerun. He didn't like sports or these new shows with singing and dancing contests, where crazy people screamed with joy and disappointment and there was no telling how things would end up. It was much better when you could anticipate and prepare yourself beforehand. Not that he hadn't been paying attention to the weather reports about this Sandy. He had the generator running and the storm windows his brother had put in latched tight, with foam and sealing tape around the edges to keep the air out. It gave him a secure feeling when he heard the little drops on the glass like the claws of hungry animals that would eventually give up and go look for shelter somewhere else.

The rain started falling harder at four. By sunset, it was a deluge. But the roof was new and tight. So he had nothing to worry about. Until the bell rang.

It was a soft, modulated two-tone, the same one his parents had put in when they bought the house in 1970. He liked it because it didn't disturb him too much when he had to get up and answer the door for a delivery. He ignored it the first time it rang because it was after seven o'clock, and who would be out on a night like this? It went a second time a half minute later and he reached for the remote to raise the volume. All his life he'd lived in Rockaway, maintaining his parents' house just the way they'd had it—plus painting the shingles every four years and putting in fiberglass insulation and a new alarm system—while the rest of the neighborhood was going to hell and the ocean was getting filthy. He could count on less than one hand the times a stranger had come to his door for a legitimate reason. Ten seconds later, the bell went a third time, like someone poking a dirty finger into his ear over and over.

He crossed his arms and crossed his ankles, and made himself all taut and tense as he leaned back in the BarcaLounger, wishing they'd just stop and go away. But of course, they didn't. The bell started ringing more frantically, the two tones on a continuous loop, so that he couldn't hear his show, couldn't think about anything except why wouldn't people just leave him alone, until he realized he was going to have to get up or else this would be going on all night.

As he went to look out the peephole, he could hear the wind howling and feel the storm trying to get in the house. Just standing by the threshold put the dampness in his bones. Someone was on his doorstep. A silhouette with long dripping hair. Like a wraith from a Japanese horror movie, with curtains of wild monsoon rain moving back and forth behind it.

"*Hello?*" it called out in a high shaky voice. "Is anybody home?"

He kept his eye at the peephole.

"I know this is going to sound crazy." The voice was girlish and, of course, untrustworthy. "But your house is the only one with a light on the block . . ."

She stopped and hugged herself, shivering as she coughed. Rain from her baggy clothes was puddling on the porch. Some kind of manacle was

on her wrist with a chain attached. One of those moronic fashion acces-
sories kids wore these days, like dog collars and rings through the nose
like a bull. He tried to see who else was out there with her. It was a trick
of some kind. The "okeydoke" they called it on police shows. Using an
innocent-sounding girl or a child in distress to get you to open your door
to home invaders. Unbelievable that someone would try to use a night
like this as a pretext.

"Sir? Ma'am? I know you're in there. I can hear the television."

She suddenly reached out and banged with the brass knocker. It had
been years since anyone had used it and he jumped back, almost slipping
on his mother's old throw rug. From the living room, he could hear the
laughter from the *Cheers* audience, reminding him of the warmth and
comfort he'd left behind. His tea and cell phone were on the coffee table.
But he knew it would be useless to try to call 911. With the way the government had been whipping people up about this hurricane, he knew the
police and fire department would never come. He was alone and totally
unprotected.

"Please," she said. "I'm begging you. It's not safe for me out here."

"Get away," he yelled.

It was awful the way his voice cracked when he was stressed and made
him sound more like his mother than his father. He should have kept pes-
tering his brother, the big New Jersey state trooper, to help him get a gun
a few years ago, instead of letting the subject drop when it was suggested
that he could drive to Pennsylvania or Florida and buy one himself with
just a driver's license. Obviously, *that* wasn't going to happen. But now
he was here by himself, abandoned and defenseless, with this *creature* at
his door, demanding to be let in.

"I know what you're thinking," she called out. "But someone is after
me. And if they find me, they're gonna kill me."

She turned sideways to look behind her and he could see a bump
under her shirt.

"Mister, it's dark out here. I'm pregnant and I'm scared. Cars are getting carried away by the water in the street."

He saw now that blood was dripping from her wrist. But someone
else could still be standing to the side of the door, where he couldn't see
them.

"What're you doing out in the middle of a hurricane?" he shouted. "Am I supposed to believe you just got lost?"

"If you let me inside, I'll explain."

"No. Leave me alone."

She lifted one foot, then the other. Then she suddenly flung her whole body up against the door. "Sir, I wouldn't be out here if I wasn't desperate." Her voice was clogged with snot and self-pity. "I know you want to do the right thing."

So what if it wasn't a trick? Did he really need trouble in his life? Some unwed pregnant teenager coming into his house and trying to make it her own. To soak his furniture and bleed on the fluffy, white bathroom rugs. She'd want to warm up in his shower and use the nice towels. Then she'd ask to go in his bedroom and look in his closets for dry clothes. Next thing he knew she'd be sitting in his BarcaLounger, using the remote to change the channel and watch her own programs.

Or worse, she would want to talk. She'd want to tell him about all the misery that happened in her life that had led to her being out on the street in the middle of a hurricane and he'd be expected to nod, listen, and say the right things in response without wanting to scream and jump out of his skin. Then she'd yawn and smile and put her hand on top of his and ask if it would be all right if she just stayed until the storm passed and the sun came up. And after that, he knew he would never be able to get her to leave.

"Get off my porch," he yelled. "I'm warning you."

He was standing a foot back from the peephole, clenching his jaw and bracing in case she hit the door again or started crying. He could hear the wind off the ocean getting fiercer now, pelting the rain harder against the side of his house, and ripping away part of the awning over the front door. It went flapping away, while his garbage cans went rolling down the street and sirens wailed in the far distance, attending to other people's emergencies.

"Sir, I'm begging you," she sniffed again. "If you can't let me in, can you please just make a call for someone to come and get me? I don't even need to dial the number myself."

From the living room, the *Cheers* crowd was laughing again, enjoying being in a friendly place where everybody knows your name.

"You think anyone's coming on a night like this?" He cut her off.

Why did he have to say that, pointing out his own vulnerability?

"Oh my God." She started to double up. "They're gonna come find me any minute."

"That's not my problem."

"But they're gonna kill me." She was weeping now.

"I'm warning you. I have a loaded shotgun here."

The shakiness of his voice betrayed the pathetic weakness of the lie.

"Shit." She sank into a wailing squat, pulling the hem of her shirt over her knees. "Why do people have to suck so much?"

"Welcome to the world," he said. "If you're not gone by the count of three, I'll shoot through the door. One . . ."

"No, no, mister. Please—".

"Two . . ."

He looked around for an umbrella or a cane to defend himself, in case she had accomplices about to kick the door down.

"Three . . ."

He shut his eyes and turned his back to the door, just wishing she'd disappear and take her sobbing and her dire needs with her. He braced again, waiting for the next plea. But there was only the sound of the yowling winds tearing planks off the boardwalk and sluicing water into the streets.

On the TV, the show was getting interrupted briefly for a weather update and a test of the emergency broadcast system. But then he heard the warm return of laughter and the tenuously hopeful piano music they used between scenes. He went back to his chair and told himself that none of this had really happened or mattered. A man had a right to be left alone. Who could hold you responsible for anyone else's bad choices? Or their bad luck. He used the remote to turn up the volume and drown out the sounds of the sirens in the storm. So he could concentrate on Sam, Diane, and their friends at the bar. A place where people cared about each other. They didn't make them like that anymore. What happened?

1

As seagulls swarmed like screeching boomerangs, Lourdes looked out toward the shore and saw two little girls making sand castles.

They looked to be about seven and five. Both with dark hair, olive complexions, pudgy knees, and the kind of bubblegum pink bathing suits Lourdes and her sister Ysabel had worn when they were young. The girls were digging with their bare hands instead of shovels and using coffee cups instead of pails to build their towers. And just like Izzy, the younger one made a point of falling on the older one's castle and wrecking it when it started looking too good.

A small wave came in and washed away the remnants, and the girls ran off, shrieking in fake horror, oblivious to the uniformed officers trying to shoo the birds away from the crime scene being processed some thirty yards down the beach.

Lourdes had just arrived at the tip of Far Rockaway, with her partner and fellow Brooklyn exile, Detective Robert "Beautiful Bobby" Borrelli. The call about a body washed up on the beach had come in about an hour before at the Queens Homicide Task Force and they had been crawling through traffic from Forest Hills because of city drivers' refusal to move over for a car with a siren.

Now they were finally at the shore, under a late summer sky with a threat of rain in the wind. A familiar ripple of dread unsettled Lourdes's stomach as she saw yellow tape blowing down the beach, threatening to catch on the gulls' beaks. The crime scene techs were working at the water's edge. It wasn't just the awareness that she was taking on responsibility for a body under the tarp, but also that the sight of the narrow channel behind them, an inlet dividing New York City on her side and Long Island on the other, set off a firecracker string of wounding memories. The fat girl who couldn't swim. Or stand to get her hair wet. Or afford to be seen in that pink bathing suit after she reached puberty. Though she was swaggeringly confident in most areas of her life, the sound of the surf could still turn Lourdes into a mass of quivering insecurities.

Don't you even think about pushing me in, blanco. She'd cocked a fist the first time she found herself poolside with her boyfriend Mitchell Vogliano.

How can you not know how to swim? he'd asked naïvely. *Half your family's from Puerto Rico. It's surrounded by water.*

Sand crept into her black shoes as she pushed through the gathering crowd of lookie-loos and marched toward the crime scene, B.B. grunting as he tried to keep up. She could hear the slap of rubber on concrete from the handball court nearby and the bark of a pit bull getting restrained by its owner. Project people living the boardwalk life. She noted empty Bacardi bottles, crushed Capri Sun juice packs, and what could have been used condoms or dead sea urchins as she stepped over the tape. Evidence of a party spot that could prove to be salient details leading to the cause of murder. If that's what this turned out to be. She remembered what she'd learned from weird old Kevin Sullivan when they were working together in Brooklyn a couple of years ago. *Never speculate, never assume. We don't know what we don't know.*

"Smell that?" B.B. looked at her sideways.

"What?"

"That rotten cheese thing—whaddaya call it . . . ?"

She wrinkled her nose. "Adipocere."

A word from the police academy classroom, but a smell from the end of civilization. Decomposing human flesh. Putrefaction, which sounded bad, replaced by saponification, which sounded worse. An odor that trumped all other odors on the beach—sunblock, salt air, gasoline from passing motorboats—and declared the supremacy of death over all living things. A smell that got inside you and stilled your own internal processes. Nature demanding deference. She saw the pit bull catch a whiff and start to pull on its leash, trying to get away from the stench. Not even considering going inside the tape now.

"Hope you had a light breakfast." B.B., still trying to be stylish in his pompadour and pinstripes, pulled a white handkerchief from his breast pocket and held it in front of his mouth. "This is gonna be ripe."

Lourdes wasn't sure how she felt about him these days. He'd been okay working with her on the high-profile murder of a lawyer in Prospect Park that got both of them promoted to the Homicide Task Force. But his aging Lothario routine was starting to wear thin, as he became less Marc Anthony and more Rodney Dangerfield. It wasn't just the graying of his hair or the thickening of his waistline causing a respect deficit. A seedy desperation had set in around the time his third marriage ended and his alimony payments ramped up. The old tricks weren't working anymore, but he didn't have the courtliness or the intuitive ability of a Kevin Sullivan to make up the difference. Instead he'd become just a little more crude and impatient as mandatory retirement drew nigh.

A young medical-legal investigator with her ponytail coming loose hustled away from the body, mouth askew and eyes streaming.

"That bad?" Lourdes tried to stop her with a smile.

The MLI covered her mouth and didn't look back. Detective Menachem "Thugsy" Braverman, the only Orthodox Jew in Queens Crime Scene and surely the only one who had once been a commando with the Israeli Defense Forces, came over, palms raised.

"Yo, yo," he said. "You guys might want to take a sec."

"What up?" Lourdes tried to see around him.

"Pit bull walker from the projects spotted something washing up on this shore at quarter past nine this morning." Thugsy nodded toward the dog and its owner lingering at the edge of the crowd. "Came over to take a look with poochie *et voila* . . ."

He thrust his chin toward what Lourdes could now see was a large black contractor bag with a few tears and strips of silver electrician's tape wrapped around it in several places.

"Can we tell anything yet?" B.B. asked.

"Only that the remains were inside a bag that was weighted down with rocks," Thugsy said. "We're thinking accidental drowning is unlikely."

"Copy that." Lourdes gave him a duck-face, lips pushed out like a bird's bill.

"We're also thinking it's been under awhile." Thugsy put a hand to the back of his head, securing his skullcap against a stiff breeze. "My cousin Shmuel used to be a lifeguard around here. The channel gets very deep in the middle. Whoever plunked the body down there probably thought it would stay down. But they've been doing some dredging this summer, and with the warm weather and storm surges . . ."

"Hey, who says climate change is all bad?" B.B. tugged on his collar, like he was playing a comedy club.

"Anybody contact Nassau County yet?" Lourdes asked.

She raised her eyes to the far shore, maybe less than a quarter mile away but a completely different jurisdiction.

The Island.

The name and the geography always seemed misleading to her. If you looked at a map, the land mass was separate from the rest of United States, mainly connected by bridges and highways that ran straight into New York City. But on the handful of occasions she'd gone to retirement parties out there for cops she'd worked with, it seemed like a far more representative slice of America than any of the five boroughs. Suburban sprawl and strip malls. Big flags, big cars, and big lawns everywhere you looked.

"Let's not get ahead of ourselves." Thugsy put a finger up. "Right now, we've got a body in Far Rock, so that's NYPD territory."

"Amen." Lourdes nodded. "Out of sight, out of mind. Any chance of an ID?"

Thugsy extended his arm, playing the gracious host. "Be my guest. Maybe someone you know."

Lourdes slowed her step as she moved past him, the smell threatening to overpower her as the crime scene detectives turned, big men in NYPD windbreakers who resembled high school football coaches without players to yell at.

She had noticed some of her brother officers giving her a wide berth these days, and not just because she'd gotten the bump from precinct detective to the task force faster than usual because of the dead lawyer case. Since her promotion, word had gotten around that she was being investigated by the Internal Affairs Bureau. A tip had been called in that she was using department resources for a personal matter. Her counterargument, if she ever got to make it, was that the disappearance of a detective's younger sister was legitimate police business.

Off a nod from Thugsy, one of the techs moved the tarp, revealing what was little more than a skeleton with patches of adipocere on it. The soft tissues had turned into what coroners called "grave wax": a grayish-white soapy covering that retained the basic contours of the body but made immediate identification of race and sex impossible. The arms were resting alongside the torso and the hands were crossed in front of the belly. The eye sockets were empty and the remaining teeth in the skull appeared to be clenched in a permanent grimace.

"The good news, if you want to call it that, is that the bag was taped tight around the body," said Thugsy. "Especially around the neck area. So between that and the grave wax, it's a little more intact than it might normally be."

Lourdes covered her own mouth, determined not to lose her lunch in front of a dozen other officers, most of them men who would talk about it for years afterward. She dropped into a crouch and forced herself to take a closer look.

"It's a woman," she said.

She caught the look B.B. was throwing Thugsy.

"And don't you be giving me the stink eye," she warned both of them sternly.

"What'd I say?" B.B. put his hands up.

"You don't have to say shit. I know what y'all are thinking."

Ysabel had been missing six months now. Every time a call came in about a female body, Lourdes found herself unable to stop swallowing until she confirmed it was someone else.

"And you know it's a woman because . . . ?" B.B.'s voice trailed off just as he realized Thugsy was shaking his head.

"Because she was *pregnant*," Lourdes said.

She pointed to the way the hands were clasped before the belly. There was a collection of small brittle bones between the fingers, which were not part of the adult anatomy. Almost like the victim was trying to hold onto a fragile little bird.

"Thugsy knows it too." Lourdes glanced over her shoulder.

"It's *possible*." Thugsy stooped his shoulders. "But let's not get over-excited and start talking about a second body just yet."

B.B. squatted beside Lourdes. "Say you're right. Wouldn't be the first pregnant girl, got herself killed." He bounced on his haunches. "Happens every day somewhere. If Daddy doesn't want another mouth to feed."

She resisted the urge to give him side-eye. There was a rumor that the third Mrs. Borrelli had asked for a divorce after getting a phone call from B.B.'s pregnant mistress—or, as she was known in Brooklyn, his *goomah*.

"But what's up with *that*?" Lourdes pointed.

"What?" B.B. hitched up his pants, damned if he was going to mess up his Italian tailoring by getting sand in his pant cuffs.

"Check out her throat, B.B." Lourdes took a pen from her pocket and aimed it. "Where did all those stones come from?"

The trachea was covered in a shell of whitish decomposed tissue. In all likelihood, the bag had gotten wrapped around the windpipe, keeping it from disintegrating. Little pebbles were lodged in the preserved tissue, clearly coming out from the inside.

"Come on, Robles, this is Detective 101." Thugsy loomed. "Look around. I already told you someone used rocks to weigh the bag down. Some of them probably just broke off and got stuck in the throat area."

"Think so?" Lourdes pressed her lips together and then relaxed them, avoiding the full duck for now.

She took out her pad and made a note about the shape and texture of the stones in the further recesses of the plastic.

"Here's my problem." She glanced up. "The stones used to weigh the bag down are pieces of cinderblock. The ones in the windpipe are relatively smooth. They're not the same."

"For real?" B.B. shrugged. "All right, so it's different stones. The bag's been underwater. There are a few rips in it. Stones from the bottom of the inlet got swished around."

"*Maybe*."

Lourdes stood slowly, hands on hips, taking in the depreciation of the flesh, the loss of identifying features and the hands in front of the belly.

"Hey, you still with us, L. Ro.?" B.B. asked.

Six months. Maybe that was long enough. Maybe getting pregnant was the reason her sister ran away. Izzy was always talking about how everybody was so nice to girls who were expecting. And that was why she wanted one herself. Maybe this body wasn't too tall to be her.

"Yeah, I'm here." The sound of the gulls broke her trance. "I'm all in."

"I'm thinking maybe we should reach out to Nassau County." B.B. stood up. "I'm remembering they had a gang case right before Memorial Day where MS-13 killed a pregnant girl they thought was snitching."

"Yeah, I remember." Lourdes shook her head. "But that was a one-off. I don't think anybody wants to make a habit of that."

"But if they did it to silence a snitch, it would fit your theory about the stones," Thugsy offered. "Seems like a definitive way to shut someone up."

Lourdes kept looking intently at the body. Still trying to reassure herself that it really wasn't Izzy. And then finding herself trying to imagine the final moments. The position of the hands over the womb. Like she was trying to protect the unborn child. Probably not where I would have my hands, if someone was stuffing rocks in my throat.

"Anyway," Thugsy said, "it's a new one on me."

"Me too." B.B. nodded.

"Makes you wonder what's up with Daddy," Lourdes said. "Doesn't it?"

"That it does," said B.B.

Lourdes straightened up and brushed the sand off her pant leg. The gulls nearby scattered and took flight as the other detectives shooed them away. The birds rose in a whitish mass like spirits deciding that the time had come to leave this sordid business of earthly living behind. The two little girls who'd gone back to the shore to rebuild their sand castles barely looked up.

2

Red flares lit the way into the woods. Their unflickering path combined with the low black sky and the sound of howling beyond clawing branches to make Kenny Makris think of a painting he'd seen in his seminary student days. When he'd solidified his conviction that sin and evil in this world were real, and the only question was whether to fight them with or without a priest's collar.

He followed the directions from a uniformed officer with a flashlight, then parked among the police cars just outside the crime scene tape. He turned the engine off and paused to collect himself. Someone was playing that pumping, noxious dance song on the radio, "Disco Inferno." The name came to him. *Christ in the Wilderness.* That was the picture in the monsignor's office. Surrounded by beasts and tested by Satan, but with angels on his side.

Kenny pushed open the door and stepped out into the chilly spring night, a thin and pale man of twenty-nine, stiff-legged and steady as a finger raised for an objection. With an oversized jaw and heavy-framed glasses on a head that seemed too big for his attenuated neck. His nostrils twitched, picking up the odor of human discharge. A young, mustached uniformed officer named Charlie Maslow wiped his mouth, done with vomiting. From deeper in the woods came the smell of pine trees and cigar smoke drifting from the silhouettes of detectives some twenty yards away.

One detached himself from the group and took his time ambling over, a stocky man with modish sideburns, a wide tie, and aviator glasses.

"You the new fish?"

Kenny recognized Detective William Rattigan, a.k.a. Billy the Kid, a.k.a. the Prince of Pain. He had seen the detective in the courthouse hallways and heard about him at the DA's office, usually referred to in quiet, wary tones. The Original Ninety-Four Percent Man—that was alleged to be his success rate in solving homicides. Though, given what Kenny knew so far, it seemed unlikely that any detective on eastern Long Island would have handled a hundred murders in the course of his career. This wasn't the city, with its street anarchy and fiscal crisis. Where the sidewalks were filthy and criminals were as free and rampant as the rats in the garbage-strewn gutters. This was the Island. Where decent people went to escape the chaos and the darker classes.

Up close, the detective was younger than Kenny had realized, maybe only in his mid-thirties. In contrast to the light-brown hair grown fashionably down to his collar, his face had a prematurely gnarled mahogany look. And even though it was a quarter to midnight, his lenses were tinted as if he'd worked in the darkness of the criminal world for so long that the distinction between day and night had lost its meaning.

"Counselor." The detective gripped and squeezed Kenny's hand. "I'm going to take a wild guess and say this is your first murder scene."

Kenny concentrated his strength into his right hand to keep Rattigan from twisting it. The natives' test. One of those crude little rituals to see if you belonged here. Even though the county had absorbed thousands of city refugees who'd lost jobs in the recent budget shortfall, if you weren't originally from the Island, you were automatically suspect. And after close to a year at the DA's office, Kenny, a son of Greek Catholics from Astoria and a graduate of Brooklyn Law School, was all too aware that he had yet to prove himself.

"Yes." He took back his hand and wrung it out. "That's why I wanted to come and see for myself."

"Have a stogie." The detective pulled a thin, inexpensive cigar from an inside jacket pocket.

"Not really cause for celebration, is it?" Kenny forced a smile.

"Don't be an asshole. It's to cover *the stink*. I don't need anybody else throwing up near my crime scene after Maslow."

"Oh."

"Brace yourself, Bridget." Rattigan jammed the cigar into Kenny's breast pocket. "Even for us old-timers, this is a nasty one."

Kenny followed the detective under the crisscross of yellow tape wrapped around the trees and out toward a trail through the woods, trying to ignore a growing tightness in his chest.

"How was the body found?"

Rattigan ignored him, taking out a small flashlight and swinging its beam haphazardly to catch bits and pieces of what the night had hidden: obscenities spray-painted on tree trunks, crushed beer cans amid fallen leaves, a black bra dangling from a spindly branch. More baggy-eyed cops trudged past them, heading out of the woods. Brighter lights were shining beyond the trees as Kenny, trying to get oriented, realized they were not far from the Shiloh High School football field.

"Girl named Kim Bergdahl, also known as Bird Dog, was due home by eight-thirty tonight," Rattigan said, a disembodied voice at least twelve paces up ahead. "By ten o'clock, the mom was freaking out, calling the local police department and organizing the neighbors into a search team. The little brother eventually coughed up a tip about Kim meeting someone behind the football field bleachers. Then the mom found the body near some bushes. That's her you still hear screaming."

Kenny realized his teeth were already clenched in anticipation. He'd thought it was just normal nocturnal disturbances.

"You've let the mother stick around the crime scene?" he asked with an involuntary shiver. "Is that standard procedure?"

"We keep sending her home and she keeps coming back," Rattigan said. "What else you want me to do, arrest her?"

Now that he knew what the noise was, each scream increased the pressure on either side of Kenny's head. As if a pair of hands were taking hold and turning him, making sure that he'd view things from a certain angle.

Rattigan's flashlight went off, leaving Kenny lost in the dark with only the football field lights far up ahead as an identifiable horizon. There was a stirring in the bushes to his right and a crackling of what he first thought were twigs and then realized was the cigar wrapper rubbing against his chest as he moved. The unseasonable sound of crickets filled the air, seeming to follow him.

"*Detective?*" he called out, his voice high and tremulous. "Where did you go?"

Rattigan's light clicked back on and arced over into his face, blinding him for several seconds. "Counselor, get your cherry-red ass over here," the detective hollered back.

Kenny stumbled toward the beam, roots on the ground threatening to trip him. The air was getting close and insects grazed off the back of his neck and crawled around the rims of his ears as he drew near.

"You ready?" Rattigan asked, with a hint of a gruff taunt.

The crimson tips of cigars and cigarettes revealed the presence of other detectives in a semicircle, smoke wafting over the deep-set crags and crevices of their faces. It made him think of a gathering of tribal elders in the dark, about to begin some kind of initiation.

"Yes." Kenny straightened the knot of his tie. "I'm ready."

"Meet Kim Bergdahl, age fifteen." Rattigan aimed the flashlight. "Take a good look, because she ain't getting any older."

The beam took its time so that all the details could register. Yellow hair with a bloody gash on the back of the head. Lowered blue jeans and a faux-Indian bead belt outside its loops. Pale white buttocks. An errant sneaker above the head. Familiar elements put together in an unfamiliar way.

"Come here." Rattigan called out, shining the light directly into Kenny's eyes again. "There's something else you need to see."

Kenny forced himself not to blink or shield his eyes this time, knowing that the others were watching and judging. He stepped carefully over the body and joined Rattigan beside a tree. The detective changed the angle of the flashlight so that Kenny could now plainly see the girl, who looked much younger than fifteen. Her blue eyes were half-opened and her head was thrown back, as if she'd been mid-howl when she died. She was grotesquely swollen around the mouth and jowls.

"Too soon to say cause of death." Rattigan cleared his throat. "We'll check to see if there was a full-on sex assault. But look what they did to this poor fuckin' child."

Kenny knelt as if he was back before the altar at St. Augustine's. "What is it?"

"*Look.*" Rattigan directed him with the beam. "No, look *close*. They jammed a fucking tree down her throat."

"What do you mean?"

The flashlight beam focused on Kim's mouth, which Kenny could now see was filled with twigs and leaves. On closer inspection, he could see the leaves were attached to stems, which were in turn attached to a branch extending from deep in the girl's throat, as if a plant was growing straight up from the pit of her stomach.

"*Jesus.*" Kenny almost fell backward.

"Okay, easy." Rattigan put a hand on his shoulder, steadying him. "I warned you not to get sick on me. Don't make me send you back to your car."

"How could they do this to her?" Kenny touched the ground with his benumbed fingertips, trying to keep his bearings. "I mean, how did they even manage to keep her mouth open long enough . . ."

"Right now we want to keep this part out of the press. So we have something that only the real killer would know about."

"Right, of course . . ." Kenny found he could not keep looking.

"So what do you say, counselor?"

"What do I say about what?" Kenny looked through the beam, trying to see where the detective had moved.

"What do you think we should do about this kind of thing?"

Kenny slowly stood, feeling slightly like a different man from the one who'd started up this path and then crouched a few seconds before. He looked around at the semicircle of more broken-in men with their weathered faces and glowing embers.

"I think we should do whatever we have to, to whoever we need to do it to, to make sure someone pays for this."

He tried to meet each gaze around him, daring all of them to laugh at his Boy Scoutish oath.

"So whatever it takes." Rattigan moved to where Kenny could see him, just a foot or two away. "Am I right?"

"Absolutely. Whatever it takes."

"Because you're either with us or against us."

"A hundred percent." Kenny nodded.

Rattigan offered Kenny his right hand again.

"Glad to have you on our side." He clicked the light off so that they shook hands in darkness. "Now take out that fuckin' cigar and smoke it already. You're in the club."

3

As soon as she entered the Queens medical examiner's office, Lourdes could feel the blood gurgling in her veins. On shelves before her were brains in jars and a glassed-in wardrobe with the bloodstained clothes people had been wearing when they died. From the next room came the sound of a saw grinding through bone, rising above the electronic syncopation of Southeast Asian dance music.

She rounded the corner and found Rakesh Wadhwa, the forensic pathologist, leaning over a naked woman's body, smoke rising from the saw in his hand as he labored to remove the top of the skull. Rakesh wore his long dark hair up in a man-bun, a mask over the lower half of his face, latex gloves, and a white coat suitable for both autopsies and butchers' shops.

The woman was more intact than the pregnant one from Rockaway. A little younger than Izzy would be now, and a little smaller. But her knees and thighs were similarly chubby, and her D-cup breasts were spilling off to the sides in a familiar way, as if trying to take refuge in her armpits. Not your baby sister, Lourdes's mind was telling her. No way she'd turn up here, even if she had been living out on the street or in a homeless shelter the last six months. The chances were literally ten million to one. Lots of people went missing and turned up alive. It only seemed like bad news had a way of beating the odds. Just the same, it felt like her heart was the size of a medicine ball as she forced herself to go over for a better look.

"Detective Robles." Rakesh tugged down his mask, revealing a trim mustache and goatee combo. "What's good?"

She came around to his side of the table. Just making sure. On a closer look, there wasn't even much of a resemblance. Tiny pleasures and sorrows had etched themselves onto this woman's face in a way that would never have registered on her sister's rounder and softer features.

"Life's good," Lourdes said. "But too damn short."

"That's why we're here. Right?"

The funky bhangra beats that Rakesh was playing encouraged her to sway her hips a little, reminding her of what a strangely lively place an examining room could be. Once you got past the particular anxiety of accidentally seeing someone you knew. All the clean, gleaming surfaces, sharp blades, and efficient drainage systems made her think of a kitchen at a high-end restaurant. There was a faint odor of chicken vindaloo in the air, as if a good lunch had been eaten close by. Rakesh himself was a smooth-skinned, dark-eyed dude from Jackson Heights, an outer-borough striver like her, the pride of a big New Delhi family. A little arrogant maybe, but sometimes she liked that. If she wasn't already living with Mitchell Vogliano, from the Brooklyn DA's office, Lourdes might have accepted Rakesh's earlier invitation to check out the hippest new dosa place on Curry Hill in Manhattan.

"I hear you got done with our vic," she said, glancing over at the sheet on the next slab, probably covering the remains from Rockaway.

"I wouldn't say 'done.'" Rakesh put the saw down. "We still haven't identified her."

"So what *do* you have for me?"

"Well, there are some unusual things about this." Rakesh turned professorial as he circled the covered form. "Typically, a body dumped in water either gases up and floats to the surface once it gets warm enough, or the crabs and fishes get their way and there's not much left after a few weeks. But here we have a perfect storm of circumstances."

"Perfect, other than her being dead, you mean," Lourdes said.

"*Quite.* For one thing, she was weighed down to sink to the bottom. And the water is very cold where she was, which certainly helps with preservation. For another thing, she was put in a bag made of very strong material and it was taped tightly around the body, presumably to make sure the heavier stones remained in place to weigh it. Then the bag got wrapped tighter by the currents. My theory is it only developed the rips recently, which delayed the fishes getting at the remains."

"Almost like whoever dumped her wanted to keep her intact," Lourdes murmured. "Right?"

"Yes. And the bag looked like it was covered in sediment, which also could have helped. Or it could have landed in a crevice and been dislodged by the dredging earlier this summer. Which would explain why the remains were so intact."

"So how long was she down there?"

"Hard to judge." Rakesh inhaled. "Could be a month, could be two years—because of all these atypical factors. We all know about the bog man who was buried in peat. I just pulled up an article about a body they found in a bay in Switzerland that had been under sediment for like two hundred years and was covered in grave wax, similar to your girl."

"So you got nothing for me?"

"Not *nothing*." Rakesh put his hands up. "I'd say we have a decent shot at extracting usable DNA from the bone marrow."

Manage expectations, she reminded herself. On the cop shows Lourdes was partial to, genetic analysis was always a slam dunk. In real life, not so much.

"Can you confirm she was carrying a baby?" she asked.

Rakesh shook his head. "Sorry, Lourdes. There *could* have been a fetus, but babies don't have enough fatty tissue for adipocere to form. So there were other bones, but I can't even help you prove there was a second body. I know you were looking for more."

"You don't know what I'm looking for," she snapped, more harshly than she meant to.

His gaze lingered on a space just above her eyes maybe a quarter second longer than necessary. Obviously, he'd understood there was a personal reason her cell phone number was at the bottom of the alert she'd put out a few months back to all local law enforcement, looking for any information about a missing female named Ysabel Robles, thirty-two years of age, five foot two, down to 143 pounds the last time Lourdes saw her, distinguishing birthmark on her left thigh and a tattoo of Alex Rodriguez, the former Yankee star, on her right shoulder.

"Sorry, hombre. I've been stressing lately."

"Yeah, I heard." He turned down the music. "You know, IAB talked to me about you using resources to look for your sister. Right?"

"And what'd you tell them?"

"I told them I didn't know anything about that and I'd only observed you being about the job."

"Thank you."

"Nothing to thank me for. You didn't do anything wrong." He dropped his voice and his brown eyes. "Listen, I didn't need to get into a hassle with the NYPD. But I'm not going to join in a witch hunt either. I'm just trying to do my job. I have enough work to do at this office."

"I can respect that." She nodded, a little embarrassed about letting her personal business get around this much. "I'm sorry if I crossed a line here . . ."

"You didn't." He looked up shyly. "But as long as we're talking about it, let me ask: Was your sister pregnant when she went missing?"

"No, but she talked about wanting a baby. Not that she was in any shape mentally to handle one." She sighed, signaling that she was ready to put this back on a strictly professional level. "*Any*way . . ."

"Anyway, if I had to make a guess at this point, I'd say this woman was down longer than your sister has been missing."

"What about cause of death?"

"The hyoid bone in the throat is shattered, which makes you think about strangulation as a possible cause of death, but makes it harder to prove."

"What about those rocks down her throat?" she interrupted, getting impatient.

His upper lip gave a little twitch, betraying slight annoyance at getting his rhythm thrown off. "It's unusual, to say the least."

"I know why I'd say that. Why do you?"

"It's not something I've ever seen before." He clasped his gloved hands. "You were right that the stones that weighed the bag down were different from the ones in her trachea."

"So is that how she was killed?"

"Can't say definitively." He shrugged. "It could've been done post-mortem. Her teeth are a little chipped. But not as much as you might expect them to be if she was locking her jaw, trying to keep someone from forcing rocks in her mouth."

"You know something else." Lourdes started to lean against a table in disappointment, but then realized a bloated old black man was already lying on it. "Don't hold out on me, amigo."

Rakesh took off his lab coat and hung it on a hook on the back of the door. "I only went the extra mile because it was you."

"Okay . . ."

"I sent a photo of the stones over to a marine geologist I know at the state university lab in Stony Brook. He said they don't appear to be rocks from the bottom of the inlet as Detective Braverman theorized."

"And?"

Rakesh picked up a specimen jar and shook it at her. A half dozen gray and white pebbles rattled inside.

"Look." He handed it to her. "These are too odd-shaped and irregular. In fact, my friend says they reminded him of the little aggregate stones he has in his driveway on Long Island."

"That's weird." Lourdes held the jar to the light, studying the rocks at a different angle. "Right?"

"People have driveways in Queens as well." Rakesh shrugged. "So I'm not jumping to any conclusions. But the whole business feels hinky."

"*How* hinky?"

"Look, given the circumstances, the first thing you think of is gang murder," he said. "The old-timers who used to work here talked about wise guys with canaries down their throats."

"Sure."

"But this is a new one. I called around to a bunch of other ME's offices and nobody had heard of anything like this either. And we're talking about people who've seen heads severed, eyes gouged out, tongues removed . . ."

"Yeah, yeah." Lourdes wasn't exactly squeamish, but she was in no mood to indulge these days. "Got it," she said. "Somebody's trying to send an old message in a new way. Same thing in the end, though. Don't snitch."

"Then why bother to sink her to the deepest part of a channel with the other weight?" Rakesh asked. "Know what I'm saying?"

The question stopped her cold. *Right.* Why send a message that no one else would ever see? There'd been something out of whack about this from the moment her shoe had touched sand in Rockaway.

"Damn," she said. "What's up with that?"

"The criminal mind is not my area of expertise." He tapped the side of his head. "It's yours. But there is one other unusual thing I wanted to point out."

"Don't stop now, my brotha. You're on a roll."

He nodded at two junior pathologists passing through the room and gingerly lifted a corner of the sheet over the Rockaway remains, exposing just the hands and belly. "See anything out of the ordinary?"

Lourdes shrugged, thinking there would be something seriously wrong with someone who didn't find all of this abnormal. "Yeah, Rakesh. We already established she could have been pregnant."

"Not that—*this*." He used a scalpel to point at the left wrist. "It's subtle but I don't think I'm making it up. The left wrist is just very slightly smaller than the right one. I took an X-ray and confirmed that the bones are closer together."

"Which proves what?"

"Malformation. Like she might have been wearing a restraining device of some kind for an extended period when the bones were still relatively soft."

"Or it could just be how she was born," Lourdes said. "Now *you're* the one reaching, Rakesh."

"No, I'm going the extra mile for you. *Again*." He regarded her frankly. "Because of the situation with your sister. And because I like you."

"Got it." She averted her eyes, at a loss for words for once.

Rakesh covered the hands with the sheet. "I should also mention that she had a hairline skull fracture that was partially healed, which indicates it was not a cause of death. A cracked right fibula that could be pre- or postmortem. And various other injuries that we're having a harder time assessing because so much of her is missing. It'll all be in my final report. Suffice to say she was young, but she'd already had a very hard life."

"Younger than thirty-two?" Lourdes swallowed.

"Again, I can't be definitive, but I'm thinking yes." Rakesh nodded. "Don't quote me on it, though."

She felt a buzz at her side, like her cell was ringing. Maybe the call that would put all her questions to rest. She swallowed again and felt around for the phone, pulled it out, pushed the button, and looked at the screen saver of her and her sister. The one she'd put on only after her sister went missing. But it was just another phantom vibration. Residual electricity from a lost connection. Registering by her left hip, in the place where Izzy usually poked her. From the time they shared a bed in the cramped old apartment at the Whitman Projects. Holding each other when the grown-ups were screaming in the next room. Or the police were breaking down the door. Lourdes holding her baby sister and saying, "Don't worry, muchacha, I'll protect you." When Lourdes was really scared enough to soak the sheets herself. "Look out for Izzy," Mami said. "Promise me you'll always do that. She's not strong like you." But Ysabel was such a fucking pest. And loco from before she was even a teenager and got her diagnosis. And then never taking her meds as often as she should have. *Mi hermana.* The wiggly little finger in the ribs. The little brown eyes following my every move. Going down with Lourdes to the Off Track Betting parlor on Myrtle Avenue to put five dollars on Lucky Day in the fourth race at Aqueduct for Mami. The two fat feet trying to wedge into my narrowest stilettos. The wrecker of my sand castles. Using Lourdes's photo in her Match.com and Tinder profiles. My family stalker. Where did you go?

Mami, during Lourdes's last visit to the assisted-living facility where her mother was gradually disappearing with early-onset Alzheimer's, had suddenly glared at Lourdes, like she was seeing her through the fog of the intervening years, and demanded, "*Why did you leave your sister behind in the park? Didn't I tell you to look out for her?*"

"Hey, Rakesh," Lourdes said. "Can you do me one more solid? And maybe don't mention this to IAB if they come around again?"

"Haven't I put out for you enough yet?" He tried to tease her with a smile.

"I want to give you a sample of my DNA."

"What for?"

"I should have done it already, but I couldn't make myself. Just in case we need to make an ID. For my sister."

"You sure you want that?"

It was only now, she realized, that she was coming to grips with the possibility that she would never see Izzy again. That she'd never feel that nudge in her side, that finger in her ribs again. Or worse. That the way she couldn't stop swallowing sometimes when she thought about her sister would become a permanent condition.

"Just give me one less distraction." She nodded toward a jar of cotton swabs. "And I'd rather know than not know. So can we just do this?"

4

Billy the Kid was leaning against a brown Ford Pinto as Kenny Makris pulled into the Homicide Division's parking lot in Hauppauge, "New Kid in Town" blasting from Rattigan's car radio. Still wearing tinted aviators under a gray sky where the presence of the sun was only vaguely implied behind the heavy cloud cover.

"Today I'm gonna give you a name," the detective said.

"Meaning you have someone in custody?"

"Yes, but that's not all I meant. I'm saying today I'm gonna help you make a name for yourself. In colored lights. The question is, are you ready to take it?"

Kenny wiped a spot off his Datsun's hood and pulled up the knot of his tie. "We've got a dead fifteen-year-old girl and a grieving mother. I'm here to do what needs doing. Just like you are."

Rattigan killed the radio and clapped him on the shoulder, almost knocking Kenny off-balance. "Atta boy."

While police headquarters had moved to Yaphank a few years ago, Homicide remained in its relatively anonymous squat building near Veterans Highway, nearly eighteen miles away, as if the department was trying to maintain some distance for plausible deniability. The building itself had no more character than thousands of other office structures on Long Island. Places so dull in appearance that no one would normally think to ask what went on in them.

Kenny followed Rattigan through a pair of slightly scuffed glass doors and into a brightly lit lobby with off-yellow walls, and without any obvious law enforcement symbols. A middle-aged woman in a floral-patterned blouse and dark slacks was in a receptionist's office to the left, smoking a cigarette and fielding phone calls.

"Dolly, buzz us through, will ya?" Rattigan called out. "I'll love you forever if you do."

She pressed a button without a glance his way. Rattigan walked across the hall and pulled open a black metal door that Kenny might have otherwise taken for a janitor's closet.

"Her husband was that highway patrol officer who got killed on Jericho Turnpike last year," the detective muttered, holding the door open. "They shot him while he was getting a plate number to write a fucking speeding ticket. The book was still in his hand when we found him. These are the times we're living in."

There was a rote quality to how he said the words, Kenny thought. Like he was reaffirming the oath they'd made earlier before allowing Kenny deeper into the inner sanctum.

"A couple things." Rattigan paused after leading him down a darkened stairway to the basement and out into a hallway with cinder block walls. "You asked if we had a suspect in custody before. And the answer is we do."

"Excellent—"

"He's in here."

Rattigan nodded to a door on the left with a rectangular window beside it. Kenny came over to look through it. Seated at a table inside was a young black man, well-built, with broad shoulders pulled back unnaturally like he was rear cuffed, a bushy Afro, an unusually long neck, and what appeared to Kenny's relatively inexperienced eye to be a light reddish bruise on a dark brown cheek. One of the heavyset detectives Kenny had seen at the crime scene was behind the man, arms folded in impatience, and in the corner an old green Peerless boiler was visible, with rusting pipes leading up to the ceiling, shaking and emitting occasional little puffs of steam.

"The boy's name is Delaney Patterson," Rattigan said. "His family moved into the area a couple years ago. In one of these low-income developments the feds threw up across the highway. I don't know how you feel about this forced integration bullshit but . . ."

"*Detective . . .*" Kenny put up a hand.

"It's okay." Rattigan shrugged. "The rooms down here are soundproof. But *anyway*, he was supposed to be some kind of badass football quarterback, who's gonna turn the team around because we were like two and eight the year before. But lo and behold, he screws up his knee at a scrimmage and is out for the season. So that's that. And instead he starts running around with the wrong crowd."

"And this connects with our little girl who has twigs and branches in her throat because . . . ?"

"Because they were both mixed up in drugs." Rattigan led him a few paces away from the one-way glass. "Kim was acting up because her parents were getting divorced and her mom's the town pump. And this Patterson because he's from the projects in the Bronx originally and he's still got family living there with the other savages. Easy for him to get pot, coke, whatever, bring it out here. We figure Kim being the white girl, knows a lot of the older white kids out here that Patterson can sell to. So she would have been the connect."

"And why the twigs and sticks down her throat?"

"You know how black guys are with little white girls. Maybe this Delaney tried something and she started yelling her head off. Then he decides he better shut her up and make sure she stays that way. Who knows how these people think? If you can even call them 'people.' All I can tell you is, this shine is good for it."

Kenny glanced back toward the one-way glass. "He already confessed?"

"Well, heh, not so fast." Rattigan rubbed the back of his neck sheepishly. "They don't call me the Hundred Percent Man *yet*. Our boy gave us a few things that are incriminating, but he's not giving up the whole enchilada. He thinks he's tough. Apparently he's had other interactions with law enforcement in the city."

"Is that why he already has that bruise on his cheek?" Kenny asked, adjusting his own glasses.

"Hey, I don't know how he got that. Maybe it's even evidence of the struggle he had with the girl."

"It looks a little fresh for that," Kenny noted. "The murder was almost twenty hours ago. And why is he not in a normal interrogation room with a lawyer present? How old is he anyway?"

"Just turned eighteen. And that's good enough for the state of New York. He's been advised of his rights and his lawyer's on the way."

"So we have nothing on him?" Kenny's voice cracked. "Why are we even holding him?"

His mind still stuck on Rattigan saying, "This shine is good for it." His sinuses made a sound like a car hitting the brakes on a rainy night as he took a long deep breath.

He had been asking around about Billy the Kid. The man was a mixed picture at best. A dogged worker, to be sure. And much admired by some of his fellow officers for his zeal and inventiveness. But Kenny distrusted inventiveness in cops. Especially when it led to wobbly testimony and judges reviewing cases on appeal.

"Relax." Rattigan took Kenny lightly by the elbow, leading him further down the hall and around a corner. "Billy the Kid's not gonna lead you off a cliff. I told you I'm gonna help you make your name today. And I'm always good to my word."

They had stopped in front of another room. The window was in the door here, instead of to the side of it. The room itself was clean and well lit, more suited to interviews than interrogations. A young man sat at a table inside, with a red bandana around his neck, a can of Coca-Cola at his elbow and the torn-off ring top on his index finger. Like Kim, the victim, he wore his greasy brown hair down to his shoulders. A yellow smiley face t-shirt peeked out between the straps of his denim overalls. His own face was round and milk-fed, with a sprinkling of acne on his forehead. An older man's beer belly was attached to his scrawny teenage frame. But what struck Kenny was a restless alertness in the boy's beady dark eyes, the tapping foot in an Earth shoe and the way he kept turning the ring top on his finger, testing the sharpness of the edge with the pad of his thumb.

"What's this?" Kenny asked.

Somehow "what" seemed more appropriate than "who."

"Our star witness, counselor. His name is Joseph Tolliver, but everyone calls him J. Or Joey T."

"And who is he?"

"The son of a police officer from the city, who moved out here a few years ago. Originally from Queens, I believe. Like yourself."

Kenny turned and cocked an eyebrow. "And how did he come to be a witness in this case?"

"Simple. He told his father what he saw last night, and his father told me."

"And what is it that he saw, detective?" The knot of Kenny's tie suddenly seemed too snug against his larynx.

"He saw Delaney Patterson go in the woods with Kim and then come out a few minutes later without her," Rattigan said. "About a quarter after eight. Fifteen minutes before Kim is supposed to be home, a half dozen blocks away."

"Which fits in with our timeline. Maybe a little too well."

"What's your problem, counselor?" Rattigan tucked his chin down. "I'm handing this to you on a silver platter."

"That's what worries me. I won't suborn a witness and abet perjury. How credible is this young man anyway?"

"I already told you. He's the son of a cop."

Kenny snorted. Some of the worst bullies and youngest alcoholics he'd known at St. Augustine's were the sons of police and corrections officers. He studied this Joey T. more carefully through the glass, not sure if this was a one-way too. The boy stopped rubbing his thumb along the edge of the ring and then picked his nose. He studied the result and then met Kenny's eye with a faintly insolent half smile.

"And how did he just happen to be in the woods behind the football field?" Kenny asked.

"Well . . ." Rattigan gave a good-natured wheeze that never quite turned into a laugh. "That's where it gets a little bit tricky."

"I don't like the sound of that."

"This is the real world, counselor. When people are hanging around areas where criminal activity takes place, it's not usually because they're looking for a quiet place to do their homework."

"All right. Out with it."

The detective sucked his teeth and winced a little. "Could be worse. We think he might have been mixed up in buying and selling drugs like the rest of them. Which is why he would've been there, waiting to buy from Patterson as well. But he's basically a good kid."

Inside the room, Joey Tolliver made a casual flicking motion with his fingers and then took a long sip of his Coke.

"*A good kid*," Kenny repeated. "Has he ever been arrested?"

"Not as an adult. He's just seventeen. Anything that happened before would be sealed as part of his juvenile record."

"And what's in his juvenile record?"

"Kid stuff." Rattigan showed capped front teeth as he curled his lip. "Breaking into people's houses. Penny-ante pot dealing. The defense would never even know to ask."

"*I'm* asking."

"And I just told you." Rattigan suddenly turned angry. "This isn't *The Bells of St. Mary's* and you ain't Bing fucking Crosby. All right?"

"I just don't want to be surprised." Kenny sniffed, trying to stand his ground. "We're talking about the depraved murder of a child. It's going to keep being in the news for months. Someone is going to spend the rest of their life in prison for it. We have to make damned sure we get it right."

Rattigan placed a finger firmly against Kenny's chest.

"Listen to me," he said. "I heard you were studying for the clergy, so let me put this in a way you can understand. This is what we do here. It's why we have a saying: 'We deal with our little demons so we can beat the devil.'"

"I'm not naïve, detective. I just want to know what kind of demon we're dealing with."

"We're dealing with someone who witnessed the murder of a blond-haired blue-eyed little girl and is going to help us make someone pay for it."

"I thought you said he only saw Patterson go into the woods with Kim and come out without her."

"He's only just started talking." Rattigan's eyes seemed to dim behind his lenses. "Who knows what else he'll give us?"

Kenny lowered his voice and turned his back to the door, in case the boy could read lips. "Are we absolutely sure Mr. Tolliver wasn't more involved himself?"

"This is a fine young man, who's made a few minor mistakes and wants to straighten himself out. So what we're gonna do is, we're gonna white-hat him and ride off into glory. And then you're going to thank me every day for the rest of your life. Remember what we said: whatever it takes."

Kenny turned and saw Joey still smiling at him. As if he'd already seen the woman Kenny intended to marry dancing somewhere without her clothes on.

"What happened to this poor little girl was the worst thing that's happened here in years." Rattigan was poking him more sharply now. "It's a nightmare not just for her family, but for everyone else's. Even with us keeping this fucked-up thing with the leaves and twigs out of the press, mothers are afraid to let their kids out of their sight. People are locking their doors. This is how homes lose their value. You put away this smoke and let people sleep sound again, you'll be made for life."

"I'm not doing this job just to make a name for myself, detective." Kenny waved Rattigan's finger aside.

"Hey, me too." The detective raised his hands in mock innocence. "All I'm saying is, it'd be nice to find yourself sitting behind the DA's desk someday. Am I right?"

"I just don't want to white-hat the wrong man."

"Oh for the love of God." Rattigan had one hand on the doorknob and the other on Kenny's back, pushing but not that hard. "We have a whole system to make sure that doesn't happen."

5

Lourdes entered the apartment with a hand on her holster.

"I have a report of suspicious activity at this location," she announced. "Sir, keep your hands where I can see them and don't move without my permission. I have a warrant to search the premises."

She cased the bedroom, checked the closet, and hit the bathroom. She emerged two minutes later wearing her old blue uniform shirt and police hat and nothing else, except for a pair of off-duty handcuffs hanging off her fingertips.

"Sir, get over on that couch and assume the position," she told Mitchell Vogliano. "That's an order from the New York City Police Department."

"My day was fine, Lourdes, how was yours?" Mitchell looked up from the living room table, where his files were in orderly stacks.

"Sir, when I need your mouth, I'll let you know. Now just lie on your back and put your hands above your head."

He complied with a head shake as she snapped the bracelets on his wrists and straddled his thighs.

Some of the more macho guys she worked with gave her shit about moving in with a skinny pale lawyer with a long nose, a high forehead, and no butt to speak of. At times, she was puzzled about what she was doing with him herself. Most of her previous men—and there'd been *a lot*—were your crazysexycool bad boy types. Mitchell was a softer proposition. A nice Italiano from Bay Ridge who'd gone to Cardozo Law School, loved his parents, hated the Mafia, and was happier handling white-collar cases than her kind of street crimes at the Brooklyn DA's office. More than once, she'd found herself looking over while he was making dinner for her and wondering when she was going to start getting restless with him. Or maybe she just didn't trust anyone who acted that good. But then he'd show he could be hard as well and that would keep her satisfied, at least for a while.

"Okay, I'm gonna search you now to see if you have a weapon." She unzipped his fly and started fishing around. "What the hell do you call *this*?"

"Not much. My girlfriend's been working all the time."

She reached in. "Is this thing loaded?"

"What does it look like?"

"Sir, I am going to ask you to submit to a field test." She undid the buttons of her uniform shirt. "You have the right to remain silent while I administer it."

"What's the charge?"

"That's what I'm trying to determine." She took him in hand and rubbed the best part of him against where she was getting warm and soft. "By the way, you have the right to an attorney."

"I am an attorney."

"*Santo y bueno.* Well and good."

She took a deep breath like she was standing at the edge of a seventy-degree pool on a broiling day, not worrying about her hair or how her butt looked, and then slowly guided him in. As her senses started to fill, she heard him gasp and groan.

"Uh-oh, am I crushing you?" She raised her hips.

"No, stay right where you are." He touched her sides, settling her back onto him. "Give me all of you. Are you using . . ."

"Just shut up and fuck me, Mitchell. Okay?"

She touched the tip of her tongue to a small bead of perspiration forming on his high, pale forehead. He laughed as she began to grind. Humping away the cares of the day. Your faithful public servant on the job.

"Kiss me," Mitchell said, soulful brown eyes staring up imploringly.

She dive-bombed him with her lips and then put a hand over his mouth. Getting down to some serious wild-ass humping as he grew firmer and stronger inside her. They wrestled, chest to chest, thighs on thighs, getting good and sweaty until she felt herself about to come. Then wouldn't let herself. *Give me all of you,* he said. But what would that leave for her?

She started to sit up, to feel more in control.

"Hey, where you going?"

He looped his cuffed hands around the back of her neck, and pulled her back down into the pleasurable chaos again. Where he could get to places deep inside her that no one else could reach. Terrifying her with the thought of losing control again. She bucked and squirmed, not wanting to yield that easily. She'd seen what happened to other women who gave up everything and never really came back to what they were. Not her. No way. Except for maybe right now. When her brain was switching off, time had lost its meaning, and she heard herself cry out like a woman about to drown, going under and joining the rush of life beneath the surface.

"*Guau.*" She threw her head back after they were done, damp ringlets sticking to her temples. "Now that's what I call . . . decent."

"That's big of you, Lourdes."

"No, it was big of you." She rolled off him and smiled, not the first time she'd said it. "Least it was until a second ago."

"So does this mean you had a great day or a shitty one?"

"Why does it mean anything?" She sat up, deliberately not looking at him. "Maybe I just came home and felt like getting laid."

She started to button her shirt, glimpsing the lights of the Verrazano-Narrows Bridge glittering across New York Harbor, connecting the land mass of Brooklyn to Staten Island. There were some definite drawbacks to living in a fifth-floor walk-up, in a Bay Ridge apartment building owned and managed by Mitchell's uncle, but she had to admit you could not beat that view.

"Come on, Lourdes." Mitchell reached after her as she stood up. "What gives? You only want to throw down like that when you want to celebrate something or you want to forget."

"I think I need a drink."

She went into the kitchen, conscious of his eyes on her ass, as she pulled down on her sweat-stuck shirttails.

"There's still chicken in the refrigerator," he called after her. "On the off chance that you might want to eat something first."

"Fucking Nassau County, man," she said, letting the cool air waft over her as she studied the leftovers and the half-empty Chardonnay bottle on the top shelf.

"What about it?" She could hear him zipping up behind her.

"I told you about that woman washed up in Far Rockaway."

"Yeah, they had it on *New York 1* today at the office. Nothing about rocks in the mouth."

"Yeah, we're holding that back. But fucking Nassau County Police called our chief of department, tryna say it's their case."

"*Wha?*"

His white boy impression of a hood rat squawk made her laugh despite the fact that she'd been ready to punch through a wall a half hour ago. "I got the message right after I left the ME's office," she said. "They want everything we have so far."

"On what basis?"

"They say it looks like a couple of cases they have on their side of the Nassau-Queens border."

"Like a pattern?" She heard him sit up abruptly. "For real?"

"Yeah, that's what I said. 'How come this is the first we're hearing about it?'" She started to shiver and took the chicken out. "But as soon as I started asking questions, everyone was like, 'Whoa, whoa, Robles. Don't start throwing around "serial killer." We don't know what this is. We're just looking into it.' So I don't know what they've got on their side. I don't know if it's more bodies found wrapped in plastic, or more stones down the throat. I just know no one's telling me shit at a time when IAB's totally on my back. And I don't like it."

She put the leftovers on the kitchen counter and stared discontentedly at the carcass in Saran Wrap. "And it looks like you took the skin off this bird. What's up with that, Mitchell?"

"You said, 'Chicken skin is the devil's work.'"

"You tryna say I'm fat?" She parked herself on a high stool and rocked from side to side, conspicuously keeping her back to him.

"No . . ."

"Sheeit." She plucked off the wrapping with her chipped red nails. "How y'all going to feel if my ass ever did get pregnant?"

"I guess that answers what I was trying to ask before."

"Which was?"

"Did you put in your diaphragm, when you went in the bathroom?"

"Mind your goddamn business." She started eating with her fingers, not needing to be anybody's example of shining motherly grace right now.

"That's not my business?"

"How did we get off on this anyway?" she asked, kicking her bare legs like a bored twelve-year-old in a classroom. "We were talking about my case."

"Right."

She could tell without even looking at him that he had that hang-dog expression he got when he was disappointed by her.

"You want to talk about one of your cases?" She went back to gnawing on her chicken leg. "That's fine. How's health care fraud?"

"It's the same. More X-rays ordered that nobody needs and more pills prescribed than anyone needs to take. Everybody's ripping everybody else off, and no one's going to prison. But we're prosecutors so we prosecute."

She turned back to the plate and squirmed some more, thinking she should have at least taken out the diaphragm before she started eating.

"Anyway, I don't feel like talking about my work," he said.

"Fine."

She hoped this wasn't about to turn into one of *those* conversations. Sometimes he was more like the girl in the relationship, the way he always wanted to talk about family and where this was going. It was one of the things she liked about him sometimes, and one of the things she couldn't stand at others. He was thirty-six years old and still had dinner with his folks at the same pasta place on 86th Street every Sunday night. Hung out with his two sisters and his brother *voluntarily*. Went to freaking struffoli parties at their houses in New Jersey and Westchester, where they made wine and pastries and played with his rug rat nephews. And never talked about work.

Everyone was so nice to her, which made it even worse when she didn't know what to say around them. And that, in turn, made her resentful because it meant she had to try to change her behavior and be just as nice when she didn't really feel like it. In her family, people had their own orbits. Which was why her father was in prison for life. Her mother was at the assisted-living facility, senile at sixty. And her baby sister, who'd idolized her so much that she'd lost seventy pounds so she could look more like Lourdes, had gone off her meds and disappeared to God knows where. And that was the gene pool Mitchell wanted her to dive into.

Part of her thought it would be nice—to be like the couples with kids on TV. But another part of her said, "Fuck that, daddy." Her life was where she wanted it right now. She was a good detective, who helped other families. Then she got to go home and fuck her boyfriend on the couch and eat chicken with her bare hands.

"So what's the next step?" Mitchell exhaled, resigned for now.

"The bosses from our department are talking to the bosses from Nassau about forming some kinda half-assed serial killer task force so they can step on our lawn and supposedly we can step on theirs. B.B. says I shouldn't beef, since I already got IAB looking at me. But I don't trust those white-bread suburban motherfuckers."

"And what does the ME say about eliminating the possibility this Rockaway woman could be your sister?"

She finished stripping the meat off the bone and dropped it on the edge of her plate. Then wiped her mouth with the back of her hand. She waited for him to criticize her manners, then bowed her head in silent gratitude. *My man gets me sometimes.*

"Nothing definitive for at least a couple of weeks." A little appalled at herself, she reached for a paper towel. "I told you I let them swab me, right?"

She dabbed her lips, worrying he'd realize it was Rakesh who did the swabbing and get jealous. He'd been a little suspicious when she mentioned her visit to the ME's office the other day. Instead, he came over and stood close behind her. She could feel his warm breath drying the curls on the back of her neck and found herself yearning for his hands on her breasts.

"I'm sorry, Lourdes. I know how hard this is for you."

"It's all right." She used a different paper towel to wipe defiantly at a wet spot forming in the corner of her eye, damned if she'd use the same one with the chicken grease. "I'm not crying or anything."

"Of course not." He kissed her behind the ear. "You're holding up better than I would have. But whenever you want to talk about it, I'm down."

"Nah, I'm over talking. What do we got in our queue for streaming?"

"We're caught up on *Master of None* and *Longmire*. Any interest in that *Handmaid's Tale?*"

"Yeah, fuck that dystopian baby mama shit. I'm not about it. I think I'd rather have sex again." She looked over her shoulder and undid the top two buttons of her shirt. "Can you handle that?"

He held up his hands as she turned around. "Could we at least take the cuffs off this time?"

6

At close range, Kenny was struck, again, by the difference between the boy's puffy features and the hungry roaming intelligence under his hooded lids. It was as if there was an older, more sharply observant man hidden inside the younger, more somnolent one. The eyes danced over the top of the menu, quick and alert, scanning the prices, monitoring Kenny's expression and reading the face of each person who came and went.

"Can I get a drink?" Joey Tolliver asked in a low deadpan, keeping the menu up like a barrier so he could continue to watch without being seen.

"No."

"Why not? I'm about to turn eighteen. I got my driver's license and everything."

"Look where we are."

They were having a victory lunch at a steak house called the Brazen Fox, just around the corner from the county courthouse. White table-cloths, brass rails, Budweiser and Schaefer at the taps, Jimmy Carter grinning on the TV in the corner. It was one of the prime gathering spots for the men who held the real power in this part of Long Island. The county executive often held staff meetings at a booth in the back and had hosted the governor here. Council members and assemblymen hovered around the salad bar. William Rattigan and a half dozen other detectives from Homicide were carousing loudly at the bar. And the district attorney himself, Philip O'Mara, the great Irish tenor, was holding court at his banquette, accepting congratulations from minions about the sudden unexpected conclusion to one of the most horrendous and notorious murder cases in the county's history.

"Look around," Kenny said. "These are people who can do you a lot of good in your life. Do you want to make the wrong impression, by being seen drinking at lunch?"

The boy loosened his tie and brushed at hair that was no longer covering his ears. Normally he would have been at his high school graduation today. But circumstances being what they were, Joey had to appear before the grand jury today instead, previewing his testimony as the prosecution's star witness in the Kim Bergdahl murder case. And, Kenny Makris had to admit, the boy had risen to the occasion splendidly, answering questions in a clear forthright voice, meeting the eye of each grand juror, telling the story of seeing Delaney Patterson in the woods in such vivid, believable detail that as soon as word had leaked to the defense about what he'd said, Patterson's lawyer had immediately asked for a meeting in the judge's chambers and had accepted the prosecution's plea deal of a twenty-five-year-max sentence in lieu of rolling the dice and facing a potential life term at the end of a public trial.

"*They're* drinking at lunch." The boy glanced toward Rattigan and the other detectives raising mugs and importuning waitresses.

"They're cops. What do you expect?" Kenny shrugged.

"And *he's* drinking." Joey turned his attention to the DA, who was raising a glass of champagne with his family and subordinates, his red face a stark contrast with his centurion's helmet of white hair.

"A lot of people from the office are here. He wants to share in the good feeling about the result."

Joey's acne-marked cheek bulged out from the pressure of his tongue poking against it, then sunk back. "So why aren't *you* drinking?"

"Maybe I'm trying to set a better example for you." Kenny unfolded his napkin and set it on his lap.

After a rough start, he'd started to like the boy. An outsider from Queens, like himself. And not a natural easy presence either. But someone who had to work for respect. They'd bonded when they learned they'd both been wrestlers at some point in high school, though Joey was of shorter and bulkier stock. They both understood that winning was not about the ability you were born with, but about practicing and refining, feigning and anticipating, and recognizing opportunities where others just saw dead ends.

"I see a lot of promise in you," Kenny said. "I know you had it rough growing up sometimes, but this is a time to turn it around . . ."

The boy's eyes became distant, as if he was thinking of something else. Possibly the fact that neither of his parents had accompanied him to court. The father was supposedly a fine man on the job, Rattigan had said. But don't ask what goes on at that home.

"You could do a lot with your life." Kenny leaned forward. "We've managed to keep your name out of the paper, by taking the plea instead of going to trial. So you can be anything that you set your mind to. A lot of young men like you go into the military and get straightened out . . ."

A small burl formed in the corner of Joey's mouth as he returned the stare, present again. "I did do good for you with the grand jury, didn't I?"

"Yes, of course. You were quite helpful."

"*Helpful?*" The corners of his eyes crinkled in a way that made him look a good ten years older. "I made your whole fucking case and spared you the time and expense of a public trial. Which you could have lost."

"Keep your voice down."

"You know it's true." The eyes grew steadier. "I put that black dude at the scene at the right time and the right place for you. I gave you the details about him brushing leaves and twigs off his hands as he walked out of the woods. And this morning I threw in that thing where I heard Patterson saying, 'Shut that white bitch up,' didn't I?"

It felt like the table they were sitting at had started to list and some of the implements had begun to imperceptibly slide toward Kenny.

"All you were asked to do was tell the truth. And as far as I'm concerned, that's *all* you did."

"Yeah, right."

The boy turned away from him, just in time to see the DA raising his champagne glass in tribute and gratitude to the two of them.

"He's running for reelection next year, isn't he?" Joey said. "Is it his sixth or seventh term? Must be—what do you call it?—a 'feather in your cap' too."

Kenny paused; what kind of teenager followed local politics this closely?

"I only care that justice was done," Kenny said.

"Sure you do." Joey reached for a breadstick. "Everyone wins now."

"I don't know what you mean." Kenny found himself smoothing the wrinkles from the napkin on his lap and looking around for the waitress who was supposed to take their order.

"Mr. O'Mara wins because this was a big case and everyone was freaking about the fuckin' moulies coming here from the city."

Kenny was about to argue but the DA was already undercutting him by giving Joey a thumbs-up and a vaudevillian wink.

"And the cops are happy because my testimony shored up their shitty case so it wasn't just squeezing some black dude's balls in the basement to get the phony-baloney ninety-four percent confessions," Joey said.

At the bar, Rattigan was yukking it up with his fellow detectives, pretending to stick his leg out to trip Patterson's defense lawyer, Malcolm Epstein, who was beating a hasty retreat with his to-go order. Then Billy the Kid mock-attempted an unauthorized seizure of a passing hostess in a short black dress. Good thing the press weren't here to see that.

"And I know you won because I saw how everyone swarmed you and congratulated you after the defense threw in the towel," Joey said. "You got it made now, don't you?"

Kenny pursed his lips and raised his water glass, as if the point was too absurd to address. But the reality was that as soon as the plea deal was announced, Phil O'Mara had taken him aside and told him he was looking for a new executive assistant. The same position the DA himself had held before he was first elected some twenty-seven years before. A change that would make Kenny the second-most important person in one of the most important prosecutor's offices on the Eastern Seaboard, and therefore, by his calculation, a step closer to being one of the most powerful men in all of American law enforcement.

He took a deep drink and put the glass down. "I guess you think you've got it all figured out then. Don't you?"

"I didn't do so good in school." Joey was brandishing his breadstick like a cigar. "But I know people."

There it was again. That thing that had bothered Kenny before. The old man within the young man. Every time he'd convinced himself that Rattigan was right, that this was a good kid who'd just made a few mistakes and was trying to start over with a clean slate now, he got the sense that this was also someone who could see to the bottom of other people too quickly, who could recognize the darkness in them and feel his way around inside it.

"So what is it *you* want?" Kenny asked, trying to tip the table back into balance.

"Me?"

"Yes, you. You seem to think you've read everyone else's tea leaves, but what is it that you're after?"

"I don't know." Joey bit the breadstick in half. "Maybe I'm just saving up for a rainy day."

Another of those perfectly natural things that the boy said, which made Kenny sit and chew his nails afterward, trying to parse it out. Who thought about rainy days at this age? But what did it matter? The case was done and justice had been served, stubby fingernails and all. Rattigan was right. This wasn't *The Bells of St. Mary's* and he'd never met a priest who could sing like Bing Crosby.

Meanwhile, the DA had been joined at his table by his wife, Renata, and their son, Brendan, who was wearing a blazer and gray flannel slacks for the same high school graduation ceremony that Joey had missed to go to court this morning. O'Mara stood up, shook his son's hand, gave his wife a chaste kiss on the cheek, and then brought his family over to the table where Kenny was sitting with the boy.

"All's well that ends well, eh?" The DA slapped Kenny on the back. "Nice work, gents."

"Thank you, sir." Kenny was chagrined to notice that instead of standing, Joey was looking down, perusing the cocktail list.

"Yo, Brendan," he muttered. "How was graduation?"

"It was all right." Kenny noticed how the DA's son averted his gaze, to the diploma under his arm. "You didn't miss much. Lot of speeches."

Kenny hadn't realized the boys were classmates. Brendan seemed so much more clean-cut and appropriately innocent for his age. A pale, earnest-looking lad with his mother's high forehead, a rep tie picked out by his father around his neck, and an eager smile that seemed to assume intentions as honorable as his own coming back at him. Born to the manor, so to speak, as the son of the district attorney. With a clearer path to a brighter future. No wonder the two young men could barely look each other in the eye. They were a study in contrasts. Brendan almost embarrassed by his privilege and Joey almost certainly humiliated at the reminder of missing an important milestone in his high school career because he'd been at the courthouse, instead of following Brendan across the stage to collect his sheepskin. The boy was still just a boy after all.

"And *you.*" The DA put a hand on Joey's shoulder, all hail-fellow-well-met bonhomie. "I hear you made quite the impression, young man."

"You mean with the grand jury?" Joey muttered. "I thought that was supposed to be, like, secret."

"Well, no public trial means no one needs to know about the role you played." O'Mara nodded. "So what are your plans for the future?"

Joey slowly put down the list, looked at the DA with his family, then over at Rattigan, who now had his arms around two waitresses at the same time, and then glanced with cursory interest at Kenny.

"I was thinking of doing what you guys do," he said.

The DA offered his hand and then nodded at Kenny. "Make sure you buy this young fella lunch today. On our office. Anything he wants."

He hooked his arms through the elbows of his wife and son and strode back to the underlings at his table, like he was leading the Easter Parade.

"Now can I get a real fucking drink?" Joey Tolliver asked.

7

"B.B., my brother, I'ma break it down for you, a-ight? We ain't in Brooklyn no more."

This wasn't even Queens with its modest redbrick multi-family dwellings and cement front yards that Lourdes had started to price out. This was Long Island. God-given White People Country. Still bristling with Make America Great Again signs nine months after the election. The island that seemed more like the mainland. Flag county. Nimbyland. Ranch houses and Queen Annes. Blue skies and boats in driveways. Backyards that deserved their own zip code a half mile from broke-ass wood-frame ghettoes with pit bulls snarling at the meter readers. Supercuts and vape shops. Giant liquor stores and mega nail salons. Best Buys and Targets. Tanning parlors and Delta transmissions. Lexuses and Infinitis flying past Mexican laborers trudging alongside the expressway in paint-spattered clothes and work boots. Houses that had yellow flags with pictures of geraniums in flowerpots like gardening was a political cause, ten minutes from homes that hadn't been fixed since Hurricane Sandy five years ago.

"Don't knock it." B.B. nodded as they came off Sunrise Highway and passed two young cops in a Nassau County police cruiser. "I'll be with NYPD thirty-five years next month. The guys probably have ten years between them and they're both making more than either one of us ever will, including overtime."

"Mall cops." Lourdes shook her head. "What's dangerous duty out here? Traffic control? Getting kitties down from the trees?"

"First of all, there's plenty of real work out here, if you know where to look." B.B., refusing to take the bait, steered them onto the Lynbrook exit instead. "Second of all, you telling me you wouldn't jump at the chance?"

"I don't know. Would I?"

"Used to be we looked down on them because they weren't real cops. Now they look down on us, because so many NYPD officers are trying to get out here and earn some real money. Fact, I'm trying to help my older boy get on the job in Suffolk."

He touched the bald spot hidden by his pompadour so self-consciously that she almost felt sorry for him. Three wives, at least five kids on an NYPD salary. No wonder B.B. was always trying to hustle security gigs on the side to pick up extra money. But she still missed working with Sullivan. Not that they'd even been together that long, but his quiet assurance centered her while B.B.'s tetchy mansplaining made her want to spike him with a stiletto heel sometimes.

"Forget about it, Robles. I live in Massapequa. And once you have kids, the suburbs are heaven. Unless you think living in the projects and going to shitty New York City public schools is okay."

"Hey, look how well I turned out."

Not that she wouldn't want to move into one of these sweet little Cape houses with shady willows, front porch swings, and backyard pools if she ever did break down and decide to have a family with or without Mitchell. They passed a store the size of a supermarket called TrainLand that just sold toy trains, and she had a vision of herself on her hands and knees laying tracks with a little boy in front of one of these idyllic homes.

But then they turned down a narrow side street and pulled up in front of an aluminum-sided A-frame with wrought-iron rails on crumbling front steps, an old-school Big Wheel trike on the patchy brown lawn, and a new navy Malibu in the driveway with a cherry-light visible in the back window. So much for daydreaming. Lourdes suspected it was the vehicle of the Nassau County police detective who was supposed to meet them here in fifteen minutes to do the death notification.

A piercing shriek came from inside the house. Lourdes rolled her eyes, unbuckled her seat belt, and got out of the Impala ahead of B.B. A droopy-faced tan-and-white boxer was at the screen door, woofing vociferously. The smell of burnt eggs was in the air. A blond anchorwoman was shouting down some liberal dweeb on the Fox News flat-screen visible in the living room. And the voice that had shrieked was now dissolving into sobs.

"Now it's a party," B.B. muttered, ringing the doorbell.

A gangly, sunburnt man of about forty-five came to the door, shield dangling from a chain around his neck, Ray-Ban sunglasses perched atop his buzz cut. "Jason Tierney, Nassau County detectives." He opened the door and offered his handshake. "And I guess you guys know this gentleman."

He stepped aside and Danny Kovalevski, Lourdes's old patrol sergeant from the Seventy-Eighth Precinct, came around the door, as unnecessarily tall and determinedly square-jawed as ever.

"Dan the Man." As surprise subsided, Lourdes forced a smile. "What are you doing here?"

"You know I transferred to the Nassau Department last year, right?" Danny said. "And when I heard you guys were coming out to look at one of our cases, I figured I stick my head in."

"Great." Lourdes gave B.B. a slight head shake.

A part of her always knew she shouldn't have kicked Danny to the curb so callously, after they'd briefly dated. But that was the kind of girl she was back then. Love 'Em and Leave 'Em Lourdes. She'd done some growing up since, but every once in a while she'd run across a heart she'd trampled on and get reminded that every goodbye had a cost. She wondered how many strings Danny had to pull to get in on this so he could give her a hard time.

"You guys get lost coming out here?" Danny asked. "I would've figured B.B. to know the route."

"We said three-thirty on the phone, it's three-fifteen." Lourdes noted the time on her pad.

"Might as well come on in." Danny made a welcoming gesture like one of the celebrity chefs on the reality shows he'd loved to watch when they were dating. "We're kind of already in progress."

The photo identifying their victim from Far Rockaway was already faceup on the coffee table. Her name, Lourdes had learned yesterday, was Renee Williams. A DNA sample from a 2010 drug conviction had helped to identify her otherwise unrecognizable body. Her mug shot was maybe the saddest Lourdes had ever seen. A girl of eighteen, perhaps a shade or wo darker than herself, barely reaching the five foot hash mark, her hair in pigtails, her eyes brimming with tears, and her mouth crooked like she was in the middle of apologizing for all the grief she was causing.

"Oh my God." A white woman with dyed red hair, approximately seventy years of age, in a Rolling Stones red tongue t-shirt, had collapsed and curled up into a corner of a couch.

A gray-haired man in a checked shirt was holding onto her, his corrugated gate of a face pulled down hard and his lumpy body shaking like he was barely keeping it together himself.

"Mr. and Mrs. Williams?" B.B. squared off, head bowed and hands clasped, like a funeral director, instead of the unregenerate pussyhound he was normally. "On behalf of the New York City Police Department, we're sorry for your loss."

"I thought I'd be relieved when I finally knew." The woman tried to catch her breath. "Now I wish you people never got here. Just so I could pretend a little longer."

B.B. gave Lourdes a little chin wag, lines like bicycle spokes leading away from the corners of his eyes. Still the worst part of the job, he'd said on the way over. "Doing it since Reagan was in the White House and it sucks every time." Like cutting the line and watching someone float off into dead space. Lourdes wondered how she'd keep breathing if someone dropped by like this to tell her about Izzy.

"I told them that we were working this case together as part of a multi-jurisdiction task force." Jason Tierney's chest heaved with a weightlifter's impatience to get his hands on the bar. "They understand what we need to do."

Lourdes caught B.B.'s eye this time: Long Island Charm School. More territorial pissing.

"Ma'am, pardon me if you've covered this already, but when was the last time you saw your daughter?" Lourdes asked, aware of Danny staring daggers at her from across the room.

"*Granddaughter.*" The gray-haired man looked up.

"I'm sorry, Renee was your granddaughter?" Lourdes studiously ignored Danny and checked her notes. "On the 2010 arrest report, she gave this as a home address."

"Her mother, Gwen, is our daughter," the grandfather said. "She stopped having anything to do with Renee when she was young, because Gwen was too busy running with the wrong crowd and getting mixed up with drugs. I'm sure you've heard it all before."

"And one of them got her pregnant: a black fella called himself Prescient." The grandmother cupped a hand beside her mouth, like she was giving up a state secret. "Which he wasn't or he wouldn't have gotten her knocked up. Then she decides to keep the baby like that would make him stay. Instead he took off like a rabbit and she went after him, left Renee with us to raise. And that was pretty much the last we heard from her. We don't even know if she's alive or dead now or if she'd even care what happened to Renee."

The grandfather studied the mug shot for another second and then pushed it away, as if that was all the reality he could handle for the moment.

"The thing I can't believe . . ." He paused to gather himself. "Is that we did everything we could to raise her the right way. I stopped drinking and running around. Held onto my job at Sanitation for another twenty years . . ."

"And I changed my habits, started going to church regular and sent her to the best parochial school in Nassau," the grandmother interjected. "And what happens? She starts doing the same thing as her mother. Missing school, running in the streets and getting mixed up with the wrong people. A girl who was reading when she was *four*. Who made us buy her books every birthday, instead of makeup or jewelry. Top of her class three years in a row. Best grades."

Lourdes saw a small collection under the TV and recognized the spines of a couple of Nancy Drews and Encyclopedia Browns she'd read as a kid, salted in among more adult titles like *White Oleander*, *The Deep End of the Ocean*, *The Heart Is a Lonely Hunter*, and the *Collected Poems of Emily Dickinson*.

"Were those books hers?" she asked.

"Yes." Mrs. Williams nodded. "She joined Oprah's Book Club, because she wanted to be smart, instead of one of these dumb hussies gets all the attention. And what does she do? Gets herself locked up for buying drugs and selling her body. Just like her mother. When she was eighteen. I swear, it makes you wonder about the life you've led."

Lourdes looked over at the mantle and saw pictures of Renee as a little girl sitting on her grandfather's lap, reading a splayed-open book. Lourdes had a picture just like it with her father, trying to read her a Grisham book right before he got locked up. There but for the grace of God go I, she thought.

"You asked about the last time we saw her. It was after we bailed her out." Mr. Williams put his hands up to the sides of his face. "She said she was going to get her life together and enroll at Nassau Community College. We gave her three thousand. About three years after the crash. End of 2011, early 2012. Most of our investments still hadn't come back. And that was the last we saw of it, and her. Until now."

"And did you have any knowledge of her maybe being pregnant?" Lourdes asked.

The grandmother went sideways as if she'd been shot. The grandfather put a hand on his chest and closed his eyes.

"I guess that's a no," Lourdes said.

Danny Kovalevski gave Lourdes a sullen look.

"How far along?" The grandfather reached for the side of the couch and tried to keep himself steady.

"We don't know," Lourdes said.

"Boy or a girl?" the grandfather interrupted.

"We don't know that either," Lourdes said. "I'm sorry I don't have a better answer for you."

Tierney, the Nassau detective, put his shoulders back and touched his Ray-Bans, like he'd just as soon flip them down and drive away at this point.

The old man reached over and took his wife's hand. "You're telling us that someone killed both of them, my granddaughter and what could have been my great-grandchild."

"That appears to be the case, sir," Lourdes said, ignoring a long sniff from Danny.

"How?"

The old man had hiked up his lower lip, so that it was trembling but holding the rest of his stoic expression in place.

"Sir, the ME is yet to put down a cause of death," B.B. said, as a table lamp caught the lacquered gloss of his pompadour.

"Don't shine me on," Mr. Williams glared. "I picked up other people's garbage for twenty-five years before I got a desk job. Tell me what you know."

Lourdes puffed out both her cheeks and let the air out slowly, hoping one of the men in the room would do the explaining. But B.B. was checking his nails, Tierney was fiddling with his sunglasses, and Danny was just standing there, looking down at his feet and feeling sorry for himself.

"There were stones found in Renee's windpipe," she said. "We don't know if it was the cause or something that was done after. But we need you to keep that under your hats and out of the media."

"*Christ.*" The old man squeezed his wife's hand harder and the boxer came over to lie by his feet.

"Who would do a thing like that?" The grandmother stared blankly.

"Ma'am, that's why we're sharing the information," Lourdes said deliberately, making sure Danny and Tierney were paying attention as well. "Does that sound like something that anyone who knew Renee would be capable of?"

"No, of course not. It's crazy." Mrs. Williams looked at her husband. "Whoever even heard of a thing like that?"

The old man was still in a head-shaking daze. Lourdes decided not to share Rakesh's theory about the shrunken wrist and the handcuff. These poor people had enough to contend with.

"Lemme ask you one other thing," Lourdes said. "You just told us the last time you saw Renee was after you bailed her out in 2011, 2012. But when was the last time you *spoke* to her?"

Mrs. Williams grabbed onto the side of the couch, like she was trying to pull herself up in a lifeboat. "You already know that. Don't you people talk to each other?"

"Ma'am?" Lourdes turned to B.B., ready to scorch him.

"Not him—*them.*" The old woman was pointing a shaky finger at Tierney and Danny. "I told the Nassau police that Renee had been calling me until five years ago, checking in and asking for money. And then all of a sudden, nothing."

"When did you tell *me* this?" Tierney's voice cracked, making him sound twelve years younger. "This is the first time we've talked."

"Hey, I just came to this department." Danny had his hands up automatically.

"I told your idiot colleagues when I reported her missing all those years ago." Mrs. Williams sat up, invigorated by her anger. "I gave them names, phone numbers, and addresses of everyone I'd ever heard of knowing her. *Five years ago*. And no response. I tried calling one of your colleagues in Mineola every week for two years, and all I ever got was a form letter telling me to stop bothering him."

Five years. If she'd really been killed that long ago, it'd be surprising if there were any remains at all. The perfect storm of circumstances, Rakesh had said. Or maybe somebody really was trying to keep her relatively intact. In a place no one else could possibly know about.

Danny looked to B.B. for sympathy. "Yo, Bobby, this is the first I'm hearing about any of this."

"We'll need to put our heads together." Lourdes patted the air, trying to keep everybody cool.

"Yeah, I think you better." The grandfather was on his feet. "Because if my granddaughter *and* my great-grandchild were murdered because of someone's irresponsibility, I'm not gonna stay quiet about it."

The boxer was baring its teeth at Danny's pant leg.

"Sir, I hear you." Lourdes softened her voice for the dog as well as the people. "And we're gonna put everything we have into this . . ."

"Now let *me* ask *you* something." The old man was hiking up his pants and shaking out his arms like he was about to take a swing at one of them. "Any of you got kids of your own?"

B.B. showed five fingers, eliding the number of women who'd produced them.

Tierney put up two fingers and grabbed his sunglasses as they started to slide off.

Danny sheepishly held up one finger, a fact that he'd curiously neglected to share when he'd been sleeping with Lourdes.

All eyes, including the dog's, went to Lourdes. "Not yet," she said quietly.

"Then how can you say you know what we're going through?" the grandfather asked.

"I didn't." Lourdes said pointedly. "Everyone's pain is different."

The old man sat down again and began to weep. His wife put her arm around him and the dog put its head on his knee.

"Don't forget about our girl," the old woman said. "That's all we're asking."

"Goddamn it," said her husband. "I am tired."

Lourdes watched them cling to each other and for a second could see them as the young couple in the framed Polaroid on the mantle, swarthy and new to love and just happy to have someone to kiss. Before they expanded and multiplied and gave their hearts a better chance of getting smashed to pieces.

She wondered if she'd ever let anyone get close enough to do that much damage.

8

Now that he'd become a cop, working midnights on Sunrise Highway, Joey liked to park his cruiser off in the trees by the side of the road and wait like a hunter.

There were never that many cars out late during the week and the dispatcher was usually asleep anyway, so basically he could do the job in whatever way he wanted to.

When cars came around the curve on the deserted stretch right before Bohemia, he'd hit the high beams so that the headlights streamed directly into oncoming traffic and drivers had to slow down to avoid getting blinded. As soon as the spotlight hit the driver's face, it was Star Time.

Sometimes it was a bunch of drunken white kids back from a club night in the city, so that was an easy DWI summons and money in the bank for overtime. Occasionally he'd lock in on a black guy going too slow or too fast or driving with a broken taillight or use some other bullshit excuse to pull him over and—what do you know?—screw your probable cause, there's a bag of weed under the front seat or a .38 in the glove compartment, and bingo, here's your felony arrest, rookie.

Praise from cops with twenty years on the job. Officer of the Month twice in his first year. A commendation for bravery in the line of duty. And, of course, quiet acknowledgment from people like Kenny Makris and Billy the Kid, who'd helped him get in the department in the first place.

We're gonna have to start calling you Blood Hound. When are you gonna start working day tours like a normal cop?

But he liked being the lone wolf, especially on nights like this. When the moon was half-hidden. And the radio was playing. And the hot chocolate was still warm in the thermos. And the cars were as few and far between as thoughts you'd never had before.

Rich people could drive back and forth on these highways every week and never have a clue what Long Island was really about. They thought it was all white beaches and clay tennis courts, summer in the Hamptons and the Montauk lighthouse, Gold Coast mansions and yacht clubs. They didn't know about the real horrors of Amityville, that the ghettos of Wyandanch and Roosevelt could be as dangerous as Harlem and Bedford-Stuyvesant, that there were shooting galleries in Smithtown and Riverhead, that you could get stabbed breaking up a bar fight in Babylon or find children starving and wandering around in soiled diapers at ramshackle houses in Flanders. There was a reason they called the Long Island Expressway the LIE.

A silver Honda station wagon came hurtling by in the eastbound lane. Joey's pulse quickened with the bass line of a new song starting on the radio. But when the lights found the driver, she was just some prune-faced bitch, nearly his mother's age, with two brats sleeping in the back seat. A few seconds later, there was a middle-aged white guy in an exhaust-spewing Chrysler Cordoba, his face as beat-up and poorly cared for as the car. Then nothing for several minutes.

Just unlit road and the song.

The chick singer trying to sound tough, threatening to harden her heart. He'd been half hypnotized watching the video on that new MTV channel the other night, at the new bar Billy Rattigan opened in Coram. The chick dressed in a black leotard, getting chased down a narrow corridor by some unseen stalker. The set as cheesy and sleazy as the saxophone that kept swanking in and out of the verses. Shitty office trailer lighting with a low ceiling and wood-paneled walls. You could almost smell the piss cakes in the urinals and the smoke from the tinfoil ashtrays. The chick in the video kept pulling on doorknobs, trying to get away from whoever was pursuing her. It was like being inside someone else's nightmare. She wasn't all that pretty, but Joey liked how scared her eyes were as she looked over her shoulder and bounced off the walls, and how she sang "harden my heart" like she was really thinking about someone chasing her with a monster hard-on. Then at the end of the video, two guys came along in tuxedos and visored helmets and destroyed the trailer with a bulldozer and a flamethrower, so there was no evidence that any of it had ever happened.

A new pair of headlights was moving slowly in his direction. The driver hesitating where the road curved, losing confidence. Just for a second. Something a woman would do, at 1:33 in the morning, on a windswept stretch of highway without a lot of houses around. She tried to pick up speed again as the road straightened out. But he was already onto her, hitting the high beams for her approach. He clocked her going maybe forty as she passed into his light.

A white Ford Escort with a female driver. Young, maybe mid-twenties. Brown hair like the chick in the MTV video. The way they did it now. All curly. Like a poodle with highlights. Skinny neck. Too much makeup. Hand up to her face, like she'd been wiping something from her eye as she passed. Lost in her own little problems. Maybe listening to the same song on the radio. Trying to harden her heart.

He hit his siren and flashers as she went by. Knowing that would give her heart a jolt. Their first physical interaction. Raising her pulse rate without even touching her. The start of a relationship. He swung in right behind her, coming up fast and filling her rearview with his overpowering beams. Her brake lights flared red. A good sign that she was slowing down right away. Immediate compliance.

"Pull over to the side please." He sounded like the voice of God on the loudspeaker.

She went off to the right, not as close to the shade of the trees as he would have liked, and then annoyed him by putting on her hazards, potentially attracting attention from passing cars.

He killed his lights and siren, then took his time getting out. All five foot ten, two hundred pounds of him, with a regulation haircut, a clean-shaven chin and arms hanging apelike at his sides with his flashlight and gun in easy reach. Giving her a chance to worry about what the problem could be.

She had a Mercy College sticker on the back window. Dobbs Ferry.

Westchester. Not Harvard. But still. A college girl. Approach with caution.

He came up to the driver's side window, took the flashlight off his belt, and shined it directly into her eyes. "Good evening, ma'am."

"Good evening, officer." She used her hand as a shield.

Up close, she was a little disappointing. A heart-shaped face already going soft around the edges. Mascara running from her left eye.

"License and registration, please."

She pulled out her wallet and reached into her glove compartment. She was dressed like she'd expected to have a nice evening out: white scoop-necked halter top, pearls, and silver earrings. Her body was okay: long neck, prominent collarbone, breasts sticking out just a little more than her stomach. He rated her a Long Island 6, which would be a Manhattan 3.

"You a student?"

He glanced back at the college sticker and put the flashlight on her license. Stephanie Lapidus. Age twenty-six. Brookhaven address.

"Part-time," she said.

"And what are you studying?"

"Political science." She sniffed. "Look, officer, I know that I wasn't speeding . . ."

"You're a long way from Mercy." He tipped the light back into her face, enjoying his own joke. "Dobbs Ferry is a good hour and a half away."

"I'm going to see my mother." She winced. "Is that against the law?"

"Nope."

She'd definitely been crying until he stopped her. Probably just broke up with a boyfriend and was heading to her mother's for comfort in the middle of the night. She probably thought the drive across Long Island would do her good. Give her a chance to clear her head.

"Do you know why I pulled you over?"

"No, officer."

"You were operating your vehicle in an unsafe manner."

"That's totally not true."

"Ma'am, I'm not going to argue. I observed you driving erratically and changing lanes without signaling."

"Are you kidding me?" she said, like someone who'd been told she was "feisty" and thought it was a good thing. "There's no other cars on the road."

He leaned in the window and smelled the white wine on her breath. The boyfriend had probably broken up with her in a bar to keep her from making a scene.

"Ma'am, how much have you had to drink tonight?"

"Hardly anything. Come on, officer. You know this is ridiculous."

He made a show of shining the light on her ID again. "Stephanie," he said. "You have any points on this license already?"

"I *was* driving safely." She looked straight ahead and put her hands on the wheel, ten and two, playing the model driver.

"Listen, nobody wants to see your insurance rates go through the roof . . ."

"Can you just give me the ticket already?" she snapped. "I don't want my mother waiting up all night, worrying about me."

In the stillness of the night, with her red hazards still blinking in the dark, the stark nakedness of the lie was obvious. Her mother was in bed. Stephanie had left Westchester around midnight, with tears in her eyes and a couple of drinks under her belt, only thinking about the solace of sleeping in her childhood bedroom. Unlikely that she even called Mom to wake her. No one knew she was out alone at this hour.

"Turn off your hazards and get out of the car, please." He turned off the flashlight and let it dangle down, heavy and long, from a belt loop.

"You have no right to ask me to do that. Just give me the summons and let me be on my way."

He almost smiled. The pressure behind her words said she already knew she wouldn't be getting to Mom's anytime soon.

Another car whipped by behind him, pissing him off by coming too close and reminding him that this was taking too long.

"I'm going to ask you again." He rested a hand on his gun belt. "Turn off your rear blinkers and exit the vehicle."

"What happens if I just say no?" Another passing car's headlights caught a faint glint of defiance in her eyes.

He put her license and registration cards in his shirt pocket. "Stephanie, you said you were studying political science at Mercy, right?"

"Yes."

Her hand was on the window frame. Now he could see she was the kind of girl who bit her nails.

"Who do you think is the most politically powerful person in the United States right now?"

"The president."

"No, it's not Ronnie Reagan." He had both hands on the gun belt now, shoulders back, thumbs outside the loops, like he was looking down on her from high in the saddle. "I'll tell who it is. It's *me*. Because I am a police officer. And right here, right now, my word is the law. I can grab you by the hair and drag you out of that window. I could impound your car. Hell, I can draw my weapon and shoot you this second if I feel threatened."

A fresh black glob of mascara had formed in the corner of her left eye and begun its grimy descent down her cheek. "Please," she said quietly. "All I want to do is get to my mother's."

She was as scared now as the chick running down the hall and looking over her shoulder in the rock video. She understood who was in charge and that it wasn't just his heart that was hardening.

"Cut your hazards and get out of the car," he said. "Or the next time I won't ask so nicely."

She pushed the button and the night stopped turning red every few seconds, leaving them alone with just the chirping of crickets and the silence of the stars winking down.

9

Danny Kovalevski looked up in alarm to see Lourdes smacking the roof of his Malibu and yelling at his window.

"Get outta that car, Danny." She slipped from B.B.'s grasp. "You and me got a problem, hombre. Big as you are, I'll kick your ass right here in the driveway."

"Robles, chill." Bobby got a hand on her elbow. "We don't know what's what yet . . ."

"Yo, fuck that, B. I got a problem with this asshole and we're gonna settle it right now."

Danny rolled down his window, as Jason Tierney looked on from the passenger seat, a cell phone pressed to his chest. "Listen, we're as confused as you are, L. Ro. Tierney's calling Missing Persons, trying to find out what happened."

"I call bullshit." She broke free from B.B. again. "You guys are holding out on us."

"We're not." Tierney looked befuddled and scared, as he put the phone back to his ear. "All right, whatever, call me back when you pull up the files. I got some unhappy campers on my hands."

"Seriously? 'Unhappy campers'?" Lourdes stuck a finger in the window. "Is that some Long Island racist dog whistle shit?"

"She for real?" Tierney eyed Danny.

"Bobby, can you ask her to chill?" Danny pleaded.

B.B. stepped back, arms akimbo, disclaiming all responsibility.

"This girl Renee's been missing five years and y'all ain't done shit." Lourdes pointed back at the house, where the girl's grandmother was watching from a bay window.

"Look, the sergeant wasn't even with the department when that happened," Tierney said. "And it wasn't my case either. We're not the NYPD, but we're a big department. I don't know everything everybody is doing."

"And now we know she's fucking dead and so's the child she was carrying." Lourdes paused to catch her breath. "Because you all weren't out looking for her."

Tierney looked at B.B. again, as if expecting an explanation for her fury. Lourdes turned just in time to catch B.B.'s hapless sellout shrug. Men.

"Can we cool down and discuss this like grown-ups?" Danny asked. "And not put all this drama out on the street?"

"*Right.*" Lourdes reached in his window and found the door lock button. "B.B., get in."

"This a hijacking?" Danny tried to smile, even as his eyes remained anxious.

"You keep talking stupid, I'll hijack your ass to Fresh Kills, Danny, and dump you there with the rest of the trash." She yanked open the backdoor as B.B. got in on the passenger side behind Tierney. "Take us around the block and stop jerking us."

"Nice job handling the city cops, sarge." Tierney looked at Danny. "Thought you said you were friends with these guys . . ."

"Don't you say shit, Danny." Lourdes climbed in and slammed the door. "Or I'll pull my gun on you right now."

"Some history here?" Tierney glanced at Danny again, as he started to back out of the driveway carefully.

"You guys dropped the ball on a missing person who's turned up pregnant and dead, with possibility of a bigger pattern." B.B. broke in. "I don't know about you, but I try to stop arguing when I see a woman's got a point."

Spoken like a man ready for his fourth and hopefully final marriage, Lourdes thought.

"So what do we know about the pattern anyway?" she said. "How come we haven't heard about it in the city until now?"

"I'm not even sure it *is* a pattern," Danny said. "Tierney and me are arguing about it."

"I say it is," Tierney countered. "No one noticed until now because most of the victims were from below the radar."

"You're saying they were prostitutes?" Lourdes asked.

"Five in the course of like fifteen years." With typical consideration, Danny used his flashers as he went around a yellow bus disgorging school kids on the corner. "Not that much, considering. I mean, being a whore has a lot of occupational hazards. Am I right?"

"Bet you wouldn't talk that way if some of them looked like your sister, Danny," Lourdes shot back.

"As a matter of fact, two of them *were* white." Danny turned off the flashers and showed her his profile. "So don't try to make this into another one of your racial things."

"Screw you, Danny. There must be something else that connects if Tierney here thinks it's part of a pattern." Lourdes put a hand on the back of his seat. "Especially if Tierney here was trying to horn in on our Far Rockaway case. Did any of these others have rocks down their throats?"

"Not as far as I know," Tierney said. "But remains wrapped in that kind of plastic? Check. Found dumped between here and the eastern tip of the Island? Check. Broken or missing hyoid bones in the throat? Check. Could be a coincidence, could be a gang initiation thing . . ."

"Or it could be one fucked-up psycho." Lourdes finished the thought. "And he could've been doing it to Renee when you should've been out looking for her."

"Come on, L. Ro." Danny interrupted. "Renee was a full-grown escort with a known drug problem who stopped returning her grandmother's phone calls. And we're supposed to drop everything and go crazy over *that* as a tragic missing persons case? You tell me there's a major police department that would make that a priority, I'll call you a liar."

"Missing person turns up possibly pregnant and dead with rocks in her throat on our beach," Lourdes said. "That's great police work."

"Well, we're waiting to see what the file says." Tierney pulled down his Ray-Bans as they drove into the direct sun glare. "But I wouldn't just come out here and automatically assume someone on our side screwed up."

"It's true," Danny said. "There are a lot of good cops out here. At least as good as the people we've worked with at NYPD. And let's not forget, not every victim is just a victim. People make choices with their lives."

"Whatever that means." Lourdes crossed her arms.

She watched the neighborhood go by. More ranch houses. Two-story houses. Oak trees. Maple trees. Two-garage houses. A playground with no trash on the ground. A couple of kids no more than nine in blue polo shirts and backpacks, walking by themselves. A porch with a rainbow flag like the one her aunt Soledad, out and proud, had in her living room in Sunset Park. *Maybe I could live out here.* Then another Make America Great Again sign on a fenced-in lawn with Beware of Dog and private security company stickers. *No, maybe not.*

B.B. reached over and tapped Danny on the shoulder. "Hey, Kovalevski, you want to do us a solid, save us some time? Could you get us the files on those other cases? And maybe the numbers for the investigators?"

Nice and easy, like he was ordering a salami and provolone hero at his local deli counter. It still irked Lourdes that she had not only worked with Danny for three years but had actually gone to bed with him a handful of times without getting anything close to this relaxed goombah rapport and assured cooperation.

"Here's the problem, though," Danny said, pulling down the car's sun visor. "I checked. Half those cases are across the county line, at the eastern end of the Island."

"So?" Lourdes hunched forward.

"So it's a whole other jurisdiction," Danny said.

"What are you, freaking kidding me?" Lourdes said. "They're your next-door neighbors. You must work joint operations with them all the time. They should be part of this task force anyway. You're telling me you don't have someone you can just pick up the phone and call?"

Tierney turned with his sunglasses down, trying to give her a badass glare from behind the shades. "All I'm gonna say is, they've got their own way of doing things out there."

"What's that supposed to mean?" she asked.

Danny put too much muscle into rounding a corner and tossed her around in the back seat. "Just go easy and tread lightly," he said. "Word is, Savak County don't play."

"Yeah, all right, that's cool, D." Lourdes straightened up and reached for her seat belt. "It's not like you might have some crazy-ass psycho Hannibal Lecter serial killer running around who might strike again at any time."

"Hey, L. Ro., not for nothing, but you may want to work on your sandbox skills out here," Danny said. "A girl could get the wrong kind of rep."

10

Everyone was surprised when Joey Tolliver showed up that morning and moseyed over to where Stephanie Lapidus's car had been found by the side of the highway. They shouldn't have been. He'd already established that he was an active young cop, eager for experience and overtime, listening to the scanner in his car during off-duty hours, just in case backup was needed to control a bar brawl or an incident on the highway.

He ducked under the yellow tape, walked up to the white Escort that was parked deep among the trees, and rested his hands on the window-sill as he peeked inside.

The half-life of last night's excitement lingered in the air. He felt like an athlete watching a highlight reel from last night's game. There were spots of dried blood on the steering wheel and the dashboard. A single cork-heeled shoe was lying next to the brake pedal. The ashtray was full of cigarettes with pink lipstick stains. She must've been smoking up a storm between Dobbs Ferry and here, listening to heartbreak songs on AM radio in the middle of the night. And of course, her purse was open with all of her stuff spilled onto the floor mat by the passenger seat: makeup compact, hairbrush, and a tube of Ortho-Gynol—a souvenir he thought of collecting and a sign that at one point she had thought the night would have a happier ending.

He leaned further into the car, sleeves rolled down to cover the scratch Stephanie had left on his right arm. Then he reached into his shirt pocket, took out the packet of Bambú rolling papers that he'd confiscated from a drug dealer named Trevor Knightsbridge and had deliberately avoided vouchering two weeks before.

He flicked it onto the floor mat by the passenger seat. But as soon as it left his hand, he saw movement from the corner of his eye. He leaned back too quickly and banged the back of his head. A cop who was supposed to be guarding the perimeter with nitwit Charlie Maslow was coming over. Amy Nelson. A new female officer they had working day tours. They called her Half-Nelson because she was so short. Probably had no business being a police officer, barely making the height requirement. But God knew she didn't have the looks to be anything else. Pointy-nosed little bitch with short hair and big ears. She looked more like a high school hall monitor. But they all had to prove something these days.

"You all right?" she asked.

"Yeah, why?" He rubbed the back of his head, dull stars bursting before his eyes.

"Looked like you hurt yourself."

He turned his grimace into a grin, not sure if she'd seen what he did. "I'm okay. How are you?"

"You shouldn't be touching the car," she said. "The crime scene unit hasn't even got here. They'll have to get a set of prints from you to make sure they don't mix them up with whoever killed her."

"Shit." He pretended that hadn't occurred to him. "Don't get me in trouble for it. Okay?"

"What are you doing here anyway?" she asked. "I thought your tour ended three hours ago."

"This is my road. I was on patrol last night. Somebody gets hurt on it, I feel responsible."

Her hazel eyes stared at him for a beat and then dropped to the interior of the car. Right where he'd dropped the papers. "You heard they found the driver strangled a mile and a half up the road?" she asked.

He shook his head and put his hands on his hips, looking up and down the road with a hard-ass Clint Eastwood squint. "I don't know what we're coming to here. A girl can't drive on her own?"

She pulled her eyes out of the car and tugged down the brim of her hat. "I'm out driving by myself all the time. And I never stop unless I need gas. So what could have forced her off the road?"

"No telling." He shrugged. "That hour, there won't be too many witnesses."

"How do we know what hour it happened?"

She aimed her pointy nose at him and cocked her narrow little pasty face at an angle. Man, you rarely saw a girl with ears that big. Most would have enough sense to grow their hair longer. It was almost like she was intentionally confronting you with the size of those flaps.

"Just a figure of speech," he said. "I'm sure it didn't happen in the middle of rush hour. Someone would have noticed."

She held his gaze for a beat longer than she should have. Then looked back inside the car, the corners of her thin-lipped mouth turning down.

"Where were you patrolling last night anyway?" she asked.

"Down by West Babylon. Quiet night."

He didn't appreciate how she kept looking just to the side of his face, like she was trying to see something behind him.

"And you didn't see this car go by with a female driver?" Half-Nelson raised her eyebrows.

"If you're not breaking the law, I'm not interested in you." He shrugged.

Billy the Kid had come staggering over. Even more hungover than usual, and wearing his tinted aviators. The man was getting to be an embarrassment, but Joey wasn't sure how much he might have seen. There was just enough detective left in him to sometimes know when to hang back and observe.

"What do we got, officers?" He patted his pockets for a notebook.

"Just maintaining the integrity of the scene for the big boys." Joey nodded. "I hear CSU's busy up the road."

"Yeah, it's ugly," said Rattigan. "Poor woman taken from her car, beaten, raped, and strangled. Her clothes are torn off and her neck is practically broken. It looks like wolves attacked her."

Joey cricked his neck, aware of how Half-Nelson was restlessly hitching up her belt and scratching a spot halfway down her throat. Like she had something she wanted to say in private. Joey put on his sunglasses to glare at her: I can see out, but you can't see in.

Rattigan clapped him on the shoulder. "Why aren't you home sleeping?"

"My road, my watch." Joey bowed his head, like the mantle of civic responsibility was weighing heavily on him. "I figured it's all hands on deck."

"Good man." Rattigan said, turning to Half-Nelson. "Stick with this guy, officer, and you'll be going places. He's a comer."

She'd already gone to start putting orange traffic cones out on the road, to keep other cars away.

Rattigan turned and gave Joey a faint smile.

"*Women,*" he said.

11

There were two ways of looking at it. From one angle, Long Island looked like a whale crashing headfirst into the rest of the United States. From another, the North and South Forks resembled the jaws of a raptor thrusting out into the Atlantic.

Either way, in the room with the map at Queens Homicide, six red dots made it look like this was a body with a series of infections.

"So what do we know so far?" Lourdes asked.

She was talking to members of the so-called Cross Bay Task Force. Which at the moment consisted of Beautiful Bobby, Danny Kovalevski and Jason Tierney from the Nassau police, a bohunk state cop named John Gallagher, a Suffolk County police inspector named Charlie Maslow who wore a handlebar mustache and kept excusing himself to go to the bathroom, and an FBI profiler named Goran Bogdan, who couldn't stop staring at his cell phone like he was either getting messages from HQ in Washington or following his stock market investments in real time.

"I still don't know if we're looking at anything." Gallagher, the state cop, dropped a pen on the gunmetal gray table. "Six dead, fifteen years? All hookers?"

"The old days we'd catch that many bodies the night before the West Indian Parade," Danny snorted, ignoring Lourdes giving him the death glare.

"*Word.*" Bogdan, the FBI agent, was now furrowing his monobrow and furiously texting with both thumbs.

Though most of these whey-faced boys didn't look like they had enough time on the job to be talking like old salts, Lourdes thought, they just assumed that dismissive tone as their natural right, passed down through the lineage of Great White Supervisors. Charlie Maslow, the one who did look old enough, got up and muttered that he was going to take a leak.

"Look, I didn't ask you all to come to the party—*they did*." She pointed at Danny and Tierney, both slouching in their chairs. "I would've been happy, minding my own, working my little Rockaway murder. Then Nassau raised their hand, said they had similar cases."

"Yeah, well, you think Long Island, you think serial killers." Gallagher rolled the pen under his extraordinarily flat and broad hand, ignoring the stack of files close by. "Joel Rifkin. Robert Shulman. Gilgo Beach. Doesn't mean every case is connected."

Gallagher was the type of a man who seemed like he was wearing a state trooper hat and a tan uniform even when he was bareheaded and in a suit.

"That's true," Danny said. "And I'm not even positive there *is* a connection—"

"But when we hear about a body wrapped in plastic, washing up just across the channel, we're obligated to check it out," Tierney interrupted. "Especially if we know about similar cases."

Lourdes nodded, even though she hadn't forgotten how pissed she was about his department not following up when Renee Williams was reported missing.

"Bodies wrapped in plastic—not so unusual," Bogdan said nonchalantly with a trace of a Slavic accent, still not taking his eyes off his phone. "What else?"

Lourdes watched his monobrow go up and down as he typed. Probably it wasn't fair to think this way, but he reminded her of some of the Balkan dudes you met in the Bronx who were a little too blasé when talk turned to ethnic cleansing and rolling bodies into sandpits with bulldozers. She tried to tell herself she wasn't just being pissy because the Bureau hadn't done jack to help her look for her sister.

"Okay, so here's what *I* see." She passed her hand in front of the map.

"I see six female victims so far, including our new girl, Renee. I see similarities in the way they were killed, according to the forensic reports Tierney has given us."

"Untrue," Bogdan said as he continued texting. "Only your Rockaway Beach victim had stones in her throat. This seems like a signature or a one-time special event. One of the others was bludgeoned. One was stabbed. The rest were probably strangled."

"That's still death by asphyxiation," said B.B., who was usually the one getting distracted by calls from his own girlfriends or ex-wives. "Let's not be so literal-minded. We're talking about victims with a similar profile, Mr. Profiler. All under forty, unmarried, with limited family connections . . ."

"All with arrest records for drugs or prostitution or both." Gallagher shook his oversized head. "Sorry, folks. I'm still not convinced this is a pattern. These were throwaway people. Marginal women living marginal lives . . ."

"Oh, so then they don't count?" Lourdes looked around, daring one of them to argue. "Or are you guys just trying to keep a lid on this so it doesn't look like the state and the feds missed a serial killer right under your noses when you should have been putting the pieces together? It's your responsibility to track these things across jurisdiction lines."

Charlie Maslow and his sleepy cowpoke expression came back in the room. Bogdan finally put his cell phone facedown on the table. Now she had his attention.

"Proceed," he said.

"*Mire.*" Lourdes pointed to the map again. "Look where these bodies turned up."

She put a chipped fingernail next to each red dot. Miriam Gonzales, age thirty-eight, found floating near Jones Beach State Park by swimmers six years ago. Yelina Sanchez, twenty-seven, stumbled upon by hikers in Wertheim National Wildlife Refuge in 2007. Anne Higgins, twenty-nine, encountered during a picnic at Westhampton Dwarf Pine Plain Preserve in 2006. Allison Forster, twenty-three, drifted up to fishermen in Sears Bellows County Park, 2005. Joyce Templeton, twenty-six, found in a Dumpster by West Babylon garbage collectors, October 2002.

"Pretty wide distribution of bodies." Danny Kovalevski shrugged. "Multiple towns and counties. It's a tough case to make that it's all the same guy killing them."

"*It is?*" Lourdes raised her voice. "Look at that map, sergeant."

She rubbed her finger back and forth across a long blue vein running the length of the Island. She saw Danny hoist one side of his mouth, like he was about to make a joke about the whole deal looking like a jerk-off rather than just sounding like one.

"All the bodies were found within a mile or two of Sunrise Highway." She raised her arms in exasperation. "The dots are all there, waiting to be connected."

Though it had actually taken her a few minutes to see it, once she put the pins in. The road, like her, began its life in Brooklyn. Then it ran all the way out, 120 miles, to the easternmost extreme of the state. Like most of the victims in the case, it changed its name and its look along the way: starting as bumpy NY 27, then slaloming out into South Condit Boulevard near the airport before smoothing and widening into Sunrise Highway, surrounded by chain stores and pain clinics in Nassau and then giving way to greenery in Suffolk as it traversed almost the entire length of Long Island, widening and narrowing along the way, before passing through the Long Island Pine Barrens and meeting up with Montauk Highway. And like the victim's lives, it ran out too soon, just as the sun met the water, ending at the eastern edge of the continent.

"I'm still not buying it," Gallagher said, parkway eyes roaming the map. "Your last victim, Renee, doesn't fit your own pattern. The beach in Far Rockaway is a good ten miles from Sunrise Highway."

"So what?" Lourdes let her arms drop. "Our killer is getting smart, finally altering his routine. Take the long view: He—and yeah, I'm assuming it's a he—is broadening his outlook and choosing his victims more carefully. In the beginning his victims were mainly white girls, who might have had more people in their circle with the means to go look for them if they're missing. As time goes on, he's choosing darker girls with fewer ties. And on top of that, he's crafty enough to dump the corpses close to the road without anybody seeing him. He does it near the highway so he can get on and get off in a hurry, be miles from the scene before anybody knows where he's been."

A silence so complete settled over the room that Lourdes could almost hear the dust gathering. Ordinary indifference she was used to. But this felt more like active resistance from a single point being transmitted invisibly from man to man, like a signal from a wireless router.

"Waste of time." Charlie Maslow finally spoke up, turkey neck quivering. "You're trying to jam square pegs into round holes to justify your budgets. Personally, I think we should be spending more money on military-style hardware, to fight urban insurgencies."

"Excuse me," Lourdes said. "What does that have to do with what we're talking about?"

Maslow shrugged, touched his abdomen gently, and left the room again.

"All due respect, I think we need to be looking at the bigger picture." B.B. looked after him. "Robles and I used to work with an old-timer named Kevin Sullivan. And his mantra was always: Close your mouth and open your eyes. And follow the map to where the facts are leading." He pointed to the pins. "And seems to me, Robles has given us a pretty good map to start with. Sully would be pleased."

Lourdes found herself shaking her head and getting a little choked up at the mere mention of her retired partner. Then cursed herself—again— for not having the nerve to call him in the last six months.

"And not to put too fine a point on it, but if these cases have been falling between the cracks fifteen years, then it's fucked up," B.B. said. "And the worst part is we may not know about all the bodies."

Of course, now that Bobby was saying it, the others were taking it more seriously. It irked Lourdes to see them slipping down in their seats and steepling their fingers thoughtfully in a way that they hadn't when she was speaking.

"We're already into our databases." Bogdan chewed his lip, more engaged now.

"Us as well." Gallagher nodded.

"You know where we're at," said Tierney.

"Where did our friend from the mysterious east go?" Lourdes asked, looking at the seat Maslow had vacated. "I thought Suffolk County was going to be a serious part of this task force. At least three of these bodies are on their side of the line and they send us the Catheter Cowboy? What gives?"

"Like I was saying." Tierney's large shoulders slumped. "A world of its own. They do things on their time, not ours. And the more you squawk and complain, the less they care."

12

AUGUST
1984

Ronald Reagan was on all the TVs above the bars at the banquet hall. He was smiling at a sea of waving American flags and upturned white faces, plastic-looking Nancy and the rest of his plastic family at his side. The Gipper said we were taking this country back. He said traditional values were returning. He said the people were in charge now. And when the crowd on TV chanted, "Four more years," he smiled, tilted his head in the Big Daddy cowboy way and said, *"You ain't seen nothing yet."*

At the Shinnecock Manor Banquet Hall in Melville, the crowd roared its approval. On the stage, a podium was getting wheeled into place and a microphone was getting tested. Banners had been strung up and balloons had been hoisted to the ceiling. And Kenny Makris, who had just been elected to the office of district attorney, peeked out from the wings, caught Joey's eye, and gave him a thumbs-up.

They were both golden now. Kenny was the law of the land and Joey, his loyal acolyte, would surely reap the rewards. Twenty-five years old. A respected police officer with a half dozen legitimate commendations under his belt, a clutch of headline arrests, and his eye on the sergeant's exam. With a Budweiser in one hand and a Cuban cigar in the other. Wearing the first suit he had ever bought with his own money.

He'd never be a pretty boy, but all the flab he'd used to have was gone, replaced by gym muscle. His stringy stoner hair was cut into a Stallone-style semi-mullet, and he wore a pair of aviator glasses about twenty dollars more expensive than the kind Billy Rattigan wore. Seventy-five dollars' worth of confiscated cocaine, which had never been turned in from various traffic stops, was up his nose. Not that the drug dealers who coughed it up when he stopped them would ever complain.

Yes, he'd been a little concerned when he'd heard that Trevor Knightsbridge's lawyers were trying to stir the pot and reopen the investigation into the Stephanie Lapidus murder. And that concern had started to shade into worry when he read in a *Newsday* article that Kenny's opponent had started talking about taking a harder line on corrupt police practices. But now the day had been saved, the investigation had presumably been quashed, and he was realizing that he might be bulletproof after all. So if he wanted to get a freeze on, who was going to stop him?

At the nearest bar counter, Billy the Kid Rattigan was clinking glasses with moron Charlie Maslow and trying to pick up one of the campaign aides. Fucking second-rater, Joey thought. A district attorney willing to give cops a free hand had been elected in a landslide. There was an open bar until midnight. And the whole banquet was full of desperate, unattached women and Billy ordered the house scotch and tried to hit on some dowdy married church lady who'd volunteered with the campaign.

Joey sneered and turned his attention to more promising prospects. There was one in a purple dress under the red exit sign just to the right of the stage. She'd been on and off his radar all night. Somehow he'd always had a sense for them, feeling them before he could even see them. The ones you could corner without too much trouble. Purple Dress had the big hair and big shoulder pads they all wore these days, to try and signify that they had some kind of power in the world. Lots of makeup, padded bra. But inside, a mouse. Nibbly, skittish, and good for experiments. He had caught her looking back at him two or three times. Like she already knew her role in this play. The chooser and the chosen.

Joey turned back toward the stage as a cheer went up and Kenny walked to the podium. He stopped and waved, put his arm around his wife, Annemarie, and their four-year-old, Christina, then tried to tilt his head and smile like the president. A twenty percent victory margin, an undisputable mandate, banners with his name all over the hall, and the man was still a stiff. Still carrying himself like the one Greek altar boy at a Roman Catholic mass. Steve Snyder, a Catholic with a Jewish name who'd just been elected county executive, came over to pat him on the back and revel in their shared victories.

Meanwhile, Phil O'Mara, the retiring DA, came over and shook Kenny's hand. Like he was thrilled he'd been forced out of the race.

Another reason Kenny Makris owed Joey for life. Like he needed more.

"My friends, this is a great night." Kenny gripped the mike, stage lights catching the red tint he'd added to his hair to cover his premature gray and look more Reaganesque. "This community has a reputation among the city elites for being provincial and close-minded . . ."

The crowd before the stage began to grumble, almost imitating the grumbles of the crowd on TV when Ronald Reagan mentioned his opponent.

"But tonight, you've made an outsider feel like an insider," Kenny said. "I promise that I will never forget any of the people who got me here tonight."

Somehow, even with lights in his eyes and the smudges on his glasses inadequately wiped, the new DA's beady eyes found Joey at the edge of the crowd. Kenny gave him a wink. Acknowledging him again, but not too much.

"Today marks a new day in Long Island law enforcement," Kenny was saying. "A few years ago, it looked like our beautiful towns were about to get overrun by the same problems that have turned New York City into the filthy, festering sewer that it is."

People began to clap and hoot.

"Not here." Billy Rattigan bellowed, hands around his mouth. "Not on our watch, baby."

Makris grimaced. Whatever goodwill Billy the Kid had gotten from the Kim Bergdahl case, he'd squandered by acting like a drunken lout in public ever since, and by being sloppy in both his police work and bar business. Which just meant more credit left over for Joey to collect on, even after Kenny Makris had helped him get into the police academy. It was getting close to the point where Joey could safely say he'd learned what he had to from the man, had absorbed his most useful traits, and it was almost time to discard the original and go with the new, improved version.

"'Law and order' used to be dirty words." Kenny turned awkwardly to the next page of his speech: the man was no natural like the Gip. "But we are going to keep our towns and villages safe. And we are going to do it on our terms. And no matter what, we are going to support our fantastic, amazing police officers."

Joey turned to look for the mouse again. But another woman was standing where she'd been. Even mousier, at least on the outside. Smaller and less buxom. Wearing a dress almost down to her ankles that was the color of a potato sack and even bigger shoulder pads than the other woman. Trying to make herself more imposing. Her hair was longer, but the big ears gave her away. Half-Nelson the hall monitor.

"What do you say there, Nelson?" He came over. "Long time no see."

"Good evening."

She was doing that stiff thing again. Trying to look around him to see something, instead of looking right at him.

"How you been?" he asked. "I think I haven't seen you since, what, the Lapidus trial?"

"I left the department after that," she said. "I'm guessing you already knew."

"How would I know?" He opened his arms, playing the life of the party. "You think I'm that obsessed with you? You must have a high opinion of yourself, officer."

"Believe me. I don't."

She cocked her head to one side, the way she'd done that day she caught him looking into the Escort with the Mercy College sticker.

"Yeah, so where you at these days?" He moved to stand closer to her, blowing cigar smoke past her ear.

"I'm with social services in Riverhead. I decided it was a better fit for me."

Not a good sign that she'd taken a pay cut to go elsewhere. Especially since Trevor Knightsbridge had been convicted of raping and killing Stephanie largely on the basis of his prints being found on rolling papers in her car.

"You seem nervous," he said.

"I'm fine."

"Have I done something that made you uncomfortable?"

"No, not at all." Her eyes danced over his shoulder; she was dying to get away from him.

"Can I ask you something?" He set down his beer bottle.

She turned her needle nose away from him. "That would depend."

Other people were moving around them as Kenny's speech droned on. They could tell this wasn't just some regular social conversation or election night pickup.

"You read any of that bullshit in *Newsday* about Knightsbridge's lawyers trying to get his case reopened?" he asked.

"I try not to pay attention," she said. "The past is the past."

"Again, with the nerves. What's the matter, Nelson? Have any of those lawyers been in touch with you?"

He noted how the tip of one of her shoes came off the floor before she answered. "Why do you ask?"

Another less-than-encouraging sign. Not yes. Or no. But a question.

"The story in the paper said they were trying to put together an appeal," he said, his suspicion fully aroused now. "Supposedly on evidentiary grounds."

"Well, I guess that's their right. Isn't it?"

Another question instead of a straight yes or no. If they weren't in a crowded room, he might have had his hands all over that potato sack dress, feeling her up and down for a wire.

"It's a bunch of crap: they've got no grounds for an appeal," he said. "We found definitive evidence that Trevor Knightsbridge was in that car with Stephanie before she was raped and murdered. It's his blood type . . ."

"Which happens to be the most common type." She immediately looked like she regretted the observation.

"And he's not just a drug dealer; he's a violent criminal . . ."

"Yes, I know." Her nostrils puckered and her ears appeared more prominent as she drew herself up, the mouse trying to be brave. "And now that you're bringing it all up, I have something I've been wanting to say to you."

"And what's that?"

"I didn't know you were the one who locked him up two weeks before, for beating up a rival in Babylon. No one told me that before I testified."

"No one was keeping it from you," he said. "The judge wouldn't allow in predicate acts until Makris proved the relevance. Would it have made any difference to you?"

"Well, it's a concern now," she said, lowering her voice.

"And why is that?"

She looked both ways, like a child trying to cross a two-way street for the first time. "This evidentiary issue," she said with a quiet intensity. "It has to do with a packet of rolling papers that was confiscated from his first arrest and never returned to him. They're saying the police held onto it and planted it in Stephanie Lapidus's car two weeks later to make him look guilty."

"Yeah, right." He feigned a laugh.

"I'm on record as being the officer present at the crime scene."

"Yeah, so?"

Her eyes became small and dark as rat pellets. "So if somebody did something they shouldn't have with evidence in that case, I shouldn't be the one who pays for that."

"Who said anybody did anything wrong?"

"I am telling you, Officer Tolliver, I am not going to prison for tampering with evidence. I've done nothing wrong."

He took a long pull on his cigar and then found an ashtray, the confident edge the coke had given him earlier starting to dull. "What exactly did they say to you?"

They had to wait as Kenny Makris said something that made everyone in the hall hoot and stomp.

"No one's said anything yet." Half-Nelson blinked her false eyelashes. "But there's rumors around the courthouse that the defense has filed a letter with the judge and is asking the governor to start an independent investigation into the whole police department."

"It'll never go anywhere." Joey expelled smoke, the back of his throat still throbbing from the coke leaking down. "Lawyers have tried that before."

"Not usually in cases with white college girls who've been brutally murdered on their way home to see their mothers."

"Trevor Knightsbridge raped and killed Stephanie Lapidus and he's going to spend the rest of his life in prison for it. End of story."

"Unless they keep looking into it," she said in a low, anxious voice. "Listen, I shouldn't be on the hook for this. But I'm listed as one of the officers who was supposed to be watching the car. You aren't. I shouldn't be held responsible."

"You want to protect yourself?" He studied the lit end. "Don't bet on long shots coming in. Kenny Makris was favored to win this race two to one after Phil O'Mara backed out. Ronnie Reagan just won in a landslide, second time around. No one loves an underdog anymore, Nelson. There's not going to be any state commission or retrial as long as Kenny is DA. Figure out who your friends are and where your best interests lie. This could be a good time for us."

The ballroom lights shimmered in her eyes in such a way that he thought she was about to start crying. Then Kenny Makris finished his speech, that "I'm proud to be an American" song came over the loudspeakers, and a shower of balloons fell from the ceiling. Joey kissed Nelson on the cheek and she teetered off like someone who'd never worn high heels before, disappearing from his sight amid the bouncing spheres of red, white, and blue.

13

Chief Joseph Tolliver's office in Yaphank was a testament to a long career dedicated to public service, culminating in a job as the operational head of one of the largest police departments in the United States.

There were photos of the chief with a mighty squadron of motorcycle cops in shiny leather boots astride dozens of gleaming hogs. Then there were photos of the chief with key political figures including the governor, both U.S. senators, and the new president himself shaking hands with Tolliver in the Oval Office. Along all the walls were plaques from Mothers Against Intoxicated Driving, framed letters of appreciation from other law enforcement agencies, headlines from *Newsday* about major drug busts and immigration roundups, and a glass trophy case full of awards and statues for personal valor in the line of duty, support for local civic organizations, and success in martial arts competitions.

No wonder we had so much trouble getting a meeting with him, Lourdes thought. We weren't offering a prize.

"Sorry it took so long to set this up," the chief was saying. "I really appreciate the two of you making the long haul to get out here."

Lourdes could see right away why he had been put in charge. He projected the air not only of a man's man, and a cop's cop, but also kind of a likeable guy. A great combination if you were going to be the head of a sprawling department overseeing a bunch of little towns and fragile egos. He wasn't a humongous dude, but he had a compact muscular physique that he was obviously proud of. As a former fatty herself, she had to respect that. His hair was shaved down to stubble and he had a Magnum PI mustache that imbued him with a serious studly authority. But he had a goofy laugh and an easy way of smiling that could help you forget that you'd just spent an hour and a half in traffic on the expressway trying to get out here. Within seconds, he had such a relaxed jokey rapport with B.B. that she wondered if they'd already been out drinking whiskey and smoking cigars at some high-end steak house.

The only thing she couldn't figure out was why something in herself was holding back and refusing to yield to his charm.

"Good ol' Charlie Maslow gave me the update and I want you to know that we take all these cases very seriously," Chief Tolliver was saying. "But we also see them a little differently."

"Really?" She found the end of her pen between her teeth. "You had three women found dead on your side of the county line. Had you already connected them to the women found dead on the Nassau side before we contacted you?"

"I'm still not really sure there is a connection," Tolliver said mildly, like it was something you could talk him out of. "I know I don't have to tell you guys that things can start off looking one way and end up being something else entirely."

"Yeah, I hear that." B.B. grinned as the chief's secretary brought him an espresso brewed on Tolliver's personal machine. "The best cup of coffee you'll have on Long Island," Tolliver had said. B.B. winked at the secretary with some of his old confidence. Like he was Frank Sinatra tipping the coatroom girl at Rao's or some shit.

"Not to tell tales out of school . . ." Tolliver lowered his voice as the secretary exited and closed the door after her. "But our neighbors in Nassau tend to get a little overexcited sometimes."

Was it just Lourdes's imagination or was the chief consciously not looking at her every time he spoke?

"You saying these aren't all murder victims?" She stopped chewing her pen.

"Of course that's not what I'm saying." The chief rocked back in his chair, arms in starched white uniform sleeves stretched behind his head. "But before we start getting crazy and making the local property owners hysterical about some alleged serial killer, let's look at some facts."

"Works for me." B.B. took a sip and nodded approvingly.

"A lot of these killings you're talking about are MS-13 related," the chief said. "Salvadoran gang members killing each other and killing their girlfriends to keep them from snitching." He paused and finally met Lourdes's eye. "And no offense, miss, but a lot of them are people who shouldn't be here in the first place."

"Why would I get offended?" Lourdes shrugged. "I'm from Brooklyn. I couldn't even find El Salvador on a map till I was in high school."

So was he dissing her because she was Hispanic or because she was a woman? Or just because she was an outsider?

"What you have to remember is sometimes bad guys move bodies after they do the deed," Tolliver said. "So we don't know where anyone actually died. A few more of these might even be New York City murders, where the bodies got dumped in our territory. So somebody could be playing a numbers game and trying to make it look like our crime rate is up while yours is going down."

"Hold the phone, chief." Lourdes gave B.B. a double take to try to remind him who he'd brought to the dance. "You think *we're* playing politics with homicide stats?"

"I'm not saying that *is* the case, but anything is possible. Am I right?" Tolliver nodded at B.B., keeping the bond going. "Especially when people are trying to protect the value of their property."

Lourdes shrugged, ready to concede that point to him. Real estate numbers in this part of the world were as important as air quality to people in the Bronx. She'd been googling real estate in Long Island on her iPhone while they were in traffic. Median sales prices for last year in the county were close to $400,000. Property taxes were some of the highest in the country. Which helped pay for decent schools, cops' salaries, and spacious offices like the one they were in right now.

"Hey, my neighbors in Massapequa don't want to hear they got a homicidal lunatic around the corner," B.B. nodded. "They got a lot of money in their homes."

"Exactly," Tolliver said. "Which is why I'm just saying let's not get caught up in smoke and mirrors." He turned to Lourdes again. "Forgive me, miss, but I'm not completely sold on your Rockaway victim being part of a pattern that started out here."

She pounced. "But you *do* see a pattern."

"Of course, *some* of these cases could be connected." Tolliver looked at B.B. as if to ask, *Where did you find this dumb chick?* "I just don't buy that it's Son of Sam all over again."

"It could be worse, because this dude could be hella smarter," Lourdes said, starting to get seriously irked.

"How do you figure?" Tolliver rested the side of his face against his palm.

She used her fingers to tick off her points. "He picks his victims more carefully. Makes sure they have minimal attachments. Changes his MO. Removes the bodies from the crime scenes and dumps them when no one's looking . . ."

"Not *that* smart." Tolliver grinned at B.B. "Or else he would have buried the fucking bodies. Right?"

"I disagree," Lourdes said. "With respect, of course. Digging a hole takes time. Just dumping them in a nature preserve or dropping them in a body of water near the highway is way smarter and way easier. Even if they turn up eventually, there's a good chance that nature's taken its course and destroyed crucial evidence."

"Then why wrap them in plastic?" The chief raised a hand to quibble.

"Listen, I'm no serial killer—I don't have all the answers." Lourdes pulled her hair back from the sides of her face. "Maybe he was planning to dredge them up and keep them as trophies at some point. Or he thought the rocks he stuck in the plastic would help weigh them down."

"Hey, the guy has got a screw loose if he's killing all these women in the first place." B.B. nodded, back on her side finally. "Who knows what he could have been thinking?"

"Look, we're pledging our full cooperation to help your investigation." Tolliver sighed. "*Mi casa es su casa,* Detective Robles. I just don't know what else we can offer."

Lourdes smiled at him but it took some effort. Again, she found herself puzzled by her own reaction. The man was saying the right things and now offering to do them. So why was something inside her hanging back outside the perimeter?

"We're thinking our man's been pretty active for a long time," she said. "We don't know if he's still out there, preparing to do more or even how many he's killed in the past. It seems like he knows enough to vary his pattern sometimes. We're thinking you may have open cases that could turn out to be him."

"Unlikely." The chief huffed like an old cushion sat on too many times. "We don't have that many open cases. Detective Borrelli, you're probably old enough to remember when this used to be the home of the Ninety-Four Percent Squad. We closed almost everything."

"I do indeed." B.B. rested a hand on his chin, a permanent groove on the ring finger that was unbanded at the moment. "Those were the days, my friend."

"Not like that anymore, brother." Tolliver's mustache curved into a wistful smile. "Our crusading DA put an end to that years ago."

Lourdes cleared her throat, not wanting them to get distracted going down some deep rabbit hole of white men's useta-be's.

"We'd like to see the files on whatever open cases you do have," she said.

"Seriously?" The chief looked to B.B., trying to drive a wedge between his visitors again.

"You just said you don't have that many open ones," Lourdes reminded him. "Ninety-four percent and all."

"Yeah, but come on . . ." Tolliver rocked back in his chair. "How many years back are we talking?"

"How many years back you got?" Lourdes asked. "We don't know how old this guy is or how long he's been doing this."

Maybe it was just her. Maybe she was pushing too hard or expecting too much. Or maybe there were greater geographic forces at work here. The tectonic plates of city and suburb pushing up against each other. All she was sure of was that there was resistance here that couldn't just be explained by entrenched rivalries or bureaucratic intransigence.

"It's going to take a while." The chief sighed and laced his hands behind his head, a man with nothing to hide. "Some of these files may not even be digitized yet. You know you're asking for the moon, don't you?"

"I do." Lourdes put the dimples in her grin. "But as Detective Borrelli will tell you, that's just the kind of girl I am."

14

The Mets were in the World Series, for the first time in seventeen years. The Red Sox were playing them, trying to beat the Curse of the Bambino and win their first world championship since 1918. But right now, all Joey cared about was getting the rookie to snort up the white line of powder he'd tapped out onto the dashboard.

"*Danziger.* What kind of fuckin' name is that, anyway?" He handed the kid a rolled-up dollar. "You a Jew, or what?"

"Sarge?"

"Simple question: *What are you?* Everybody's something."

Since the promotion, Joey had started paying an almost scientific attention to the people he worked with. He'd always been detached and observant, even as a little kid, when he figured out how to play his parents. But now that he was moving up, he was keying in on assessments. Learning to evaluate others for their strengths and weaknesses. There was a pecking order and a food chain. Everyone had their malleable spots. A place where they could be pushed in and manipulated. Everybody could be gotten to at some level. And then used. You just had to sound the depths and figure out where to drop the hook.

They were near the end of their tour, close to midnight, parked behind a "We Buy Gold" pawnshop in Smithtown. Not quite cooping but not really on patrol either. Just hanging out, observing, and categorizing for future reference.

Any cars passing by with white guys at this hour were in the market for drugs or whores.

Any woman out on her own was selling what her mama gave her.

And any rookie who'd pass what Joey thought of as the reverse integrity test by leaning over a line of blow never officially turned in was as vulnerable to his sergeant as a hooker shivering in a twenty-dollar minidress on a thirty-degree night. An object to be used, not a fully sentient human being like himself.

"Lutheran," Danziger said, watching Joey aim a rolled-up twenty-dollar bill at the line.

"Ha?" Joey snorted.

"You asked what I was. My parents raised me Lutheran. It's part of the church."

"If you say so." Joey offered him the rolled-up bill.

"It *is*. Comes from Martin Luther. You know? He came out against the indulgences."

Joey gave him a deadpan stare. "Why would anybody do that?"

Danziger was a lanky, lantern-jawed kid who had no business being out on the street at this hour or any other hour. A farm boy from Patchogue, said to be going to night classes at LIU and thinking of getting his law degree. A Kenny Makris type, only not Greek and maybe not as smart. At first, Joey had bristled when he got assigned to show the kid the ropes. The last thing he needed was an altar boy in his vehicle cramping his style.

"He didn't believe you should just be able to buy your way out of punishment for your sins," Danziger said, eying the bill nervously.

"Hey, you gonna do this or what?" Joey nudged him.

"Uh, sarge, I don't know. I never did drugs."

"Then how can you work on the streets or understand what we're dealing with?"

"I thought we were supposed to be locking people up for doing drugs," Danziger said.

"Look." Joey put a heavy hand on the officer's shoulder. "We went into the 7-11 together and you didn't pay for your soda, right?"

"But you said we didn't have to."

"And we got drinks on the house the other night from Harrigan's. Didn't we?"

"You said cops drink for free in there." Danziger was starting to look scared. "Every night."

"We're working out here together. You're expecting me to put my life on the line for you, as your sergeant. And you're gonna leave me hanging out here, because I gotta worry that I did something in front of you that you might tell somebody about? How can I ride with you if I can't trust you?"

"I don't know, sarge."

"Put this in your fucking nose, and get going." Joey handed him the bill. "We're not in a Lutheran church right now."

Just like that, the kid took the bill, leaned over, and inhaled the half a line his sergeant had left for him.

"Hey, you got a little dribbling out of your nose." Joey swiped a thumb across Danziger's lip, just to show he could touch him whenever he felt like it.

"Uh . . . Thanks, sarge."

"You know what I say? 'Clean up your act before you start telling anyone else what to do.'"

Meaning: I own you now, *bitch*. The rookie looked stricken.

Static and hyped-up voices poured from the radio, interrupting the announcer who was talking about the Mets game going into extra innings.

"I didn't get all that." Danziger turned up the volume, trying to catch the tail end. "What's going on?"

"Bullshit domestic dispute call on Edgewood Ave.," Joey translated. Five years in the department, he was one of the only people who could consistently understand the dispatchers. "At least one gun in the house and kids are involved."

He turned down the game, switched on the engine, and tore out of the lot, the car almost going up on two wheels as they made the abrupt U-turn onto West Main Street, then hit seventy-five going under the train trestle, pasting the rookie back against the passenger seat. Danziger struggled with his seat belt and tried to hang on to the ceiling strap as street lights and gas stations hurtled by like they were going into hyperspace in *Star Wars*.

"Uh, sarge?" The rookie was trying to speak through gritted teeth, as residual coke from the dashboard flew back into his face. "Shouldn't we be letting Emergency Services take the lead on this?"

"We're in the vicinity," said Joey, pushing harder on the gas to make sure the rookie was properly daunted. "He's got a gun and kids in the house."

Putting the newbie through the rush, and not giving him the chance to turn around and ask questions about what they'd just done. It never failed. Probe. Breakdown. Bond. Build up. Repeat. And never forget: everybody has done something they don't want other people to know about.

The house was a tidy ranch from the 1970s, with a patched asbestos roof, storm windows, and a two-car garage. Even at night, it was plain to see that the exterior needed a fresh coat of white paint and that some of the black shutters were in need of repair. The neighbors, middle class but starting to slide, were out on the sidewalk in their bathrobes, hugging themselves against the autumn winds and looking spooked.

"And I swear, to look at them, this is the all-American family," a woman was saying as Joey got out.

The thing was to demonstrate to the rookie that he had no fear of anything. Especially not a subordinate officer turning on him. The drugs were doing their job, pumping him up, making him hard all over, like every vein in his body was erect. He felt as if he was ten feet tall and hung like a prize bull.

"Whose house is this?" he asked the woman who'd spoken, a frowzy brunette loudmouth in pink bunny slippers.

"Randy Carter. He's gone crazy since he got laid off at Northrop Grumman. You should see the empty liquor bottles in the garbage . . ."

"Did someone call in that he's got a gun?" Joey asked.

"At least two, maybe more." Bunny Slippers wagged a finger. "My husband's been to the shooting range with him and . . ."

"How many others inside?" Joey asked, making sure Danziger saw him taking charge here.

"Five. There's Randy, his wife, and the three kids. And the cat. The kids are twelve, ten . . ."

He put up his hand, having heard enough.

"Sarge, ESU is at least seven minutes out," Danziger called out the window. "Maybe we should hold off till—"

Joey was already on the move, past the jungle gym in the front yard, unswept leaves on the stone path to the porch crunching underfoot and prematurely announcing his arrival. He pulled his service revolver from his belt, rapped sharply on the front door, and then stood to the side in case a bullet answered.

"Police, Mr. Carter. Open up."

There was no reply. A name like Randy Carter, a neighborhood like this, he could be white or black. Not that it made any difference to Joey. Just that it was easier to find justification for shooting a black man than a white one. But really they were all just chum in the water. Bone and blood. A means to an end. He put an ear to the window and heard the moron ranting at his family inside. Probably drunk. Or high. And never mind the irony; Joey could handle his poisons.

The wife was audibly begging and crying. She must have been a mongoloid herself for marrying such a loser. And having his imbecile children, who were screaming and sobbing as well. Good argument for enforced sterilization.

He tried the handle and found the door was unlocked. No warrant but guns plus kids equaled exigent circumstances.

He stepped in with the gun raised and both hands on the grip. The hallway lights were on. Kids' baseball caps and warm-up jackets hung on hooks. A bottle of Mr. Clean sat on the floor that needed to be stripped and polyurethaned big-time. Arguing family voices competed with the sound of the World Series on the kitchen TV. God forbid they should turn it off in the middle of a crisis.

Through the open door at his back, he could hear Danziger outside on the sidewalk, calling more frantically for backup on his radio. Good that he didn't have the guts to come in yet. More reason for him to feel ashamed and thimble-dicked later.

Joey followed the sound down the hall, checked the side rooms, then got an angle to see into a kitchen with lots of counter space and a good high ceiling. There was an empty quart of some dumb-ass redneck bourbon next to a pizza box on the Formica counter. The freezer door was open. The cat was eating something off the floor. The wife was waving her arms frantically. And the three children were huddled in a corner near the dishwasher, weeping hysterically with wet swollen faces like they had been caught in a shipwreck. And these were *white people*? What happened to being the master race?

"Don't do it, Daddy." The oldest kid, a blonde like her mother, was crying the hardest. "Please put the gun down. We love you."

Joey stepped into the kitchen with his weapon raised. The smell of burnt rice put him back in his own childhood home for a half second, and a shot of searing hot rage went through him even as the sports announcers on TV nattered on.

"Daddy, please don't hurt yourself," the little girl was saying. "We need you."

The father had a .45 pressed to his temple. Maybe a SIG Sauer. It would leave a hole to be sure.

He was a big galoot who'd been drinking for a while. Tall and broadshouldered, with a burgeoning beer belly and an unshaven face that was getting much too fleshy for the amount of hair he had left.

Randy.

He didn't deserve that pneumatic, hard-bodied wife he had looking at him imploringly. Not much of a face but she almost made up for it with those tits in a red tube top and tight little buns in show-off spandex shorts. Like she was working double-time to keep herself together while the alleged man of the house was falling apart.

"Sir, you want to put that weapon down." Joey aimed at Randy's center body mass. "Right now."

Randy's sluggish expression became more animated for a second as he took the gun away from his temple and aimed it at Joey instead.

"Get the fuck outta my house," he said. "No one wants you here."

The hand with the .45 wasn't as brave as the voice. It was trembling. This kind of loser could probably put the barrel right under his chin and miss. But a gun was a gun, and with only twenty feet between them, there was a chance he'd hit something: shoulder, neck, chest, groin.

Joey still felt strangely numb, though. Both in the midst of the scene and ten miles above it. Even as he heard Danziger scampering up the hall behind him. The freeze spreading from the membranes in his nose to the rest of his body. Cold and in control. Because he truly didn't give a shit. Didn't care about any of them. Whether the whole family lived or died meant nothing. As long as he came out of it undiminished in the eyes of the rookie, who would then tell the rest of them that the sergeant was the man. He'd learned from the house he grew up in that you were either the dominant or the dominated. And it was better to be the dominant. Weakness was worse than fatal in a situation like this. Because a bullet could kill you instantly. But shame took its time doing the same thing, and that was worse.

"Officer Danziger, please get the rest of them out of here," he said in a calm, commanding voice. "We don't want any accidents."

Joey kept his eyes locked onto Randy's, letting the man know he could see everything he had and thought little of it.

"Go on now." Joey glanced at the wife, so she'd understand who had taken charge. "Take care of your children."

She threw an anxious look at her husband, who was weaving in place a little, and then at Joey. She knew who had the balls in the house now. And so did Danziger. He hustled the rest of the family out, leaving the two men pointing guns at each other while the Shea Stadium crowd on TV grumbled and the cat licked the linoleum floor.

"Pussy," Joey said.

The front door slammed and Randy looked startled, like it was a shot coming from another direction.

"You heard me," Joey said. "You're a fuckin' pussy."

"Yeah? Would a pussy do this?"

Randy put the .45 in his mouth, deep-throating the barrel. His legs were still unsteady and there were dark circles under his eyes, but there was nerve in them that hadn't been there a moment or two before. With his family out of the house, he could complete the action.

With a sudden thud in his own chest, Joey realized that this wasn't what he wanted. No credit or glory to an officer arriving and failing to prevent a suicide. The wrong kinds of questions might come up afterward with the Firearms Board. And Danziger, without proper deference, might say the wrong thing.

"This is how you want your kids to remember you?" Joey asked, trying to get the upper hand back. "Dead from a self-inflicted gunshot?"

Randy took the barrel out of his mouth. "They're better off without me," Randy said in a 16 rpm slur. "I've messed up everything. My wife doesn't even know the half of it . . ."

His elbow rose as he pressed the muzzle against the side of his head. Joey felt three more thuds in quick succession echoing within his own chest cavity.

"Sir, I need you to put the gun down."

"Or else what? You're gonna shoot me?"

"I will if I have to."

"Go ahead. We're upside down on our mortgage and hundreds of thousands in debt to the Money Store," Randy said. "Our life insurance is the only way out."

Joey looked around the house, both hands on his pistol grip, doing the math with the current market.

"How much is the policy for?"

The question startled Randy as much as the slamming door. "What's it to you?"

"Just answer the question."

The elbow lowered a little, but the barrel stayed at Randy's temple. "I don't know. I think a million point five. I got it right before I got laid off. What's the difference?"

"And you've been keeping up with the premiums?"

"Yeah, but I'm about to miss the next payment."

"Your family doesn't get the money if you fucking kill yourself, idiot."

It felt good to drop the mask and speak in his real voice for a second. Randy flinched a little, like he'd just heard the feral growl of some beast in nearby bushes.

"What'd you just say to me?"

"Didn't you read the fine print on your policy?" Joey readjusted his grip. "They don't pay off on suicides within the first two years. And I bet it hasn't been that long."

In his raging stupor, Randy was trying to recalculate. He looked like someone with a shellfish allergy, realizing he shouldn't have ordered the shrimp cocktail.

"What am I gonna do?" He wailed, face crumpling. "I can't even think straight anymore."

"Just listen carefully," Joey said, mind racing as his voice stayed even. "Lower the gun but don't let it go."

Sirens were approaching in the mid-distance. Emergency Services would be here any minute to break the door down and take away his control of the situation.

"Don't let it go?" Randy looked confused, his barrel away from his temple and aimed uselessly at the ceiling.

"Point it at me," Joey said.

"What?"

"You heard me. Someone may be looking in that window right now, watching us through binoculars. The only chance you have to get that money is if I help you."

"By shooting me like it's in self-defense?"

Joey tried to get away with a subtle nod, in case anyone outside could hear them. But that wasn't going to be enough of a cue for Randy.

"If you want to commit suicide by cop, you wouldn't be the first," he said slowly. "And no one else will ever know."

He saw the gun rise in Randy's hand again and then stop at his side, as he tried to think this through. "Would that even work?" he asked, hesitating.

"I'll make sure it gets put in the right way," Joey said with growing urgency.

The sirens were almost out front, and once ESU entered the house, it was all over.

The .45 started to come up again and then stopped at Randy's hip. "But what's in it for you?"

He was losing his nerve again, his natural chickenheartedness re-emerging. He needed to be pushed to follow through. The sirens were right outside now, the bright emergency lights washing into the kitchen.

"What's in it for me? Honestly?" Joey managed a half smile. "I'm gonna screw that blond little wife of yours till she forgets your name, beat your kids like they were my own, and live off your money in your house after you're gone."

"Hey, fuck you," Randy said, as the gun finally came up with purpose.

Joey pulled his trigger twice, striking him in the chest both times.

Randy looked aggrieved as he dropped his gun and clapped both hands to his blossoming wounds. Like he'd just figured everything out. He fell in stages and collapsed on the floor as the crowd cheered and the announcers screamed something about Buckner letting the ball go between his legs and Mookie getting to first base. The cat stayed focused on licking up whatever remained.

15

"Shouldn't you be getting home to your man?" Kevin Sullivan asked. "Or are you looking for excuses to stay out on a school night?"

"Maybe I just want to check in on my old partner." Lourdes stuck her chin out. "What's so funny 'bout that?"

They were in Sullivan's house in Windsor Terrace, Brooklyn, a predictably humble two-story row house among the more blatantly grand townhouses. It was the first time she'd ever been to his home—no great insult since most of the guys she worked with had never been there either. She'd been hoping to see a couple of photos of the wife and kid he spoke about so sparingly.

"Maybe I just heard you were moving and figured you could use a hand packing up." She leaned against a blank wall, trying to guess what kind of furniture might have been there.

"Most everything's in storage or at Goodwill," he said, tearing off another strip of duct tape for a wardrobe box.

That was Sully: wrapped up tight and self-contained. Sixty-five years in a house he'd inherited from his parents, forty years with the NYPD, and he didn't ask a single person to help him move.

The big man had more institutional knowledge than the Smithsonian, more street wisdom than Iceberg Slim, and—as she was given the privilege of learning in the brief time they worked together—more depth of feeling than three generations of family in a Spanish-language soap opera. But you'd need a rubber hose, third-degree lights, and a vial full of truth serum to even find out that he'd once been married.

"But if you came by just because you wanted to talk, that's okay too," he said, all gruff diffidence as usual.

"How much did you get for this place anyway?" she asked, deflecting, feeling a little reticent herself at the moment. "If you don't mind me asking."

"A little over two, though I probably could have held out for more. Needs a new kitchen. New bathrooms. But the bones are still good and it's just down the street from Prospect Park. Good place for someone just starting a family. Sorry you didn't make an offer?"

She half smiled and cast her eyes to the side. Might as well have a target on my chest. Sully getting right to the heart of the matter, as usual. That's what you get, going to see an old-school detective first grade with something on your mind.

"Where you moving?" she asked.

"I got a distant cousin with a family up in Albany, says she wants to spend time with me. But who the hell knows? Sixty-five-year-old widower living in your attic? Who needs that? But at least I'm handy around the house."

Lourdes realized that at least half the reason she hadn't checked in on him lately was because of her own fear. You heard too many stories of old cops who hit mandatory retirement age and were dead within a year or two. She made a mental note to see if he kept his gun unpacked and within easy reach.

"So what's doing with the job?" he asked.

"That Far Rockaway thing with the body washing up on the beach?"

"Yeah, I figured you'd be in on that." He nodded. "Never did lack for ambition, did you?"

Somehow it sounded more like a compliment than a dig, coming from him.

"How's Borrelli been on it?" he asked.

"You know . . ." She let her voice trail off, no need to spell out that it would have been different if he was the one working with her. "It could be connected to a bunch of Long Island murders going back fifteen years, with bodies buried up and down Sunrise Highway."

"Uh-oh."

"Why do you say that?"

"Nassau *and* Suffolk County?" His bushy Irish eyebrows shot up like matching apostrophes.

"What's the matter? You've done cases out there?"

"As infrequently as possible." He went to an open box and fished out two lowball glasses.

"And what's your beef?"

"I'm not saying there's no good people in those departments but . . ."

"But?"

He pulled a half-empty bottle of Four Roses Single Barrel from a cabinet above the refrigerator.

"A ninety-four percent confession rate? Gimme a break."

"Yeah, what's up with that?"

"I'll tell you what's up. They do whatever they please out there, with hardly any accountability. It's another world. They never had a Knapp Commission to make them clean up their act. Just some kind of state investigations commission that got buried thirty years ago."

"And why's that?"

He rubbed his hands together and held up his palms, like a magician showing he had nothing up his sleeve. "No one knows. It was just on and then it was off. A woman named Martinez called me once to ask about a case I had with them and then I never heard from her again. Maybe she got taken off it, maybe she didn't find anything. All I know is that Suffolk's had the same district attorney for at least thirty years and he lets his little favorites in the police department do whatever they want."

"Wait. The DA doesn't run the police department. They're separate entities."

"Not as much as they should be out there. In the city, we work with the prosecutors, but we fight them sometimes as well. Out there it's hand in glove. Which rarely makes anyone better at their jobs. Any case I had with them I tried to keep my distance. That ninety-four percent baloney that Long Island juries let them get away with don't play in Brooklyn, *chica*."

It still cracked her up to hear this old Irishman with Starsky-era sideburns finally going gray talking el barrio with her. But then she looked up and saw that his old .38 Smith & Wesson service revolver was on the same shelf where the Four Roses bottle had been. He saw her looking and shut the cabinet door.

"Yeah, well, I got at least six bodies between here and Montauk, so B.B. and me gotta work with them, the state police, and the FBI on a task force."

"Six?" Sullivan whistled. "*Dayum*, girl."

"Tell me about it. I was just in the Suffolk chief's office asking if they had any other open cases and this Joseph Tolliver looked at me like I had just named him as my baby daddy."

"Tolliver? Name rings a bell." Sullivan rubbed an earlobe and looked up. "He ever work in the city?"

"Not that he mentioned. In fact, he kicked us out of his office as soon as he could."

Though come to think of it, she'd gone out first and B.B. had lingered behind for almost a full minute with the door half-closed. Like the two big men were hanging out and having a laugh at her expense. Hard not to get an attitude.

"Yup, that's how they roll out there," Sullivan said. "They've stopped claiming the ninety-four percent confession rate, but they'd still rather deep-six a case or shift it to another category than have anyone looking over their shoulders."

"Any advice on how to deal with that?"

He poured two bourbons neat and handed her one without asking if she wanted it.

"Save your outrage for the victims," he said. "And the doer if you ever find him. Any leads?"

"Not much. Our man's slick. And sly. He changes up his approach every once in a while."

"What else? What are the basics? Concentrate."

"The victims are all women. And they're getting darker, more isolated and vulnerable." She swirled the liquid around in her glass without lifting it. "Most of them were working girls."

"Uh-huh."

He let that breathe for a second, waiting to see if she was going to say more. She looked up to see him sitting on a radiator, draining half his drink and then resting his glass on his knee. Expectantly. Giving her room. A lot of detectives had a gift for talk. Not that many had his gift for silence.

"So we've started reaching out to the local escort services—again." She put her head back. "And you know how that goes . . ."

"Yep . . ."

"If they weren't that eager to help with a personal matter, you know they're not going to roll out the welcome mattress when it's an official murder investigation."

"Let's not jump to any conclusions," he said.

"It's just common sense. A prostitute's not going to help a cop unless he's paying for her time . . ."

"I'm saying let's not jump to any conclusions about your sister being involved," he broke in. "I know that's what you're thinking."

"How do you know what I'm thinking?"

"It's what I'd be thinking—if I was you."

She rested both shoulders against the wall and looked up at the ceiling. Useless to argue. Sullivan was the first cop, besides her aunt, who she'd told about Izzy being in the wind. Even before the twenty-four hours had passed so she could call Missing Persons. He was retired nearly two years but he was still the best investigator she'd ever worked with. He took it as seriously as his own child being gone. Knocking on doors, reaching out to his contacts at the precincts and beyond, tapping into the databases, walking the streets in the middle of the night.

It was Sully who'd generated the only viable information they had so far, finding a photo of Izzy online. A picture Lourdes herself had taken about a year before her sister disappeared. Ysabel glammed up and posing in their mother's bedroom. Wearing a red dress that Lourdes could barely fit into herself. The formerly tubby girl smoking hot with false eyelashes and hair extensions. It pierced Lourdes to the heart, remembering how they'd been vamping it up for Izzy's OkCupid profile. Her sister finally coming out of her shell after a lifetime of depression and bipolar delusion.

Back in May, Sullivan had found the picture on a Sugar Daddy website based in Ronkonkoma. For younger women "seeking arrangements with older men of means." Baby steps toward prostitution. Sully knew it was true as well. By the time they got to it, the email address Izzy had used to open the account was closed and the cell phone number she'd posted was no longer in service.

"You think she's dead?" Lourdes asked Sullivan, not for the first time.

"I don't know."

He'd promised he'd never lie to her.

"But how likely is it that she's alive if we haven't heard anything in all this time?" Her hand tightened around the glass.

"Don't you think you've got enough riding on this case already?"

"Can't help myself." She put the drink down. "How do other people stand it? That's what I'd like to know."

"They drink. Some of them."

She knew it was crazy to blame herself. But then again the whole family was crazy. Except for maybe her and Aunt Soledad. Mami in assisted living, Papi upstate, Georgie, the brother she barely knew, dead from an OD, and Izzy until recently living in a fantasy world, overeating in front of her computer and telling everyone she was going to marry either Derek Jeter or Alex Rodriguez of the Yankees.

After the fallout had settled from the dead lawyer in the park case, Lourdes had thrown herself into a family reclamation project. Finding a facility out on the island that could handle Mami's dementia on her benefits, paying a couple more visits to Papi in prison, and pulling together a team of doctors for Izzy.

For a while, it worked. It was like having Mami taken care of deprived Izzy of justification for being a mess. She went on new medication, dropped a ton of weight, started auditing classes at John Jay, and began hinting that she'd met "someone nice" online.

But then the drama started all over again. She claimed Lourdes was jealous of her weight loss (which maybe she was, a little bit). She started staying out late and refusing to say where she'd been. She accused Lourdes and Soledad of trying to control her and stopped taking her meds. And then one night she didn't come home at all.

"A lot of prostitution outcalls go from the city to Long Island," Lourdes said.

"True enough."

"She could have run into the same psycho."

"And if your aunt had a mustache, she'd be your uncle."

"Fuck you, Sullivan. My aunt *has* a mustache."

"Sorry."

"Look: not that many sex workers in New York. Izzy could've gone on one of those calls."

"Say there's about a hundred thousand sex workers in the area, and each goes on an average of two calls a night. It's *possible*, but not likely."

"So you admit it. It's not *im*possible. She could be wrapped up and lying in some swamp off Sunrise Highway right now."

"Jaysus. And they call me a morbid bastard? She could also be alive, you know."

"I'm just trying to be real and prepare myself for the worst."

"If you want to be real, then you can't be prepared."

She looked out his window, dusk falling over the men gathered outside Farrell's bar across the street, the dwindling tribe of cigarette smokers. A couple of them were leaning against her car, and it was hard to resist the urge to open the window and yell at them to get off it.

"How's my Camry?" Sullivan came up to look over her shoulder.

"*My* Camry now. And it's still running, thank you very much."

"You changing the oil regularly?"

"Yeah, of course." It annoyed her, thinking about how much Mitchell had to take it to a garage instead of doing it himself.

"How's the alignment?"

"The alignment's good and so's the tire pressure."

"You keeping up with the other contracts?"

"Oh, for crying out loud, it's a twelve-year-old car, Sullivan. No one's gonna steal it or strip it."

"Still a good car, if you're taking care of it."

"Yeah, though I'm thinking of trading it in and throwing the extra money at an SUV."

He grunted in disapproval as she turned around. "What do you need a bigger car for? You planning on buying a dog or starting a family?"

"Fuck you. Are you just saying that because I'm a woman in her thirties?"

"That and the joke about naming the chief as your baby daddy."

"It was *a joke*, Sully."

"And the fact that you brought it up last time we had lunch."

"I did not."

"Your eggs had just come. You said, 'How can I even be thinking of having a baby with how loco the rest of my family is?'"

"Oh . . ."

"Listen." He finished his drink. "If I'd lost someone, I'd look for something to take their place."

"But you *didn't* look for anything after you lost your wife, except to get into a lot of crazy," she said sharply. "So what the fuck are we talking about?"

He pressed a fist to his chest like he had heartburn.

Nice.

Why don't you ask him to break out those photos of the wife and kid? Remind him of all the mad man stories you heard about how he tried to get himself killed after they passed?

Maybe ask how many rounds he's got left in that .38 he keeps in the cabinet.

"Well, it's getting late." He looked at his watch. "I'm sure your young man is wondering where you are."

"He's all right," she said. "He's used to waiting."

He started to take the glass from her. "Well, it won't do for you to be showing up with liquor on your breath if you're supposed to be working late with Borrelli on a serial killer case."

She thought of Mitchell looking up as she came in, questions in his eyes he was starting to be afraid to ask. She held onto her glass.

"I am working." She finally took a sip and cringed. "We were talking about how to get these other departments to cooperate."

"We were?"

"I was going to ask if you know anybody you could reach out to, help us get what we need on these open cases if we get stonewalled."

"I'll look into it." He set his glass aside, instead of refilling it. "And maybe I can do a little more as well. Wouldn't mind a side project. Stay out of the relatives' hair for a while."

It was getting dark in the house. She realized he'd unscrewed most of his light bulbs either because he wanted to save money or because he didn't see any point in replacing them. Whatever. The man needed to work.

"Are you really going to move upstate?" she asked. "Can't see you getting up early to milk the cows."

"Maybe I'll go to Long Island instead." He shrugged. "If you're telling me true, prices ought to be falling off a cliff."

16

Do I know you?

Joey, now a lieutenant, was on the witness stand, testifying at the Lonnie Donges trial when he noticed the slightly washed-out blonde in the back row staring at him.

"And how many years have you been with the department, lieutenant?" Brendan O'Mara, the prosecutor on the case, was trying to keep him focused.

"Eight years, next month."

"In that time, is it fair to say you've been involved in numerous investigations?"

"It'd be fair to say 'hundreds.' I was very active on patrol. And I've stayed active as a supervisor. I never ask my men to do anything I wouldn't do."

He stared back, trying to key in on her. She wasn't his type at all. Too tall, too old, too fully formed. She was wearing a white blouse and a blue blazer. Not too much makeup or attention to brushing her hair. Like she didn't care all that much about people evaluating her by her appearance. Who the hell was she and why was she looking at him like this?

"In those hundreds of cases, have you ever encountered the scene of a crime that was so wantonly brutal and vicious?" Brendan approached the stand, blocking Joey's view.

"No, although . . ."

"Objection." Lonnie's lawyer, David Dresden, was on his feet, ponytail bouncing over his suit jacket collar. "That's not even a leading question. It's an invitation to deliver a soliloquy."

Smartass Jew York lawyer who didn't have any business trying a case out here. Probably was barely breaking even between his piddly public defender compensation and the cost of gasoline he spent driving out here.

"I'll allow the question," said the judge, the Honorable Edward J. McCarthy.

The People's murder case against Lonnie Donges was in good hands with Fast Eddie in charge. Especially since officers on Joey's watch had used their discretion not to arrest the judge for domestic violence, when Mrs. McCarthy called them to the house in Port Jefferson and showed them her blackened eye and bruises on her neck.

As Brendan moved, Joey saw the blonde was still giving him that X-ray stare. He wondered if this could be a divorce lawyer for the judge's wife, looking for leverage to use in the settlement.

"Can you describe the scene to us?" Brendan asked.

"Certainly." Joey put his hands on the rail of the box, asserting his authority. "The victim was found in a wooded area behind a Toys 'R' Us department store in Babylon. Her clothes had been torn off and her head was at an unnatural angle because her neck was broken. Her legs were covered in blood and it was obvious that identification was going to be a problem because her face was so badly disfigured."

Thinking about it on reflection, he realized that putting the remains in a construction trailer and setting them on fire had not been worth the trouble. It didn't look like that old MTV video and those volunteer firefighters had somehow arrived within ten minutes of him dropping the match. He'd barely had time to hide behind the darkened Dairy Queen across the road, to see what the response was going to be. The flames barely had a chance to consume the flesh, let alone scorch the bones. If he ever did this again, it'd be simpler just to find a safe place to wrap her up and dump her near a highway. With a chart of everybody's schedules, he could be reasonably sure of when the roads would be empty.

"It was actually less difficult in this case to identify the suspect." Brendan raised his voice. "Wasn't it?"

"Yes."

"Can you tell us why?"

Joey shut his eyes and started nodding, knowing the jurors would mostly interpret this as a dedicated public servant deeply moved by his duty to speak for the dead. In this case, a plump failed nursing student named Angela Spinelli, who, given his own limited interaction with her, no one was sincerely going to miss.

"An intact crack pipe was found near Angie's body." He knit his brow to show how he was still affected by the sight. "Our crime scene technicians were able to lift useable fingerprints from it. We eventually were able to match them to Mr. Donges's prints, which we already had in the system from a previous arrest."

Lonnie, dark as sin and skeletal from his crack habit, started muttering loudly to his lawyer: "Buncha lyin' motherfuckers. How's everything gonna burn except a fuckin' crack pipe . . ."

"Mr. Dresden, tell Mr. Donges to stifle himself or I'll have him removed," the judge said, noticing that the jurors had started to shake their heads. "I know city courtrooms are like zoos these days, but out here we show respect for the law."

Was that blond bitch in the back smiling like this was some kind of joke? Joey leaned to the side, trying to get a better read on her. But then the courtroom doors opened and Kenny Makris came in, the DA trying to make a statement to the jury with his presence, and sat right in front of her.

"Lieutenant, you were on duty at the station when Mr. Donges came in voluntarily and agreed to give a statement without a lawyer," Brendan said. "Is that correct?"

"Objection." David Dresden stood again. "He was dragged into the station with a bloody mouth, tortured in a basement room, and denied his right to counsel. And he's since recanted that statement."

"Overruled." The judge didn't even bother to look at the defense table. "Lieutenant, you may answer the question."

"Yes, I was present. Though Detective Rattigan was in charge of the interrogation."

The former Prince of Pain was slouching in the first row, having testified earlier and basically thrown up all over himself under intense questioning from Dresden. He looked like he was passed out now. The presence of the DA in the courtroom was intended to assure the jurors that the office still solidly believed in this case. And Joey's testimony was going to be crucial for its redemption. But how long were they going to keep carrying this lush?

"At any point did you see Detective Rattigan strike or in any way physically abuse the defendant for the purpose of obtaining a confession?" Brendan asked.

"Absolutely not."

Joey curled his lip, to show the jury that any such suggestion was beneath contempt. Which it was. Since William Rattigan was no longer in good enough shape to get down on one knee and squeeze a defendant's testicles hard enough to get an incriminating statement. Joey himself had donned the rubber glove and performed the honors himself. Another reason to saddle Billy the Kid's horse and send him riding off into the sunset.

"No one forced Mr. Donges to do anything," Joey said. "He abducted, raped, and killed an innocent woman before he put her in a trailer that he set on fire. Then he put himself at the crime scene with his own ill-considered words."

"Fuck *all*, y'all." Lonnie slapped the defense table and turned away.

"Judge, really . . ." Dresden was more weary and perfunctory as he rose this time.

"Overruled."

Lonnie was shaking his head. "Y'all the ones shoulda been burned up . . ."

"Okay, that's enough." The judge brought the gavel down. "Mr. Dresden, we're going to take a break and discuss this in chambers. Mr. Donges, you're going back to the pens."

There was a bright red Dodge Challenger next to his white Camaro IROC Z in the parking lot. The first sign of trouble was that he could see the Challenger had its hood up. The second and third signs were the pair of black spiked heels he could see beneath the front bumper.

"There a problem?" He made sure he was smiling as he came around on the driver's side.

Of course, it was the blonde from the back row. She'd been waiting.

"I must have left my running lights on, because now my battery is dead." Her skirt, way too short for late October, was tight across her butt as she bent over the engine block, one minor concession she'd made to the honey pot role. "Could you give me a jump?"

He straightened up to his full height, nostrils twitching slightly, like a dog trying to tell if it was a deer or a coyote he sniffed close by.

"Why not?"

He went to get his cables from the trunk, deciding to play along for now and see what she was after.

"I can never remember where to attach them," she said as he came back. "Positive goes to negative?"

He squinted again. She wasn't set up to play dumb. There was too much rangy intelligence in her eyes and she moved too athletically when she unfolded herself to stand up to him. There was nothing scared and helpless about her, he noticed, as he clamped the jaws on her outputs. She seemed like a woman who could check her own spark plugs and change her own oil filters.

"Impressive," she said as he raised the Camaro's hood to attach the cables to his own battery.

"Really?" He went to unlock his door and start his own motor. "I'd think anyone in this lot could've done that."

"I was talking about your testimony in the courtroom."

He didn't like the confident way she came over and stood by his open door, hand on her hip, looking down at him.

"Just the facts, ma'am." He gave her his best Joe Friday. "That's all it was."

He fumbled a little, putting his key in the ignition. *Bet you could find it if it had hair around it,* his father used to say. He jammed it in and twisted it a little too hard, almost flooding the engine.

"Guess you better get in your own vehicle and see if it'll start now," he said.

"There's nothing wrong with my battery, lieutenant. Turn your motor off."

He shut it down and looked up at her, sun glare over her shoulder turning her into a looming silhouette. She took her time detaching his cables, shutting her hood, and then coming to the driver's side of his car to hand them back to him.

"What's this about?" he asked, no longer grinning. "Who are you?"

"Leslie Martinez." She handed him an ID. "I'm with the state investigations commission. I've written to you and left several phone messages. I thought I'd try to see you in person."

"You don't look like an investigator." He gave the card a cursory glance and gave it back to her. "Or a Martinez."

"It's a married name. And I promise you that I am an investigator. With a particular interest in your department."

"Okay, so now you see me," he said. "What can I do for you?"

He was conscious of everything now. The position of his hands in his lap. The tilt of his shoulders against his seat. The pressure of the sun on his eyeballs, which made him long to put on his shades. The awareness that there had been talk about the state investigating the PD, taking a closer look at the confession rate and these bullshit allegations about so-called innocent minorities getting abused.

"I'd like you to come in and answer some questions for us," she said.

"And why would I do that?"

"It would help our investigation."

"There's no reason for your investigation. Except to harass good cops."

"Let me ask you something: Do you think that was credible testimony today?" she said.

"Ask me what you need to ask me and let's get this over with," he said. "Because I'm not coming in. And you've got no cause to compel me. This is my car and my time, and I've got places to be."

"I'm sure you do." She stood back, pretending to admire the ride. "Funny thing, what you said on the stand today. Reminded me of another case."

"Yeah?"

"Do you remember Stephanie Lapidus?"

She moved so the sun was more directly in his eyes, forcing him to squint more intently.

"Student from Mercy College, found raped and strangled down the road from her car?" Leslie Martinez did not make this sound like a question.

"Yeah, I remember. Long time ago now."

"Some striking parallels to this case. Don't you think?"

He faced forward and furrowed his brow just enough to make two distinct lines on his forehead. Like the thought had never occurred to him.

"What are you thinking specifically?" he asked.

"Both Stephanie and Angie Spinelli were young white women traveling alone late at night. Both were abducted, taken to secluded areas, and supposedly killed by drug-addicted black men."

"Nothing 'supposed' about it. Trevor Knightsbridge is up in Attica for life for what he did to that poor girl. If there was any real justice, the state would have fried his ass by now. Instead of wasting taxpayers' money harassing honest, hardworking cops."

"You feel like I'm harassing you, lieutenant?"

"Say what you have to say."

He'd be well within his rights to ask for his union delegate or a lawyer now. But only guilty people asked for lawyers. He'd said it himself a thousand times. Besides, he needed to find out how much she already knew. Mentioning a lawyer would end the conversation too soon and leave him hanging.

"In both cases, incriminating evidence with the defendants' fingerprints was found at the crime scene," Leslie Martinez said.

"Yeah, that's how it usually goes with real police work. You find evidence, follow leads, and get people to tell you things that they shouldn't. You might want to try that some time. Instead of swallowing a bunch of crap you've been fed by scumbag defense lawyers."

"You didn't let me finish." She put one stiletto heel on the driver's side doorstep. "The other parallel is that in both cases, the defendants had been arrested several weeks earlier. And both say they had possessions confiscated by the police that were never officially vouchered."

"Boo-hoo. Call the American Civil Liberties Union."

"The point is, that same evidence later showed up at the crime scenes, with their fingerprints. Like it was deliberately planted to incriminate them."

"What do you expect them to say? Jesus, lady . . ."

She was encroaching further into his car, having herself a good look around. Almost as if she was mocking him. Daring him to lose his cool and tell her to back off.

"The rolling papers in Stephanie's car and the crack pipe by Angie's body. Some coincidence. Don't you think?"

"Drug paraphernalia at crime scenes." He refused to look at her shiny knee coming at his face. "It's like popcorn at the movies. Just what you would expect."

Someone was talking. Two cases, seven years apart. Why would this Leslie even think to compare them unless someone had tipped her off?

"Here's what you wouldn't expect." She held onto the top of the doorframe. "The same officer involved in both of the original arrests. And the same detective at both crime scenes."

"You're trying to turn me against Billy Rattigan?"

"You know how it works, lieutenant. You or him. Maybe you want to come in sooner rather than later."

"I don't know where you're getting all this garbage, but I'm innocent. I don't even remember locking up Trevor Knightsbridge. And for your information, with Lonnie Donges, I wasn't the arresting officer. I was the supervisor. See these bars on my collar? Means I'm a lieutenant."

"Which is why you just happened to be there when they found Angie's body. But why were you there when they found Stephanie's car seven years earlier?"

"I wasn't."

"Sure about that?"

"Yes. I'd just been working the overnight tour."

"I thought you didn't remember the case that well."

He realized he'd been still and stiff for so long that his joints would audibly crack if he tried to move too quickly now.

"It's coming back to me," he said.

"Then you remember standing by Stephanie's car when it was found. Even though, as you just said, your tour was over."

For a half second, there was nothing between now and then. He was back beside the highway. The smell of grass and auto exhaust in the air. Bambú packet in his shirt pocket. Billy Rattigan distracting everyone as he staggered over with a hangover. Amy Half-Nelson in her baggy uniform, putting her eyes where they should not have been.

He turned and looked up at Leslie Martinez, not giving a damn if she heard a crick or a pop in his neck now.

"You ought to be ashamed of yourself," he said.

"I should?" She looked incredulous, a finger above the blouse button where he could see the black lace bra she was wearing.

"Running down good cops so you can get ahead. They got a name for what you are."

"I'm more interested what you think they should call you, lieutenant. And by the way, how's that new place in Smithtown working out for you? Funny that I can't find the report with your blood alcohol content after the shooting."

"Get your leg out of my car before you lose it." He slammed the door, nearly catching her ankle.

He rolled the window down and spat on the asphalt near her shoes. "You want to talk to me again, it'll be with a lawyer."

"Nice meeting you too."

He rolled the glass up, restarted the engine, and drove away.

17

The first surprise was that anybody from the Suffolk County District Attorney's office called Lourdes back, after she'd been getting cold-shouldered by Chief Tolliver's people. The second surprise was that when she showed up at the records room with B.B. expecting to collect some files from a second-tier assistant, they were instead ushered in to see the DA himself, Kenneth Makris.

His office was a more austere affair than the chief's. Instead of all the civic awards proudly displayed, he just had a few spare diplomas on the wall and a framed, yellowing *Newsday* headline celebrating his first electoral victory in 1984. In fact, the most noticeable items in the office were pictures of a much-younger Makris on a stage with his wife and daughter and a large white cross on the credenza behind his desk.

Makris himself was a thin, white-haired man in horn-rimmed glasses and a bow tie, outwardly gracious and polite but inwardly severe, bordering on ascetic. Like other DAs she'd met, he seemed more like an administrator than a politician or a lawman. Someone who was happier wielding power in a quiet office rather than on a stage or in a courtroom. It was a minor wonder he'd managed to get elected at least eight times. His opponents must have had about as much charisma as kelp.

"So I hear you folks have already been to see Joey," he said, surprising Lourdes by trying to turn her hand as he shook it.

The old cop-testing ritual. Sullivan had shown it to her when they worked together. If you could twist someone's wrist while you were shaking hands, you might have yourself a cooperator.

"Joey?" Lourdes closed one eye.

"Chief Tolliver at the police department." Makris forced a grin. "I heard good things."

"Did you now?"

She glanced at B.B., who was back to being his old spiffy self today, shoes polished and suit pressed, like he was here for a job interview.

"So what can I do for you good people?" The DA took a seat behind his desk. "I'm always happy to help out my friends at the New York City Police Department. We've solved a lot of great cases together over the years."

"We certainly have." B.B. grinned, his teeth noticeably whiter today as well. "I think you and I worked together on a Gambino heroin case back in the nineties, counselor, where they were dealing out of the back room of a pizza place in Smithtown . . ."

"*Aaanyway*," Lourdes interrupted before this got as white and boring as a golf tournament without Tiger Woods. "I'm sure the chief told you that we were looking at these Sunrise Highway murders going back a few years."

"Yes, those are Nassau County's cases." Makris had started vigorously nodding before she was done talking. "I heard all about those from Joey."

"Well, they're not *all* Nassau County cases," Lourdes said. "Some of the bodies were found on your side of the line, which is why we—"

"See, this is what we have to be careful about," Makris said over her. "We don't want to get our lines of communication crossed and put the wrong message out there."

"And what message is that?" Lourdes asked.

"That we have a major crime problem in our community," the DA said. "Which we do not. Except what's caused by some illegal immigrants. Who will soon be gone, thanks to the efforts of my office with the federal government and the police."

Lourdes glanced at B.B., who was just standing there with his hands clasped and an ingratiating smile on his shiny face like he was auditioning to be a greeter at one of the more expensive Vegas hotel-casinos.

In a way, she got it. They had their carefully maintained little American dream out here, with green fields and good schools and rising house values, and the idea of a serial killer running around destabilized the whole image. Not like the neighborhoods she came from, where you expected every day to be a struggle and where just lying down in your bed at night in a housing project without getting shot through the window was a triumph. Making everyone feel safe and not rocking the boat was why Makris kept getting elected.

"Forgive me, Mr. Makris," she said. "I think we've had a misunderstanding. We didn't ask for this meeting because we're worried about a local PR problem. We asked for it because we're concerned there might be a serial murderer running around and we're getting very limited cooperation from the police department. Our bosses thought you could maybe help because your office has done its own investigations into some of these cases."

"Definitely." The DA nodded. "I have some of the finest investigators in the business. Some of them come here straight from the Suffolk County Police Department, and go right back after working with us. Though we maintain our independence. So tell me exactly what you're looking for."

"Anything that could help our case," B.B. said, finally sounding like a detective doing his job. "When we start thinking about serial killers, we think either of people who've never been caught or people who've been caught for something else and are out now. Maybe your office successfully prosecuted someone in the past who could be our suspect now. Especially if the dates line up with when they were in and out of prison."

"And Joey couldn't help you with that?" Makris looked up, his desk lamp catching the smudge of a fingerprint on one of his lenses.

"Well, he's pledged his assistance, but time is of the essence," Lourdes said. "And we were hoping that because of the close relationship between the DA and the PD out here, you might be able to encourage the chief to be more responsive."

"Heh, heh, well, Joseph Tolliver does things on Joseph Tolliver's time." Makris laughed and used a handkerchief to wipe his glasses off. "But tell me something, detective. Who else is talking to you?"

"Sir?" Lourdes looked at B.B. as if she needed translation.

"You've been looking into these murders. Where are you so far?"

Under normal circumstances, it would have been a perfectly reasonable question. The head of an important prosecutor's office asking a couple of visiting detectives what they had so far. But again, she had that halted feeling. Almost like an arm in front of her chest, keeping her from plowing ahead heedlessly.

"Well, we're still in the early stages," she said. "But all our victims so far were prostitutes who worked on Long Island, so anything anybody can give us as background is going to be helpful."

"Yes, yes, I can see that." Makris nodded. "I'll have my people start pulling case files as soon as we're done. But please, share whatever you have with us. It's all about creating dialogue."

Lourdes tried to catch B.B.'s eye, to see if he was as disconcerted as she was. Why were these people pretending to be helpful and then doing nothing? Were they just worried about looking like they'd been asleep at the switch? She was beginning to understand what Tierney and Sullivan meant when they'd said that this was another world.

"And I'll reach out to Joey at the police department and let him know we've spoken," Makris added. "And you should let him know what you have so far as well. We all want the same thing here."

"I hope that's true," Lourdes said.

"Of course it is." Makris gave a kind of flabbergasted smile as he stood up to show them out. "Why would you ever doubt it?"

18

Billy the Kid was riding low in the saddle again. Rattigan was clinging to the end of the bar at a place that had changed its name from the Brazen Fox to Cheers Too. The white tablecloths were now checkered, Guinness and Heineken ran from the taps, and the Irish soda bread and crisp breadsticks in the baskets had been replaced by day-old Pepperidge Farm rolls.

But the waitresses were mostly the same, if older and more pulled-on, and Rattigan was still on his customary stool, wearing his tinted aviators indoors. Only now the darkened lenses served the purpose of keeping him from detecting the increasingly contemptuous stares aimed his way, the rag on the counter the barmaid had just thrown at him to fend off his halfhearted advances, and the ruined bloat of his body threatening to tumble off his perch as he demanded the staff switch the TV from East German protestors on CNN to sports in the middle of a weekday.

"Look at him." Joey took off his own aviators and glanced over his shoulder. "Can you believe there were people on this job who once respected that man?"

"I thought you were one of them," Kenny Makris said, eyes on the lunch special blackboard, hand wrapped around the glass of pinot noir a waitress had just brought over.

How times had changed. The DA having a drink of his own in plain view of Steve Snyder, the hail and hardy county executive, sitting in a booth across the room. Under the same roof where Kenny nearly had a heart attack because the star witness in the case that had made his career dared to want his own glass filled. The miserly hypocritical fuck. So much for gratitude. Well, he'd be paying today.

"Anyway, we were talking about this state investigations commission." Joey turned back, catching his own reflection in the mirror.

He liked the way he was coming into his look. More beefy and square-jawed than his old man. Clear-eyed and thick-necked. Closer to the central casting look of a man of authority. Someone not to be questioned.

"I got a call from the judge in the Spinelli case and thought I should come down and speak to you about it right away," Kenny said. "Apparently, Leslie Martinez has been in touch with him about irregularities in procedure."

"The nerve of this broad, Kenny." Joey dropped his voice and his chin. "The friggin' balls on her. Trying to stick her big fat foot in my car and up my ass."

"I understand." Kenny paused to wave uncomfortably at a passing legislator. "But there are questions that have to be answered now."

The wineglass was suspended halfway to his lips. The scared little altar boy in him not completely at ease, even running one of the biggest local law enforcement offices in the country.

"A lot of people have a lot of nerve," Joey grumbled. "And not enough memory."

"Is that referring to something?"

"What do *you* think?"

Kenny looked away, put the glass down, and raised a hand for the waitress to come over to take their orders. They both asked for the pasta special and Kenny tucked his tie into his shirt, already worrying about it getting stained.

"So what are we going to do about this Martinez bitch?" Joey asked as the waitress scurried off.

"I have no control over what a state investigations commission does. For all I know, they could be looking at my office as well as the police department."

"You better hope not."

Two judges passed by and Kenny draped a napkin over his wineglass. As if it had just occurred to him that after years of sliding into the habit of having the occasional discreet drink at the banquette he'd inherited from Phil O'Mara, he had to be on guard against spies from the state.

"Look, I'm proud of the work we do here," he said quietly. "But the governor is worried about the next election and he doesn't like some of the stories he's been seeing in the press. He wants to look like he's doing something about corruption."

"By conducting a witch-hunt, led by actual fucking witches."

"Could you keep your voice down please?"

Joey had his back to the room, but he could see the reflections of the county executive and the judges watching them in the smoked mirror over Kenny's shoulder.

"I got nothing to be ashamed of," he said. "And I'm not taking the fall for anybody."

"Then let's be honest: How much of a problem do we have here?"

"Who said there was any problem? It's just the same old bullshit with the high and mighty from the outside trying to tell us what to do."

"Joseph." Kenny took off his glasses and set them aside, near the wineglass. "This is me talking. I've known you since you were a teenager. I've vouched for you. I helped you get into the police department. I've encouraged the chief to move you up on the list. I need the truth now."

Joey expanded his chest with a deep breath through his nose. "You know what you need to know."

"But what I'm hearing about these investigations is troubling," Kenny pressed on, trying to sound steely and resolute in his low-key way. "*Twice* evidence that wasn't properly vouchered showed up later at crime scenes. What am I supposed to make of this?"

"Nothing. Present it to the jury and let them decide."

"I will not allow the reputation of this office to be tarnished." Kenny tapped a fingernail on the tablecloth, his face turning red. "The integrity of the process has to be protected. Especially when the legislature is talking about bringing back the death penalty for cases like this. I'm not going to be involved with innocent men getting executed."

"Oh please." Joey wrinkled his nose. "Don't talk to me about 'the integrity of the process' when you took cases with a ninety-four percent confession rate."

"We're not doing that anymore. Not with a state commission turning over every stone."

"Then say goodbye to your pristine little track record, Mr. Law and Order." Joey waved. "Because you're going to start letting the animals roam free."

"Look." Kenny turned his head in both directions before he started speaking in a lower, more heated voice. "This goes beyond procedure. They're looking at individual behavior. And it doesn't help that a highly regarded officer just moved in with the widow of a suspect he shot in Smithtown."

"That's none of anybody's business."

"At the same house, Joey? Really?"

"That was three years ago and I wouldn't be talking about anyone else's real estate arrangements if I was you, Kenny," Joey warned him. "I heard about your office dropping the investigation into Port Jefferson Mortgage Brokers right before you got the loan from them."

The blood drained from Kenny's face. "Who told you about that?"

"That's not important. People talk."

"I've done nothing improper." Kenny held the sides of the table, as if trying to maintain his balance. "There wasn't enough evidence to sustain a case against the bank."

"Yeah, keep telling yourself that." Joey grinned. "How's Judge McCarthy's old place working out for you anyway? Annemarie putting in a new kitchen? Better schools for Christina too, right? I hear you got yourself a nice break on the interest rate for the loan. Two percent on a thirty-year mortgage?" He licked his lips to whistle. "Man, I'm impressed."

The district attorney put a finger on the tabletop. "Joey, why do you want to put me in this position?"

"*Because* I put you in this position." Joey laughed. "*Get it?* You wouldn't be the fucking DA if it wasn't for me."

The finger on the table began to shake and turn white from Kenny pressing down so hard.

"I'm going to ask you something now that I didn't want to ask in this setting," Kenny said, struggling to maintain his composure. "But I need to get to it. And I want you to answer it quietly and straightforwardly. Did you plant evidence in either one of these cases in order to incriminate these defendants?"

"Who says I did?"

"Answer my question first, lieutenant."

So it was "lieutenant" now, instead of "Joey" or even "Joseph." Trying to distance himself. Like they weren't inextricably linked. Like spattering mud only went in one direction.

"Trevor Knightsbridge murdered Stephanie Lapidus and Lonnie Donges killed Angela Spinelli." Joey hunched forward on his elbows. "Anyone says otherwise is a liar."

Conversation around them died away, leaving ferns swaying in the air-conditioning and Billy Joel singing "My Life" prominently on the sound system. In the mirror glass, Joey could see that half the restaurant was looking at them now. They had kept their voices down, but the presence of two grown men speaking so intensely without laughter or a glance at the bar TVs meant that either a large sum of money was involved or a fight was about to break out, or both. Even Billy Rattigan was sitting up and paying attention.

"So I guess I'll have to accept that," Kenny said. "For now."

"So exactly who is talking to this commission? Where are they getting this bullshit about the chain of evidence?"

The district attorney put his glasses back on and forced a smile, as if they were going back to a normal conversation. "You know I can't tell you what they shared with me without jeopardizing the independence of their investigation."

"Fuck you, Kenny." Joey kept monitoring reactions in the mirror. "You were reminding me of how much I owe you? Let me remind *you* of something. You wouldn't be where you are if it wasn't for me. I was your star witness in the case that made you. I kept the players where they needed to be. And as a police officer, I've helped drive down the crime rate to make you look good."

"I haven't forgotten."

"It sounds like you have. So let me remind you of something else. There's no statute of limitations on murder. If your star witness comes forward years later and says: 'Hey, the prosecutor pressured me to finger this poor fucking black kid, instead of the real doers' . . ."

"You would never do that."

"Don't be so sure, Kenny. You may not know as much as you think you know. If the whole shit house goes up in flames, you can't predict who's gonna get burned."

"This is beneath both of us."

"Who is talking to them, Kenny? Don't make me ask you again."

The waitress brought them their specials, lava spills of tomato sauce covering up Prince Spaghetti Day, and finally gave Joey the bottle of Coors he'd ordered twenty minutes before.

"One of the officers who was at the Lapidus crime scene may have seen something out of the ordinary." Kenny spoke in a barely audible voice, hiding his mouth behind the napkin for a moment as he tucked it into his shirt collar. "It's a developing situation."

Joey looked down the neck of his beer bottle, vapor rising like smoke from the barrel of a gun.

"She say who else was there?" he asked.

"Look, I'm getting this secondhand and I shouldn't even be speaking about it."

"But you're not denying it was a female officer talking to them. Half-Nelson tell them *he* was there too?" Joey looked over his shoulder again at Rattigan, who was trying to play slap-my-hand with the reluctant barmaid. "Both cases."

"You're not seriously talking about throwing Billy the Kid under the bus?"

"I'm just saying what's true." Joey started picking the label off his bottle.

"After all he's done for you?" There was something genuinely hurt and surprised in Kenny's expression.

"He's had his day. You and me have our best ones ahead of us. Or we could, if this state investigation goes away."

"All right, enough." Kenny tried to sort through the tangled strands on his plate. "I need to ask you something else now."

"Okay."

"Is there anything I need to know about what happened to these women?" Kenny asked.

"What are you saying?"

"You know." Kenny lowered his face toward the steaming pile, barely raising his volume. "There are other open cases and I've heard officers talk about what happens on these roads after midnight."

Joey stopped picking the label and laid his hands flat on the table.

"How can you even ask me that?"

"I have to. You know I do."

Joey took his time answering. He inhaled deeply through his nose. Then studied the back of his hands, a spot on his knife, candle wax spilled on the tablecloth that hadn't been cleaned up, and the mass of whorls on his plate. Then he looked at Kenny, whose glasses were still clouded from the steam off his own plate. Despite Billy the Kid's pleas, the East German protestors were back on CNN, asking for the Berlin Wall to come down. Things had to change, Joey realized. He needed to be more careful about what he picked out. And more fastidious about what he left dangling. He picked up his fork and began twirling it through the strands.

"There are bad people in this world," he said softly. "And there are good people. If you can't tell the difference, I don't know what we're doing sitting at the same table."

19

The former self-proclaimed President of All Long Island Pimps lived in a one-story shotgun house in Wyandanch with vacant lots on either side and a sticker on the front door for a security systems firm that had gone out of business years before.

The "president" himself was a pale, long-haired, doe-eyed law school dropout named Ronald Alan Meltzer, who was sitting at a card table in the front room, looking over the photo array Lourdes had just put out for him. He was wearing a Gold's Gym t-shirt with the sleeves cut off to display the muscles and tattoos he'd collected during his two prison bids for "pandering" and selling Viagra to clients without prescriptions. From the other rooms came sounds of simulated female ecstasy.

"Don't sweat it, Lucky," Ronnie said when he saw the suspicious look Lourdes was giving B.B. "I ain't pimpin' no more. It's just podcasting from the studio I set up down the hall."

"You mean like you got girls doing live-streaming?" B.B. appeared consternated, palming the back of his pompadour.

"It's not video and it's not live." Ronnie looked slightly put out. "It's more like an audiobook that you can download and listen to whenever you want. Like in your car."

That would explain why there was so much traffic on the expressway, Lourdes thought.

"We may need to check that out," B.B. said, a little too avidly. "Your parole officer know what you're up to?"

"Maybe we can hold off on all that," Lourdes said, trying to keep everyone focused. "Ronnie here says he's trying to help us with our murder cases, so let's keep our minds on the victims."

A breeze coming through the open window ruffled the white drapes and the five photos on the table. The Suffolk police and the DA still hadn't helped. But through patient searches of cell phone records and newspaper clips, Lourdes had pieced together that at least two of the dead women in the pictures were escorts who'd been repped and promoted by Mr. Meltzer, formerly of Westhampton Beach. However, Ronnie himself was not a suspect at this point because both Allison Forster and Joyce Templeton had been killed while he was locked up.

"Recognize any of the other girls?" Lourdes passed a hand over the array. "Bear in mind that obviously they could have had different names and somewhat different appearances when they worked for you."

Ronnie studied the photos more closely and then shook his head at Lourdes. "I feel you, Lucky. No one's ever who they say they are."

"Who's 'Lucky'?" she asked. "You know me or something?"

"I *thought* I did." Ronnie gave her a cloudy look. "Didn't they used to call you Lucky?"

Lourdes shook her head, ignoring the way B.B. was snickering behind his wrist. It was going to be a long goddamn ride back to the squad. And an even longer couple of days at the squad after that. "*Hey, the President of Pimps said he worked with Robles before. Showed total respect for her as a 'professional.'*" Every ringtone in Homicide would be changed to that song, "*I'm up all night to get lucky.*"

"Well, if it wasn't you, it was someone who looked like you." Ronnie gave her a crooked love-me-anyway grin.

"You tryna say you worked with a girl who looked like me?" Lourdes felt a flutter in her chest. "Like as an escort?"

Ronnie stared back, calculating his legal status on parole. "Nah, I don't work with escorts anymore. That's not my thing. I manage *performers*. My bad."

"You sure now?"

"Yeah, I'm sure."

"Anyway, you were asking me if I recognized some of these other girls, like Allison and Joyce." He went back to davening over the photo array.

"Man, I don't know. These girls do so much to themselves you can't recognize them. They get their tits done, their lips blown up, their fat sucked . . . Gets to where I could sleep with a girl, run into her six months later, and have no idea who she is anymore."

Don't get distracted, Lourdes reminded herself. Don't be thinking about Lucky being your sister or when this dude could have met her. That's a shot in the dark anyway. You're here about *these women.*

"Stay with me now," she said. "I was asking you about any clients your girls might have felt unsafe around."

"My girls never felt unsafe because I was always looking out for them," Ronnie said, tattooed arms crossed defensively. "I never sent them out on calls except with a driver, who took them to the call and then brought them back. If she gets hurt, it's bad for business. I lose my thirty percent and the driver loses his ten."

"My girl only gets sixty cents on the dollar?" Lourdes raised her voice to a squawk. "Oh *hell* no. What kinda shit is that?"

"Come on, my man." B.B. chided. "We're talking about men paying for sex. Your girls must have run into some freaks."

"Everybody pays for sex." Ronnie shrugged. "One way or another."

"True that," B.B. said, with a sad look at Lourdes, probably thinking of his wives and mistresses.

Lourdes jumped in, to redirect them. "What I think Detective Borrelli is saying is that your girls must have reported back threatening situations so you could avoid booking those customers and endangering your other assets."

"Yeah, like, *duh.*" Ronnie's face went slack. "What kind of asshole do you think I am?"

B.B. wagged his chin at Lourdes: no need to swing at that pitch.

Ronnie caught the byplay. "You want to know who the scariest freaks are?" he asked, getting an attitude. "*You guys.* The police."

"Yeah, right." Lourdes pretended to be more concerned with the state of her manicure.

"I'm serious. Cops are the most twisted with the girls." Ronnie looked at B.B., as if expecting confirmation. "Not that I'm knocking all police officers. Some of my drivers were retired Long Island PD. And some of my best customers, and the biggest tippers for the girls. But you want to talk about *freaky*. Hoo boy. People who've got easy access to handcuffs and batons are off the hook."

Lourdes felt her face get hot, remembering her own unauthorized use of police gear with Mitchell.

"Were any of these police officers violent with the women you knew?" she asked.

"What happens if I say yes?" Ronnie stuck a lip out.

"What do you want, a little gold star?" B.B. drew back his hand as if to smack him. "Answer the lady's question."

"I start talking about cops choking out prostitutes, who's gonna protect my ass?" Ronnie hugged himself.

"From who?" B.B. asked.

"Who do you think?" Ronnie said. "The police."

"*We're* the police," Lourdes said. "And you got nothing to worry about if you answer our questions honestly."

"I'm not talking about you, Lucky. I'm talking about the police out here. I'm taking a chance just speaking to you about this."

"That's ridiculous." Lourdes rolled her eyes. "In the first place, you're not doing anything wrong at the moment—you're just assisting an investigation. In the second place, it's paranoid. How would any other police even know you're talking to us? Think you're that important?"

"Uh, you want to look out my front window?" Ronnie said drolly, pointing out the window with a tatted-up arm as heavily illustrated as a comic book. "They've been here like five minutes."

"What the fuck," said B.B., staring.

Lourdes pushed aside the curtain and saw two Suffolk County police officers in Ronnie's driveway, standing behind the Charger they'd borrowed from Queens Narcotics after the transmission on their Impala had punked out this morning.

"They come by all the time," Ronnie mumbled. "I think they're expecting freebies or something."

"Hey, guys." Lourdes gave a friendly wave, trying not to be unnerved. "What's up?"

The officers, both white and both gym rats, took turns hate-fucking her with their eyes and then went back to studying the rear of the Charger. One was holding a license plate reader and the other was taking notes.

"NYPD." She displayed her shield, trying to contain her annoyance.

Be fair. A Hispanic woman in plainclothes at a known pimp's house. Could she blame them for wondering?

The officer taking notes looked at the shield and made it clear he was rating her as a chick anyway. "Everything all right in there?"

"Yeah, we're good," she said.

The other officer was still looking her up and down like he didn't buy she was a real cop. "What are you doing out here?"

She resisted the urge to tell him to mind his business. "Just chasing a bum steer. You know how that goes sometimes."

Both officers looked nonplussed.

"We just like to know who's in the hood," said the one with the license plate reader.

He didn't sound like he was in a particular hurry to smooth out the misunderstanding. B.B. moved to stand beside Lourdes, showing solidarity but not bothering to display his own tin. "And so now you know," he said. "Thank you, officers."

They took their time going back to the RMP parked curbside as Lourdes puckered her lips, signifying for B.B.'s benefit. Just like to know who's in the hood?

"What did I tell you?" Ronnie pushed back from the photo array. "I can't be seen talking to you all."

"Well, you already have been seen." Lourdes gave him full-on duck-face. "So don't worry about it anymore."

"That's supposed to put me at ease?" Ronnie asked. "Fuck that. I'm so done."

From the other rooms, the industry of pleasure was continuing. Though Lourdes noticed that some of the women were starting to sound bored and resentful.

"Just give us the names of the girls who had a problem and you can go back to satisfying your subscribers," she said.

"Actually, we have *advertisers* too." Ronnie sniffed. "But never mind about that. I just want you guys out of here."

"Names, phone numbers, and email addresses," Lourdes said. "Sooner we get them, sooner we're out of your hair."

"And where you gonna be if this comes back on me?" Ronnie asked in an imploring voice. "You see how they're watching."

B.B. glanced out the window, making sure the cops were gone, and put his hands in his pockets. Maybe a little spooked himself.

"We're part of a task force that has state police and federal agents on it," Lourdes said, dispensing with all prior sweetness. "If they start going through the other rooms in your house, asking for IDs and green cards, you're not going to be doing any more podcasts. In fact, we talk to your parole officer, you'll have way bigger problems than the local PD taking down license plate numbers."

Corny TV cop crap. Ronnie, as a former law student, knew as well as she did that they wouldn't bother. But who needed the further hassle?

"You're so cute, Lucky." Ronnie threw up his hands. "Why you gotta be so mean?"

"Get us those names and numbers," she said.

20

It was almost eight o'clock on Halloween night in Riverhead and Amy Nelson was having another sinking spell. One of the worst in a while. Which was more than irritating, since nothing that dramatic had happened to her that day—just a half dozen home visits, typing up reports for Family Court, and forty-five minutes buying candy for the office costume party that always ran on too long. But somehow she hadn't gotten around to eating anything herself and now she was suffering for it.

Her blood sugar was dropping. She felt weak and shaky. The back of her mouth was dry. All she wanted to do was get in the front door, scarf down some leftovers, don her favorite bunchy wool socks, and watch an episode of *Hunter* with Fred Dryer and her secret crush Sgt. Dee Dee. She reached into her shoulder bag to get her keys and then stopped.

The blue garbage can with the bungee cord on the lid to keep out the raccoons who lived in the woods at the end of her cul-de-sac was to the right of her front door.

A natural southpaw, she almost always put it on the left.

Something fluttered in the bushes separating her place from the neighbors. Cicadas were chirping. The waxing moon appeared to have an iridescent aura around it in the autumn chill. Candles flickered in the jack-o'-lanterns on the neighbors' porch, but they were all out trick-or-treating at the more populated end of the street. Of course, it was possible that she was just a little muddleheaded from having low blood sugar. But she made sure the gun she'd carried since her cop days was where she could reach it in her bag before she unlocked the door.

The Teenage Mutant Ninja Turtles had just arrived at the Boys and Girls Club in Port Jefferson Station. Leonardo, Donatello, Michelangelo, and Raphael. Kicking shell and taking names. The kids at the club, mostly eight and under, screamed with delight as the Turtles began tossing out candy. And of course, everyone wanted to touch Leonardo's sword.

All the lights were off in the house, except for the one she always left on in the living room. She told herself that its purpose was to discourage burglars by making them think there was always someone home. But lately she'd begun to wonder if she wasn't doing it more for herself. Pretending it wasn't just the hamster and the parakeet waiting for her. The lamp had become a little beacon of faith that she wanted to keep lit. A sign that as she closed in on forty, with her last serious relationship three years behind her, she still held on to hope that she wouldn't be alone for the rest of her days. Yes, she still had work in the social services. But what did that amount to? Taking care of other people's families. Half a life for Half-Nelson. She just prayed her mother wouldn't call tonight and make her feel worse by asking if she'd met anybody.

The candy bowl in the foyer was still full, and it was probably too late to expect any ghosts or Power Rangers to come calling. The kitchen clock seemed abnormally loud in the dimness of the house. She turned on the hallway light and was relieved to see that her road bike was exactly where she'd left it, leaning against the wall. But why did the seat look raised? Like it had been adjusted and pulled up so the stubby legs on her five-foot-two frame wouldn't quite reach the ground?

She really did need to get something in her stomach as quickly as possible.

She walked into the kitchen and flipped on the light switch. The glare off the linoleum floor hurt her eyes. The oven clock was blinking 5:23 over and over, as if the power had gone off and come back on at that time.

Had she really left that Snoopy-and-Woodstock coffee mug next to the sink, instead of in it? From the corner of her eye, she saw something go past the window over the kitchen sink. A knot formed in her stomach. It was just the shadow of the dogwood in silvering moonlight.

The hamster cage was on the kitchen table, with Herman running frantically on his wheel inside it. Orange juice was what was immediately required for the low blood sugar. She opened the door of the refrigerator, thinking she'd just drink straight from the carton without getting a glass. The one benefit to living alone. The Minute Maid full pulp quart was exactly where she'd left it. But the little glass insulin bottles were beside it, instead of on the lower shelf where she normally kept them. But why was the one on the left already empty? And why would she have put it back if she'd used it up?

"The Katana is a great and noble weapon. It must be handled with a sense of great responsibility."

Leonardo, the leader of the Ninja Turtles, had taken his mask off, revealing Joey's face to the kids as he showed off the plastic sword he'd brought to the Halloween party.

"Am I right, Michelangelo?" he called out to Danziger, still wearing his shell and his mask as he tried to organize pin the tail on the donkey.

"Don't eat too many caramels," said Raphael, a.k.a. Kenny Makris, hanging out around the punch bowl, trying to pick up votes for '92 already.

"Hey, can we get a picture with everyone and the sword?" Joey asked, trying to rally Kenny as well as Charlie Maslow, who was giving a little too much attention to two little blond girls on his lap in the corner. "Donatello, get your mask on and get over here, dude."

Charlie got up and lumbered over, pulling his mask on even as his droopy mouth registered that Joey now had something on him as well. He put his arms around Leonardo and Michelangelo, posing with his fellow crime fighters and six kids going into sugar comas as a Polaroid flash went off and an XL-70 camera slid out the image like a damp, thin tongue.

Someone was behind her. She felt his breath on the back of her neck as cold air from the refrigerator wafted over her from the front. An arm went around her throat. Her feet left the floor, losing one shoe and then the other. A wave of blackness came rushing up at her. There was a sting in the crook of her right arm.

She tried to fight back, but biology and chemistry were against her. Her vision began to blur as she went into shock, the world already receding. This was all she would ever know and all she would ever be. The last things she knew were the fan in the refrigerator, the lonely hum of the 60-watt kitchen light bulb, and the spinning of the hamster wheel.

21

The third girl Ronnie Meltzer told them about lived in a trailer that was part of a religious encampment near Jericho Turnpike, in Coram, behind a Kohl's and a Laundry Palace. She called herself Mary Magdalena Lenape, which kind of figured to Lourdes, since half the locations out here got their names either from the Bible or Indians.

"You're talking about this dude they called J," she said in a smoky rasp. "But really they were all in on it."

She was a light-brown woman, maybe close to three hundred pounds, wearing stretch jeans, an XXL "Y'All Need Jesus" t-shirt, and a large white crucifix the size of a cell phone around her neck. Her nappy hair was piled high on top of her head; it looked like it would fall below her waist if she let it down. But she had a way about her, Lourdes thought, a kind of careless gypsy-eyed sensuality that made even an old-school ladies' man like Bobby Borrelli sit up and take notice.

"All right, stop, rewind, go to the top again," B.B. said. "Who is this 'they'?"

Magdalena gave a heavy sigh. "I never talked about this before," she said. "But maybe the Lord sent you here for a reason, to hear my story."

She gave Lourdes a beatific smile—one big girl to another hopefully not-quite-as-big girl. The trailer was cramped and stuffy. It smelled like incense, cats, cheap weed, and small children. It felt like a firetrap with too many extension cords and too few sockets. The eyes of Jesus followed you from a 3-D picture among the finger paintings on the fake-wood-paneled walls. There was a yellow bong next to a votive candle by the sink. Unopened bills sat under a plastic vase of traffic-light-red roses on the table. Someone was smoking cigarettes and listening to gospel in a back bedroom.

It also felt a little bit like home to Lourdes, which wasn't necessarily a good thing. "So you were, like, an escort at the time we're talking about, right?" she said in the high, girlish, not-too-serious voice she employed to get unpleasant facts out of the way.

"I wasn't always." Magdalena adjusted a scarf over a lamp. "I was studying mortuary science at the community college in Garden City and I needed to make some extra money because I was the sole support for my family. I mean, no one grows up *wanting* to be an escort. But I ran into Ronnie at an off-campus party and he started talking to me about it. He had just dropped out of Hofstra and he was like, 'You only have to do it once. And if you don't like it, you never have to do it again.'"

"This was how long ago?" B.B. leaned across the tiny table.

"Dunno—early nineties?" Magdalena blinked; for some reason, she'd put on false eyelashes and heavy makeup to talk to them. "I was a lot younger and a lot skinnier then. But you know how that goes, sister. Hard to keep them pounds off. A-ight?"

They were sitting so close together that Lourdes couldn't afford to duck-face or even self-consciously pluck at her own belly roll. The scale said she was down to 152 this morning, so what was this bitch talking about?

"So you got into the life and you ran into this guy J, who was violent with you," Lourdes said. "Where was this?"

"North Babylon, of course." Magdalena fingered her crucifix. "It got that name for a reason."

"Okay, and this was an outcall that you went to with a driver or what?" B.B. asked.

He posed the question with a sort of off-handed impatience that made Lourdes think he'd probably had some personal experience with prostitutes in breaks between the wives and mistresses.

"Neither," Magdalena said. "It was a party some of the other girls told me about. We thought we'd all go together and cut Ronnie and the driver out of it for once. I mean, we're doing all the work."

"Absolutely." Lourdes nodded. "And where was this? Do you remember?"

"Private house, not too far from Sunrise Highway." Magdalena half closed her eyes. "I don't remember what street, but it was near Southards Pond Park."

Lourdes shot a darting glance at B.B. The day before they'd found a *Newsday* story about a woman named Cheri Weiss, age twenty-nine, who had been found raped, beaten, and strangled near the same location in 1992, right after Easter. Much earlier than the other murders they'd been looking into, and still an open case, as far as Lourdes could tell.

"You know what? I think I might have said too much." Magdalena, catching the look, let go of the cross she'd been holding.

"What's the matter?" Lourdes asked.

It was her bad, not covering her reaction better. Magdalena had seen the silent exchange and knew it signified complication for her.

"I know what you're thinking of," Magdalena said. "I may be crazy but I'm not dumb. You're asking me to talk about a violent cop who may still have connections."

"It was a long time ago." B.B. tried his easygoing Tony Bennett smile. "And what we're talking about isn't that big a deal."

"No?" Magdalena sat up, nostrils flaring. "Then why y'all drive so far from the city to ask about something that happened twenty-five, twenty-six years ago?" She looked from Lourdes to B.B. and then back again. "It *must* be a big deal or you wouldn't bother. You're asking me to go against powerful people who could still come after me. And my family. My neck is on the block. I got my son and five little kids living in this trailer with me, on land we don't own. Two of my daughter's while she's in rehab, and three of my son's kids. Who's going to be looking out *for us?*"

"Maybe we can help." B.B. reached out for her arm with his hairy and heavily ringed hand.

Magdalena looked askance. She knew enough not to trust a man who looked like Bobby. Her eyes went to Lourdes instead, searching for a different kind of assurance.

"We'll do whatever we can," Lourdes said. "There are federal agents on our task force. Maybe we could ask them to help you get in the program to relocate."

"You swear you'll do that?" Magdalena asked.

"Listen," Lourdes said. "I come from a religious family too. I was raised to always do the right thing . . ."

Dios mío. She didn't even sound convincing to herself. When her sister disappeared, Lourdes first suspected the reason was to get away from their mother and the other church ladies speaking in tongues with Winstons in their mouths and oxygen cannulas up their noses.

"*Swear on the life of your unborn child,*" Magdalena said abruptly.

"What?" Lourdes gave B.B. an incredulous headshake.

"You're pregnant, ain't you?" Magdalena let her eyes drift gently down to Lourdes's belly. "If you're being straight with me, swear on the life of the child you're carrying."

Lourdes's bottom jaw did a slow circle beneath the upper one. There would be no living with B.B. after this. He was studying her with a distantly amused look, to see how far she'd be willing to go to make this case. But Kevin Sullivan always said a good detective could be whoever he or she needed to be at any given moment. And the courts had long ago affirmed that police had the right to lie to get a statement. But, man, this felt like a deal she had no business offering.

"Yes, I swear," she said.

As if saying it quickly made it a less binding promise. She heard a sharp intake of breath from B.B., as if he was somehow both pleased and disappointed in her.

"Why'd you say you'd be going against 'powerful people' if you talked about this?" Lourdes asked, eager to get to it.

"You should've seen the house where all this happened." Magdalena fanned her face. "I was like *damn*. I saw girls going in and out of like six bedrooms with some of these guys. The cars in the driveway and out on the street were all, like, new model Audis and BMWs. Some of them had those special plates and placards so they could park wherever they wanted."

"Pretty observant, aren't you?" B.B. scratched the side of his mouth.

"I told you I was studying mortuary science," Magdalena said. "Before I was a ho."

Somehow she packed a quarter century of self-loathing and self-betrayal into the last syllable. An assessment so brutal and unsparing that Lourdes almost grabbed Magdalena's arm in a show of sisterly solidarity.

But someone who'd been handled in exchange for money wasn't going to buy into easy solace from a cop.

"You saying these were police placards they had in their cars?" Lourdes asked, trying to nail down the details.

"Of course." Magdalena stared. "Because a lot of them *were* cops. Or something else in law enforcement. Or politicians. Or businessmen who had deals with people like you. Come on. You know what this was."

Lourdes didn't need to look at B.B. this time. They both knew they were edging out onto thin, crackling ice now.

"Do you know what the occasion was?" Lourdes asked.

"They were celebrating. This J had just gotten some kind of medal or promotion. He wasn't any Schwarzenegger, if you know what I mean. More like a dumpy average guy who'd been to the gym a lot and made himself into something. He wasn't in uniform but you could tell how much the others all looked up to him, calling him 'loo' and 'boss man,' and all that. Giving him cigars and bottles of scotch. And—*oh yeah*—lines of cocaine."

"There were drugs at this party," B.B. said evenly, as if this was no big deal in and of itself.

"*Definitely.*" Magdalena nodded more vigorously. "That's the secret behind the other secrets. The girls were doing lines as well. It was always like this at these parties. Those guys would be huffing it up, like it was nothing. Like the law didn't apply to them. And you know that's not a drug that makes a lot of people more humble or clear about who they are, or what they should be doing. Not that that's any excuse for what happened. Or what he did to me."

"And what did he do to you?" Lourdes asked, instinct telling her not to start taking notes yet.

"Oh, he just tried to fucking kill me. That's all."

She said the words so lightly and nonchalantly that someone passing through the room in a hurry might not have stopped to take them seriously.

"And how did that happen?" Lourdes pressed on deliberately.

Just get the facts on the table, next to the dying flowers and the unpaid bills.

"It started off fairly normal," Magdalena said. "Or as normal as you can get at a party like that. He knew what I was there for and I knew what he was there for. So we ended up in one of these big marble bathrooms, doing lines off the sink. Then he came up behind me and started rubbing me. Grabbing my breasts and all. Then he turned me around and put me on my knees. I remember because the marble floor was cold . . ."

Lourdes looked over and saw B.B. starting to reach into his pocket for a pad. She shook her head at him but knew what he was thinking. The cold marble floor made the story a little more solid and persuasive: an incidental detail most people wouldn't even think of inventing.

"After like five minutes, he still couldn't get hard in my mouth, so I was like, 'Forget about it.'" Magdalena curled her fingers in front of her chin, hesitating. "I think my actual words were 'Looks like you're not really up for it.' And that's when everything changed."

"Changed how?" B.B. asked.

"It was like here's the big man with the girl on her knees in the bathroom. And he can't get it up. And then I say something like, 'Maybe you're not such a big man.' And just like that." Magdalena snapped her fingers. "He switched. It was like he turned into someone else. He got all red, grabbed me by the face, and started yelling, 'You shut your mouth. You shut your fucking mouth.' And when I started yelling back at him, he got me by the throat and started choking me."

"Choking you?" B.B. raised his hands. "Like this?"

"Yeah, like that." Magdalena raised her eyes, as if she was somewhere other than this trailer for a few seconds. A different girl with a different body and a different name.

"It was all so fast. It was like a frenzy." She started to breathe hard, like it was happening right now. "He's getting on top of me, crushing me with his full weight, and I'm struggling to breathe. I try to yell but no sound comes out. No one can hear me. The music is too loud anyway. He lets go for a second and I start to scream my head off. Then he grabs me again, by the windpipe. He's trying to kill me for real now. I'm thinking, *I'm really going to die in this marble bathroom.*"

Her hand went to her throat and tears rolled down her cheeks.

"And he's getting off on this. I can tell from how he's breathing and moving on top of me. And I'm starting to black out and lose control of my body because I'm not getting any air. And the last thing I'm thinking is, *God, if you let me out of this, I swear I'll turn my whole life around. I'll dedicate my life to you and becoming a better person.* And then, right at that second, there's a knock at the door and I hear one of the other girls who brought me to the party, yelling, 'Lemme in. I gotta pee.' It was like Jesus pressed on her bladder at just the right moment."

"And what did this J do when he heard that?" Lourdes said, realizing she'd been starting to sweat as if the trailer had gotten more humid while she was sitting there listening.

"He got up." Magdalena let her breath out. "I guess he figured he was trapped and had no choice. How would it look if he opened the door to leave and there's a dead girl? So he gets off me and I start to say something. So he takes a wad of dollar bills and tries to stuff them in my mouth."

"In your mouth?" Lourdes did not dare to look at B.B.

"Yeah, in my mouth. To shut me up. And remind me that I'm just a whore. Like one way or another, he's gonna shut me up, even if he has to pay for it. But by then I'm all balled up in a corner sobbing with my arms in front of my face. So he just drops the money on the floor and walks out. Like nothing happened."

Lourdes nodded slowly. It could just be a coincidence. She'd heard of men sticking money in all kinds of places. But she heard B.B. exhale and knew for once they were on the same page. Thinking about how the stones in the Rockaway victim's mouth hadn't been in the media, so Magdalena couldn't have heard about them.

"Did you ever learn this officer's real name?" B.B. asked, maintaining a deadpan expression.

"No." Magdalena grabbed a Kleenex to dry her eyes. "But I know he stayed a big man on the job for a long time. I used to see him around the First and the Fourth Precincts, telling other cops what to do."

"Uh-huh." Lourdes nodded, trying to stay neutral. "So you were still in the life, *after that?*"

"Yeah . . ." Magdalena sighed and left the crumpled tissue on the table. "It took me a long time to keep my promise to Jesus. I had to go through a lot of other men, a lot of drugs, and a lot of money to find my way back to Him. Took me the better part of my life, in fact. But He never stopped watching over me. Or else I wouldn't be here, talking to you."

Lourdes put the heels of her palms against her eyes, spent from just the effort of taking this all in.

"But you want to know something?" Magdalena exhaled, like she was free from the burden. "I don't put it all on J or whatever they call him."

"Why not?" B.B. asked.

"Because all the other men who were there knew what was up," Magdalena said. "They saw me come out of that bathroom with tears in my eyes and marks on my throat. They knew he'd tried to hurt me and no one said anything. None of the other cops. None of the lawyers. None of the politicians. And none of the businessmen. I even had to call my own cab to get out of there."

"Wait a second—how do you know what these other guys did for a living?" B.B. put a hand up to redirect her.

"I've seen their faces on the news since then, over the years," Magdalena said. "But don't ask me about names. I'm not so good with those. I smoked and snorted a lot of stuff I shouldn't have. And now I can't remember shit, except my verses from Bible study."

Without a doubt, this was not an ideal witness. An unstable former prostitute and drug addict, dodging bills under a made-up name and taking her marching orders straight from Christ. If this ever came to trial, she would have close to zero credibility testifying against a ranking police officer. Particularly one who was as well regarded as the one she described. But there was also no doubt in Lourdes's mind that almost every single word of this account was true.

"Thank you." Magdalena turned to Lourdes.

"For what?"

"For giving me a way to get all this off my chest. I've been carrying this for a long time. I feel better now. I knew you'd understand, since you have enough faith to bring a child into this fallen world."

"So does that mean you'll testify for us at a trial if we get this guy?" Lourdes asked.

"You help me get my family out of this place, we'll talk," said Magdalena. "Maybe the Lord sent you to help me start the process. If He can move mountains, maybe He can move us out of this damn trailer park."

22

Things were different since their last meeting, five and a half years before. For one thing, she was calling herself Leslie Jesperson now, instead of Martinez, as if she'd gotten a divorce and gone back to her maiden name. For another, Joey was ready for her. He was a captain now and in the conference room with his union lawyer to help defend him. Somehow, with a new governor in office, she'd managed to revive this witch-hunt with the state investigations commission, getting enough of a budget to afford a JVC camcorder to videotape these interviews at a conference room in Albany and a young staff lawyer who had hair like Slick Willie Clinton to sit in and take notes.

"Before we get started, I'd like to make a statement." Joey looked at the camera, making sure that the recording light was on. "I'm here voluntarily . . ."

"Actually, you received a subpoena from this commission," the Slick Willie–type butted in.

"I'm here on my day off to answer questions," Joey pressed on. "But I just want to put on the record that I believe this interview is a farce and the result of a vendetta being pursued by Investigator Leslie Martinez or Jesperson, or whatever she calls herself these days. And that I believe she alters evidence as easily as she alters her name to suit her purposes."

"Your objection is noted," said Leslie, who now had close-cropped hair that she was allowing to go silver in a way that both intrigued and disgusted Joey. "Captain Tolliver, you have been a police officer since 1981. Is that correct?"

Joey looked at Brendan, representing him for the union. "Can I answer that?"

"This is not a formal proceeding." Leslie pulled on the lapels of her blazer. "We're just gathering information. There's no need to stand on ceremony."

Brendan nodded. "Yes, I believe that's correct," Joey said. "I have fourteen years on the job so far. Should I list my awards and commendations as well?"

"That's not necessary either." Leslie opened a thick file on the table. "And in your early years on the job, did you sometimes patrol the local highways?"

"Yes, that was part of my assigned duties."

"Would you have been on that duty the night of September 13, 1982?"

"You have my file, Ms. Martinez-Jesperson. I assume that date is correct."

"Actually, we've only been given partial records." She looked at her counsel and then at the camera. "There's been a conspicuous lack of cooperation from your department and the DA's office. We're hoping that will change now. My question has to do with the case of a Stephanie Lapidus. You're familiar with it. Aren't you?"

Joey leaned sideways in his chair, not liking how it creaked beneath him. He was getting too settled and heavy the last few years. He needed to start moving around more, to keep himself lean and alert.

"Yes, of course, I remember the Lapidus case," he said. "It was in the newspapers. I believe a drug dealer named Trevor Knightsbridge is still in prison for killing her."

"You did not testify at the trial, did you?" Leslie licked a finger and turned a page in the file.

"There would have been no reason." Joey shrugged. "I wasn't involved."

"You say that, yet there are officers who recall seeing you at the crime scene where Ms. Lapidus's car was found," Leslie said.

"We're talking about thirteen years ago," Brendan started to object.

"Never mind, I'll take this." Joey screwed up his mouth knowingly.

"It's the same thing over and over. They're trying to pin the tail on the donkey again. They've got these so-called eyewitnesses who saw me somewhere supposedly doing something, but absolutely no proof. We've been here before."

"Are you aware that some of these witnesses were police officers?" she said.

"Was one of them a former detective William Rattigan?" Joey feigned a yawn. "I think we all know Billy the Kid resigned in disgrace years ago because of his mishandling of evidence in a number of cases. His struggles with alcohol are well documented. I wouldn't take much that he says too seriously."

He could see where this was going. Leslie had obviously stroked some horny old legislator's thigh in the state capitol and gotten herself some new funding for this ludicrous adventure. And she was trying to enlist bitter Billy Rattigan, who'd been involved in the Angela Spinelli case as well and was somehow still alive, as a soldier in her campaign.

"Actually, I was going to ask you about an officer named Amy Nelson, who was listed as one of the officers securing the Lapidus crime scene," Leslie said.

"Rest her soul, poor girl." Joey shook his head. "I hardly knew her."

"Yet we have an affidavit from a former clerk at the police department who recalls you looking at her personnel record, shortly after the first time I spoke to you."

Leslie removed two stapled pages from the file and slid them across the table.

Joey gave them a cursory glance and passed them to his lawyer. "I don't recall this clerk and I don't recall making any such request."

So this was the new information she was using to come at him. A black retired clerk named Jessica Wallace had been recruited as a witness against him. He'd never paid her much mind before, but he would now. If she didn't have a DWI or an arrest for passing a bad check that could be used against her, somebody in her family would have a problem that could be leveraged.

"You're aware that there was information in Officer Nelson's record about her having diabetes," Leslie Jesperson said, with a growing flush on her normally sallow cheeks. "Aren't you?"

"I don't recall looking at the file." Joey made himself still and looked her in the eye. "And I certainly didn't monitor Officer Nelson's health concerns."

"You were aware she was left-handed, though. Weren't you?"

"I can barely picture Officer Nelson." He shrugged again. "Where are you going with this?"

"I'm just noting for the record that previously there was no reason to question the circumstances of Ms. Nelson's death several years ago, since the fatal insulin injection went into the correct arm."

Joey kept his expression blank. What'd she want him to do? Smile because she was complimenting him for being halfway intelligent about getting rid of a problem?

"Is there a question here?" Brendan asked.

"Yes." Leslie nodded, playing to the camera. "Can Captain Tolliver account for his whereabouts on the night Ms. Nelson died?"

So here it was. What they'd been waiting for. The hook in the water. The bait barely concealing the sharp edge. Joey glanced at Brendan, who took the manila envelope out of his briefcase and slid it across the table.

"You're talking about Halloween night almost six years ago," Joey said. "Please open that envelope and look at what's inside."

Leslie undid the clasp and took out the pictures. Four Mutant Ninja Turtles in yellowing Polaroids. Dumb-ass Charlie Maslow and Tommy Danziger both had their masks on, but Joey and Kenny Makris had kept theirs off.

"There's lots of witnesses from the Boys and Girls Club in Port Jefferson who'll back us up on the time and date." Joey shrugged, not needing to be unduly smug. "We're there every other year. Maybe you should have checked that out before you called us up here, Ms. Jesperson. By the way, does that state commission compensate me for the cost of gas?"

"Here's what I know," she said, trying to hold herself steady as she put the pictures back in the envelope and passed them to the staff attorney. "The revival of this commission isn't about holding just one person accountable. It's about looking at an entire system that's allowed corruption to flourish. Those who decide to cooperate sooner rather than later can expect to be treated more leniently."

"Is that a threat?" Joey looked at his lawyer, comfortable enough to allow himself a smile. "Because I don't see how you have much to back it up."

"This isn't over, Captain," Leslie Jesperson said. "Someone once said the arc of history is long but it bends toward justice."

"Then they must have had their head up their ass." Joey stood up and signaled for Brendan to do the same. "Come on, counselor. We've got a long drive back to the Island."

23

Lourdes slipped into the back of the darkened ballroom just as Joseph Tolliver was beginning his speech to the American Police Chiefs Association at the Marriott Marquis in Times Square. Almost immediately, a group of white-haired men began trying to wave her over to their table, assuming she was a waitress who could refill their glasses.

She ignored them and rested an elbow on a bar counter, as Tolliver stood ramrod straight at a podium some fifty yards away, sounding as if he was running for higher office. His voice was deep and commanding as he moved deftly between true blue oratory and seemingly off-the-cuff remarks about the challenges facing twenty-first-century policing.

He spoke about illegal immigration and the opioid epidemic. He spoke about stifling political correctness. He spoke about the "Ferguson Effect" and how omnipresent video cameras wielded by so-called social justice warriors inhibited his officers from doing their jobs. Then he spoke about duty and dedication and answering the call to public service.

He received a thunderous ovation afterward and accepted handshakes all around before Lourdes tailed him into the bar downstairs, waiting patiently as he glad-handed his fellow chiefs and handed out business cards. She nursed a club soda for a few minutes and then sidled up to him as he went to the bar to ask for menus since the waitresses were overwhelmed.

"Nice speech," she said. "I've been thinking some of the same things myself."

He turned and looked down. He actually wasn't that much taller than her, but he carried himself like someone who'd displace a lot of water when he jumped in a pond. He snapped his fingers.

"Detective Robles, NYPD." She helped him. "I came by your office with Detective Borrelli last week, to talk about those Sunrise Highway murders."

"Riiight." His eyes got small as his index and middle fingers pressed together. "Didn't my records guy get back to you?"

"We're still waiting."

"Sorry about that." He pulled out an iPhone. "Let me set a reminder to give Charlie Maslow a *zetz* tomorrow."

"That would be great. Because, you know, we've called your office like six times since we saw you and sent three long emails."

"Yeah, sorry about that as well." His mustache pulled back into a smile and his eyes danced past her to see if the chiefs he'd left at the table were watching. "Things have been kind of crazy at HQ, preparing for this speech and working on the budget numbers for next quarter. You don't have to worry about this stuff when you're a working detective. A piece of advice? Don't try to do what I did and move up the ladder. You'll miss real police work."

"I don't think that's ever going to be an issue." She laughed, to maintain the illusion that this was just a friendly conversation. "No one's ever said I'm administrative material."

"So what brings you to our little gathering, detective?" He was still smiling, but there was unmistakable tension gathering in his jaw. "The event is supposed to be invitation only."

"Like I said, we hadn't heard back from your office and when I saw you were speaking in town, I figured I'd stop by."

"And how's the investigation going?" he asked. "I heard you stopped to see the DA."

"Oh, you know." She kept her voice light, just floating above the cocktail chatter. "We're following the steps, tracing the circles. Developing a sense of direction."

"And where's that leading you?" he asked, giving special attention to the lower part of the menu.

"Into some tricky areas, which is why I wanted to speak to you directly." She put a fist on the counter, where she was sure he could see it.

"A few things are becoming clear. One is that there may be a few more murders than we first realized and two is that they may go farther back than we initially realized."

"Really?" He sounded only moderately disturbed, like she'd just offered a ridiculous sports prediction. "How far back?"

"At least twenty-five, twenty-six years. To the Cheri Weiss case. Maybe even earlier. Angela Spinelli. Stephanie Lapidus . . ."

"Wow, that's what I call reaching." Tolliver shook his head. "You're going deep, aren't you? Sure you're not just looking for connections between things that aren't connected?"

"It's possible." She shrugged. "But it's also possible that there are connections other people have overlooked."

"Like what?"

She leaned over and kept her voice down. "Look, I don't want to start pointing fingers. But we can't ignore the pattern in the things we've been hearing. About violent cops and prostitutes."

"Officers from *my* department?" He splayed a hand against his chest, as if offended.

"It could be. We have to look into every possibility."

"So what are you asking me for?"

"It would help to get a look at some of your Internal Affairs reports."

"For what possible purpose?"

"To see if you had officers accused of abusing escorts in the past."

He looked back at the other chiefs waiting for him to come back to the table with the menus. One tapped his wrist, as if to say, *Time is money.*

"You're seriously talking about things that happened in the eighties and nineties?" Tolliver inhaled.

"We are."

He shut both eyes and gave her a quick little headshake, like this conversation was using up all his powers of patience and forbearance. "And exactly who is giving you all this information?"

After their little encounter at the DA's office, she'd decided not to say any more about looking into the state investigation report from '89. Gallagher, the state cop, was supposed to be reaching out to get ahold of this Leslie Martinez, the lead investigator who'd been driving it.

"We're at a sensitive stage of the case," Lourdes said. "We don't want to endanger anyone by putting their names out there before we're sure we can protect them."

"But you have no problem coming here, asking me to violate my officers' right to privacy by opening up their personnel records? You know that there's a state law that protects *them*. And you."

His elbow brushed her side. Hard to tell if he'd done it deliberately as he waved back at his fellow chiefs, to let them know he hadn't forgotten them.

"Chief, we're talking about seven murders and counting so far," she pointed out. "Puts a different light on it, don't you think?"

"Jesús, Robles. You're talking about a department of almost three thousand officers and files going back thirty, thirty-five years. Can you narrow the field a little? What are these allegedly upstanding citizens in the prostitution field telling you?"

"An officer called J has been mentioned. He'd just become a lieutenant in the early nineties. And he was apparently well liked and well respected within and outside of the department."

"Hey, my name starts with a *J* and I was a lieutenant in the nineties." He laughed. "Does that mean I need to hire a lawyer? Seriously, Robles. What is it that this guy is supposed to have done?"

She opened her mouth to answer but a wave of noise crashed down on her. It suddenly felt like the music had been turned up and the conversation had gotten more raucous around them. A waitress threw herself against the counter and began sliding empty glasses at the bartender with undisguised aggression. Someone dropped a crumpled cocktail napkin with a lipstick stain on the other side of her. It felt like the world conspiring to distract her, but she had studied her own reactions enough to know that something else was going on. This was her personal warning system.

"He attacked a woman at a party near where Cheri Weiss was found," she said carefully. "And he did it in a manner consistent with how our Rockaway victim was found."

Nothing about his face or body language had changed. He was still regarding her with friendly interest, not leaning in too close or back too far, keeping a respectful distance while still listening. It was more something inside her that was different. An urge to draw together her knees

and cover her chest. A sense that she was no longer just talking to a col-
league, but being minutely observed and sized up through a microscope.

"'A woman at a party'? 'A manner consistent'?" He affected a look of
earnest concern. "Could you be a little more vague? What the hell are we
talking about, Robles? Some whore got choked out?"

"I never said anything about choking." Lourdes looked at him more
closely.

"Whatever." He shrugged. "Shit like that happens all the time. It's
probably going on right now, upstairs, at this hotel. Should you and me
go break down every door?"

"Chief, we're just following the leads where they take us. And there's
a plausible connection to our other cases. If you can find a way to share
some of those IAB records, I'm sure we can find a way to share more of
our information."

Of course, she could have told him more. Pulled him into the process, made him a stakeholder. But something was distinctly holding her
back.

"So you're playing games with me, detective?" He nodded with a
knowing half smile. "I scratch yours, you scratch mine? Let me remind
you: I'm a chief and you're a detective."

"And I'm working with a federal task force that could demand records from your department and subpoena individual officers," she warned
him. "But I'd rather not get to that stage."

"Don't worry, you won't." He gave her a light pat on the arm. "My
department likes NYPD telling us what to do about as much as NYPD
would like outside interference. I'll be interested to see what you come
up with."

He waved toward his fellow chiefs, who were throwing their hands
up as if they'd been waiting for him to come back to the table since the
first Gulf War.

"Chief, don't do this," Lourdes said. "You make us keep digging on
our own, you might not like what we come up with."

"Excuse me." He gave her arm a squeeze. "I need to get back to my
friends. And by the way, good luck looking for your sister. I saw the alert
with your name on it. I'll have my guys keep an eye out."

24

Beth looked surprised when Joey walked into the bedroom wearing the same suit he'd had on in Albany. Like after five years of living here he was still a stranger in this house.

"What do you think of this?" he said.

He was showing her a picture he'd ripped out of a magazine at the dentist's office the other day. Madonna with short blond hair in a leather bra, biker shorts, fishnets, and a blindfold.

She paused from folding the kids' laundry on the bed. As hard-bodied and oblivious as she'd been on the night when he first walked into this house and shot her husband Randy in the kitchen downstairs.

"Why you asking me?"

"I'm just saying." He shrugged. "As a look you could try."

It didn't seem that unreasonable. Normal people probably had conversations like this. And as far as he could tell, he'd been pretty much acting the way normal people should act for a long time now.

"You want me to cut my hair?" she asked.

"I'm saying, think about it. Be open."

"So I could look like *her*?" She took the page and gave it an incredulous squint. "Like seriously?"

More like Leslie Martinez, he was thinking. Now Jesperson. All the way back from Albany in the car, he'd been thinking about her and the questions she'd asked. The way she thought she had him cornered and ready to submit. So now he had a little film loop that wouldn't stop running in his head. Leslie facedown on a mattress, with him giving it to her from behind until she screamed and begged for mercy.

"But I've always had long hair." Beth tossed her blond tresses self-consciously.

"Maybe it's time to try something different."

"But it's how the kids have always known me." She put stacks of their underwear on the dresser.

"If you loved me, you'd do it for me," he said.

"That sounds like something from a movie."

"It's how people who care about each other talk."

It had been months since they'd even tried to have sex. Certainly not much since the wedding two months ago. Her fault, he reckoned. When he'd first moved in, a couple of years after the shooting, they'd been at it at least once a month. Like normal people. Just the way he'd told her husband it would be before he pulled the trigger. Promising to screw the man's wife, beat his kids, and live in his house once he was gone. The memory of that moment had gotten him off more than her body or even the size of the house. Temporarily relieving his urges and keeping him out of trouble on the street. So he could focus on building his career and elevating himself to where he needed to be. He'd looked at it analytically, and every man who'd ever gotten to be chief had a home and a family. And most of the so-called serial killers out there had been loners and obvious freaks. So he'd accepted that he had to rein himself in because he couldn't get to where he wanted to be without appearing to be "normal."

"It's weird," she said, putting the picture on the night table.

"What is?"

"That it means so much to you."

There were scissors in the bathroom. He could force her down and cut the hair himself. Then do it to her like he was doing it to Leslie Jesperson. Who wouldn't be trying to pin him down or talking about reviving some old investigation then. She'd be sobbing into a pillow and asking him to stop. But then the kids would come running and banging on the door, and then he'd have to put them in their place and next thing you knew the neighbors would be calling 911 and there'd be an awkward conversation with his own officers responding. And then having something on the boss, instead of the other way around. Exactly the opposite of what he wanted.

Why was this so hard? He just wanted to have a life that looked like other people's, so he could do what he wanted the rest of the time. In a way, he blamed his parents as well. The lack of structure when he was growing up. He'd been a latchkey kid back in the day. Prone to tantrums from the start, it was true. Prone to lying as well. Prone to getting others to take the blame for what he'd broken. And prone to coming home early from school to skip Little League practice and watch *Dark Shadows* on Channel 7 instead. A soap opera about a vampire, who could sap the blood and overcome the will of weaker souls. Which is why he happened to be home early sometimes to hear things he wasn't supposed to hear and see things he wasn't supposed to see.

Sometimes he'd go out to Rockaway Beach on his own afterward. He'd stand there and watch the tide go in and out. First one wave would crash in and haul off all the seaweed and abandoned toys on the sand. Then another would come in and overpower it, snatching away everything in the first wave's grip. Over and over, smashing and then receding, leaving cracked shells and misshapen pebbles in its wake, and then taking them away. Until there was just clean and shining gray shoreline that looked like the back of some giant mammal for a few seconds.

This was the world. This was life. You had to keep crashing in with overwhelming force. To dominate and demand submission. Maintaining command and control. And never yield. Because there was always a bigger wave out there, ready to rush in and drag away whatever it was that you thought you had.

"Lie down on the bed," he told Beth.

"I'm still doing the laundry."

"What, I have to ask you twice now?" He put the strength in his voice, so he didn't have to raise it or show her a fist. "Get your fucking pants off and lie on your stomach. And don't look at me."

"Joey, come on. The kids are home."

"Then I guess you better not make a lot of noise."

The key was to overcome all resistance. Like the wave overtaking the sand. He took off his pants and got on top of her. But now things had changed and the thought of Leslie Martinez Jesperson kept him from getting hard. It was the way she said she was going to take him down eventually. Thinking she was the tide, inevitable and unceasing, trying to take away what he had, a little bit at a time. Until the whole beach eroded. A bigger wave had to come down on top of her. To show her what was stronger.

This was how it should be, with a man and a woman. The strong over the weak. In and out. Conquering the vulnerable with the force of your will and your body. The moon controlled the tides. And the tides were tied to how women acted. And since you couldn't control the moon or the tides, all you could control was women. He'd overcome his mother and he'd overcome Amy Nelson before they could take away what he had. So he'd overcome Leslie Martinez or Jesperson or whatever she called herself now, and any other wave of disturbance that came after her.

"You're hurting me," Beth said in a muffled voice, her face mashed into the pillow by his hand pushing on the back of her head.

No kidding. That was what was finally making him hard. Along with the sounds of the kids scampering around the rest of the house looking for her in frantic concern and the thought that her husband's ghost was hovering somewhere in this room. I'm fucking your wife and then I'm going to scare your kids, and then I'm going to go downstairs and eat the rest of the apple pie in your refrigerator, and there's nothing you can do about it, because I am alive and you are dead, and I am the sea and you were a tiny ripple that no one remembers anymore.

In the meantime, Beth had gone limp beneath him. No longer clenching and tensing, but just lying there like she was surrendering as prey to a larger predator. Without the struggle, the excitement was gone. He pulled out and released, more out of boredom than exhilaration. Then he rolled onto his back and looked up at the bedroom ceiling, spent and disappointed. The ceiling was higher and dingier than he realized. The light fixture was old and one of the bulbs was dead.

Beth sat up on the side of the bed. "Do you ever think there might be something the matter with you?" she asked.

"No. Why?"

"It's just sometimes, I don't know where your mind is."

He stood up to look for his pants. "There's nothing wrong with my mind. Or my body. The problem is you."

This was what he wanted. It was what made him different and better than the Zodiacs and the Son of Sam types, who idiots like Leslie Jesperson might think were the same as him. But they weren't the same. He wanted to have a normal relationship and a normal home. Not just as a cover, but as part of another life. In a separate compartment.

There was a knock at the door. "Mom, I can't find my science book."

Stacy, the oldest child. The one who cried the hardest the night her father died and the one who'd been the coldest and most suspicious since Joey had moved in.

"Your mother will be with you in a minute," he said sharply. "We're talking."

There was open defiance in how the girl stomped away across the landing and in the way her mother looked over her shoulder at him now, brushing her hair out of her eyes.

"She could use a father, you know," she said.

"Her and everybody else," he grumbled, pulling his jeans on one leg at a time.

It was no good, he realized. Living here with the family and the ghost under the roof. Better to tear it all down and start over. Or better yet, get rid of the family and keep the house. Give himself a better chance to get it right this time. In and out with the tide. Once this Leslie Martinez Jesperson was off his back.

25

The retired detective lived in what looked to Lourdes like a creepy old farmhouse on a deserted stretch of road not far from the Long Island Pine Barrens. If B.B. wasn't already with her, she would have radioed for backup before entering.

The ex-detective himself spooked her even more. He seemed like someone who should have been dead. Or who already was dead but didn't know it yet. He reminded her a little of one of those ancient rock stars you saw sometimes late at night on cable TV. Faces like splintered old wood, molasses-colored hair spilling from the tops of their shrunken heads, eyes hidden behind tinted glasses, and withered mouths telling stories of superhuman drug consumption and surviving impossible falls down steep flights of stairs.

"Remind me how you guys found me again?" William Rattigan looked from Lourdes to B.B.

Lourdes took a deep breath. "We're looking at a bunch of old murder cases out on this part of Long Island," she said, repeating what she'd already told the retired detective on the phone virtually word for word. "Most of them are unsolved cases where the bodies were found in the vicinity of Sunrise Highway. Others were solved cases from the same general area. In looking at the files, your name came up as lead investigator several times."

"Because I was the best!" William Rattigan grinned, showing teeth as mismatched and discolored as Indian corn. "All the unsolved cases must have been from after I left. Because when I was on the job, we had a ninety-fucking-four percent confession rate! Beat that, NYPD!"

They were in an ancient bachelor's basement. It smelled like mildew and brands of liquor that weren't manufactured anymore. Dented gray file cabinets were pushed up against fake-wood-paneled walls with footprints along the baseboards, as if Rattigan liked to lie sideways on the stained carpet and pretend to walk to walk on them.

"You know what you people should investigate?" Rattigan's hand shook as he pushed in a flesh-colored hearing aid. "You should investigate why I was forced to retire at the height of my game! I made these people what they were! Kenny Makris? He was a fucking little pissant ADA when I gave him his name! Joey Tolliver? He was a fucking juvenile delinquent when I found him! And Tommy Danziger? Don't get me started. Okay?"

"Okay." B.B. raised his hands and offered a tolerant smile, all gentlemanly Italian charm, glad not to be the aggrieved and disrespected party for once. "We can get into all that. But right now, we're looking for some other kinds of information."

"What do you want to know?" asked Rattigan, calming down a little now that a male cop closer to his own age was talking to him.

"Most of these murder victims were prostitutes working in the area," B.B. explained. "We started looking for patterns of violent johns, who could have been victimizing them."

"Yeah, so far so good." Rattigan nodded, hiking his pants halfway up his flannel shirt.

He was one of those alcoholics who got skinnier and more desiccated as they got older, Lourdes noticed, rather than bloated and immobilized. By her count, he must have been about eighty years old, only about a decade and a half over Sullivan's age. But physically he seemed like he was pushing closer to a hundred.

"And one of the leads we're pursuing is that there was a police officer who'd been violent with some of the girls," she interjected. "It's unclear whether your IAB would have brought him up on charges."

B.B. looked down at his polished shoe tops and did that disapproving little tut-tut wag with his chin. Like he didn't like her timing. But with the way this Rattigan looked, they could end up questioning a pile of dust and bones if they didn't keep up a brisker pace.

"I don't know anything about that." Rattigan adjusted the '70s-style aviators that hid the expression in his eyes. "I'm not aware of any working girl ever lodging charges against me. I always paid full price. Not that I ever really had to . . ."

"Hey, hey, no one's saying you did anything, Detective Rattigan." B.B. put his hands up reassuringly, the barren light bulb in the basement catching the glint of his many rings. "We're just looking for you to assist our investigation."

"Oh yeah, right, okay." Rattigan snuck a quick look at Lourdes, as if making sure she wasn't about to claw him. "I just get touchy sometimes after the way these guys forced me out."

"And how was that?" Lourdes asked.

A lesson she'd learned from Sullivan. If somebody doesn't want to talk about your main subject, get them to talk about whatever they want. Then circle back.

"They accused me of 'mishandling evidence.' You believe that?" Rattigan shook his head at B.B., the shellacked quality of his hair convincing Lourdes that it was a wig after all. "They said I tampered with evidence in the Stephanie Lapidus and Angela Spinelli cases and gave me the option of retiring early or getting put under the microscope by some fucking state investigations commission. They sacrificed me to help their own careers. How's that for gratitude?"

"Who sacrificed you?" Lourdes asked. "What are we talking about? Orient me here, detective."

"Oh for Chrissake." Rattigan's glasses almost flew off as he snapped his head toward B.B., getting even more worked up. "Will you tell this dizzy broad what's what?"

"I don't know what you're talking about either, old man." B.B. shrugged. "We're not from around here, remember?"

"Fucking Kenny Makris, Joey Tolliver, Steve Snyder, and all the rest of them." Rattigan threw his mottled hands up in frustration. "They made me pay for *their* sins. Fucking Steve Snyder. Who's talking about running for Congress now! In my district. Who I arrested when I was a patrolman and he was a thirteen-year-old punk shoplifting at E. J. Korvette's. And fucking Joey Tolliver! Which is ten times worse. I was with that kid since he was a little shitbird witness in the fucking Bird Dog case."

"What's the Bird Dog case?" Lourdes turned to B.B.

Rattigan froze with his arms in the air. His shoulders tilted forward and he bent at the waist. Lourdes could detect some eyeball movement behind his tinted lenses. A general air of gravity and incredulousness had pervaded the room.

"You're kidding me, right?" Rattigan's jaw went up and down a couple of times, like he was trying to break apart something too dense to swallow.

"No, I have no idea what you're talking about." Lourdes glanced at B.B. "Do you?"

B.B. stooped his shoulders and tugged on his collar, back into his beleaguered *I don't get no respect* mode.

"Was this some big Long Island case?" She turned back to Rattigan.

Something had changed in the last few seconds. He'd taken the beat you never wanted a subject to take in an interrogation room, making himself just still enough to do an internal inventory and calculate where he stood in relation to the rest of the world.

"I don't think I want to talk to you guys anymore," he said.

"Why, what happened?" Lourdes asked. "Did we say something wrong?"

"I'm just thinking about what's right for me." Rattigan was looking down, touching the side of his phony hair over and over.

Lourdes glanced at B.B., trying to figure what this old crank was on about. Or what he hoped to protect. From the brief look they'd had upstairs, there was no Mrs. Rattigan and no other family to look out for. He was the sort of man, convinced of his own greatness, who had probably long since driven off anybody who would have conceivably cared about him and was now surviving on his own pointlessly.

"I could still have skin in the game," Rattigan said abruptly, as if he'd just been shaken from a slumber. "Kenny Makris is still the DA and there's no mandatory retirement age for investigators. You know, I just put an application in the other day. How's it going to look if I'm going around talking trash?" He turned to B.B. "You might want to consider that as well. You look like you aren't getting any younger yourself."

Lourdes waited for B.B. to deflect him or say something to turn the conversation back in a comfortable direction. Instead, he just looked down at his shoes again. As if the suggestion of time running out had shaken him as well.

"Go on, get out of here." Rattigan shuffled toward the stairs to show them the way out. "I've said enough already. In fact, I've said a lot more than I should have."

"Can we at least leave a card?" Lourdes asked. "If you change your mind about talking to us."

"Hell no!" Rattigan raised his arm as if he wanted to backhand her. "Watch your step getting out of here. The ceilings are low."

26

The last time Leslie was out in this part of Long Island, the pub was called Cheers Too. Now it had been turned into a TGI Fridays with a standardized menu, Marilyn Monroe on the walls, Tiffany lamps, stripes instead of checks on the tablecloths. But the seats of power were still at the banquette in back, where she sat facing the district attorney, Kenneth Makris, during a relatively quiet happy hour.

"You know I really would have preferred to have had this meeting at your office or at another more discreet location," she said.

"Why?" The district attorney raised a glass of wine. "I don't have anything to hide. Do you?"

"Sir." She rapped her knuckles on the table and then realized she needed to pace herself. "We're not talking about me. We're talking about Captain Tolliver and his history."

"You have most of his service record." He gestured at the file on the seat beside her. "I've always known him to be a dedicated public servant. He's brought us a lot of good cases and has always testified credibly."

"I was at the Lonnie Donges trial several years ago." She pushed aside the plate full of wilted salad leaves that she hadn't touched. "I did not find that testimony credible in the least. In fact, I'm surprised your office didn't initiate an investigation on its own into whether Tolliver perjured himself on the stand."

Kenny frowned, as if his hamburger was giving him indigestion. "Ms. Martinez . . ."

"It's Jesperson now."

"Ms. Jesperson. I thought you'd already looked into this back in '89 . . ."

"When I was pressured into filing a report prematurely and shut down after one of my key witnesses died under suspicious circumstances."

"I looked into Amy Nelson's death personally and found nothing questionable about it. And I believe Captain Tolliver and his lawyer went up to Albany and answered your questions personally. I was told that they presented incontrovertible evidence that he could not have been involved . . ."

"Yes, I know. I saw the Halloween pictures. You're part of his alibi. But we're developing some evidence to undercut that."

She'd known she was going to get resistance, trying to jump-start this investigation again. Especially since there were stories of an unholy alliance going back years between Makris and Tolliver. But she had a feeling that the DA would sever his ties under the right circumstances.

"What kind of evidence?" Makris asked, glasses slipping down his nose.

"Let's just say it's early days, but some people are talking who might have been afraid before."

It was only a partial bluff. She'd reached out last week and had coffee with Tom Danziger, one of the other officers in the Ninja Turtles photo. He had served under Tolliver and still seemed deathly afraid of him. But he'd definitely perked up when she said she had connections with the incoming state attorney general's office, and she had a feeling he could be leveraged into opening up about Joey T. if she played him right.

"You sure it's not just sour grapes?" Makris put too many teeth into his smile. "There's a lot of older cops who are bitter about being leapfrogged by Joey and all too willing to talk trash to an attractive female investigator."

The compliment landed like unexploded ordnance. Inexpertly delivered and wide of his mark.

"It's not just sour grapes," she said. "It has to do with Tolliver's history. Isn't your office supposed to independently investigate police-involved shootings?"

"In certain situations." He pushed back his glasses with a touch of defensiveness. "Why do you ask?"

"Did you ever take a second look at the fatal incident involving Tolliver and Randy Carter in Smithtown?"

"No need." Makris shrugged. "Everyone agreed Mr. Carter had multiple guns in the house and he was waving one of them around when Joey and the other officer entered."

"So you never reopened the case, even after Tolliver moved in and got married to the widow?"

"That was long after." Makris waved a hand. "And I'm not in the business of investigating officers' off-duty lives—"

"Well, maybe you should be," she interrupted, picking up the tempo. "My understanding is that the neighbors have called 911 several times recently after overhearing disturbances in that house."

"My, aren't you the little busybody?" He rested a hand on his cheek.

She bristled almost literally, close-cropped hairs rising on her scalp. "I'm telling you, there is a pattern of troubling behavior from an officer you've been closely associated with throughout your career. I wouldn't keep my star hitched to his wagon if I were you."

"Are you threatening an elected official, Ms. Jesperson?"

"I'm giving you fair warning," she said through a locked jaw. "Especially since I hear you have higher aspirations of your own."

"Are you sure I'm the one with 'higher aspirations'?" He crooked his fingers and offered a smile edged with contempt.

"The wheels are about to come off. You may want to get out in front of this."

"You're suggesting I hop aboard your wagon instead?"

"Joey Tolliver is bad news, Mr. Makris. This time, I'm going to get him."

"You aren't the first, and I'm sure you won't be the last. If nothing else, the man is a survivor."

A waitress came over to check on them. Leslie scared her off with an Iron Lady glare. This had been a mistake, she realized, trying to get the district attorney on her side for this. Makris would not be enlisted or even neutralized.

"Why are you protecting Tolliver?" she demanded, losing patience. "What does he have on you?"

He looked down, as if befuddled to find his napkin still neatly folded next to his plate. He picked it up and shook it out with a fury that did not seem purely connected to the present conversation.

"I'm on the side of any law enforcement professional devoted to doing his or her job," he said, not meeting her eye.

"Then why aren't you helping me?" Leslie asked.

"I'm sorry, but I can't," he muttered. "I need to ask you to respect my position."

"How can I? We're talking about at least four women dead and at least two men wrongly in prison."

"I think this conversation is done."

"We're still sitting in a restaurant." Leslie turned her head from side to side, looking at the other customers. "And neither of us are done eating. Should we just finish the meal in silence?"

"No, let's just get everything to go." Makris raised his hand. "Check please."

27

When the white car first appeared in the upper right-hand corner of her mirror, Lourdes ignored it.

They had been way the hell out on the Island the day after seeing Rattigan, trying to track down some of the girls who'd been at the party where Magdalena said she'd almost been choked to death. Two of the three were no longer at the addresses and phone numbers she'd provided. The third was married with children in Syosset and had made it clear that no way was she ever talking about that part of her past, and if they didn't get out of her driveway, she was calling the local bulls on them.

By the time the sun was starting to set on Sunrise Highway, B.B. was fed up. Too restless to sit in traffic back to the city, he had Lourdes drop him off at the nearest LIRR station and agree to sign out for him at the squad. He claimed he had a cousin he wanted to drop by and see near Massapequa. Which Lourdes translated to mean that all the talk of hookers and cocaine had gotten him nostalgic and horny, and he was probably headed off to see one of his old girlfriends.

Not that Lourdes honestly minded having time on her own to listen to her own music and think about the case on the way back to the city with windows down and the breeze in her face. Having the chance to finally put her eyes on these Long Island parkways, nature preserves, and wildlife refuges where the bodies were found made the cases feel much more real to her. Someone had actually done this over and over again for several decades without getting caught.

Other guys in the squad were going to have trouble swallowing that a cop could have done this. Even the suggestion would be heresy to some. But Lourdes was starting to warm up to it. She'd known a few head cases who had somehow made it past the NYPD psych services exam. And whoever did this was sharp enough to evade detection as he selected his victims, murdered them, and got rid of their bodies. But the question that nagged at her as she hurled past the Olive Garden, Dollar Tree, and Dunkin' Donuts with Nicki Minaj blasting, was, how could he have managed it on his own if he wasn't someone as high up as Tolliver?

At least ten bodies and counting in thirty years. Somebody must have seen or noticed something suspicious in that time. She put pedal to metal and turned up "Anaconda" until the chassis shook as she began to focus in. Chain outlets and auto body shops gave way to wooded areas along the side of the road. Why would anyone keep quiet for so long? Talking to Rattigan had got her thinking about the nature of conspiracy cases, which normally were about money and power. It was only worth protecting someone if they had enough juice to make it worth your while. Serial killers weren't usually big into the Favor Bank. They were lone wolves, which was why you never heard about Ed Gein and Jeffrey Dahmer handing out money and patronage jobs. Why would anyone literally enable a homicidal maniac?

The road had gotten dark and twisty. She realized it had been several minutes since she'd seen a streetlight or an open store. Nicki Minaj and the big snake were getting buried and lost in radio static. Her headlights caught the android-green eyes of a deer standing by a copse of trees on the right, getting ready to dash out onto the road. She pulled out her iPhone to check Google Maps and her messages. There was a voicemail from John Gallagher, the state cop. She listened to it through the Bluetooth on the dashboard.

"Hey, I just talked to a lawyer named Ford upstate. He had news for us about the state investigations commission's report and Leslie Martinez. Long story short, don't hold your breath waiting to have an informed conversation with her. It's a dead-end. Ms. Martinez left this earth a while back. Call me back, I'll explain."

She "*left this earth*"? The words struck her like a severed hand through the windshield. Why did he have to say it like that? Instead of just saying she *passed*. Her chest got tight and her scalp felt cold. She tried to call him back and had to leave a message when it went to voicemail. The road curved in the other direction and turned darker. Feeling lost, she called Mitchell, who was out, and then Sullivan.

"Yeah?" As usual, he picked up like they were already half an hour into a conversation.

"What's a Bird Dog?" she said.

"Come again."

"I told you we were going to see this old detective Billy Rattigan and he said he'd known Chief Tolliver since he was a witness in something called the Bird Dog case. I've been trying to look it up and not finding anything. You know what he's referring to?"

"Sure he hasn't lost his mind?" he asked. "I hear that happens with old cops who have too much time on their hands."

"You don't say . . ."

She moved into the left lane and slowed down a little, noticing that the headlights in the corner of her rearview had flipped up to high beams. She realized the white car had been lagging behind her for several miles, without her paying too much attention to it.

"Uh-oh," she said.

"What's the matter?"

"I think someone is tailing me."

The headlights started to get bigger and brighter in the glass as the car accelerated toward her. There were fewer cars on the road now and the lights increased to migraine-level intensity as they moved toward the center of her mirror. Her hands tightened on the steering wheel and she checked her side mirror to see where it was trying to pass her. Instead it dropped its velocity to stay directly behind her. Colored lights burst on, triggering her internal alarm system and removing any doubt that this was a police car.

"Damn," she said. "It's the police."

"You're the police."

"I'm not in the city. I'm out here."

She put on her directional signal and switched into the right lane, hoping the police car would just go by. Instead the driver flicked the high beams on and off, making his intention as blindingly clear as the reflected lights stabbing into her eyeballs.

"*Pull over,*" the voice on the loudspeaker said.

"I heard that," said Sullivan. "Leave the phone on while they're talking to you."

She placed her phone in the recess between the seats, slowed down, and put on her rear flashers with an unmistakable sense of déjà vu. Like something like this had happened before, not necessarily to her, but somewhere around here. Part of a collective memory. The high beams went off as the police car pulled in behind the borrowed Charger she was driving. She could see two male officers get out.

She watched their approach in her side mirror, their silhouettes appearing and disappearing in the tick-tock red glow of her rear blinkers. Of course, they'd picked a spot where the signal was weak. These guys had this down to a science.

"Good evening."

The officer who came up to her driver's side window already had his hand on his gun. She was almost sure that it wasn't one of the gym rats who'd taken down their license plate number outside Ronnie Meltzer's house. But that was worse; it meant there were more of them. This one was stockier and sturdier, and he spoke with what sounded to Lourdes like a very slight Mexican accent. Clever that they would send another Latino to do this. This way, no one could say it was racist profiling.

"Good evening." She started to reach for her billfold. "How you guys doing?"

"Ma'am, keep your hands where I can see them please. On the steering wheel."

They weren't playing. Not even a pretense of friendliness.

"I was going to show you my shield," she said. "I'm on the job, like you are."

"When we want your ID, we'll ask for it," said the other one, who was standing by the passenger side window.

He sounded younger and whiter than his partner, and more eager to prove something.

"Is there a problem, officers?" Lourdes asked, playing it straight and polite, knowing they were looking for excuses.

With their headlights off and both cars parked in the shade of the trees, a dashboard camera in the vehicle might not see much. And she doubted they had turned on any body cameras. But they might be recording the exchange on audio with an idea of editing it later to make it sound like she was being belligerent and combative.

"You know that you were texting while you were driving, right?" the officer at the driver's window said.

"I was?" She remembered Sullivan was silently listening.

"We saw your screen was lit up from behind you and then you switched lanes without signaling."

"I'm sorry, officers. I didn't see you when I looked at the phone."

She realized it was going to be a while until she got to hear the Leslie Martinez story and see what work her predecessor had done out here previously. And whether she'd been tailed and messed with similarly. A little more information would be useful right about now.

"So—like, what?—you only follow the law when you think there's a cop watching?" The one at the passenger side was plainly trying to gin up a reason to get furious with her.

"No, sir."

That they were going to fuck with her now was a foregone conclusion. The open question was how far they would take it.

"And you know you were weaving all over the road," said the one with the accent.

"I don't see how that could be true, officer." She raised her chin, trying to meet his eye without challenging him. "Is that what you recorded on your dashboard camera?"

"Never mind what's on camera," said the one at the passenger window. "Are you gonna argue with us?"

It was difficult to read his face in the dark. But he sounded hard and closed off. Like he was determined not to deviate from the steps needed to escalate this encounter.

"I'm not arguing," she said. "I'm just trying to—"

"You want to fight this, there's two of us and one of you," he spoke over her.

The interior of the car had begun to feel humid and close, even with both windows open. As if they had found a way to suck the air out of the vehicle.

"Look, can we just start over?" She spread her hands against the top of the steering wheel. "As a matter of professional courtesy, could you just—"

"You want 'professional courtesy'?" said the one with the accent. "How about showing a little deference first? You ain't in New York City anymore, sistah."

Boom. There it was.

"It's *detective*." She sat up. "And when did I say I was from the city?"

The question stopped them for a second. Two cars went by behind them, both doing eighty easily as they chased each other in and out of lanes. Neither of them even looked. They had her boxed in and they weren't letting her go now.

"What's really going on here?" she said. "Is the highway even your jurisdiction?"

"Why don't you let us worry about that?" the one closer to her said, tapping two fingers on her windowsill. "We know where we're supposed to be."

"I'm just saying, can we get real about this?" she asked, trying to banter with them. "Who did I piss off? The chief tell you to pull me over?"

"Right now, you're the one pissing *us* off with the attitude." The one at her window looked across at his partner. "Officer, do you detect the smell of anything unusual in this vehicle?"

Lourdes sank deep into her seat, the dashboard appearing to rise before her eyes.

"Yes, sir," said the one at the passenger window. "I'd say there's a distinct odor of marijuana emanating."

"No, no, no." Lourdes began shaking her head. "This isn't happening."

It was just like a nightmare, this sense of total helplessness in the face of events that seemed both utterly inexplicable but completely inevitable. They were going to do her good.

The officer at the passenger window clicked on a flashlight and aimed it, just as she knew he would, at the floor where B.B.'s feet had been resting not fifteen minutes before.

"Got something," he said.

He reached down and picked up a small glassine envelope that was revealed in the flashlight beam to be filled with white powder. She realized that he must have tossed it in when she was turned around talking to the other officer. And there was not a damn thing she could do to prove it.

"Really?" she said. "We're really going to do this?"

The last couple of years, when there was all this bad press about cops doing illegal stops and shooting unarmed minority civilians, she'd tried to stay out of the controversy. Kept her head down and her mouth shut at Starbucks and the nail salon whenever she overheard these heated conversations. Because if you really knew what it was like to be a cop these days, you didn't need anybody to tell you. And if you didn't know, there was no way to explain it.

Now it was happening to her, though. She'd thought that having a badge, which was all she'd ever really wanted in life, would save her from being treated like ghetto scum. But she was outside city limits and they were acting like she was lower than a common criminal, like she was just a Puerto Rican skank who should have been on her knees in front of them. She felt sick and clammy, her gut throbbing like her heart had just fallen into her stomach.

"Get out of the car please," said the one at the passenger side window.

"You motherfuckers," Lourdes murmured.

"What was that?"

"I cannot believe you would pull this on one of your own."

"I got news for you," said the one closer to her, who had now taken his gun from its holster. "You ain't one of ours. And if you don't stop resisting, you're going to find out what real trouble is."

"I'm not resisting. I've complied with everything you've asked me to do."

"Again, with the mouth." The one who'd pretended to find the bag clicked his flashlight off. "I think we need to charge her with resisting and possession with intent to sell."

"I want a lawyer," Lourdes said evenly, her pulse racing as she reached for the door handle. "And I want to talk to a supervisor."

"Just keep your hands where I can see them and tell me where you carry your gun." The one at the driver's window reached to unlock her door and then opened it. "Now get out and assume the position."

28

The sky had turned gray, threatening the return of the snow, while she was inside the Price Chopper on Central Avenue in Albany.

A hundred and six dollars for just a week's worth of groceries. Two boys and a girl were eating Leslie out of house and home since the divorce. How she was going to afford even state colleges for them on an investigator's $76,000 a year was beyond her. But her ex was determinedly not working and scholarships weren't likely with their grades and athletic performance, so somehow she would find a way.

As she pushed the shopping cart over the cracked and icy parking lot asphalt, the rattle of its cage and the crunch of salt under her boots reminded her that she needed to somehow trudge on and hold things together. There were no savings to fall back on and little chance of advancement at the Department of Investigation, unless she could prove that the time and expense of the Long Island investigation had been worthwhile. She just needed to keep moving forward somehow. Especially since she had a constant sense of eyes on her back. She'd even felt them in the supermarket as she perused the frozen foods aisle.

Joey, still trying to get the hang of PowerPoint, clicked the switch and the image of a clown with a rictus grin filled the screen.

"John Wayne Gacy," he said. "A bozo. Literally."

The members of the class tittered. Fresh-faced recruits. Mostly local kids, with associate degrees and a couple of years' working experience in other jobs. Mostly white, mostly male, mostly unlikely to be superstars in the department. But he liked to keep teaching, to get a feel for them early on, to see who could be trusted and who had to be watched.

"Democratic Party operative, member of the Jaycees, KFC franchise manager, owner of his own construction company, married father of two, with a sideline entertaining hospitalized children as Pogo the Clown." He clicked to the photo of Gacy's baggy-eyed and unshaven 1978 mug shot. "And also the murderer of thirty-three young men, most of them buried in the crawl space of his home."

The tittering died away. Somehow these twenty-four people wanted to be police officers but had never heard of one of the most famous serial killers in the country.

"How did he get away with it?" Joey moved in front of the screen. "Was he a mad genius, like the kind we see on movies and TV shows?"

The class gave each other knowing looks, though none of them had a clue where he was going with this.

"Well, he wasn't a complete idiot." Joey, in short sleeves to show off his biceps, opened his arms. "He finished high school. Managed a couple of more or less successful businesses. And was able to avoid detection for several years. But a genius? Gimme a break."

He clicked to Gacy's clean-shaven 1968 mug shot. "The dude had been arrested and convicted ten years before for sexually assaulting a fifteen-year-old boy. And then paying another kid to mace the vic and beat him up to keep him from testifying. The neighbors saw him coming and going in his car at odd hours. And at least two other boys told the police Gacy had handcuffed them and raped them without it leading to an arrest."

The cadets were starting to mutter among themselves.

"So it's not like this was a criminal mastermind," Joey said, clicking to a picture of David Berkowitz. "Son of Sam, in the city, 1977. Thought a dog was talking to him." He clicked to a photo of Jeffrey Dahmer. "The Milwaukee Monster. Borderline personality disorder with psychotic tendencies. Liked to drug his victims, rape them, and cut their heads off. And occasionally fry up their body parts for dinner."

A couple of the cadets made faces and covered their mouths. Had these people been living in caves that they hadn't heard of this?

"Drilled a hole into one kid's skull while he was still alive and injected hydrochloric acid into it," he said. "The cops found the boy sitting naked on a street corner. And what'd they do? They walked him back into the house where Dahmer had another corpse rotting and then left so Dahmer could finish the kid off. Brilliant. Right?"

He noticed that they had stopped shifting around and murmuring to each other.

"He was finally arrested two months later for basically starting to do the same thing again when the cops found a shirtless guy wearing a handcuff outside his place," Joey said. "So what does this tell us?"

She popped the hatchback of her Honda Civic and started to load her bags. Something passed in the right side mirror. Too slow for a bird, too fast for a car just getting out of its space. She turned and found herself staring at another harried mother, this one younger than her, but more bony-faced and dead-eyed in that upstate way she was still getting used to. Two sleeping twins in a creaky double-stroller. Leslie tried to give her a sympathetic smile, but the woman just bared more of her upper teeth. As if to say, *Why isn't anyone helping us?*

Leslie went back to putting bags in the car, wishing she hadn't parked in this remote part of the lot, just to be near the exit onto the service road. Everything seemed a little harder than it needed to be since her transfer up north. Long Island hadn't exactly been warm and friendly. Especially when she started digging into the relationships between the police and the politicians out there. But the winters weren't as bleak and brutal with six-foot snowdrifts, plows that never made it to the unpaved road where she'd finally found a house she could afford to live in with three adolescents, and frequent power outages from fallen wires.

Since her aborted lunch with Kenneth Makris, the investigation had hit more roadblocks. Tommy Danziger had stopped returning her phone calls, all of her budget requests had been steadfastly ignored, and Beth, the widow of Randy Carter, had given her the finger as she pulled out of her driveway and spotted Leslie parked across the street from the Smithtown house. Wearing sunglasses after sundown, like she had a black eye. Joey Tolliver strikes again. As if he'd been tipped off by his old friend, the DA.

Leslie finished putting the bags in the car and slammed the hatch. Then she came around on the driver's side to get in the front seat. She saw him clearly in the left side mirror now. The brown hooded sweatshirt with shades and hands in the front pouch.

Joey killed the projector and turned on the classroom lights. The newbies rubbed their eyes and looked around, like they were each coming out of some collective nightmare.

"It tells us that these people did the same thing over and over in a ritualistic fashion." He leaned against the lectern. "Like they did not adapt and adjust after their close calls with law enforcement. Because they were in the grip of some obsessive behavior that they could neither control nor explain. And what does *that* tell us?"

Again, blank scared looks all around. A mixed blessing. Because they were larva and somehow he'd have to supervise them on the job. On the other hand, he knew he had nothing to fear from them. Not a Sherlock or even a Kojak among them.

"It means the police were not doing their jobs," he said. "They had no system to absorb information and learn from it." He slammed a fist on the lectern, to wake them up a little. "Adapt or die, people. That's what it's all about in this life. Those who don't learn from the past are destined to repeat it. Until they get caught or until they realize they missed the opportunity to prevent a murder."

Finally, one of them shyly raised a hand. Dudley Do-Right in the first row. With goggly eyes, floppy hair, and an oversized cleft chin.

"Yes?"

"Um, is it possible sometimes all these people don't get caught because someone's helping cover their tracks?" he asked.

"Son, what's your name?"

"Gillispie, sir. Paul Gillispie."

Joey made a note of the name on the side of his lecture notes. "Well, Paul Gillispie," he said. "I hesitate to say anything is the dumbest thing I've ever heard because I've heard so many dumb things in my career. But you're in the big time now."

The class cracked up and Gillispie sank down in his seat, embarrassed.

Joey underlined the name. Determined to remember it and make sure the kid never got an assignment anywhere near him.

Leslie turned just as he pulled out the gun. He fired twice before she could reach for the Glock in her shoulder bag. The first round glanced off her collarbone. The second struck her in the middle of the forehead.

    She fell against the car and landed on her back on the asphalt, flakes falling fast and melting on her unblinking eyes.

29

They took her gun. Then they took her prints. Then they took shoelaces so she wouldn't hang herself, and put her in a protective custody cell in Central Islip.

At least she'd been able to get a call out to Mitchell to tell him what was going on before she lost reception again. Presumably he had called her squad and they had reached out to One Police Plaza to let the upper echelon know about this crap being pulled on an NYPD officer pursuing a legitimate investigation in another jurisdiction.

But right now, none of that made any difference. The reality was that it was almost two o'clock in the morning, it would be seven hours until she got to see a lawyer before arraignment court, and she was stuck by herself in a twelve-by-fifteen cell with Styrofoam white walls, a gray cement floor, and a black camera eye in a corner of the ceiling.

She'd been flaked and screwed and there wasn't a damn thing she could do about it. And she still couldn't quite believe the reason. Yes, she'd been narrowing her focus down onto a cop who preyed on prostitutes and other vulnerable women. But the question still nagged: If Tolliver was involved, how could he have gotten away with it for so long? Other people would have had to know.

She got up from the bench and put her back against the wall, thinking of doing some of her yoga exercises just to relieve the stress, made worse by the microwave-like hum of the lights. But she couldn't bear the thought of the guards cracking up as they watched her on the closed-circuit TV monitor outside. Fat female cop doing downward dog in the pens. Comedy gold. Within hours, it would be on every laptop in every police station in the county. And then it would go viral and nationwide, worse than the YouTube clip of her and Erik Heinz in the city.

On the other hand, maybe they weren't covering for a serial killer. It could have been simple resentment. Nobody likes an outsider coming in to tell you how to get your house in order. Pointing out where you messed up and let a dozen women get killed. And perhaps finding out about a bunch of other corruption in the process. Magdalena had said there were politicians and businesspeople at the party where this J tried to strangle her. That would be enough reason to try to shut down an outside investigation.

There was a sharp buzzing sound, a series of metallic clicks, and then a doughy female guard led in a new prisoner. A hulking figure was deposited in Lourdes's cell and as the guard exited quickly, opening an outer door, Lourdes could hear other women in the main holding pens. It sounded like there'd just been a major prostitution-and-drug sweep. The ladies were clearly high off their asses, shout-singing and cursing raucously and laughing like it was someone's retirement party and no one needed to worry about going to work tomorrow.

Then the outer door closed, the locks clicked, and Lourdes found herself alone with her new cellmate.

The microwave hum was louder now, bringing with it a renewed sense of menace. For a second, it appeared that a large and belligerent man had been left with her. Brawny and crewcut, with the sleeves torn from a lumberjack shirt to show off beefy tatted-up arms. A pair of baggy denim shorts ended just above two clam-like kneecaps and hairy shins backed by bulging calf muscles. The feet were encased in black Doc Marten workboots without laces, which looked like they might have had steel toes. The head was lowered in the position of a bull about to charge.

The words *"I'm a friend to the LGBT community!"* came urgently to Lourdes's mind. Followed quickly by *"I have an aunt who's gay and butch!"*

But any idea that this might be an encounter about gender identity or tolerance dissipated as the cellmate dropped into a drastic deep squat in the corner, massively callused hands clenched into fists in front of her face, a lunatic cackle escaping behind them. She began to bounce lightly on her sizable haunches, like she was riding a man sexually, and began to sing to herself.

"*Ma hump. Ma hump. Mahumpmahumpmahump . . .*"

Lourdes looked up at the ceiling camera and slowly shook her head. You bastards.

"*Whatchoo gonna do with all that junk, all that junk inside your trunk . . .*"

The woman lowered her fists, revealing a rough longshoreman's mug and an unnervingly steady glare.

"What you looking at?"

"Nothing." Lourdes patted at her side absently, wishing she at least had her Taser on her.

"Dumb bitch." The callused hands rested on the knees. "You say something to me?"

"No, I didn't say nothing."

It was a shock to hear her fourteen-year-old ghetto girl voice come out of her thirty-five-year-old mouth. This was like one of those conversations she'd learned to dread in the stairwells of the Walt Whitman Projects in Fort Greene. A few stray words while you were passing someone on your way to do something more important and then next thing you knew a kick in the ass sent you flying down a flight of steps where you landed facedown on the landing with a bunch of two-hundred-pound girls stomping the living shit out of you.

"Hey, you hear what I said?" The cellmate stood and shook out her arms, which had matching dragons tattooed on them. "I called you a 'dumb bitch.'"

"Yeah. Okay."

The large woman swaggered up to her, fists hanging at her sides, mouth twitching like she was thinking of all the things she wished she'd said to everyone who had pissed her off. She stopped within six inches of Lourdes, deliberately disrespecting her personal space, forcing Lourdes to flatten herself even more against the wall. Even without the Doc Martens, she would have been a solid six feet tall. At close range, though, her lips were pink and feminine and her nostrils were small and surprisingly delicate as they sniffed.

"What's that I smell?"

"I don't smell anything."

Lourdes began to slide away sideways, but the woman put up a log-like arm on either side of her, penning her in.

"I smell dry cooch. Don't you?"

"I didn't think dry cooch had a smell." Lourdes thrust her chin out. "But I don't get down there that often."

"You saying I do?"

"No."

"You calling me a dyke or something?"

"All right, can you back up or put your arms down?"

"You saying that because of how I look, right?"

"I'm not judging anyone or anything, but you're crowding me."

"Shit." The big woman looked down and laughed, but kept her arms where they'd been. "I'm more of a woman than you'll ever be."

"Whatever. If you say so."

Lourdes tried to turn away with a demure smile, but the cellmate followed her with her face, keeping her hemmed in.

"Hey, look at me when I'm talking to you," the big woman said. "What's wrong with you?"

It was obvious what this was. They'd placed someone with a serious mental illness in the cell with her, trying to provoke a physical confrontation when she was forced to defend herself. Then they could tack on assault charges to go with the drug evidence they'd planted on her. To further discredit her by making her look unstable. And if she didn't fight back and got her face stomped again, losing two teeth and getting her jaw fractured like she did at the Whitman houses, well, that wasn't the fault of the guards. Was it? Just them dumb crazy bitches going at it in the pens. Same as it's always been.

"I want to know what's inside you." The cellmate leaned in, their chests almost touching as Lourdes smelled the remnants of weed, beer, and maybe crack. "Can you tell me?"

"Same thing that's inside everybody else." Lourdes kept her profile turned to the woman.

"Yeah, but you're a cop." The woman's nose was almost mashing into Lourdes's cheek. "They told me that you're a cop."

"If they said it, then it must be true."

"Hey, I said, *look at me.*" The woman suddenly grabbed Lourdes's jaw with one hand and twisted it as she squeezed. "Are you afraid?"

"Don't touch me." Lourdes batted the hand away. "I'm not your bitch."

The guards were definitely all crowded around the closed-circuit monitors outside, watching this instead of UFC reruns. The best show in the facility.

"What would you do if I got all up in your business?" The woman pressed her mouth up to Lourdes's ear, her breath hot and heavy. "If I got my fingers in there, would you be all hard and rough like the inside of a police car? Or would you be all soft and wet like a lady should be?"

"All right, you need to back the fuck off and give me some space *right now.*" Lourdes ducked away from her and slid along the wall. "I think we just established that I'm a cop."

"Except now you're in here, *chiquita.*" The woman cornered her again, in the place where two walls met. "So we're the same now. You said it yourself. There's no difference inside."

It was not going to be good if this got physical. On the street, Lourdes could handle herself decently. She got down and dirty in the gutter with a few perps. But that was when she had mace and cuffs and a partner to back her up. And of course she'd shot that lowlife Tyrell Humphries in the scrotum when he'd tried to hold up a beauty parlor where she was getting her hair done. But here: no partner, no gun, no physical parity. She could be rolling on the cold floor for hours with this hag and the guards would claim they'd been tied up handling a bigger disturbance in the main cells.

"You know what?" The cellmate put the tip of her right boot against the tip of Lourdes's left shoe. "I used to be prettier than you."

"I said, *back the fuck off.*" Lourdes tried to push her away with both hands, to little effect. "I'm not gonna tell you again."

"I had a man who was twice the man you'll ever have." The woman was exhaling and staring down at Lourdes with a kind of unyielding interest, like she was already thinking about taking pleasure without asking for consent. "He bought me clothes. He bought me shoes. He took me away. He poured champagne all over my body, Moët Chandon, and licked off every inch of it with his tongue."

"Then why you bothering me?" Lourdes tried shoving her harder but it was like trying to move the Great Wall of China.

"Because they arrested my man for selling drugs out of his car, then they beat him until he wasn't a man anymore. Then they locked me up with a bunch of fucked-up psychos where the only way I had to survive was to become like I am now."

"Oh."

Lourdes felt some of the air go out of her fear. Even as the woman laid a gentle finger against her lips.

"So you stay cool, baby," she hastened her whisper. "Everything ain't the way it looks out here. There's some scary people who'll do you right in the end. And rotten-ass skanks who'll smile in your face and stab you in the back. But if they end up doing you like I think they will, at least you'll know you got a friend on the inside. I'll look out for you if you look out for me. Deal?"

"Deal." Lourdes nodded.

"But if we both go to prison, don't forget to slip me some sugar once in a while. Your big bad mama's got a sweet tooth for sweet thangs."

She kissed Lourdes hard on the mouth and then went to lie down on the bench. Leaving just enough room for Lourdes to sleep sitting up beside her.

30

The bar in Central Islip was called Legends. It had dartboards and Never Forget posters on the walls, Led Zeppelin on the jukebox, and off-duty police and corrections officers three deep at the counter, letting off steam. When Mitchell Vogliano walked in with Kevin Sullivan that night and tried to order a glass of red wine instead of a domestic beer, it nearly caused an international incident.

"A *cabernet*? Here? Seriously?" The bartender, with a boiled cabbage complexion and an accountant's eyes, nodded toward the taps. "You're drinking Bud or Guinness."

"Read the room," Sullivan muttered.

"I'll just have a seltzer then," Mitchell Vogliano said, ignoring the commotion he'd set off around him.

"Christ," said Sullivan. "Like we're not going to have enough trouble."

They'd driven out from Brooklyn together to try to get Lourdes out of county lockup. But the night sergeant said he didn't care what they heard when they called ahead; courts were closed for the night, arraignments were in the morning, anyone in was staying in. And yes, this so-called Detective Robles was being held in protective custody.

Sullivan made a few calls and arranged to meet a local bail bondsman he knew slightly at the bar and now here they were, strangers in a strange land, and semi-strangers to one another. He'd had Mitchell Vogliano as an assistant district attorney on one drug murder case back in

Brooklyn where the defendant pled out right away and had heard he was good at his job. Otherwise, he was mainly aware of him as Robles's fancy man, a choice he found himself puzzling over as he pointed toward the Guinness harp and settled on a bar stool.

"Ever hear the expression 'go with the flow'?" he asked. "Or 'when in Rome'?"

"I don't like beer." Mitchell sat down beside him. "And I don't change my stripes to fit in."

"Good for you. I suppose."

Typical nose-in-the-air prosecutor arrogance, Sullivan thought. Let the world come to me. As opposed to your work-a-day cop adjusting to circumstance. On the other hand, now he could see a little bit of what Lourdes liked about this skinny young white fella. He wasn't exactly a street fighter, like she was, but he wasn't a pushover either.

"I'm a little surprised she called you first," Mitchell said forthrightly, like it was something he'd been sitting on during the mostly silent car ride out here.

"I'm sure she tried you." Sullivan shrugged. "Or was about to."

"Maybe I should say that I'm jealous. That you were who she thought to reach out to when she knew she was in trouble."

"I just happened to be on the line when they pulled her over. I wouldn't read too much into it."

"Shouldn't I?" Mitchell rested an elbow on the counter. "There's a lot I don't get out of her. Like I wasn't aware you guys were that close, or had worked together for that long."

"We didn't," Sullivan said. "But in this job, sometimes you just click with people or you don't."

"Maybe that's why I'm jealous." Mitchell nodded. "You got to be in the car with her. For all those hours."

But you get to be in bed with her, Sullivan thought. Another one of those regretful things he'd never say aloud. Especially not now.

The jukebox was playing "Babe I'm Gonna Leave You." And even though it was a weeknight, the officers at the bar balled up their fists and threw them in the air every time the song switched from its sad acoustic part to the bludgeoning electric sections.

"She's a good woman," Sullivan said quietly. "You're a fortunate man."

"Am I?" Mitchell's eyes had started to drift like he was sinking into worry. "I wonder how long I'm going to have her sometimes."

"Well, I doubt you'll ever really have her, son. But you're fortunate to have time with her. That's all you really have with anybody."

Sullivan watched the bartender tilt back a glass and fill it under the taps. For some reason, he remembered playing his wife some other Zeppelin album and trying to explain to her why white men loved "Stairway to Heaven." She was, of course, a Latina and a dancer, so classic rock made absolutely no sense to her. But he adored the way she laughed when Robert Plant sang about the bustle in the hedgerow.

"So what do you think?" Mitchell leaned over. "Am I going to lose her?"

"To another man or to the job?"

"Actually, detective, I was more anxious about the immediate situation with her being in custody." The younger man almost smiled as he looked around. "These people are a little scary. No?"

Sullivan eyed the crowd. It was true that police were police in most places. And there were plenty of good cops from the city who'd come out to work here. But experience had taught him that within every constabulary force was a core of officers who were suspicious of democracy and preferred authoritarianism. And that this was a group that was particularly hostile to outsiders and people who didn't look like them, and they were very dangerous to drink around.

"She should be all right," he said, looking toward the entrance to see if his bail bondsman had arrived. "But I'll feel better once she's headed home with you."

"You don't really think they'd plant evidence on her and try to send her to prison, do you?" Mitchell asked.

"You challenge the powers that be, they'll rarely thank you for it."

"So it's true," Mitchell lowered his voice. "You think this could go up the ladder as well? I mean, that the higher-ups could have been involved in what happened to these women?"

"It's hard to imagine, but maybe. Once you decide it's more important to protect the system than the people in it, then anything is possible." He turned as the bartender brought them their drinks. "Excuse me, sir, were you on the job out here?"

"Was I a police officer in Suffolk?" The bartender fingered his blue denim work shirt and smiled to himself. "For about five seconds. Till they put me on midnights on the highways. Not for me, brother. I'm a talker, not a loner."

"Kevin Sullivan, Mitchell Vogliano. We're out here from the city." Sullivan offered his hand. "Mind if I ask you something?"

"Go ahead." The bartender returned the grip firmly. "I'm Paul Gillispie, by the way." He ignored a couple of drunken officers waving their empties at him. "I always say that I serve these guys, but I'm not their servant. Some of them get confused sometimes."

"You ever hear of something called the Bird Dog case?"

"Are you putting me on?" Gillispie asked. "You're talking about the Kim Bergdahl case?"

"That would be the one." Sullivan snapped his fingers. "Now that you're saying the name properly, it's starting to come back to me."

"Then pull your stools closer and order another round," Gillispie said.

31

The state investigators came to talk to him three days after Leslie Jesperson was killed. They found him on a Saturday morning loading up the station wagon in the iced-over driveway of the Smithtown house.

"Captain, can we get a minute?" The taller one was built like a hockey player, hefty but easy on his feet, with a trace of a Canadian border accent. "I'm Chris Sinclair. My partner's Ernie Barbaro."

Joey waved them off when they started to show tin. No need to make a bigger thing of this with the neighbors watching.

"Going somewhere?" Barbaro was eying the equipment in the back of the station wagon.

If his partner Sinclair was the point man, Barbaro was the enforcer. Lower to the ground and chunkier. More a brawler than a skater.

"I'm supposed to referee a hockey game at the rink this afternoon," Joey said. "I'm bringing the pads and sticks and balls and all the other equipment. But if you need me, the lady of the house can step up."

Beth was watching from behind the half-open door, giving all three of them the evil eye. He had made up his mind to shed her and the kids as soon as he got the bump to chief. The internal buildup was getting too hard to manage without release and the family was getting in the way.

"Anyway, what can I do for you guys?" he asked.

Sinclair and Barbaro exchanged a look, as if they'd scripted for more resistance.

"We're hoping you could come by the barracks and help us out with a case we're working on," said Sinclair.

"Happy to oblige." Joey reached into his pocket for keys. "State police have been great about helping out with our cases. I got another car in the garage. Should I take it or go with you?"

"Don't you want to know what this is about?" Barbaro thumbed the side of his mouth.

"Sure, if you want to tell me." Joey looked back at the house. "Or we can wait till we get to the barracks. Whatever works for you guys time-wise."

"You spoke to an investigator named Leslie Jesperson a while back," Barbaro said. "You remember that?"

"Of course. She used to be Martinez. I saw her up at the commission. I wish I could say 'nice lady,' but to be honest I never got around to that side of her. What's up?"

It would have been ridiculous to lie about knowing her. They could get the video of the interview he'd done with his lawyer present.

"She got shot to death in Albany a few days ago," said Sinclair. "In a supermarket parking lot."

"Ho shit." Joey unhinged his jaw. "I saw something about a cop getting shot upstate, but I didn't think . . . Do we have any leads?"

The driveway was slightly slanted and both state officers looked unbalanced now on the slippery ice.

"Not yet," said Sinclair. "We're hoping you could help us check off a few boxes, so we can move more quickly."

"Absolutely." Joey nodded. "Let's go. Whatever you need." He looked toward their Buick, parked across the street. "By the way, what day was she shot?"

"Wednesday afternoon," said Barbaro. "Witnesses saw a man in a brown hooded sweatshirt driving away in a white car." He took his time, looking at the black station wagon Joey had loaded up and then glancing at the garage.

"Wednesday afternoon?" Joey feigned a double take. "Yeah, that's why I didn't hear about it until later. I was tied up all day in a seminar."

"Seminar?" Barbaro shot a worried glance at Sinclair.

"Yeah, I teach a class about securing crime scenes at the academy in Brentwood from one to five every Wednesday afternoon." Joey shrugged. "They gotta learn somehow."

"So you were with a bunch of recruits on Wednesday afternoon?" Sinclair asked, the smooth skater tripped up.

"Yeah," Joey said, playing it out. "A couple dozen cadets. Good class this year. Why do you ask like that?"

The neighbors had come out to see what was going on. The Hansons, the Armitages, the McCarthys. All the people who'd been there the night he showed up to deal with Randy and who had kept their distance the whole time he'd been living here. He looked back and forth between them and the investigators, pretending to be surprised and embarrassed.

"You guys weren't thinking I had anything to do with this." He composed a hurt expression. "Were you?"

"Nah, nah, nah . . ."

Their voices were a cascade of denials as they broke into awkward grins. Flea-brain Staties. Better suited to flag duties than homicide investigations. He couldn't believe they thought they had a right to even stand near his lawn.

"We just need to look at everyone and everything," Sinclair said. "You understand, right?"

"Totally." Joey nodded. "And I'll get you the names and numbers of every student I was with, so you can confirm. But really, guys? You thought I was good for this? All the time I have on the job?"

"Hey, captain." Barbaro had taken on a sort of disappointed hedgehog look. "Wouldn't you have done the same thing if you were us?"

"No doubt I would, my brother." Joey slapped him on the back, making sure it smarted. "Can't blame someone for doing his job."

32

The courtroom used for arraignments in Central Islip was packed as Lourdes was led in.

At first she tried to tell herself that it was crowded because of the sweeps the night before, which had the holding pens bursting with home-less women and streetwalkers too insane or desperately drug-addicted to have enough sense to sell their goods online instead of outside. At least two rows were taken up by fed-up relatives or restive pimps or johns who'd been shamed into showing up with cash bail.

But everyone else was clearly there for Lourdes. It was like a night-mare version of the old TV show her father used to talk about: *This Is Your Life*.

Mitchell was in the front row, looking slightly shell-shocked and even more pale-faced than usual. Aunt Soledad, from Brooklyn Narcotics, vice president of the NYPD Hispanic Women's Society, was beside him wear-ing a suit jacket and white blouse, instead of her customary Hawaiian shirt. Lourdes's captain from Queens Homicide, Rashid Ali, was in the pew behind them, and just across the aisle were functionaries from One Police Plaza, including a deputy inspector she'd met at a promotion cer-emony a couple of years ago and a sergeant from the public information office, both out of uniform. There to observe and report back to the com-missioner, while avoiding making a statement of support for an officer ac-cused of transporting drugs in another jurisdiction.

Sullivan and B.B. were nowhere to be seen. But Rattigan was here, in his checked shirt and aviator glasses. And just to remove any doubt that she was well and truly screwed, the back rows were jammed with media people taking notes and staring at her like some weird zoo exhibit. The cops from out here had obviously leaked this and bloggers were probably already posting notices about her disgrace.

"Ms. Robles, how do you plead?"

She looked up after the preamble, still dazed from a mostly sleepless night. The Honorable Thomas Danziger was presiding, a gawky high-voiced man with the appearance of an aging farm boy. Everything was in the wrong place. She should have been on the prosecutor's side of the courtroom, where the two officers who'd arrested her were sitting behind an assistant district attorney. Some dog-faced mope should have been where she was standing, hands crossed behind her back, with a lawyer she'd never met from the Detectives' Endowment Association there to speak for her. How could it be the People versus Lourdes Robles? She was supposed to be on the side of the People.

"Ms. Robles?" the judge prompted her again.

"Not guilty, Your Honor."

The judge looked slightly surprised, perhaps even disappointed as he looked over at the prosecutor. "Bail, Mr. Harris? What say we?"

The assistant district attorney, a balding, potato-shaped man who looked too experienced to be handling arraignments, put aside the papers he'd been shuffling.

"Your Honor, we're opposed to any bail," he said loudly. "The charges in this case could not be more serious. The defendant was pulled over for driving erratically. Officers then detected a strong odor of marijuana coming from inside the vehicle. On cursory visual inspection conducted from outside the car, they spotted a bag that appeared to contain drugs near the driver's feet. Initial lab analysis revealed it to contain a mixture of heroin and fentanyl totaling more than eight ounces."

"They flaked me," Lourdes whispered to her attorney, Anthony Brigati, who looked more like a mob capo than a police lawyer in his pinstripes. "Assholes . . ."

He put a hand up, silencing her, as murmurs rose from the spectator gallery and knees knocked wood as people crossed their legs.

"Under the state penal code, that amount brings us to criminal possession of a controlled substance in the first degree, which is an A-1 felony," Harris said. "And we may be adding trafficking charges, pending further investigation."

Lourdes shook her head in disbelief at the justice seal above the judge's head, struggling to keep her mouth shut. She knew there was little chance she could end up getting convicted. But her body was reacting like she'd just received the maximum sentence: stomach groaning, mouth going dry, pores secreting clammy sweat.

"As Your Honor knows, we're dealing with an opioid epidemic on this part of Long Island," the prosecutor continued. "And most of those drugs come from the city. The defendant is a nonresident with no ties to our community, facing serious time. She has the motive and means to flee. We're asking you to remand her directly to a county facility, to be held until trial."

Without even turning around, Lourdes could tell how different factions were reacting. Mitchell was looking over his shoulder at the doors, as if he longed to flee. Soledad was probably ready to launch herself over the balustrade and smash the prosecutor to the floor with a flying tackle. And the media people were writing down every word.

"Your Honor, all due respect, but this is absurd," said her lawyer, Brigati, with a trace of a Long Island-by-way-of-Brooklyn accent. "Number one, this wasn't even her regular vehicle . . ."

"We're not trying the case here," Harris interrupted. "We're setting bail."

"And number two," Brigati bulled past him, "Detective Robles is a fourteen-year veteran of the New York City Police Department with numerous commendations and many ties to the local law enforcement community. We're confident that these charges will be ultimately dismissed and her reputation will be restored . . ."

Restored? The word landed on her like a freight elevator. Had her reputation been lost already?

"We're asking that she be released on recognizance," Brigati said, turning to glare at Harris the prosecutor. "And we're expecting a full apology from the Suffolk County PD and the district attorney's office for besmirching the detective's good name."

"Don't hold your breath." Harris looked past him and shook his head.

"We've convicted other NYPD officers for drunk driving and even robbery in this courthouse. A badge isn't always a shield."

"Yeah, thanks for that." Brigati half smiled. "Judge, this accusation would be laughed out of court in any of the five boroughs. Detective Robles is obviously the victim of a vendetta of some kind."

Lourdes stared at her lawyer, aware of a sudden hush behind her. Whatever trouble she was already in had just been made worse by this posturing and dick-waggling.

"We're very confident that these charges will stand up." Harris winced like a bad breakfast was repeating on him. "And since Mr. Brigati brought up these so-called ties Ms. Robles has, here are the facts: Detective Robles has a mixed service record. In addition to her commendations, she was disciplined several years ago for her role in an incident where she stood by while another officer berated a cab driver with racial epithets."

Bonehead Erik Heinz, her one-time partner at the seven-eight squad, had embarrassed both of them by getting caught on video screaming slurs at an Arab driver who'd cut them off in traffic. The video had gone viral and Lourdes, who'd made the mistake of keeping her mouth shut during the tirade, had found herself on extended assignment watching monitors in housing project basements as punishment.

Harris went in for the kill: "It may also interest the court to know that she is the daughter of Rafael Robles, a well-known drug dealer from Brooklyn, currently serving a life sentence for murder in Attica. We believe she was selling these drugs to help pay for lawyers appealing his sentence . . ."

Lourdes found herself paralyzed, as raw and exposed as a toddler falling face-first on pavement with no chance to put her hands out. This was the silent scream before the pain arrived. The openmouthed horror of anticipation. The skin had been scraped off and the nerves were out in the open and ready to transmit. This was going to hurt. For a long time. And maybe leave a scar.

"All right, *enough*." The judge put a hand up.

The whispers and scribbling from the gallery felt like infections spreading through her bloodstream.

"Mr. Harris." The judge looked at the prosecutor. "I appreciate your dilemma in bringing yet another city police officer into this courthouse.

I applaud the integrity of your office and the depth of your preparation on such short notice."

Lourdes shook off the cobwebs and glanced over her shoulder, wondering who could have tipped them off about her father. They couldn't just have started randomly searching for people named Robles in the state prison system.

The absence of Sullivan and B.B. was weighing on her more heavily by the second. Had one or both lost faith in her? Or did it mean that something even worse was coming?

"These charges, if proven, would be a gross violation of the oath Ms. Robles swore as a police officer," the judge said, getting caught up in the sound of his own voice. "On the other hand, denying bail altogether seems like a drastic measure."

In other words, he was worried about creating an obvious issue for a future appeal.

"So I'm inclined to go the route of King Solomon and split the baby evenly," the judge said. "I'm setting the amount at fifty thousand dollars, cash bail only."

Lourdes heard a whistle from the back of the courtroom.

"Holy sh—" someone started to say before the court officers hushed him.

She felt warm air on the back of her neck as if the spectators had given off a collective whoosh.

"Your Honor . . ." Brigati took a moment to catch his wind. "Wow. *Cash bail?* Don't you think that's . . . ? Where are we supposed to get that kind of money on short notice?"

The judge gaveled him into silence. "Mr. Brigati, we've already established that we're not trying this case today. Your client can either post bond or get used to eating the bologna sandwiches we serve at our facilities. If she has dietary restrictions, she can tell the sheriff's office."

People were moving around behind her, pushing past one another in the aisles, grumbling *excuse me*'s and *goddamn*s like they were fleeing the scene of a disaster, their heels on the granite floor tapping out the Morse code urgency of her situation.

The deputy inspector and press officer were probably already out in the hall, calling the commissioner's office at One Police Plaza. Within the hour, she'd be on modified assignment, if not officially suspended. And even with her aunt rallying the Hispanic Society, Mitchell putting the arm on his relatives, and B.B. passing the hat in Homicide, there was no way any of them could scrape together fifty grand on short notice. Or even come up with ten percent to give a bail bonds company in the unlikely event they could find one to put up the rest in cash.

She was sunk. Her joints going rigid, her shoulders turning inward. Like she was preparing to curl into the fetal position to endure the ferocious beatdown she was sure to get as soon as word got around the county lockup that there was a police officer among the prisoners.

Her chin came down with the weight of her shame. Your father's daughter, after all. She saw her own lawyer brush off his lapels and start to edge away a little in his Bruno Magli wing tips. Like he was already on the hunt for better prospects. Then he looked toward the back of the courtroom, waved, and smiled.

She turned to see what he was looking at and her heart shot up into her throat. Kevin Sullivan was standing up in the back row. Somehow she hadn't seen him until now, or perhaps, in his semi-mystical trance-inducing way, he hadn't allowed himself to be seen.

He walked slowly and a little stiffly toward the well of the courtroom, like the Golem in one of those old silent movies Mitchell liked to make her watch on TCM. Her protector, appearing like she'd conjured him. In his right hand was a worn and torn leather briefcase, as weathered and pockmarked as his face.

My man. She had to consciously restrain herself from vaulting over the balustrade and throwing her arms around him. Instead she discreetly rubbed a knuckle into the corner of her eye, noticing that the court officers who would normally never allow unsanctioned personnel to traverse the well made no effort to get in his way. He reached across the barrier to put a hand on her lawyer's shoulder and then spoke a few quiet words in his ear.

Brigati turned and gave the judge and bailiff a quick thumbs-up. Lourdes turned to mouth "thank you" but Sullivan was already on his way out, having left the briefcase on her side of the barrier.

33

The party to celebrate Joey's long-awaited promotion to chief of the department was at Legends, and it looked like half the Island had shown up to kiss the ring.

There were cops, lawyers, judges, legislators, Chamber of Commerce glad-handers, insurance agents, investment brokers, waste management consultants, homebuilders' association reps, Knights of Columbus, Rotary Club members, and pretty much every other variety of power groupie you could find on Long Island. All looking to "strengthen the relationship" and make their little deposit at the Favor Bank, in the hope it might pay off later. The head of the state investigations commission had stopped by, and so had various members of the defense bar, eager to make sure the arrangements still stood for getting their business cards distributed to potential clients. And of course, the union grifters were out in force to get their spoons in the soup while it was still warm.

There was money to be made here, if you weren't a complete idiot, and not just from the higher salaries. Every time you made a collar for a DWI or a DV, and the sap began to wail about "where am I going to find a good lawyer?" any cop in this department with half a brain would have a card in his pocket with the name and number of a local barrister who could be counted on to kick back a hundred dollars of his fee to the arresting officer. Now that Joey was chief, some of that would be coming his way. Or maybe some enterprising officer would do what he did and earn a little pin money by passing along some license plate information to the local wise guys or tipping them off about an upcoming State Liquor Authority raid at one of their bars along the North Shore that served underage kids. At least twenty-five percent of that would be his now.

This was his coronation and rightful reward. This was what he'd worked for and rightfully deserved. He sat swollen with pride at a banquette in the back, drinking Moët Chandon instead of Coors tonight, accepting congratulations, as Kenny approached with Steve Snyder, the county executive, and Snyder's new tanned and redheaded second wife.

"Look at this kid." Snyder grinned with his big white teeth, a halo of salon-style gray-white hair setting off his own phony tan. "Can you believe this, Kenny?"

Kenny shook his head, as if there were no words. Joey raised a glass and smiled back at the county executive, who had officially approved his promotion and let it go through.

"Sit down, Steve. And tell your beautiful wife to park herself on the other side of me."

They did as they were told. Snyder had been on and off Joey's radar screen for about twenty years. A small man trying to turn himself into a big man. Always presenting himself as a concerned good-government type at Town Board meetings and high school graduations, talking about the nobility of public service and how it was just as important to attend to the potholes on people's streets as it was to make speeches in Washington while he was raising money to run for Congress. Always had a hand in your pocket at campaign time. No one got a serious meeting or a real job around here unless they'd paid up ahead of time.

As Snyder and his wife slid in on either side of him, Joey let the back of his hand graze the wife's bare knee, as if by accident. He noted that she did not draw away immediately.

"Tell me something, Kenny." The county executive looked up. "Does he deserve this?"

Kenny laughed and put his hands up. "Hey, I'm just the DA. I don't appoint police chiefs."

"Come on," Snyder said in that braying coercive way that politicians had when they'd been overserved. "Tell me why we let this go through. We could've stopped it."

"What can I tell you?" Kenny tried to play along as the good sport. "The man paid his dues."

Joey rested his hand on the wife's knee more firmly now.

"What else?" said Snyder. "Why did you recommend him personally?"

"Chief Tolliver is a dedicated officer who has given his all to this job," Kenny said. "And he understands the system in a way that few others do."

Saying the words dutifully, instead of convincingly now. That was all right, Joey thought. Better to be feared than loved. People remembered their fear better anyway.

"What else?" Snyder rocked against Joey, trying to enjoy himself in a drunken way even as the champagne on his breath smelled like horse shit. "Remind me what this sonovabitch did to deserve his shot."

"He turned the vote out." Kenny nodded. "Every time."

"That's right." Snyder raised his champagne flute in tribute. "Every campaign, I know I can count on Joey Tolliver to knock on doors, get on the phone, and make sure our support from the rank and file of this department never slips below eighty percent."

"I look out for people who look out for people." Joey raised his own glass and clinked it against Snyder's in a perfunctory way. "Kenny knows that. Right?"

"Indeed, I do." Kenny glanced over his shoulder and waved to Brendan O'Mara, who'd just walked in. "Chief Tolliver never forgets where he came from or how he got to where he is."

"The greatest story ever told." Joey took a sip while under the table his other hand slid a couple of inches up the wife's thigh, his knuckles just brushing the hem of her short skirt.

She was trying to look him in the eye, either to warn him to stop or to let him know she was getting off on him having the nerve to do this in front of her husband.

In the meantime, Beth was off talking to a bunch of other cop wives in the corner, none of them with any idea of what really went on in the world.

"Hey." Snyder leaned close on the other side. "Pretty soon we could be taking this act to Washington," he said in a husky whisper. "I won't forget the people who made our towns safe again."

Joey squeezed the wife's leg, daring her to react and force her husband to do something.

"It's wonderful." She nodded blandly. "Steve always remembers his friends."

Her hand was on top of his wrist. Not grabbing it and throwing it off. Just registering he was there. Like she was frozen and unable to react in response. Which was all he really needed. He knew he could fuck her anytime and not have to pay for it.

He turned back to her husband. "Glad to hear that, Steve," he said. "It's hard to believe that we started off where we did and wound up here."

A not-so-subtle reminder that he knew about Snyder's little juvenile delinquent caper stealing Yes albums from the local E.J. Korvette's department store. He saw the flinch in the county executive's eyes and began to slide his hand further up and under the wife's skirt. And the rush of the sensation filled him up so much that he almost felt the need to loosen his belt to accommodate it. Because once a man realizes that others just have to shut up and take it from him, that they feel utterly compromised in his presence, he can be whatever he wants to be.

But in that same instant, a part of him was bored and restless. Asking, like in that old song, is that all there is? Because already he was starting to realize that the big desk could be a trap. Yes, he had the power and the position now, but he also had the added scrutiny. Even as he sat here, he couldn't get up to take a leak, because too many people kept coming up to shake his hand and slap him on the back.

It would only be worse at work. The endless budget meetings, the CompStat strategy reviews, and the village council powwows. The bureaucratic days stretched out like anonymous tombstones between here and the end of his time on earth. No, it was intolerable. What was the point of having accumulated all this wealth if you couldn't spend it?

"Congratulations, chief," said Snyder. "And it's only the beginning."

Joey looked the county executive straight in the eye and put his hand exactly where he wanted to, knowing no one was going to stop him now.

"Steve," he said without even looking at the wife. "In all honesty, I couldn't have done it alone."

34

SEPTEMBER
2017

The day after her release, Lourdes found Sullivan living out of suitcases at a motor inn in Commack, just off Jericho Turnpike.

The room was distinctly un-Sully-like: a downy white quilt on a round waterbed, smoky triple-X mirrors on the walls and ceiling, a heart-shaped tub in the bathroom.

"*Por que*, big man?" Lourdes stood on the threshold marveling.

As usual, her language brought a blush to his naturally ruddy complexion, which contrasted with the crow-black hair he'd obviously started dyeing again.

"They're giving me a good monthly rate," he said sheepishly. "I just needed a place to keep my things until I figure out my next move."

"I'm saying, why you bail me out, Papi? Ain't you got nothing better to do with your money?"

"If I do, it's slipped my mind." He looked down at his stockinged feet on the shag carpet, like he was embarrassed to be seen without proper shoes. "I guess you better come in."

She stepped across the threshold and he closed the door after her.

"I repeat," she said. "What the fuck, Sullivan? You come up with fifty G's on short notice to bail me out. What am I supposed to do with that?"

"Forty of it came from the bail bondsman me and your boyfriend met up with the other night. The rest I had on hand from selling the house. You could just say a simple thank-you and leave it at that."

"Why are you being so good to me, my man?"

"What can I tell you?" He stooped his still-broad shoulders. "An elephant never forgets. You stuck up for me when things went south on the Dresden case and the bosses wanted to put me out to pasture before my time."

"*De nada*," she said. "They wouldn't have let me anywhere near that murder in the first place if it wasn't for you."

He looked even more embarrassed and awkward now, the gruff old cop exterior giving way to the appearance of a shy, lonely widower.

"Well, you're gonna get your money back from the court, so don't worry about that." She sat down at the end of the bed. "My lawyer says we're gonna get the charges dismissed by the end of the week."

"How is he going to be able to manage that?"

"Since we can prove we were borrowing another team's car from Queens Narcotics, the cops in Suffolk can't even prove where those drugs came from. Which is a good thing for them, since the truth is they probably took them from their own evidence facility before they planted them on me."

One side of Sullivan's mouth went up in a cynical half smile. "And it all gets swept under the rug and we live happily ever after . . . except for all that dirt they spread about your father in the press."

She sucked her teeth and a rotting taste filled her mouth, like an old piece of food had been stuck behind a molar. Made her want to spit. The media had been given stories to run about her getting cleared, but she hadn't even started to deal with the fallout emotionally.

"So now it looks like there's peace in the land and the spirit of cooperation reigns between the NYPD and the police out here," Sully said.

"Can't prove it by me." She pursed her lips. "Gonna take me a long time to get over this. And I'm still wondering who tipped them off about who my father was. At first I thought it was Danny Kovalevski, but the more I think about it, the less—"

"Don't get sidetracked," he cut her off. "Have you asked yourself exactly why they went this far, pulling you over and flaking you in the first place?"

"Uh, duh. Only about every five fucking seconds."

He winced. "Do you mind with the language, Robles?"

"Oh, excuse me." She pretended to smooth the wrinkles from her lap.

"I forget my manners when other cops start airing all this dirty shit about my father."

"What's the answer?"

"Obviously, Tolliver and the rest of them are looking to intimidate me and undermine the credibility of an outside investigation," she sighed. "They're playing defense to keep control."

"Yes, but have you asked yourself *why* they're playing so hard?"

"I'm guessing you're gonna mansplain it to me now." She folded her arms.

"Your boyfriend tell you about the conversation we had with the bartender?"

"He said that Bird Dog was a nickname for a girl named Bergdahl."

"It's been nagging at me since you started working on this case." He frowned, making his face craggy with memories. "The pregnant girl that washed up in Rockaway with the stones in her throat."

"That's not supposed to be public information," she said.

"It reminded me of something but I couldn't quite put my finger on it."

"My man Rakesh over at the medical examiner's office told me he'd never even heard of anything like it," Lourdes said.

"It would've been before your time, and his as well." Sullivan nodded. "And it didn't happen in the city anyway. I only remember because I'm old. But I was talking to this Gillispie and all of a sudden it came back to me. Twigs and branches."

"Wha'?"

"He didn't need to say the rest. One minute the thought wasn't there, and the next minute it was. Like when you smell apples and realize you're not in love anymore."

He was starting to get that other expression she remembered, what she used to call his Cochise look. When the intuitive Irish detective became the mystical Apache warrior channeling the database of the dead. Other cops claimed these were the trances of a hungover drunk or an acid casualty, but Lourdes had learned to give the man some room when he wanted to go into this state.

"They shoved twigs and branches down this poor girl's throat," he said.

"What 'poor girl' are we talking about? You gotta give me some context, Sullivan."

He seemed to come back to the room briefly. "It wasn't anything I was involved in personally as a police officer. It was just a case I read about in the newspaper, like any other citizen."

"You remember a newspaper story you read forty years ago?"

"I know, I'm like the head of an old vacuum cleaner that needs to be cleaned. Some things just stick with me. But you'll be the same someday." He handed her a file full of papers. "Yesterday, after the hearing, I went to the town library and found the story on the microfilm. About a fifteen-year-old girl found dead behind a football field in Shiloh with twigs and leaves down her throat."

Lourdes opened the folder and started to read. The top sheet was a smudged photocopy from a newspaper called the *Long Island Press*. The paper was slick and thin; it had clearly come from an old microfiche machine at a seriously underfunded local branch. Didn't Sullivan know these things were online now? But then she noticed the date on the article was 1977, possibly before everything had been scanned in.

The headline read: "Defense Takes Plea in Shiloh Girl Murder Case."

"Look, Sullivan, for real, I'm not following you here." Lourdes looked up after a few paragraphs. "This says a black high school football player named Delaney Patterson took a plea for killing a fifteen-year-old white girl named Kim Bergdahl on Long Island. What's that got to do with Chief Tolliver or any of our cases?"

"I thought you were supposed to be smart," he said with sudden harshness. "One night in lockup and you lose fifty IQ points?"

"*Hey.*"

"Read the damn article." He loomed over her, jabbing a finger at the sheet. "And read it more carefully, for Christ's sake. Who was the prosecutor on this case?"

"It says the district attorney was Philip O'Mara." She kept reading, a little stung by his tone. "And the assistant district attorney handling the trial was a . . . Kenneth Makris."

"Who is currently the district attorney for the whole county," Sullivan reminded her. "And has been since 1984."

"Yeah, *I know*, Sully. B.B. and me talked to him. He gave us nothing. But so what? Somebody else went to prison for this murder. There's no connection to our cases."

"Look *harder*," Sullivan insisted. "It says the defense folded after witnesses testified before the grand jury."

"So . . . ?"

"So I called Gillispie back and he gave me the scuttlebutt. Which is that the defense folded after they saw the grand jury testimony of a teenage witness. By the name of Joseph Tolliver."

"Are you shitting me, Sullivan?"

He placed a hand over his heart. "Language, Robles. Do you mind?"

"*Sor-ree.*" She huffed, trying to get her wind back. "But are you serious? Tolliver was a 'witness' in a case from forty years ago with a similar MO?"

"It would appear so. The grand jury testimony might be sealed, but Gillispie said the rumors had been around for a long time."

"*Wait.*" She put out her arms like she was directing traffic at the foot of the Brooklyn Bridge, cars rushing at her from every direction. "Let's not get ahead of ourselves here. You're telling me that the chief was a witness in some sicko murder case when he was a kid."

"Right."

"And most witnesses aren't kindergarten teachers. They're usually at the scene of a crime, because they're involved."

"That would be my experience, over the course of forty-odd years," Sullivan said.

"But Joseph Tolliver became a police officer." Lourdes held a finger up, wanting to parse this carefully.

"Everyone who testifies before a grand jury gets transactional immunity." Sullivan shrugged. "Or maybe he was never charged with anything because he came forward. All we know is that this case made Kenny Makris's career and put him on the map. And according to Gillispie, Makris then rewarded Tolliver by sponsoring him to get into the police academy. And it's been like this ever since. One hand washing the other, until one gets to be the DA and the other gets to be chief."

"Okay, but so what?" Lourdes shook her head, knowing she needed to stress-test this. "A police officer and a prosecutor have a relationship. That doesn't mean either one of them is a killer."

"Of course not. But it certainly raises some questions."

"Still a stretch. We're talking about a crime that happened forty years ago. And this Patterson kid already pled guilty to the 1977 murder. The article says he got sentenced to twenty-five years in '78."

"And if he served all twenty-five, which he probably did if he's black, he couldn't have murdered victims who were found dead in that period," Sullivan said. "And he may have been coerced into taking the twenty-five deal after Makris and Tolliver buried him. We both know it wouldn't be the first or the last time that happened."

Lourdes rubbed her chin. Like most police officers, she didn't have a high tolerance for gray area discussions when it came to perps. If you pled guilty, you were guilty. False confessions might be possible, but she had never seen one with her own eyes. Over time, she'd become convinced that the vast majority of people who were in prison were there for a reason. Including her own father, who was doing life for killing a rival drug dealer.

"You already knew you might be looking at a cop for killing these women," Sullivan reminded her.

"Yeah, but *a chief*?" Her voice went high. "Of a major department?"

She thought again of her own visceral reaction in the Marriott bar that night. Right after he said, "Hey, my name starts with a J," and his mustache split as he laughed. The way the noise crashed in around them but left him unaffected. And most of all, how she found herself wanting to take cover even though he hadn't done anything.

"If it's one person who killed all your victims, haven't you asked yourself how he could've gotten away with it for so long?" Sullivan said. "A cop would know what other cops would be looking for as evidence. And if he was high enough up, he'd know how to control an investigation and direct resources so that no one suspected him."

"This is still just a theory," she said, trying to stay steady and methodical.

"Yes, but it fits. Especially when you start asking how he could have done it alone. The answer is, maybe he didn't."

"Whoa." She threw her hands up. "Now you're really running wild. You're saying other people knew *the whole deal*?"

Even as a world-class consumer of crime novels and TV shows, she couldn't get there from here. Conspiracies were notoriously difficult to pull off, because people couldn't keep their mouths shut. A good reason for serial killers being lone wolves.

"I'm not saying other people were covering up the *acts*," Sullivan clarified. "But people close ranks when they think they need to protect the *institution*. True in our world and everyone else's."

She was still struggling to get her mind around this. It wasn't that she was totally in denial about dirty cops. No one who'd come up hard in the projects like she had could be. But on the night her father got arrested, she'd thrown in her lot with the good guys.

So she could easily accept that an individual psychopath had gotten on the job and used his shield as a license to commit crimes. But the idea that others, including good cops, had not only missed it but perhaps had semiconsciously aided and abetted a murderer blew her circuits out.

"All I'm saying is you need to look into it." Sullivan picked up the article again. "You're not doing your job if you don't."

"And what happens if it *is* true?" she asked, the pit of her stomach dropping as she thought through the full implications.

"Then you've got real problems." Sullivan looked grave. "This isn't a regular skell, but, like you said, the chief of a major department who commands a lot of people and a lot of loyalty. If you come after him, he's gonna hit back with everything he has. The traffic stop might have just been a warning shot. He has the ways and means to put a much worse hurting on you and yours."

"Yo, I'm starting to get seriously freaked out," she said. "Remember you told me about a call you got from an investigator named Martinez a long time ago?"

He nodded slowly. "The one from the state investigations commission?"

"I just heard from the state cop on our task force that she was killed back in the mid-nineties. Supposedly by an angry ex-husband, who's still in prison for it. Which is why she had a different name and it took us a while to track her down. Now I'm beginning to wonder. If somebody else did time for the Bird Dog murder, then . . ."

"We don't know what we don't know." Sullivan raised a hand, to caution her. "But the circumstances bear looking into."

Lourdes felt herself starting to shake, as if the mental process of letting go of so many conventional assumptions at once had started to physically destabilize her.

"You could still be wrong, you know," she said. "I could go after this Tolliver with everything I have and it could all blow up in my face. And then what? I'll be out of a job, with my sister missing and my mother in assisted living. My life will be a wreck. Maybe you can afford that, but I can't."

"What's your alternative?" He shrugged. "You know you can't back down now."

"Spoken like a man who already has his pension."

"If you just want to turn a blind eye, go ahead," he said. "But I didn't think that was what Lourdes Robles was all about."

"Oh my God. What a shit show."

She felt like she was looking up at King Kong menacing her from the top of the Empire State Building. If it all came down, it wouldn't just be the big ape crushing her, but the entire structure. Stone and glass, flesh and blood, office upon office, oh the humanity. This would all bury her, taking countless others down along the way, and even after they got done digging they'd never be able to separate her remains from the rest of the damage.

A wave of physical exhaustion washed over her. She realized he was right, as usual. But she'd slept maybe a total of four hours in the last two days and now it was all catching up with her. What she needed to do was go home, run a hot bath, watch movies with Mitchell, get a little lovemaking off him, and do a major reset before plunging into this case head-first again.

"I guess I should thank you now." She put the file in her bag. "And not just for paying my bail."

"It's what we do." He was back to not meeting her eye. "And it's not just for you, you know. I hate what a man like that does to the job."

She stood and looked around. "You took this room for a month?"

"Where else am I going to go? NYPD made me retire on my sixty-third birthday. I made too many enemies at the DA's offices to get hired. And that niece I was going to stay with upstate decided she'd rather renovate the attic for her kids than have me living in it."

"Sounds like you're looking for an excuse to keep working."

"You'd be doing me a solid," he said.

"Yeah? Come on, Daddy. You still got fuel in the tank. What about teaching at the academy or something?"

He cast down his eyes. "I don't want to talk about this, but I've been to the doctor."

"Can you give me a little more?"

"I'd prefer not to. Let's just say I let a little too much time pass between certain kinds of exams."

"We talking about your prostate or something, Sully?" She took a step toward him, thinking to put an arm around him.

"Oh for the love of God . . ." He put his hand up. "Just let me be. Okay? All I want is to be useful. Can you grant me that? And allow me my privacy?"

"Of course. But if there's anything I can do . . ."

"I'm fine for now." He cut her off. "On your way, you."

She kissed him chastely on the cheek, touched him on the arm, and left.

35

The girl who had just been led into the conference room looked like a smaller, less durable version of her sister. Her name was Brittany Forster and she was fifteen years old. She was lighter in complexion and had finer features than Alice, who was twenty-three at the time of her disappearance. Brittany's youth was emphasized by the Destiny's Child t-shirt she was just beginning to fill out, as well as her tiny gym shorts and the gum she did not bother to stop chewing as she was being introduced to the police chief.

The detective who had brought her in, Gary Mullins, put an Arizona Lemon Iced Tea down in front of her and sat beside Joey on the other side of the conference table.

"Good afternoon, Brittany." Joey reached over to take her hand and test her grip. "Do you know why I asked to speak to you personally?"

"Um, no? Not exactly?"

Her palm was damp and she had picked up that annoying suburban white girl habit of making her voice go up at the end of random sentences, as if she was asking a question instead of making a simple declarative statement.

"Normally, people who are involved in a case the way you are wouldn't meet with the chief," Joey explained. "But I wanted to make an exception here for a couple of reasons. Number one, I know your mom has been telling people this department doesn't care what happened to your sister because she's a woman of color. And I want to tell you that isn't so. Okay? We care equally whether you're from Wyandanch or the Hamptons."

"Uh . . . okay?"

She snapped her gum and snuck a sideways glance at Mullins, like he was another student in her remedial math class.

"The other reason is that you reported getting a phone call from your sister's kidnapper." Joey leaned forward, careful not to throw an "alleged" or a "supposed" to indicate he didn't believe her. "That's something we take very seriously. I want to hear personally what was said to you so we can determine how many resources we can devote to this investigation. Do you understand?"

"Kinda?"

He was beginning to think it wasn't just age difference. She was legitimately not as smart as Alice, who for all her other faults had a sort of insolent street corner intelligence. Maybe the product of a different father. Wouldn't be that surprising, Joey thought, since the mother looked like she might have been half a hooker herself back in the day, before she got addicted to meth and welfare.

"And we asked your mother to wait outside because we thought there might be aspects you'd be more comfortable describing privately," Joey said. "Things to do with your sister and her lifestyle. Is that all right with you?"

This time Brittany just nodded, too shy to meet his gaze. Or maybe too afraid.

"Now, I know you've already discussed some of this with Detective Mullins, but I'd like to hear about this call from you directly," he said. "How long after your sister's disappearance was this?"

She tipped back in his chair with her legs apart in such a way that the shorts rode up on her tanned thighs.

"Um, it's kind of hard to say how long?" She stored the gum in her cheek, licked her lips, and glanced at Mullins like she needed his permission to continue. "Like sometimes we wouldn't hear from Alice for a long time anyway? You know, like sometimes, we wouldn't even know like where she was staying? Right? But I got this call like a few days after we reported her missing because she'd stopped answering her phone, which she like never did?"

The sight of her pink tongue had primed his pump for a second, but all those "likes" made him feel like reaching across and strangling her.

"I understand someone called your number using her phone," Joey said, recomposing himself carefully. "Is that correct?"

"Uh, *yeah*." She went back to chewing and he knew he'd have to keep an eye on the gum to make sure it didn't wind up on the underside of the conference table. "At first, I was like all excited because I thought it was Alice calling."

He picked up his pen and clicked it several times, monitoring his own response to her. Was it worth the risk to have her sitting here? He'd never gotten this close to the edge of discovery before, and it was a new kind of kick to be sure. She was so dopey and innocent. Like a fawn in the clearing. It made his hunter's heart beat faster. Another head to put on the wall. He could already feel the blood rushing to his extremities. But there might be other predators in the woods. The phone call she was describing might be a trap he could fall into. He had to slow down, think carefully. It wasn't just about the thrill now, but about keeping control of the investigation and making sure it didn't go the wrong way.

"By any chance, did you record this phone call?" he asked,

"Uh-uh." She shook her head. "When I saw it was Alice's number, I was just so glad. She's more like my mom than my mom is. You know what I mean?"

"I think I do," he said and nodded, pushing away thoughts of his own mother and what she'd tried to do to him. "So what happened when you picked up the call?"

"There was like this guy talking. He asked if I was Brittany."

"He already knew your name?"

"Yeah." She put her legs together and looked down. "It made me feel weird right away."

"What did his voice sound like?"

"Uh, I don't know." She smiled, inappropriately, as if he'd embarrassed her by asking the most obvious question in history. "He just sounded like a man."

"I think the chief is asking if you can be more specific," said Mullins. "Did he sound old? Young? Black? White?"

"I don't know." She squirmed and crossed her legs. "He just sounded regular."

She brought her seat down and looked at Joey like she was peering deep into a cave.

"He sounded a little bit like you," she said.

He stared back at her, letting out a long stream of breath. There was a definite animal threat in the air now. The prey had somehow gotten behind the hunter and started to show its teeth.

"Tell the chief exactly what he said," Mullins prompted her.

"At first I was like, 'Hello?' And he was like, 'Hello, Brittany.' And then I was like, 'Whoa, who is this?' And he says, 'I'm someone who's been spending time with your sister.'"

"That's really what he said?" Joey threw a dubious look at Mullins.

"Yeah."

"How do you know?" Joey said. "Did you write it down?"

"No. But I remember."

"Tell the chief what happened next," said Mullins.

The detective was one of those perpetually tired-looking men who could sound wry without being particularly acute. Which was one of the reasons Joey had promoted him.

"I asked if Alice was all right and if I could speak to her." Brittany was chewing harder. "He said I shouldn't worry about that. He was taking care of Alice."

Joey paused with his pen in mid-click. "Come again?"

"He said, 'I'm taking care of Alice.'"

He put the pen down carefully, with a distant ringing in his ears. "Those were his exact words?"

"Definitely." She nodded, her voice not going up for once. "I'll never forget how he said it. Because it made like the little hairs on my arm stand up."

"Go ahead." Mullins nodded at her. "Tell the chief the rest of it."

"Oh yeah, right." She looked down as if he'd shamed her. "He said he'd been spending a lot of time with Alice and doing a lot of things with her. And it got him thinking he'd like to do things with me."

"Is that true?" Joey glanced at the clock above her head, trying to ignore the rapidness of his heartbeat.

"Yeah, of course." She kept chewing nonchalantly.

"What were his exact words to you?"

"The ones I just told you." Her mouth cracked like she was trying to blow a bubble with regular Wrigley's gum.

"No, I'm asking for the *exact* words, Brittany. It's very important."

"What I just told you." She tipped back in the chair again, showing more of her thighs. "He said he'd done things with her and he'd like to come do things to me."

Joey looked at Mullins and then at the clock on the wall, as if he was losing patience. His own short hairs were standing up now. Like he was realizing it was not just the prey that had slipped up behind him, but another hunter.

"Stop tipping back and stop chewing that gum." He snapped his fingers. "You think this is a joke?"

The girl and Mullins both abruptly turned like they'd heard a gunshot.

"We're trying to find your sister and make sure she's okay," Joey said. "Why are you making up stories?"

"I'm not." Brittany brought her chair down.

"Of course you are." Joey waved his hand. "Tell the truth now. There was never any man on the phone. No one said they want to 'do things' with you. No one's coming for you. Why are you trying to make this about yourself?"

"I'm not lying," she said with a sullen pout.

"Then how come no one else got a call like that?" Joey demanded. "What makes you so special?"

"I don't know." She hung her head, mumbling into her developing chest. "Maybe because I'm her sister?"

"More like you're jealous of her. Right?" Joey pointed a finger, as if he was waiting for her to join the growing consensus. "Because Alice always got all the attention when you were growing up with her loud mouth and her stupid boyfriends."

"That's not true." She began to bang her knees together rhythmically.

"And what else did this mystery caller allegedly say to you?" He rolled his hand over the top of the pen, letting her know that whatever she was about to say wouldn't be worth writing down.

"Um, I'm trying to remember but you've got me so rattled." She wrinkled her big beige forehead, trying to concentrate. "He said I sounded sweet and he was looking forward to seeing me. And that Alice missed me a lot."

"And that was it?" He threw a dubious look at Mullins.

"Um, I think so."

"Sure about that?"

"Can I go?" she asked Mullins. "I told him everything, like you said I should?"

"Yes, why don't you step out a minute and talk to your mother," Joey huffed. "I need to speak to Detective Mullins on our own. And please close the door after you."

She got up and walked out, pulling down the hems of her shorts as they started to ride up her ass cheeks. Imagine the mother letting her come in like that. He held on to his armrests, trying to collect himself in light of what he'd just heard.

"Think maybe you were a little rough on her, chief?" Mullins asked.

Good old Wrong-Way Mullins. Always ready with the wrong question at the wrong time.

"She's a goddamn liar," Joey said. "Or maybe I should say a natural-born liar, now that I've got an eyeful of the mother."

"You know there was a phone call to her from the sister's phone, on the day she's talking about," Mullins reminded him. "It came from the Jamaica train station at rush hour."

"Exactly." Joey nodded. "Which shows it was just Alice calling to say she was going away. This is what it looks like. Nothing more. Nothing less. Big sister cutting her ties with the family and saying goodbye for good. And now that we've seen what a horror show the mother is, we know why. Baby sister is just creating drama to make herself the center of attention."

"So you want to just leave it as a missing persons case?" Mullins asked.

"Not even." Joey picked up the pen and dropped it, to show his disgust. "Alice is an adult. She'll probably turn up any day."

"And what about that call we got from Nassau PD about that other missing girl from Atlantic Beach?"

"Leave it be. Nothing in it for us. Just another dumb-ass runaway who's probably out there turning tricks. We supposed to track every pigeon that flies the coop?"

Mullins gathered his files and stood up with a heavy sigh.

"Sad fucking thing if Alice just took off like that," he said. "You can see how much the little sister needed her."

"What can you do?" Joey barely looked up. "People are who they are."

36

OCTOBER
2017
"Hang on a minute, B.B."

Lourdes hit the door-lock button in the Impala, just as Borrelli was about to get out.

"What's up?"

B.B. rested his hands on the wheel, trying not to appear unduly alarmed that his partner had just kept him from exiting the vehicle.

They'd come straight from a meeting at One Police Plaza, where they were assured that this business with Lourdes getting arrested and then released out on Long Island had all been an embarrassing mistake, and the brass had talked it out and everyone was ready to put the mess behind them. All the time that Dave Pritzker, the chief of detectives, and Carolyn McGuire, from Legal Affairs, had been talking positively, Lourdes was thinking: *Fuck*. Everyone is saying they have my back, and nothing has changed but one little mistake and that'll be me smashing down through the floorboards.

"You weren't at the arraignment out on the Island," Lourdes said, breaking the silence that had stayed pretty much intact from lower Manhattan to this part of the Bronx.

"Yeah, I thought you heard. I was following up with Gallagher to find out what happened to this Martinez woman. I figured you'd understand."

"You're not lying to me now, B.B. Are you?"

"Why would I be lying?"

She noticed how his callused knuckles flexed involuntarily on the steering wheel.

"You know, you haven't been right since the jump with this case," she said.

"What are you talking about? I've been working my ass off, just like you."

"How is it you happened not to be in the car when I got pulled over?" she asked.

"What are you, fucking kidding me? I was banging a broad I know in Massapequa Park. I really have to spell that out for you after all this time we've worked together?"

"Yeah, you do. Especially when I get flaked and locked up and you're not in court the next day."

"All right, I'm sorry—okay?" He gestured operatically at the wheel. "I felt bad I couldn't be there. Now can we get past this?"

She settled back in her seat, letting him know she wasn't going anywhere right away.

"What?" he said.

Even though he was still wearing his starched collar, French cuffs, and pressed Italian pinstripes, he had the voice of a man leaning out a window in a sweat-stained wifebeater on a ninety-degree night.

"You said your kid was trying to get a job with the Suffolk PD," she said. "You told me that right before we ran into Danny Kovalevski and Detective Tierney at Renee's grandparents' house."

"I don't remember saying that." B.B. shook his head.

"You think I haven't noticed how kiss-ass you were when we were talking to Tolliver and Makris? Or how interested you looked when Rattigan mentioned there were jobs for investigators your age at the DA's office."

"This is crazy," he said. "I talked to them like I talk to any other witness."

"Someone told them about my father, B.B. And I never told Danny who or where my old man was."

B.B. crossed his arms and drew his chin back, refusing to look at her, but as defensive in his posture as any skell in an interrogation room.

"You've got no basis for any of this," he said. "All the years I've worked with you."

"Maybe you didn't say anything. Or maybe you didn't know they were going to flake me and lock me up. Maybe they said they were just looking for a little edge and that's all."

"Never happened," he insisted. "There was no conversation behind your back."

She stared at the side of his face, remembering how he'd lingered in Tolliver's office after she walked out.

"My eye is on you, B." She unlocked the door. "I ain't playing."

They got out of the car and entered the community garden through a chain-link fence door, exhaust from the nearby Cross Bronx Expressway filling the sky.

Lourdes had never been much of a nature girl, so she couldn't name most of the things she saw growing on the stakes and in the soil beds. She was pretty sure those yellow flowers were daffodils or black-eyed Susans. It was possible those blooming items over by the chain-link fence were either cherry trees or crab apple trees. And she had a sneaking suspicion that those ascending stalks reaching for the clouds were marijuana plants, except they smelled more like mint than skunk when she got close to them.

She was absolutely sure, on the other hand, that the sphere-shaped brown man with the long neck sticking out of dusty farmer's overalls was the ex-con they were looking to speak to. She could see it in the hesitant way he parked his wheelbarrow, looked around, and bent down to heave a rusty bed frame off a flowerbed. Like he was waiting for a guard's permission before every move.

"Delaney Patterson?" She pulled back her jacket, to show him the shield clipped to her belt, which somehow felt a little less real since her night in custody.

"Joshua Ben-Levi." He straightened up.

"Your name's Ben-Levi?" she asked, starting to share an incredulous look with B.B. and then stopping herself, since they no longer had that kind of rapport.

"*My lawyer's* name is Ben-Levi." Delaney Patterson reached for a rake. "That's who you should contact if you want to speak with me."

"You're not in any trouble," B.B. said.

"You don't say," Patterson drawled, hand on hip in a mocking Scarlett O'Hara stance. "Well, let me just drop everything I'm doing because the po-lice have always been so good to me."

B.B. gave Lourdes a hooded told-ya-so look. They both knew this was going to be a heavy lift. No one does twenty-five years in a state prison and jumps at the chance to assist an investigation.

"It has to do with the Kim Bergdahl case," Lourdes said.

"Everything in my whole damn life has to do with that case." Patterson leaned on the rake. "From the time I was nineteen until I was forty-four. And now you want me to talk about it some more? Oh, happy day."

He was a big leathery man who'd developed lots of layers. Like most people she'd met who'd been in prison. Including her own father. There was a layer of sarcasm, and just beneath that a layer of searing, defensive anger, which barely covered a layer of inconsolable hurt and a layer of fear. It got to where you had so many layers that you had no idea what was underneath them all except an emptiness you didn't dare show anyone.

"We're looking at something more recent that might be connected," B.B. said, falling into the reflexive impatience of a cop talking to a former inmate.

Patterson fished a cell phone out of the front pocket of his overalls and displayed it to them—an iPhone 4, maybe, with a cracked screen.

"See this?" he demanded. "I did twenty-five fucking years. I've been out of prison since 2003 and I always have one of these with me. You want to know why? It's so I can always prove where I've been. In case one of *you people* comes around asking questions again."

B.B. clicked his tongue unhelpfully, no doubt still keyed up from the tense conversation in the car. This was starting to harden up into a useless confrontation, Lourdes realized. Bad enough that they weren't getting as much cooperation from the rest of the task force since her arrest on Long Island. Even with the charges dismissed, the chilling effect on the investigation had been achieved, and it was going to take some effort to get the momentum going again. She pulled out her own cell phone and showed him the picture she'd downloaded from the newspaper website.

"You know who this is?" she asked.

Reluctantly, Patterson put away his phone and pulled out a pair of reading glasses. The lenses were crooked and a strip of gray tape on the centerpiece held the frame together. She sensed he was one of those quietly dignified men she'd encountered at homeless shelters, who preferred to mend their own things and keep their sad stories to themselves.

"White police chief with a dumb-ass moustache," he said after a cursory glance. "Supposed to mean something to me?"

"Do you remember a Joseph Tolliver?" Lourdes asked.

"What kind of question is that?" Patterson drew back. "Of course I remember that lying motherfucker. He got up in front of that dumb-ass grand jury and made up a story about something that never happened. Ruined my whole life."

"Could this be him?" Lourdes thrust the screen at him again. "Just asking you to look."

Patterson gave a little sigh as if questioning the value of his own forbearance and then angled his frames. His eyes focused. His features became very still. His nostrils puffed out with a quick angry expulsion of air. He took the glasses off and wiped his eyes with his forearm.

"Well?" Lourdes asked.

"Yeah, that's him." His lower lip came out and covered his top lip; then he turned away with a sharp sniffle.

"You're sure now?" asked B.B.

Patterson turned his back to them, his fingers slipping through spaces in the chain-link fence, gripping the wires and shaking them.

"You didn't know he'd become a cop after the trial," Lourdes said. "Did you?"

"Nope." Patterson still wasn't turning around.

"You gonna look at us while you speak to us?" B.B. asked.

Lourdes gave him a headshake. After all, they had no leverage on this dude. But some cops and street guys were like cats and dogs. They went at each other instinctively with no regard to practicality or common sense.

"Sir, I do not want to turn around," Patterson said, his voice growing firm and deliberate over the honking of Bronx traffic. "Because I do not want you to see the full extent of my reaction."

"Why's that?" Lourdes asked.

"Because I thought nothing could cause me as much pain as having both my parents die while I was locked up. But seeing what you just showed me . . ." He gripped the fence harder and shook it. "Seeing how this so-called man was *rewarded* for destroying my life . . ."

His voice got choked off and a couple of the white middle-aged ladies who managed the garden started over with concerned looks. B.B. scared them away with a stern glance.

"Man." Patterson took a deep breath, still not letting go of the fence. "I know it shouldn't matter after everything I've been through, but it still *hurts me* to know that's how it is."

"What can you tell us about him?" Lourdes said.

"Joey?" Patterson tried a laugh, but it stuck in his throat. "He wasn't shit."

"How well did you know him?" she asked.

"We were the FNG at Shiloh High School." Patterson finally turned around. "The fucking new guys, both come out to paradise from the city. Because our folks wanted to make a better life. See how well that worked out?"

Lourdes exchanged a look with B.B., warning him not to break the rhythm.

"We were both on the football team," Patterson said. "He was the center who was supposed to snap the ball to me and then block. But he only did the first part, so there went my knee when I kept getting sacked and then there went my scholarship to Rutgers. So then he comes to me and says, 'Hey man, I got a connection with this white girl out here in the tenth grade. You should go back to the projects, get some pot to bring out here, and we can make a fortune selling to these suburban brats, enough money to both buy cars for college.' And you want to know who his tenth-grade connection was?"

Lourdes kept up a deadpan to hide her reaction. "Kim Bird Dog?"

"She was a white girl, but she was a straight-up punk." Patterson took off his glasses and pocketed them. "And I don't mean that in a music way. I mean that in a street way. That girl was nasty. Her mother let her run wild because she had no control over herself. Carried a Swiss army knife she liked to wave in your face and a Zippo lighter that she let Joey use to light cat tails on fire. I never knew they made little white girls like that. But she didn't deserve what happened to her. Sticks and branches down her throat. Who even thinks of that?"

"You weren't interested in her as a girl?" B.B. raised his eyebrows.

"Oh hell no," Patterson said emphatically. "She'd cut your dick off if she even thought you were looking at her that way."

"So you didn't kill her?" Lourdes said, just making it official.

"No, I wasn't even near the football field that night. Tell you the whole truth, I was helping to rob someone's house two miles down the road. Which was why my lawyer didn't want me to testify, but . . ."

"Then why'd you plead guilty?" B.B. interrupted, not buying it.

A look of childlike befuddlement cleared the creases from Patterson's face. "Because I thought I had no choice. This Detective William Rattigan got a partial statement out of me, saying I was there, by beating me up and squeezing my balls while I was handcuffed to a pipe. The judge refused our motion to suppress it. Then Joey goes and tells the grand jury—the *all-white* grand jury—that he saw me in the woods with blood on my hands. My lawyer said I'd get life if I didn't take the offer that was on the table that day only. And my family was going broke paying him. I didn't find out until later that both the judge who took my plea and the DA, Mr. O'Mara, had been his law partners. That's why I used to blame Joey for everything. But now I think he was just part of the system that had been set up."

Lourdes noticed that B.B. had stopped taking notes, like this was just the usual skell nonsense. But she could hear the sound of truth in it as plainly as a bat hitting a ball at Yankee Stadium nearby.

"Why do you think Joey lied about you?" she asked, being careful not to make it too much of a leading question.

"To cover up his own part." Patterson fussed with a frayed denim strap of his overalls. "Before he made me throw in the towel, my lawyer said there was a good piece of evidence for our defense. The police found one of those red bandanas Joey used to wear at the crime scene."

"They did?" Her jaw went slack and she looked at B.B. So much for the poker face.

Her mind was already rocketing toward getting subpoenas for retired officers and laying her hands on every other piece of evidence imaginable before the chief caught on and had it deep-sixed. For someone who'd been in public life more than three decades, he was surprisingly elusive and hard to get a grip on. They'd recently confirmed that Tolliver had been married once, to a woman with three kids, who had dropped off the grid at some point in the last ten years.

"Yeah, don't get too excited," Patterson said wearily, wiping the back of his neck with a handkerchief. "My lawyer's dead now, and he probably wouldn't have cooperated with you even if he was alive. I found that out when I tried to file papers to rescind my plea. And you know what else I found out? Most of the physical evidence from that case is gone. A flood at the warehouse. Funny how the water always lands on the boxes they don't want you to see."

Lourdes found that she couldn't look at B.B. this time. Knowing if he had anything to do with fucking this case up, she might be tempted to shoot him.

"He did it again, didn't he?" Patterson said.

"Did what?" B.B. asked, a hint of a challenge in his voice.

"He did something else fucked up." Patterson looked back and forth between them. "Otherwise you all wouldn't be here, asking about him."

"Sir, we're not at liberty to talk about an active investigation," B.B. said, retreating into cold police language. "You'd be wrong to make assumptions based on anything we've said."

"Except you told me this had to do with something more recent," Patterson reminded him. "I always knew there was something wrong with J. Just the way he looked at you sometimes. Like you were a thing, not a person to him. You know what I just remembered? What he told me once, when we were in high school. He said, 'I wanna be a cop. Not because I want to help people. And not for the benefits. But so I can do whatever I want.'"

Lourdes took the note and made sure B.B. heard it as well. Nothing admissible here, but they were moving in a definite direction.

"You know what I just realized?" Patterson picked up a shovel. "I'm wasting my breath talking to you all." He looked from Lourdes to B.B. "You're not here to help me clear my name. You're here to help J cover up for what he did."

"Sir, that's not true," Lourdes started to say.

"Just get the fuck out of here." Patterson turned his back to them and started digging into the soil. "I need to get some work done while I still have the sun."

37

Joey stumbled in late after Tommy Danziger's retirement party. He parked the Jeep in the garage and switched the light on, intending to slip in quietly through the side door. There were tall stacks of cardboard boxes along the walls. The light went on in the kitchen and Beth came out wearing her blue terry cloth bathrobe, furry slippers, and a resolute expression.

"What's this?" he said, still so coked up from his private little after-party in the car that he could barely get his keys back in his pocket.

"You're done," she said. "We're done."

"Done with *what*?" He was having trouble modulating his voice. "You're not making any sense."

"You're moving out. It's over. Your stuff's in these boxes."

"What'd I do?" He raised his hands in mock surrender. "Read me the indictment."

"I don't want to get into it." She shook her head, the harsh overhead light showing that she was letting her roots grow out. "I must have been insane to let you move in here in the first place."

"Will ya . . ." He put a hand in front of his face, shielding his eyes. "Will you tell me what's going on?"

"I've realized this whole period of my life has been madness," she said. "I had a husband who lost his job and then lost his mind. And then I let another man take over, because he seemed to know what he was doing."

He leaned heavily against the table saw, trying to get his bearings.

In the distorted reflection of the blade, he saw a balding, baggy-faced man. Certainly not chief material. He realized he was sweating like an ox, even though it was freezing in the garage.

"Could you please give me some fucking idea what you're talking about?" he said deliberately.

"I don't know everything you've done, Joey. But I know enough, and I can guess the rest. I know you leave the house in the middle of the night sometimes when you think we're all asleep and you come back right before dawn. I know you put something in my tea sometimes so you think I'll stay down longer and not notice when you're gone. I know you buy and throw away cell phones like Kleenex, and you have a bunch of bank accounts under other names. I know something funny has been going on with you and the DA for a long time. And I know you know more about some of those girls they found then you've let on."

"Shut the fuck up." He smacked the table. "You don't know what you're talking about."

"Keep your voice down. The kids are back from school and sleeping inside."

"They should know their mother is having some kind of psychotic fit." He saw his breath in the cold garage air.

"They know you're leaving. And for your sake, it's better if they don't know why."

"Why are you doing this to me, Beth?" he said plaintively, thinking of getting the gun out of his ankle holster. "And why now?"

"*Why now?*" She looked a little chipmunky, showing her front teeth as she laughed. "What do you care? You don't need us anymore. You got to be chief. And we helped you look normal enough to pass."

He was slowly getting oriented, realizing that the fourteen or fifteen boxes had his name written in Magic Marker. Thank God he kept anything that could send him to prison in a storage facility in Huntington. But now that he was understanding that she was serious about this, his anger began to gather in earnest.

"Let me ask you something, Beth," he said. "If even a tenth of what you were talking about had any reality to it, why would I let you throw me that easily?"

"Because of what I know about you, Joey." She put her hands on her hips. "I've been keeping a diary for a long time, writing times and dates when you come and go. I'm sure if somebody smart put them together with times and dates for when some of these girls got killed, you might have a problem."

"Are you threatening me, Beth?"

He let his arms hang heavily at his sides and turned his wrists out toward her, suggesting the primitive menace that he'd used to keep her and the kids in line in the past.

"I've made copies of my diary," she said calmly, like this was a speech she'd practiced in front of the bathroom mirror. "And I've put them in envelopes and given them to a bunch of people I know—and not the ones you would think of, Joey. If anything happens to me or the kids, there are instructions for those envelopes to get opened."

"Where did you get this from? Some stupid Lifetime movie?"

"Never mind about that." Her face got more deeply lined as her mouth got tighter. "What you need to worry about now is money."

"What about it?"

"I'm going to sell this house and keep all the proceeds. Then I'm going to move somewhere and leave a bank account number. I know you've been making money on the side through all your crooked deals, so I'm going to expect monthly direct deposits. I think you can manage thirty-five hundred a month easily. And other than that, I don't want to hear from you ever again."

"You're shaking me down?"

He scrunched his eyes three times and shook his head, like he was trying to recover from being sucker punched.

"Don't act so surprised," she said. "And don't try to claim the high ground."

"You fucking bitch."

"Poor you. You're really the victim here."

"I'm not leaving this house," he said.

"You will. And you'll give me a divorce without contesting it—with alimony along with the other payments—because you want to keep being chief and you know it's not worth the risk to try me."

He leaned against the Jeep. "I can't believe I was with you all this time and didn't know what you were capable of."

"I want you out of here by the end of the week," she said. "Maybe I can ask the kids to help you move the rest of your things."

38

The morning was already off-kilter when Lourdes approached the religious encampment near Jericho Turnpike, the day after talking to Delaney Patterson. For one thing, the sky was the color of drying cement and she'd thoughtlessly put on the boots with heels when she dressed, forgetting that she had to cross a field to get to Magdalena's trailer. For another, she was working with John Gallagher, the state cop, instead of B.B. today, because she felt she could no longer trust Borrelli.

"Here's your problem," said Gallagher, whose blocklike head and self-conscious swagger gave him a stature that his investigative abilities hadn't earned him so far. "Your whore says this J tried to choke her out at a party more than twenty-five years ago. We're showing her a picture of Chief Tolliver from five years ago. How's she even going to recognize him?"

"First of all, why is it *my* problem, instead of *ours*?" she asked. "Second of all, what's this 'your whore'? That's not who she is anymore."

"*Touchy.*" Gallagher strode ahead. "I still say ID is going to be a problem. Chief Tolliver's got a good reputation out here. He always backs up his men."

"Let's just keep an open mind." She hustled to catch up, soft ground sucking at her heels. "Anybody could be anything."

"What about giving a fellow officer the benefit of the doubt? There's us and there's them, detective. So be fair. When you got locked up, I figured there had to be a good explanation."

"Yeah, that was generous," she muttered.

"Hey, I'm riding with you today, instead of demanding they throw you off the task force. Which is what some people think should happen. So why can't you give the chief the benefit of the doubt as well?"

As they followed the firmer part of the path toward where Magdalena's trailer was parked, Lourdes could see a local police car idling on the other side of the grounds some two hundred yards away. An officer in shades was using a pair of binoculars, as if it was standard practice to be hanging out at a trailer park without an obvious call to respond to. It didn't look like any of the cops she'd encountered out here before, but from this distance, it was hard to be sure, and his unexplained presence turned her ribcage into a fluttering pigeon coop.

A group of children were hanging out in front of Magdalena's trailer. Five of them, between the ages of three and nine, different hues and different sizes, but some commonality in look. They all wore dark sweat clothes that didn't quite fit and the stunned expressions that Lourdes had seen on abandoned children in the hallways of Family Court.

"Oh shit." Gallagher stopped. "What is this? A ghetto funeral?"

Lourdes went up to the oldest, a chubby girl in a *Yeezus* hoodie and khaki shorts; her weight and grief made her old before her time. "Excuse me. You know Magdalena?"

"My grandmother." The girl turned and pounded the trailer door. "Yo."

The sky dimmed to a lighter shade of charcoal. Midday traffic hummed with indifference to personal tragedy on the nearby freeway. The cop in the squad car had put down the binoculars and picked up a cell phone, holding it in front of his face as if filming them.

The inside door of the trailer opened and Magdalena appeared behind a screen door, wearing a baggy black tracksuit with double stripes on the arms and legs.

"You again, huh?" She gave Lourdes a cold once-over, big white cross swinging from her neck. "I know you been calling, but I'm not answering."

"Ma'am, we'd like to just come inside and show you something real quick," Gallagher said, jumping into the breach. "Won't take more than a minute or two."

"Ain't nobody got time for that." Magdalena showed him the flat of her hand against the screen. "I need to get my ride to the beach and spread my son's ashes on the water."

"Oh." Lourdes put a hand to her chest. "Oh my God. Your son. What happened? I'm so sorry."

"You should be." Magdalena glared at her without pausing now. "They killed his ass three days after I spoke to you."

"Who did?" Lourdes asked.

"The police." Magdalena scowled toward the officers in the Suffolk County police car. "Like you didn't know. Shot him at the Exxon station just down the road. After they pulled him over for some bullshit crack in his back windshield. His girlfriend was right next to him when he pulled out his phone to tell me what was up. And then they shot him right there. Said they thought he was reaching for a gun. Those lying motherfuckers."

Gallagher put his hands up like he was about to caution her about talking this way in front of the little kids, but Lourdes shook her head at him. They'd probably heard way worse. By their age, she had.

But this was beyond what she'd gone through. Because when she'd decided to become a cop, it was because she had some vague idea that there was a system that could protect people, if it could only be made to work properly. From the looks on the kids' faces, she could see they had no such illusions. The system was there to hurt them and take what little they had, and they were learning that there was nothing they could do to change that.

"Twenty-four years old." Instead of crying, Magdalena gave a pugnacious sniff. "Left me with three goddamn grandchildren to raise on my own. Because their mothers are all babies themselves. Like he was. And now I got his ashes in a jar. Do you know what that's like, miss?"

"I do," Lourdes said quietly, hanging her head.

She could picture herself on tiptoe as she tried to hoist Izzy high enough to kiss the urn on the mantle that held their brother Georgie's ashes. The ritual. Good night, Georgie.

"Yeah, I believe that." Magdalena opened the screen door and spat at Lourdes's feet. "Same as I believe you're pregnant, like you told me the last time. How come it looks like you lost weight? Lying bitch."

Lourdes's hand dropped from her chest to her belly.

"Fool me once, shame on you. Fool me twice, shame on me," Magdalena said. "I'm done talking to you. Get the hell away from my door and don't come back. Some of us have real families."

She slammed the inner door, shaking the trailer and leaving Lourdes to deal with the weight of everyone staring at her.

39

Joey's father's house was on a dead-end street, near the ocean side of Rock-away. Jamaica was on the opposite side of the thin peninsula, less than three blocks north. The front yard was bare concrete but it was surrounded by a brick wall, like a convict's arm around a plate of prison food. But that was the old man. Acting like he had something to hide, when no one really cared enough to take what he had.

The old man had always been a little suspicious and paranoid. Which was why he'd collected so few friends from the job. After he'd moved back to Queens, following the divorce, he'd only got worse. Shades drawn all day in the three-story house with one gable peeking from behind another, as if trying not to be noticed. Three standard locks and a heavy padlock on the front door. A Beware of Dog sign on the mailbox—even though his dog had died back in the Clinton years.

The neighbors always knew enough to avoid him, since he muttered conspiratorially to himself on the street and only went to the beach when it was empty. When he fished in the bay, he brought a boombox on his rowboat and turned it up to max volume to drive other boats away when they got too close, not caring if the fish scattered as well. Inside the house he was a hoarder, naturally, living with stacks of old *Life* magazines, ammo boxes, gallons of water, saltine crackers, flashlight batteries, and various other doomsday items that he'd accumulated in anticipation of blackouts or race war. Both of which he thought were inevitable.

When he died, no one found him for a week. He was only discovered when a Con Ed meter reader detected a foul odor from the porch. It took Joey months to get rid of the smell. Not that he came that often, at first. It was a long way from the place he'd moved into in Babylon after Beth kicked him out and there were a lot of bad memories on this side of the city border. On the other hand, the house was his now, no other family members to claim it, and it was a piece of property that might eventually be worth something when the real estate market came roaring back from the recession.

More important, there were vacant lots on either side and nothing across the street, at least at the moment, which meant he could do what he wanted without drawing too much attention. After the close call with Leslie Martinez and the bad bust-up with Beth, he'd decided he needed to cool it awhile, let time pass, show some restraint. Most people who'd done this never seemed to have asked themselves the hard questions. But he was in a separate class from the disorganized dirty car drivers on one end of the spectrum and the hyper-ritualized, obsessive-compulsive fetishizers on the other end. His deal was different and, to be honest, better. He'd read the books and watched the video confessions, he'd lectured about serial killers at the academy, he'd seen where they tripped up and gave themselves away, like they wanted to be caught all along if the cops hadn't been busy looking in the wrong direction.

He waited several hours after he was done at work and then drove to Queens under cover of darkness. He parked the Jeep in the garage his father had built behind the house and went in through the rear door. Nearly three years he'd had the place, he was fairly certain that no one on the block had ever seen him. The kitchen was more or less the way his father had left it. Same Whirlpool refrigerator and gas range from the mid-eighties. Same crappy peeling linoleum on the rotting floor that he had to get around to replacing himself one of these days.

He got out his keys and unlocked the door to the basement, a blanket under one arm and a paper bag in his other hand. The landing was as bad as the kitchen, just four splintered planks of lacquered wood that would surely give way if he put his full two hundred pounds on them. He took care to step over them to get the ladder and extend it down to the basement. He'd torn out the regular stairs when he dug out the cellar floor to make it deeper and less accessible from the upstairs. Then he'd put egg cartons on the ceiling for sound muffling and attached a metal handcuff bar to the wall he'd replastered over Memorial Day weekend.

"Honey, I'm home."

Corny joke, but if you couldn't make corny jokes under your own roof, what was the point of having a second house? The rungs made a homey grumping sound as he descended. The lived-in creak of a man in his proper place, the king returning to his castle and escaping his worries about sending money to his vicious ex-wife. This was the sound his own father probably longed to hear, if only he could have stilled the noise in his own head. If only he could have controlled himself, controlled his woman, and had the family he really wanted.

"You miss me?"

She'd seen a t-shirt with the saying before she knew it was part of a poem: "Hope is the thing with feathers."

But now she was starting to think that was wrong.

Hope was the thing with teeth.

It tore into you and wouldn't let go. And once it got in deep enough, you couldn't pull away without losing a piece of yourself and nearly bleeding to death.

She'd given up on her family a long time ago.

She'd given up on friends coming to rescue her.

She'd given up on this being any kind of normal situation where some official person like a doctor or a lawyer would come in and say, "What the hell, man?"

But she hadn't quite given up hope that she would somehow get out of this alive. And that was what kept her on edge all the time, every minute of the day, like some feral beast had clamped its jaws on her leg.

"How's it going?" he asked.

Like this was some kind of normal situation. Like she wasn't handcuffed and connected by a fifteen-foot-long chain to a cuff on a handicap bar he'd installed on the basement wall. Like she hadn't been living for who knows how many weeks in this dampish underground dwelling with a toilet and sink he'd put in the corner and the half windows above her head filled in with bricks.

"Oh, you know." She held up her cuffed wrist. "Just living the dream."

She'd decided to stop cursing and crying for now. Just like on the outside, calling someone "stupid" and "diseased" didn't get you treated better. The difference was that in here, being mouthy didn't just get you backhanded or thrown out of a bar before closing time. It meant you didn't eat for two or three days. That you might not get soap or toilet paper. That you might get tortured and abused in ways that even the skuzziest truck stop whores couldn't imagine in their worst nightmares, so that you might yearn for sudden death as much as your grandmother's forgiving embrace.

He dropped a thick red quilt on the filthy mattress in the corner.

"What's that?" she asked.

"Something to make you a little more comfortable. I know it gets cold down here nights. Sorry about that. I did most of the work myself. And I can't hire a plumber to put in radiators, because, well, you're here."

She smiled like she understood and didn't blame him. Which in a way, she didn't. She'd been so high on heroin when he found her on Cherry Street in Wyandanch, right before Independence Day, that he could have brought her to the moon and she wouldn't have noticed. So it was kind of her fault. Like the circumstances of everything in her life. The mirror he'd put on the wall was gone now; she'd smashed it the night after he brought her here. Because she couldn't stand to see all the bad history and grade-A mistakes reflecting back at her.

"It's cotton," he said.

"What?"

She started to rub her itchy nose on her forearm and then stopped, remembering he didn't like her doing that.

"The quilt I just brought. It's forty-five percent cotton. Fifty-five percent polyester. It breathes. So you don't wake up sweating like a pig in the morning."

Her heart leaped at the mention of morning. With all the bricks in the window, she couldn't tell day from night anymore, let alone how much time she'd been down here.

"Where'd you get it?" She started to reach for the quilt.

"Target," he said. "They had them on sale."

"It's pretty," she said, barely able to brush a corner with her fingertips because of how the handcuff held her back.

He smiled, which made his already beady eyes look smaller. Like dice dots, she thought. The rest of his face wasn't that weird. His regular expression had that half-sluggish, half-hungry look she'd seen on other cops and regular schmoes who came into the Squire when she was stripping there. Like they were sleepwalking through life until they saw something they wanted and didn't want other men to have.

"Thank you." She rubbed the fabric between her thumb and forefinger, glad to have something clean to hold. "I think it's going to help a lot."

"You know, it's still possible that I'm going to kill you," he said, so casually and offhandedly that she wasn't sure that she'd heard him correctly.

"Pardon me?"

"You hear something dripping?" he asked. "I just fixed those fucking floors upstairs before you moved in."

"Excuse me? What'd you just say to me?"

"I just don't want you to get the wrong idea. I might still kill you. Or I might not."

He turned back. His smile was more distant now, his eyes even smaller.

"What's going to make you decide?"

She pulled up the corners of her mouth, like she was smiling back at him. Like this was a running joke between them. But her skin felt fake on her face, the way it did when she smoked PCP or inhaled bath salts. Like her flesh was some thin plastic barely covering her skull that could easily be peeled off.

"Hard to say." He tugged up on his gun belt. "Sometimes it's just a feeling you get."

"You've done this before?"

Her voice, bouncing between the poured concrete floor and egg carton ceiling, sounded eerily calm and unaffected. But then her outside never had much to do with her inside. People were always telling her she looked good when she felt bad, and thinking her natural monotone and blank expression meant that she was in control of herself.

"Yeah. Maybe once or twice. Maybe more."

"And did you ever let anyone go?"

"Sure. I got a few out there that I see from time to time."

"I don't think I believe you."

"Why don't you try yelling your head off again and see how much good that does you? But I don't think you liked the results last time. Did you?"

She sank to the stone floor and covered her scraped-raw knees with the remains of her tattered denim miniskirt, her wrist developing a worrying dark purple ring from the cuff being on too tight.

"I think you're going to kill me no matter what." She looked up at him.

"But you can't be totally sure."

"Why would you let anyone go after you did something like this to them?"

"Because there's a relationship." He stared down at her. "Do you even know what that means?"

She hissed—half in contempt for him and half for herself.

"Yeah, dude. I know what it means."

"I'm not talking someone sticking their dick into you once in a while or you giving blow jobs to pay the rent. I'm talking about really getting to know and accept someone, so they can just be themselves around you."

"Who the fuck are you to say that?" She yanked on the handcuff chain. "Doctor Fucking Phil?"

"Hey." He raised a foot like he was about to kick her in the head. "What'd I tell you about having the wrong attitude?"

"All right, all right." She flinched and curled away like a prawn. "You got me. I don't know anything about relationships. Teach me. Please."

She was starting to see what he wanted. He liked the moment when she gave in, especially if there was a buildup.

"That's better." He breathed in, as if submission had a good aroma. "What I'm talking about is getting to a level of trust."

"Okay."

"That's what I want in my life, at this point. A mate. Someone I can come home to. Can you understand that?"

She nodded, as if this made perfect sense. Like this was the most logical thing she'd ever heard and she wasn't scared out of her freaking mind every single second she was in his presence.

"But you know there's a little bit of fear in every relationship," he said.

"I mean, let's be honest about it. It might be fear that the other person is going to abandon you. Or that they're going to cheat on you with someone else. Or, I'm just saying, as a for instance, go nuts and cut your throat for no reason."

"Sure." She nodded more rapidly, like a dashboard bobblehead going over an unpaved stretch of road.

Who knew where this was really going?

"My folks were kind of like that." His thumbs went inside the gun belt. "Always were on edge with each other. Sometimes one was up. Sometimes it was the other."

"Yeah, my grandparents were like that too," she said, trying to keep her voice steady. "When they were trying to raise me."

Maybe this was a new route. Just going with it. Acting like you could accept and relate to whatever he said.

"Did I ask about your fucking grandparents?" he said, his voice suddenly turning cold. "I was talking about *me*. Okay?"

"Okay. Right. My mistake."

"My mother was a beautiful woman, like you are . . ." His eyes drifted up toward the window and then stopped. "Actually, she was kind of a whore. Like you."

"I'm sorry. That must have been really hard for you."

It was like she hadn't spoken. "Maybe she cheated because my father cheated first." His tone turned more ruminative. "Or maybe she did it because she thought he was going to abandon her with a kid she couldn't control anyway. And she thought she could hook up with someone strong who could knock me into line."

She tried to tell herself that it was good he was opening up to her this way. Like for some reason he could be at ease around her. Being himself. And perhaps she could get him to the point where he'd be relaxed enough to change their arrangement. Letting her go on the condition that she never told anyone about this place and what he'd done to her. It wasn't impossible. If she could make him feel like he still had the power to come here and do what he wanted and let his hair down, then he might let her live.

"But she didn't have to do what she did," he said abruptly. "I mean,

Jesus Christ. My father's a cop investigating drug dealers and my mother starts banging drug dealers? Because she's doing drugs? I mean, what is that?"

"I don't know." She blinked, starting to feel nauseous again, following the twists and turns he was taking her through.

"It's *sick*. That's what it is. She was a sick, sick woman. And I was her only child. And she took everything my father was, everything he worked for, and she destroyed it. Totally. She humiliated him in front of his friends and his colleagues because everyone on the job knew what she was doing. Okay? So what choice did he have except to beat her to within an inch of her life and mess her up so that no one would ever want to fuck her again? *Right?*"

"Uh-huh." She hugged her knees tighter, afraid to look at him at all now. "I guess."

"It *is* right. Because someone had to show her that a man should be strong. And never allow himself to be humiliated like that."

"Definitely." She nodded. "None of that should have happened." She felt like the girl in a monster movie, looking away from the gargoyle gnashing its teeth and dripping venom. "Your parents should have taken better care of you."

"Who the fuck asked you?" He crouched down and slapped her. "You're talking bad about my parents? Who the hell are you to judge?"

The sting made everything go white behind her eyes. "But you just said . . ."

"Maybe you misunderstood." He smiled, showing lots of teeth. "Maybe you got it all wrong. Maybe I was feeding you false information to see how you'd react. Maybe *I* was the one who beat my mother. Because my father was too broken to do it and I knew I wouldn't get in trouble because I was twelve and a mother wouldn't send her only son to get locked up."

"I don't know what to say now." She was starting to shake. "Just tell me what you want me to say."

"Who said you needed to say anything?" He suddenly screamed, turning bright red. "Maybe I just wanted to hear myself talk. Maybe it gets me hard to make you listen. Or maybe you're just a thing to me and I won't even remember you in a couple of months."

She began to sob, face against her knees. No one would remember her, she realized. No one was even looking for her now.

"You're not going to let me live." She forced herself to look back at him. "Are you?"

He still hadn't quite figured out why he hadn't gotten rid of her the way he'd gotten rid of the others.

He hadn't targeted her or stalked her. He'd just found her one night, six weeks ago, shaking her good thing and offering it for sale in Wyandanch. It had been a while since he'd done this, but he expected to go through the business of scaring her, tying her up, getting off, and then dispatching her and dumping the body. But instead something weird had happened. Maybe it was because both his parents had died and he was free now. Maybe it was just getting older and having some of the natural rage burned out of him. Or maybe it was the fact that he'd tapered off the drugs and finally gone cold turkey a few months before. But for the first time that he could remember, he'd been able to have sex with a woman in a somewhat normal way, no trouble getting it up for once, and now he wanted to keep her around, at least temporarily. If only as a trophy to remind him of his success.

"Anyway, I brought you Chinese food." He held up a takeout bag he'd brought down. "Moo shu pork and egg rolls."

"I'm allergic to MSG."

"Oh well." He put the bag down on the card table he'd set up in the corner opposite the toilet. "Guess you don't eat then."

"You didn't ask what I wanted."

"Excuuuse me."

"If you're not going to kill me, how long are you going to keep me?"

"Told you." He pulled apart the stapled top of the bag. "Depends."

"Depends on what?"

"Depends on how much you don't piss me off by asking a lot of stupid fucking questions."

She roused herself to stand up and pad over. Once she got within a foot of the table, she put a hand on her stomach, stuck her tongue out, and made a retching sound. "Ugh, that smell. Where did you order from? The town dump?"

"No one's forcing you."

"No one's forcing me?"

"No one is forcing you *to eat*," he said pedantically. "Believe me, it doesn't look like you've been missing too many meals."

"That's mean."

"You don't know what mean is."

"Why do you act this way?" she said. "Haven't I given you everything you wanted?"

She pulled the shirt tight from the bottom, so he could see the outline of her nipples against the material. Acting like a whore. This conversation was starting to remind him of the way his parents talked to each other.

"*Hey*." He grabbed her by the jaw and squeezed. "What did I tell you? I can get any woman I want, any time I want."

"Yeah?" She snorted defiantly, even as he smushed her features together. "Then what do you need me for?"

"I'm starting to ask myself the same question." He twisted her head sharply and then let her go. "You're a fucking pain in the ass. That's what you are. You're not worth the trouble."

She rubbed her jaw and looked up at the ceiling, ten feet overhead, just out of reach with her short stature, even if she could stand on a chair.

"Go ahead, scream again." He pointed at the egg cartons. "No one can hear you. Scream your fucking head off. See how much good that does you."

"You know, you should ask yourself some questions," she said. "About why you keep doing this."

Somehow she had a way of pushing his buttons but stopping just short of insolence. Of being just provocative enough to get his attention without quite pushing him over the edge and making him blow up.

"You want chopsticks?" he asked. "I'm not giving you a knife or a fork. I bet you can understand *that*, can't you?"

"Answer the question."

"What's the point?" He suddenly turned and raised his hand as if to slap her. "So you can fucking psychoanalyze me? You *can't*. Don't you get it? It'd be like a dog trying to understand its master."

Instead of flinching like the others did, she kept staring with those eerily unblinking eyes.

"I'm not a dog," she said. "I'm a person. My name is Renee Williams. I have grandparents who love me." She spoke louder as he pretended to clap his hands over his ears. "I haven't taken any drugs since I've been here. How could I? You made me go through withdrawal on my own. I was alone when I was sick with night sweats and throwing up and diarrhea. But now I'm clean . . ."

"Oh, what do you want, a medal?" He waved his hand, not wanting to deal with what she was trying to conjure for him.

"I want you to see me as *a human being*."

She was right about the drugs, of course. Her skin had cleared since she'd stopped using and she looked both younger and more intelligent than she had when he first brought her in here.

"Save your precious breath, because you're gonna need it," he warned her. "I already told you. You cannot understand me. And you cannot put a label on me. I know all the mind games and reverse psychology. I'm not some little sociopath with no executive function. I could kill you right now and sit down to eat these egg rolls. Just means more food for me."

"I don't believe you."

He sat down on a folding chair, snapped the chopsticks apart, and began deftly handling pork and pancakes. "You can believe whatever you want. I'm just being honest, because I'm free. And you're not. I own you. I feed you. I house you. But you're nothing to me. You don't matter. In fact, I don't even think we're the same species."

"I don't think that's true," she said evenly.

"Yeah, why's that?" He gave her a lopsided smile, a rolled-up pancake halfway to his mouth.

"Because one species can't usually make another species pregnant," she said. "And I'm carrying your baby."

40

Mitchell Vogliano came home feeling ragged from a long day at the Brooklyn DA's office. His bureau chief had treated him like a chew toy in the morning and in the afternoon the judge in Supreme Court had spoken to him like a five-year-old when he asked for another week to prepare arguments in his latest health care fraud case.

He let himself in the Bay Ridge apartment, wishing he had a full-fledged family to come home to. A wife and kids to greet him like a conquering hero at the door, dinner ready in the kitchen, news of neighbors and relatives to be shared over the meal, and maybe a loving shoulder rub before bed. But here he was, thirty-six years old, salad for dinner in the fridge, barely covering his bills on a civil service salary, and living with a woman who didn't even want to get married at this point. On the subway coming home, the one thing he looked forward to was taking off his shoes, hanging up his coat, and doing a little yoga in the spare room before he settled down to work on his briefs after eating.

But as soon as he walked in, he saw Lourdes had her coat already hung up and the light was on in the yoga room. He pushed the door open and found she'd turned the studio into her personal workspace. She was in a t-shirt and jeans and surrounded by pieces of paper and index cards taped up on the walls, all profusely illustrated with charts and dates in her near-perfect Catholic school penmanship. There were strings of red yarn to demonstrate connections between the items, and for some reason he wondered first where she'd gotten the yarn since he'd never even heard her mention knitting.

"Lourdes," he said, deciding to keep the question to himself. "What the hell?"

"Mitchell, I think I almost got this." She waved at the walls a little too excitedly. "I just needed to lay all the pieces out to start to see the bigger picture."

"This looks like an insane asylum. Or a scene from *Homeland*."

"Right." She capped the red Magic Marker she'd been using and wiped her hands on her shirt front. "That's where I got the idea."

"But the woman on that show has a mental illness." He put a hand to the small of his back and arched it.

"Okay, but crazy isn't always wrong," she said. "Look what I got here."

She stood next to the beginning of the timeline she'd laid out with the cards. "In 1977, Kim Bergdahl is found dead with twigs and branches down her throat. The ADA on the case is Kenneth Makris. And the main witness before the grand jury is Joseph Tolliver, age seventeen."

"Whoa." Mitchell stopped her. "I thought that was just a rumor."

"I'm still checking it out, but here's what I know for sure . . ." She pointed to the next card. "In 1981, Joseph Tolliver becomes a police officer with a letter of recommendation in his file from Kenneth Makris."

"Does it mention this girl with the twigs in her throat case?" Mitchell asked.

"No, of course not." Lourdes waved him off a little too manically. "That would be too easy. But check it." She pointed to the next series of cards. "In 1981, Joseph Tolliver becomes a police officer. In 1982, Stephanie Lapidus is found dead near Sunrise Highway. In 1989, Angela Spinelli. Tolliver had highway duty or supervision for both cases."

"Circumstantial." Mitchell pinched the bridge of his nose.

"Joyce Templeton, 2002. Allison Forster, 2005. Anne Higgins, 2006. Yelina Sanchez, 2007. Miriam Gonzales, 2011. All within his jurisdiction. And mostly when he was chief and could control the chain of evidence."

"Also circumstantial. Not nearly enough to sustain an indictment against the chief of a major department. How would he have gotten away with it for so long?"

"He had help." She began pointing to an alternative timeline she'd laid out beneath the Tolliver cards, like a parallel history. "In 1984, Kenneth Makris becomes DA, partly because of the Bird Dog case and increased arrests against black and Hispanic residents. Same year that Joseph Tolliver becomes a sergeant. By 1988, he's a lieutenant and helping to turn out the vote not only for Makris but also for Steve Snyder, the county executive. Then in 2003, Snyder supports Tolliver becoming the chief of the department."

"Lourdes . . ."

"I'm telling you, Mitchell. It's all part of the same deal."

"They were all in on it?" He raised his eyebrows. "Is that what you really believe?"

"I'm not saying they all hired prostitutes and strangled them," she rattled off. "I'm not that paranoid. But did they all find a reason to look the other way, because Joey was making them look good? I'm thinking yes."

"Sorry." Mitchell shook his head, feeling a soreness at the base of his spine. "I'm still not buying it. For one thing, you told me yourself that Tolliver has alibis for some of these murders."

"He's *chief*. He can alter time sheets, get people to vouch for him. You don't have to be so literal."

"And for another," Mitchell rattled off, knowing he had to talk fast to get in everything he had to say before she butted back in. "Where's the connection to your Rockaway case? Not only is it farther away from Sunrise Highway, the MO is different from all the others, except the Bergdahl case. None of the others had anything stuffed down their throats, except for Renee Williams and Kim Bergdahl. And none of the others were pregnant, except for Renee. I say you're talking apples and oranges. Forgive me, Lourdes. I know that's not what you want to hear from me, but I love you too much to lie to you."

"But you admit it's still possible, don't you?" she said, with some edge-of-the-fingertips desperation.

"Sure it's possible. But 'possible' isn't proof that will stand up in a court of law." He came over and put an arm around her. "Look, I know how much you put into this. But is it also possible that with all this thinking about your sister, your lines have gotten a little blurred?"

"Later for you, Mitchell." She pulled away gently. "My lines are still straight. You're just mad I took over your little yoga room."

"Actually, I was hoping one day it might be a baby's room." He looked sadly at the rolled-up mat in the corner where he'd envisioned a crib standing.

"Whatever." She started writing on another card. "But don't tell me that I'm the one getting ahead of myself."

41

Everyone had gone way over the top worrying about Hurricane Irene last year and, aside from a few flooded streets and lost homes, it hadn't been that big a deal. Joey, who as chief had pressured the local politicians to close the schools for safety reasons, wound up getting more of an earful from mothers bitching about having the kids home from school all day and husbands pissed about how much the police were getting for overtime.

So when the hype started up again about this Hurricane Sandy being the storm of the century, he didn't lose his mind right away. They lived in a place where natural disasters didn't hit as often as man-made ones.

Just the same, as head of a major department overseeing some three thousand officers and responsible for the safety of a million and a half people, he knew he'd have to be on duty or at the very least reachable for most of the day and night to coordinate emergency procedures, rescue efforts, and the prevention of looting.

The girl was insulated from all of this, in the basement with no access to TV, radio, or Internet. She probably didn't even know about the neighbors' preparations, since he'd bricked up the basement windows and the nearest standing house was at least fifty yards down the block. But she started asking questions when she saw him bringing down extra jugs of bottled water and a high-powered flashlight with new batteries, and then watched him install a camera in a corner of the ceiling that transmitted images to an app on his cell phone, so he could keep an eye on her while he was at work.

"Seriously?" She rattled the chain at him. "You ever think of talking to somebody about your control issues?"

He was still torn about keeping her around. Back in the day, he would have disposed of her by now, killing her, covering her up and putting the memory in a tidy box, so he could take it out and stroke it once in a while.

But it was getting more complicated. Part of it was procedural. When he'd started, there were no cell phone pings or GPS devices to track your every move. No search engines. DNA couldn't reveal your identity by a mere sweaty touch or an accidental spray of spittle. Nowadays, it was getting close to the point where you could just talk in a room and someone would be able to prove you'd been there.

But it wasn't only fear and caution keeping her alive. He wasn't at the mercy of such weak emotions. And it wasn't just wanting to toy with her and torture her a little longer. Pain and helpless terror no longer excited him the way they used to. Something in him had shifted because something in her had shifted. What he'd made was inside her now. A presence that could enter a room without going through a door. A miracle. The idea of it made him feel as powerful as he did the first time he put his headlights in a woman's face.

He'd wondered how he could make this work in the long run. Typical domestic arrangements were out of the question. How could he let her out and about after all that had happened? What was the alternative, though? You saw stories about cretins and fanatics keeping women hostage for years in such circumstances and then photos of the women stumbling into daylight, blinking like moles, and stumbling into the arms of waiting relatives who hadn't tried that hard to find them.

He was much smarter and savvier than any of the so-called masterminds. Maybe he could stay under the radar while monitoring every aspect of her environment, create the home and family he'd always wanted, to make sure everything came out right this time.

All that was required was diligent attention to detail, total resistance to outside influences, and unyielding vigilance.

All the same, he had an uneasy feeling when he left her with three ready-made meals in the basement that late October morning. The radio in the Jeep said the storm was still at least three miles out at sea, but the clouds were already holding a black mass in the eastern sky and the tide was already rushing in further and faster than usual, splashing up between the boardwalk planks.

As soon as he arrived at headquarters, he was under siege, fielding a constant stream of emails, texts, and calls from local mayors, town supervisors, and police substations working with volunteers to reroute traffic, barricade roads with poor drainage, and help keep the beaches deserted. His desktop screen was split into multiple views of major intersections and potential trouble spots while subordinates barged in and out of the office with minute-by-minute updates on the storm forecast and street conditions.

By four o'clock, it was plain that this was no longer a drill. The governor had shut down mass transit in the city the day before and now schools were closed, emergency shelters were open, and there were mandatory evacuations in the surge zones of Babylon, Islip, Southold, and Fire Island. His office was turning into a war room with rising voices, nonstop phones ringing, and everyone's screens flashing with more and more dire alarms. The Weather Channel was talking about twenty-foot waves and raw sewage in the streets. Then reports came in about fallen power lines sparking in the gutters and homes without electricity starting to catch fire. He tried to project cool-eyed authority behind the desk, but hundred-mile-an-hour winds were howling outside, shaking and battering the windows.

Every few minutes, he pulled out his cell phone to check on the transmission from his father's house. The image of the pregnant girl chained up in the basement was oddly reassuring. Sitting there barefoot, tenderly holding her belly and moving her mouth as if she was talking to the unseen presence within. A cold hand gripped his heart. He realized that this was in danger of turning into one of the emotions other people always talked about. Somehow he had been tricked into caring about what happened to her. And the realization scared him as much as the sight of a patrol car's lights drawing near before a body was buried. Because now he had something to lose.

The image froze and refused to refresh. Leaving the still life of his prisoner Madonna on his phone. He tried turning it off and back on but the connection was broken. The power had gone off in the neighborhood and the generator hadn't kicked on. Probably no one's cell phones were working. She was alone in the house with the baby in her womb. And soon she would know about the water.

42

With Mitchell fed up with her—temporarily, she hoped—and B.B. on her personal no-fly list, Lourdes elected to go out to Central Islip on her day off to look through court records and see if she could find anything about Tolliver in the Kim Bergdahl case file. Unsurprisingly, the clerks hemmed and hawed, made furtive phone calls, and pulled out endless forms to be filled out by hand. And then said they had nothing.

When she came out to the parking lot mid-afternoon, there was a sharpened screwdriver stuck in the left rear tire of the Camry, which she'd taken because B.B. was holding on to the squad car for the day.

She had to call around to a nearby tire shop and then call into the squad to make sure they'd pay for the replacement. Then she made another call to the chief of detective's office, getting permission to hatch a plan she'd had cooking in the back of her mind for a couple of days.

Despite the bartender's antipathy toward the chief, Sullivan had heard that Tolliver sometimes hung out at the bar called Legends. She called Sully at the Motor Inn and lured him out with the prospect of a drink and interesting conversation.

Tolliver's eyes got wide when he saw the two of them walk in, just after seven o'clock that night. The chief had been sitting at a round table with droopy old Charlie Maslow and a couple of women in slinky dresses who looked like a million dollars from the back and fifty dollars from the front.

"Hey, chief, I think I have something of yours." Lourdes walked up to the table.

"What's that?" Tolliver tried to keep the party going in his eyes.

The bar was crowded and the music was loud, but everyone was watching. Obviously he thought that by smiling he could make it look like this was a normal conversation and she was just another chick he'd banged.

Lourdes put the sharpened screwdriver on the table in front of him. "I think you might have misplaced this," she said.

The two women got up from the table. Charlie Maslow angled his chair away.

"I have no idea what that is." Tolliver maintained his bon vivant grin. "But pull up a chair, detective. You look stressed." He glanced over her shoulder at Sullivan. "And tell your older friend to take a load off. I'll buy you both a round."

"Yeah, that's nice," Lourdes said. "But I don't drink when I'm working."

"You working now?" Tolliver turned down the corners of his mouth. "Aren't you the dedicated little public servant?"

"Actually, I was spending a little extra time out here because I had to change a flat on my car. My friend, Detective Sullivan over here, agreed to meet me here after some asshole stuck a screwdriver in my tire."

"How's it going?" Tolliver gave Sullivan a halfhearted wave.

Sully dead-eyed him, the full fearsome Golem.

"Anyway, I figured you might have been missing your tool." Lourdes glanced down at the screwdriver. "It's got some rust on it, but it still has an edge."

"Not mine." Tolliver shrugged and shook his head. "I know where all my tools are."

"Do you?" Lourdes let her voice go high. "Hard for me to imagine it could be anybody else's. But maybe you have people that work for you that don't do such a good job cleaning up after themselves."

Maslow took that as a cue to rise and slide away. "I'll get us another round."

The women followed him away, leaving the chief on his own.

"What are you trying to accomplish here, detective?" Tolliver asked. "Are you trying to embarrass me on my home court?"

"I'm not after embarrassment, chief. You know that as well as I do."

"Okay, then clue me in. What are you after?"

"I'm letting you know that I'm pursuing a lead on this Sunrise Highway case and I'm not going to be intimidated," Lourdes said, playing it out. "Not by a phony traffic stop and not by somebody giving me a flat tire."

"If you want roadside service, you've come to the wrong place." Tolliver raised a half-empty stein. "This is a bar, young lady."

"I'm just interested." She leaned down so her face was inches from his. "You're not just focusing on me because I'm the girl in the squad, are you? Because that would be messed up."

He gave her a smile so glassy that she could have sworn he wasn't just half-drunk but high on drugs. "I notice none of your regular male colleagues are in here with you," he said. "At least none who are young enough to still be with the NYPD."

"Can't buy me off with a job in your department, chief," she said.

"You thinking of somebody we know?" Tolliver asked.

From the corner of her eye, she saw Sullivan give a subtle headshake, discouraging her from running down B.B. when she was recording the conversation on her cell phone.

"I can't speak for any of them," she said. "But I'd hate to think it's because you have some deeper problem with women."

"Believe me. I got no problems with women." He broadened his grin. "In fact, my only problem with women is that I have no problem with women." He glanced at Sullivan, as if he wanted to share the joke. "You know what I mean, big guy?"

"The lady is the one talking to you," Sullivan grumbled. "Not me."

"You're barking up the wrong tree." Tolliver turned back to Lourdes. "A hundred percent."

"Yeah, that's what Delaney Patterson said as well. About your testimony putting him away."

Tolliver's eyes drifted and his lip curled ever so slightly, revealing the bored delinquent still inside him.

"That's history." He yawned. "Nothing to do with anything going on now."

"We'll see about that, chief. We're not excluding any possibilities."

Everything else in the bar seemed to have faded away. It could have been just the two of them trapped in a stalled elevator.

"Let me ask you something, Robles," he said, no longer playing the smile for the room. "Are you still on this case or is this just a personal matter now?" He stared at Sullivan. "And why is this old-timer with you? Is he sweet on you? Or is this something more serious?"

"It's not just personal, chief," she deflected, as stone-faced as she could get with dimples. "We're pursuing the leads where they take us. Even when one of your officers shoots the son of a potential witness at an Exxon station."

"That matter is under investigation by the DA's office." Tolliver shrugged. "But I can assure you my officers did nothing wrong. That young man was reaching for a gun when he was shot."

"Sure it wasn't a screwdriver?" She pointed at the tool still lying in front of him.

"Let me ask you one more time: *What are you trying to accomplish here?*"

He absently picked up a thin red cocktail straw that one of the women had abandoned at the table. Then he slowly wrapped it around a finger like he was strangling a vein. She halfway hoped he would spit in her face or try to shove a napkin down her throat, or do something careless that would give her a sample of his DNA that she could try to match to one of the crime scenes.

Or, failing that, maybe she could goad him into making another mistake after the fact, like calling someone later tonight, whose phone number they could discover through a subpoena.

"I'm just letting you know that I know who you are," she said.

He stared back at her, not just sober but unnaturally focused. As if he had only now decided to finally give her his full undivided attention. It reminded her of the first time she'd been close enough to a tiger at the Bronx Zoo to see that its eyes really were yellow and inhuman, and that its interest in her had a strong element of hunger.

"I know who you are," he said. "You're a shitty little affirmative action hire who only got promoted to fulfill a quota who couldn't make it in a squad with any real standards. So why don't you get your fat ass off your high horse before you break its back?"

"Watch that," said Sullivan.

"Or what, grandpa?" Tolliver waved for the women to come back to the table. "Gonna kick my ass? You couldn't get your leg up that high. Or any other part of you."

"Classy," said Lourdes. "You may want to think of stepping down now. To focus on your personal and legal issues. But I want to let you know in the meantime: if I find another screwdriver where it doesn't belong, you're gonna have a more immediate problem."

"Hey, miss, look around you." Tolliver made a sweeping gesture. "This is my world. You are here as guests. If you wish to stay, my offer to buy you a drink still stands. Otherwise, we can continue this conversation in my office, with a recorder running, in the presence of my lawyer. Is that clear to you?"

"Yes, it is."

"Thanks for stopping by to give me the update." Tolliver pulled out a chair for one of the returning women. "And be careful drinking and driving out here. My officers are out on the road and an NYPD courtesy card won't get you out of a ticket."

Sullivan tapped her on the shoulder, signaling that the time had come. They walked out together, passing the wary eyes and tight mouths of local off-duty cops packed in at the counter, narrowly resisting the urge to pull her gun when she heard someone mutter, "What a pair, huh?"

43

She didn't know what time the water started coming in, because there were no clocks in the basement.

With the windows above her head all bricked up, there was no way to distinguish between morning, afternoon, and night either; the only demarcation was when he would show up. Otherwise, she was adrift, with no defined edges, sleeping for hours and waking up in terror, with no idea where she was or whether anyone was looking for her. She didn't know if they'd had the election or who was president now. There were imaginary conversations with people who weren't present and hallucinations involving rodents doing the Macarena and armies of singing cockroaches. And of all the things he'd done to her—the handcuffs, the beatings, the weird sex, even the way he'd roofied her and brought her down here in the first place—stealing the sun and the moon was the worst. Because it deprived her of the one thing every man and woman on earth deserved: a sense of time passing.

So she'd taken it back. Or maybe it had been given back to her. The life growing inside her was a clock. It reestablished a schedule for her. It put order in her life. The baby slept in the day and kicked at night. It told her when to eat and when to rest. It demanded she pay attention to the moment and forget about the past and the future. Especially now, as the water seeping between spaces in the bricks began to stream down the wall. She looked around and saw it was leaking through in other places, dripping from the egg cartons on the ceiling and dribbling from cracks in the other walls.

"Hey, what is this?" she called out to the camera he'd put up in a corner of the ceiling—no idea whether it had a microphone. "You seeing what's happening here?"

She heard a spatter and saw that more water was spilling down over the landing where the stairs had been torn out.

"Hey, yo." She waved at the camera. "I think you must have left the bath running upstairs or something."

She looked down and saw there was already an inch on the floor, rising up toward her bare ankles. Something scurried behind the boiler in the corner; it could have been one of the rats she'd seen earlier, making its escape through a tiny hole. Water bugs were crawling along the badly plastered spots on the walls. Because he'd done most of the work down here himself, the basement had a hurried, slapped-together look. And if he'd done an equally crap job with the plumbing, this could be a burst water pipe. But then it dawned on her that a pipe wouldn't be gushing from so many different places at once.

It was pouring from the brickwork filling the window frame, dribbling down onto the toilet in the corner, and running freely down the opposite wall near the refrigerator where she thought she'd seen the face of Jesus in the growing mold.

"Hey, a little help here?" she yelled, pulling against the handcuff chain. "There's a fuckin' pregnant woman in this house."

The water was almost up to her knees. It was brownish from the sediment on the floor and it had squiggles in it that she hoped weren't worms or live bacteria of some kind.

"Yo, for real now," she cried out. "Somebody help me. I'm all alone."

How was an old black gospel lady's voice coming out of her mouth? Her mother had no religion except for dollars and crack, and her grandparents had only managed to drag her screaming and kicking to church three or four times before she cut loose.

The basement was flooding more quickly now, water rising up and soaking the baggy blue running shorts and the sweatshirt he'd given her.

"Oh shit." She stood on tiptoe and gasped from the cold. "Shit. Shit. Shit."

Soon the level would be up to her mouth. She remembered being afraid to put her face in the water when her grandfather took her for swim lessons at the YMCA pool. Saying this was one black girl who was going to learn how to stay afloat. Barely took off her water wings or let go of the kickboard before she quit that as well. But now she was starting to panic as the water came up to her chin.

"Oh my God, oh my God . . ."

Muscle memory got her legs bike-pedaling and her arms dog-paddling. *Come on, come on.* She panted, trying to stay above the surface, catching a whiff of raw sewage in the air. The steady patter of rain was more distinct now, and she could hear what sounded like the sustained yowl of a monster in the distance. A broken-off piece of brick floated past her eyes. She looked up to see where it had come from and spotted water rushing through a new gap in the bricked-up window frame.

She kicked her legs harder, trying to get to the gap as more of the basement flooded. She realized the house must be near a large body of water; otherwise the flooding couldn't be happening so quickly.

The bottom of the window frame was less than a yard overhead. She reached for it, to have something to hang onto, but her arm wouldn't extend. The long handcuff chain came a few inches out of the water and then stopped. She realized she was still attached to the bar below the dark swirling surface.

"Oh no." She yanked, her hand achingly close to getting a hold. "Fuck me . . ."

She thrashed and struggled against the shackles, her legs starting to hurt and grow tired. The egg cartons on the ceiling were disintegrating from the water coming through. She cursed him all over again, not just for keeping her captive, but for cheaping out with his slipshod amateur construction.

She reached again for the gap in the bricks but the chain held firm, stopping her within inches of getting a safe handhold. She began to sink down in fatigue and despair. But as soon as her head went under the surface, the baby began to kick, as if it was protesting, *"You had your life, now let me have mine."*

She flailed spastically back to the surface one more time, gasping and tilting her head back to keep from swallowing more contaminated water. Something wriggled by that could have been a snake. A purple-pink piece of egg carton drifted after it like a piece of heart tissue.

Her body gathered itself in for one last burst. She paddled closer to the wall and braced her bare feet against it. She bent her knees, grit her teeth, and with an expulsion of breath pulled with both hands and all her might.

Something was starting to come loose.

The handcuff at the other end of the chain was still hooked to the bar somewhere below the surface, but it felt like the bolts had been poorly secured behind the plaster and were now partway out. She almost laughed in demented-little-girl glee at her own strength, but then a slap of dirty water went in her open mouth and down the back of her throat.

She swallowed, put her feet flat against the wall, and pulled harder. Both sides of the bar were breaking free from the sodden plaster. She could feel it. She pulled a third time and the whole bar came loose. She raised her arm out of the water, and the bar and shackles came with it. She realized he must have had the other cuff on so tight that it wouldn't just slide off the bar.

She put her shoulders back and buoyed herself higher, rising with the water until she could get a part of her butt resting on the windowsill. Then she pulled on the chain until she had the bar in her hands, with rusty bolts hanging off either end.

She banged it against the brickwork in the window and saw red powder fly out. Then she wedged one end into the gap where the water was coming in and started to pry it loose. Making her way out into the black roaring night, piece by piece.

44

Lourdes knew it wasn't a good sign when she walked into the squad the next morning and saw that the captain's office had been commandeered by the NYPD chief of detectives, Dave Pritzker.

"You want to come in and shut the door?" he said—telling, not asking. "I don't think you want a lot of people to hear this."

"Sir?"

He was a short, restless man, hard of eye and firm of mouth, who had gotten ahead by knowing exactly who had the power in any room and being willing to move decisively against those who didn't.

"Sit down," he said. "You know what this is about."

"If it's about Chief Tolliver, then . . ."

"Of course it's about Tolliver. What'd you think I came to talk about? Your goddamn sister?"

"Sir." She closed the door and sat. "Before we get into this, I want you to know that we're making real progress in the larger investigation."

"Give me your phone." His eyebrows descended.

He was a man defined by dark outlines: black hair, black brows, black suit contrasting against a pale complexion.

"What?"

"I said get your phone out. I don't want this recorded and showing up online." He snapped his fingers. "Let's go."

She turned her phone off, showed him the black screen, and put it facedown on his desk.

"There are two conversations we need to have, official and unofficial. Got it?"

"Yes, sir."

"Officially, this is still an ongoing investigation and we're still working cooperatively with other members of the task force and local law enforcement agencies."

"But unofficially?"

"Unofficially." His pupils, dark and small as dice dots, strayed to her phone on the desk. "Are you fucking kidding me, Robles? This is the head of one of the biggest police departments in the country and you confront him in the middle of a bar full of his subordinates?"

"Sir." She sat up, trying, as she always did in these situations, to assume the proper posture of an English horse lady on a wild-ass bronco. "My understanding is that my strategy had been cleared through channels and you were aware of it."

Of course she wouldn't have done it on her own. One Police Plaza micromanaged everything to the point where you needed an okay from headquarters to requisition a paper clip.

"I called your office yesterday, after my tire got shanked," she said. "And I thought that we all agreed it'd be a good idea to shake him up and see how he'd respond."

"Well, I have no paper trail to support that." He stared at a spot somewhere over her head. "And certainly no one spoke to me directly."

"*For real?*" She gripped her armrests, feeling like she'd been grabbed by the ankles, swung around, and dropped back into her chair. "Sir, everyone knows you signed off on this."

"You calling me a liar, Robles?"

"No, sir, but . . ."

Her voice died in her throat. Fourteen years on the job and basic bureaucratic injustice could still make her feel like a child struck speechless by discovering her father's first lie.

"I didn't do anything wrong." She tried for a reset. "I'm sure you know we're getting subpoenas for all his personnel records, to see if he reaches out to an accomplice . . ."

"*Nope.*"

"Sir?"

"Those subpoenas just got quashed by a Supreme Court judge out in Riverhead."

He dropped a file on the desk, the slap of paper like five fingers across her face.

"I don't understand," she said.

"You had a prosecutor named Mitchell Vogliano help draft the subpoenas." Pritzker slid the file to her. "Are you living with him?"

"Yes," she said, pissed and embarrassed that he had gotten that far into her business. "But I don't see why that matters. Mitchell's in the Brooklyn DA's office. The subpoena was signed by an assistant U.S. attorney for the Eastern District. Why does it matter who helped?"

Though now she was deeply sorry she'd dragged Mitchell into it after their little yoga room argument, when she'd pressured him to use his federal friends as cover.

"Well, now it's blown up in all our faces." He pushed the file at her with a hiss of disgust. "The judge found you'd overstepped by a country mile, asking for the records of a police chief without probable cause."

"We *have* probable cause. We know Tolliver was on duty as an officer and in the vicinity for at least three of the murders we know about. We're trying to show his photo to the prostitute who said she was choked by him at a party . . ."

"That's not good enough, Robles. Those were all Long Island cases and you are a New York City police officer. Not only are you operating outside your jurisdiction, you're accusing the chief of a major police department of multiple A-1 felonies when it's more plausible that most, if not all, of these are gang-related cases. And if that wasn't bad enough, now Tolliver's people are saying you have an ax to grind because you got pulled over with drugs in the car."

"Which they planted on me."

"Let's not get into that, Robles. We all know your side of the street isn't completely clean either."

"What's that supposed to mean?" she asked, challenging him.

"Meaning Erik Heinz and Raffi Robles. Nuff said?"

From the corner of her eye, she saw B.B. drift by and give what was probably supposed to be a sympathetic nod, before he plopped down at his desk and took out his cell phone.

"Sir, all due respect, but if I'm getting too close too soon it's because everyone else has been dogging it for too long. These murders have been going for decades without anyone seeing the pattern."

"And you've done good work, connecting some of the dots. But now you need to take a step back."

"Ain't just 'dots,' sir," she said, no longer able to hide her disgust. "At least one of them was carrying a baby."

"Okay, then let me say this more plainly." He raised his voice and cast a look at the door, making sure it was closed. "You're way off the reservation. Rein it in."

In a TV show, or maybe even in a college classroom, she'd be turning this around on the boss. Standing tall and accusing him of letting down the victims. And calling him out on this "reservation" shit in the process. Straight-up racism, that's what that was.

But this being the real world, and her wanting to hold on to her job, the only job she'd ever really wanted, and one that would provide her with a healthy pension if she could hang on another seven years, she was going to take her aunt Soledad's advice. She was going to put the ass on her lip and keep her mouth shut. Like every other grown-up in the real world who wanted to maintain their paycheck and their health benefits.

"Listen," the chief sighed, taking it down a notch. "I know how you're taking this seriously, but there's a whole other level to it. It isn't our world where most of this is happening. They've got their own way of doing things out there. It's a machine and none of us have the access codes."

"I don't know if I can access your *code*," she answered. "What are you telling me?"

"I'm telling you that the judge who quashed that subpoena used to be a prosecutor working under Kenny Makris, who's still the DA out there."

"And Makris owes Joey Tolliver for helping him win his first big case," Lourdes said.

"Perhaps." The chief nodded. "But what you need to bear in mind is that Kenneth Makris helped Steve Snyder become county executive out there. And then Snyder became a congressman. And now he's the junior senator from our august state. Do you know how that happened?"

"Should I?"

"Yes, because he won his congressional race by two thousand votes. Which is how many police officers Joseph Tolliver turned out at the polls for him. And which is what gave him a leg up when he ran for the senate."

"Oh."

"'Oh' is right, detective. Did you know that Steve Snyder is now a key ally of the president, serving on several key committees that oversee appropriations for our state and our department?"

"Yeah, but . . ."

Lourdes put her fingertips to her temples like she was trying to keep two halves of her skull together.

"Sir, we're talking about seven or eight bodies," she said. "Minimum."

"I know what we're talking about, detective. Believe me."

"Do you? Because, sir, all due respect, we're only beginning to get the picture here. I think this guy had accomplices."

"Accomplices?"

"Yes, sir. Both after the fact and maybe ahead of it as well."

"Like little *assistant* serial killers? Robles, get off the hard stuff."

"I haven't nailed it all down, sir. But I'm certain he couldn't have acted alone. It's how he managed to have alibis for some of the murders. And when there are accomplices, it means there could be a chance to turn someone . . ."

"I said, rein it in. You need a hearing aid, detective?"

"So we're just gonna look the other way? Because of politics?" She started shaking her head. "*Really?*"

"Don't put words in my mouth, Robles. No one's talking about looking the other way. But only one of those bodies was found within city boundaries. And even that was iffy. And you damn well know it."

"So we're gonna let outside agencies tell us who gets to work a case? That it?"

"Oh, will you please . . . ?"

He stopped himself and in the clenching of his fist she could see a lifetime's frustration with women like herself coming together.

"Look." He tried to start over. "I'm not here to litigate with you. You ran your little number in the bar and now Tolliver is going to argue you have it in for him."

"Because he *is* our guy. All we need is the rest of those records to prove it."

"The other members of the task force are all over that."

She looked out the glass and saw B.B. still on the phone, hunched over in his chair, hand on his forehead like he wasn't still keeping an eye on her.

"So we're just going to hand over the whole case?" She looked around, like there was someone else in the room to share her outrage. "That's not what I signed on for when I joined this department."

"Spare me the diatribe. It's true that you connected the bodies, but it's a multi-county investigation, which technically should make it a state police case. The FBI has the expertise in serial killers. We're lucky we were even on that task force."

"And now you're pulling me off it?"

"No one's pulling anything," he said. "You're being asked to play more of a support role. Let Detective Borrelli be more the face of this investigation. For now."

She turned and saw that B.B. had his back to the window, so she was looking right at the bald spot beneath his comb-over.

Obviously, he'd gotten to Pritzker before she did, short-circuiting any argument she could have made about him being fatally compromised. Sullivan had already told her to leave this alone now, and so until she had proof, she'd have to go along to get along.

"If that's the way you want it, sir." She stood up. "Will you excuse me to tie up some loose ends?"

"You're excused." He already had his phone out, ready to deal with other problems.

45

When Renee finally got outside, it looked like she had stumbled out onto the lip of an active volcano.

There was fire in the air and water in the streets. The muffled roar she'd heard from the basement was five times louder out here. She staggered away from the house, trying to figure where she was and what had happened. It was night. All the lights were out in the street. But there was a full moon. Flaming embers passed in front of it, then sizzled as they hit the water. The flood was coming from two different directions and nearly up to her waist. The wind was making her hair a riot. Something brushed against the backs of her thighs and she realized that it could have been a fish.

Feet numb and teeth chattering, she turned toward where she could see cars and houses outlined in silver by the moonlight. A red station wagon came toward her with its lights blinking and its horn blaring over and over. She waved her arms to get the driver's attention. But then it kept coming, right at her, and she had to lunge left to get out of the way.

"What the fuck?"

The vehicle swayed and rocked as it went past her, indifferent. Floating, instead of rolling, with no driver at the wheel. Like the three cars drifting after it, lifted off the ground by the rising tides. The smell of salt water filled her nostrils. She realized she would drown if she stayed still or he'd come back and find her outside the house.

Rain pelting her in the face and the baby kicking her kidneys like tiny soccer balls, she waded toward where there appeared to be more houses. Two more cars came at her, going cockeyed and back end first. She heard a *thonking* sound and saw a large chunk of boardwalk hitting the side of a house where the hedges were barely peeking over the swampy surface.

She pushed on, smelling gas mixed with the salt water now. Patio furniture and plastic hampers came floating by. She realized her left arm wasn't weighed down quite as much as it had been. The cuff with the chain was still on her wrist, but the bar at the other end must have slipped off. There was more of a main road ahead, perpendicular to the street she was on. A yellow light glowed a few blocks away on the left, while a faint red light was in the farther distance on the right. She sloshed toward them, more frantically, the colder water up to her midriff now. Her legs were starting to go numb. It felt like she was in the no-man's-land of a war zone, no side willing to claim her.

A part of her just wanted to give up, stop moving, and sink to the bottom. But the baby kept squirming and poking, insistently reminding her that she had to think for two now. She took a deep breath and tried swimming toward the street corner, doing a kind of half-assed breast stroke, the one she'd learned at the Y.

Unmanned boats jostled with drifting cars on the avenue. Sirens wailed behind the almost-solid curtain of rain, signs of life buried deeper in the night. She clawed toward them, gasping and snorting after she put her face in the brackish water. A shower of sparks fell from a tower up ahead, as if a transformer had just blown out.

She stopped short and tried to stand again, afraid of what would happen if a live power line fell in the water. Would every living thing get electrocuted?

She gave out a long, fierce, inarticulate scream, a gutbucket howl of terror and frustration. When it was done, she heard other human voices. Not answering her, but calling out to each other. The water had receded a little, to just below her waist, and she fought the current as she splashed to the corner. She looked right and saw flashlight beams swinging and searching. It looked like a scene from *Titanic*. A half-dozen people were clinging to a long rope stretched across the avenue, hanging on to each other and dear life in the floodwaters. She called out, like she was trying to rejoin the human race.

A wave knocked her sideways and pushed her under. She flailed and bubbled beneath the surface as it dragged her along, glimpsing a baby doll and a wicker chair as her eyes opened underwater.

When she finally found her feet again, the people were no longer in sight. She was in another part of the neighborhood. The water was only up to her hips here. But her body was that much more exhausted from the effort. She began to weep from having been so close to rescue, her tears indistinguishable from the rain. She now realized the roar she'd been hearing was from the street drains overwhelmed by the deluge, the mouths only able to take in so much.

But then she saw another light in the distance, less steady than the yellow one she'd seen earlier. It was so faint and flickering at first that she thought it might be a boat getting tossed across the bay. But then it began to grow stronger as it leveled off and came toward her. It split, defining itself as a pair of headlights, one seemingly brighter than the other. A car with a driver in it, heavier and sturdier than the ones she'd seen floating away. Maybe a Jeep or a Land Rover or a truck of some kind.

She raised her arms, praying it would stop and pick her up. She remembered the people she'd just seen clinging to the lifeline and to each other. She'd tried to tell herself that was the brighter light of human nature. That more people would help you than harm you, given a choice. That even most of the men who'd paid her for sex were just lonely and desperate, and no more cruel than they had to be. Some were even kind enough to give her a ride when she needed one. It was her own fault for drawing the darkness around her. But that was over now. There was a life growing inside her. She was no longer blocking the blessings. She threw her arms up as the high beams washed over her like a movie star.

The car stopped about ten yards in front of her and the driver's side door opened. She saw the silhouette of a man getting out and coming toward her.

"Renee," he said.

The water she was standing in seemed to get warm and then become instantly frigid. She turned and started to run.

46

Joey had two separate files open on his desk when Officer Octavio Ramirez came in and closed the door behind him.

"Have a seat, officer. This shouldn't take long."

Ramirez settled before him, a boxy man with a round face and a flat affectless stare that had probably served him well on the handful of undercover gang assignments noted in his file. But that burgeoning paunch was clear visual evidence to his chief that the officer had spent too much inactive time in his car for highway patrol or sitting around the dinner table with his extended Mexican family in Brentwood.

"Sir?"

Joey donned a pair of reading glasses, turned the pages of the personnel file, and stroked his mustache thoughtfully. "How you doing there, Octavio?"

"Fine, sir. Thank you for asking."

"Not too bothered from the fallout of that Robles arrest, are you?"

"No, sir. Bad press comes with the territory. Like you always say."

A part of Joey still wondered if he should have had Charlie Maslow or some other mid-level supervisor handling this conversation. To put another layer of insulation and deniability between what was said in this office and what was done on the street. Usually it was better if the buck stopped *there*, not here. Management 101. But he'd been through this before, and the cost-benefit analysis said to limit the circle. Don't bring in more eyes and ears than you need to.

"I just want you to know how much I appreciate your dedication and discretion," Joey said. "And I want to continue to encourage you to take the sergeant's exam, to move you up in the ranks."

"Thank you, sir." Ramirez nodded. "I'm planning on it."

"Meantime, I have another job for you."

Ramirez became very still in a way that reminded Joey of how livestock acted right before they got a second branding mark.

"Sir?"

Joey liked the way the officer's voice changed as he spoke. The little servile upturn. Like he knew that despite his uniform and the house he'd worked so hard to give his family, he could be reduced to Mexican peasant status in the blink of an eye.

Joey opened the first file and held up the Missing Persons alert. "Officer, have you seen this notice before?"

"Yes, sir." Ramirez took the printout. "We've had it for several months. Like most of the other police departments in our area."

"Do you recognize the woman in the picture?"

Ramirez dutifully narrowed his eyes. "Not personally, sir. But I'm assuming she's a relative of the woman we arrested on the highway. There's a family resemblance."

"It's Detective Robles's sister, Ysabel. We have reason to believe she was working as an escort on the Island at some point in the last eight or so months. I want you to ramp up the search for her. I know you have contacts at some of the local homeless shelters and outreach centers in the various communities."

"Yes, sir. My wife works in a soup kitchen and my sister-in-law is involved with a number of church groups."

"I know that," Joey said. "And these are resources most of our regular Anglo officers don't have. Maybe some of the local day laborers have been with her. Maybe she's been living on the streets or sleeping in someone's van. I want you to tap into those resources immediately. I'm sure you have a group of officers you can trust to assist in this. If they can keep their mouths shut, there's money in the budget for them."

"Sir, shouldn't we be doing that anyway in partnership with the other departments?"

"Octavio, ol' buddy, can I let my hair down a little?" Joey smiled, passing his hand over his shaved pate. "This needs to be done off the books. Do you understand?"

"Sir?"

"If you find her, I don't want her put into the system. I want her brought to me and I want no official paper trail on her. Understood?"

It was no easy task reading Ramirez's slightly squashed expression with his small black eyes hiding deep in their prematurely weathered sockets. A man who'd retreated deep inside himself to attend to his private sorrows.

"Sir," he said after a long pause. "Is that all right to do?"

"I'm your chief. I'm directing you to do it."

"I understand—but permission to speak freely?" Ramirez waited for the chief's nod. "I could get in a lot of trouble for that, couldn't I?"

"Why's that?"

"I mean, there's already a lot of questions about the highway stop we did with Detective Robles. I don't want to get put in a position where I get fired and then can't get hired by another department."

Joe reached for the second file, having guessed pretty much where this bump in the road would come.

"Officer Ramirez," he said. "Haven't we discussed the tragic death of your son recently?"

"Yes, sir." Ramirez swallowed. "Heriberto got hit while he was helping my brother change a tire on the Southern State Parkway last year. It's one of the reasons I asked to get transferred to the highway unit. To make sure things like that don't happen to someone else's children."

"Very admirable." The chief nodded. 'I spent a lot of time on highway patrol myself. Important work out here."

"Yes, sir."

"And have we discussed the other family you have living with you?" Joey took his time removing the letter from the school board in his file. "An Eduardo *Cardenas*. Am I saying that right?"

Joey smiled as if he was proud of pronouncing the name with an appropriate Spanish flourish, though truly he was more enjoying the way Ramirez was beginning to shift and cross his ankles with unease.

"The son of my aunt," Ramirez mumbled. "He's a good boy."

"Yes, it's coming back to me." Joey nodded as he pretended to read.

"Ten years old, smuggled here from Juarez. Better prepared than most. Speaks good English. Works at your wife's flower store on weekends. Able to handle eighth-grade-level math . . ."

"Yes, sir, and I'm grateful that you didn't report him to Immigration earlier," Ramirez said, referencing the conversation they'd had right before the chief ordered him to pull over Robles on the highway.

Joey took his time turning to the next page and drawing out the officer's discomfort. "And look at this. It says here that he's keeping up with kids four years older than him at your son's old middle school. His math teacher says he's killing it in trigonometry."

Ramirez turned sideways and looked out the window, as if he was starting to see where this was going. "*Que deseas?*" he murmured. *What do you want?*

"The problem is that Immigration is tightening up a lot lately. Before it was just a matter of nobody going out of their way to report him. But now that he's in the school system, he's much more vulnerable to deportation. It says here that his math teacher admitted the boy was here illegally and was going to school under your dead son's name when she was questioned by another cop responding to a recent incident at the school building. Is that true, Officer Ramirez?"

"Chief, I think I'd like to talk to my union lawyer."

"Now let's not get too carried away." The chief took off his reading glasses. "Obviously, you're trying to do right by your people, taking this poor kid in and giving him chances your own son never had."

Ramirez took a long breath in through his nose, knowing the dive was only getting deeper. "Sir?"

"The worst-case scenario for your family is that this gets played by the book, and our police department reports this child who's here illegally to ICE and he gets deported back to a war zone. I'm sure you're aware that we're living in a time when the president is threatening to withhold federal funding from sanctuary cities. A lot of people could suffer for that."

"I do understand that, sir." Ramirez nodded as if an unseen hand was on the back of his neck.

"So what shall we do?" The chief spread his arms, in mock bewilderment. "Shall we break the law and look the other way all the time? Knowing that thousands of dangerous criminals flood into our country because of lax border enforcement? Or do we think about this more humanely and try to make the occasional exception to the rule?"

Ramirez bowed his head. "Sir, I'm hoping we can find a way to let the boy stay," he said.

"You do know that would involve bending the rules, officer. Don't you?"

"Yes, sir."

"So you believe it's necessary sometimes to bend the rules to do the right thing?"

"I do."

"Then you're an intelligent officer and intelligent officers can do well under this administration," Joey said, shoving the Missing Persons notice back at Ramirez. "This person could help an investigation we're conducting. We need to find her as soon as possible, by any means necessary. And we need it quietly. *Comprende, amigo?*"

"Yes, sir. I understand."

There was almost no chance that Ramirez would be recording this conversation, given the situation with the nephew living here under an assumed name, but it never hurt to measure your words. Ramirez got up to leave and then stopped.

"Sir?" he asked. "Does this mean we should keep the boy home from school so he doesn't get picked up by ICE?"

"Of course not." The chief waved him off and went back to his paperwork. "Keep sending him. This is America. He can be anything he wants."

47

OCTOBER
2012

Plunger got the call right as the storm was hitting, boats rocking at the marina, weather people in ponchos on the TV. But here was "the Chief" on the line, pushing his buttons, telling him to put his galoshes on. There was another girl on the loose, and if someone else found her first, it was going to be a problem.

Just like that, Joey could reach past thirty-five years, through the double-glazed storm windows of a two-story woodframe house in Atlantic Beach where the mortgage had just been paid off, and into a recently renovated kitchen that was equipped with jugs of fresh water and flashlights with fresh batteries in case the power went out. Just like that, he could pull the string and make his old friend Plunger feel like they were back in the woods behind the football field, covered in clammy sweat, bugs crawling all over his arms and mosquitoes buzzing around his ears. Another lifetime but still on the hook for it.

Plunger found his raincoat and made sure there was gas in the generator and food that wouldn't spoil for the rest of the family. Then he got his keys, climbed into the Land Rover he used to take the kids to soccer practice, and drove out into the miasma.

The wipers could barely go fast enough to clear away the fat drops blotting his windshield. Maybe ten feet of visibility even with the fog lights on. Not another soul on the road. Who in their right mind would be out on a night like this anyway? Every time the wipers cleared his view for a half second, it looked like the world was getting washed away. Black sky, roiling mist, smeared red lights through the glass.

He prayed the Atlantic Beach drawbridge would be up and give him an excuse not to make it into Rockaway. It looked like Reynolds Channel was overflowing onto Bay Boulevard and Rescue Road. But no, goddamn it, both sides were down. Because what kind of lunatic would be out trying to pilot a boat during a hurricane? Only someone who had absolutely no choice except to obey. A human toilet implement thrust down into the muck to suck out some hideous problem no one else would touch. He dropped down to ten miles an hour, visibility down to maybe three feet, as he edged across the span, wipers on double time, water halfway over his wheels, as he tried not to lose control and crash into the side rails. The lights were on at the toll plaza but the booths were unmanned as he steered around the barriers, heart in his mouth so he could almost taste his own blood.

Far Rockaway looked post-apocalyptic as he made the turn onto Seagirt Boulevard. Rowboats and garbage cans floating in the streets, stray trash bobbing on the surface, lighter cars drifting unmoored into his path. There was an orange glow in the sky to the west and between weather updates 10-10 WINS on his radio said houses were on fire in Breezy Point, at the other end of the peninsula. Plunger's vehicle kept hydroplaning as he followed the directions Joey had given him, the Land Rover threatening to spin off the road and into a lamppost, or maybe someone's living room.

This was madness. The ocean and the bay were joining together over the peninsula, and his headlights were nearly underwater. Even if he did manage to make it to the address, the girl would surely be gone with the tides. Probably facedown and drowned somewhere. And therefore no longer a problem. He made the turn onto Rockaway Beach Boulevard and thought of turning around. But then the water began to recede a little and he saw a lone figure in the distance, a staggering silhouette in his high beams.

He kept his speed at a steady twenty miles an hour, going over ruts and potholes, afraid he'd stall out if he went slower. Lank dripping hair told him it was probably a girl. Pale brown. Holding her arms out at her sides, with a handcuff and a chain off one wrist. Looking around in a daze, as if she didn't know where she was. Wearing an oversized white t-shirt, like the one J had described. Tiny and hollow-eyed. Under normal circumstances she'd be as scary as a sparrow. But in these conditions, she was a grotesque incomprehensible thing that had to be destroyed.

She froze in his headlights as the water cleared enough for him to stop. He got out of the car slowly and left the motor running, so he wouldn't have trouble starting it again.

She was younger than he'd expected. And softer looking. He thought J preferred hard, angry women who wouldn't be missed by anybody. But this one was a heartbreaker. Which was what made her a danger to both of them.

He said her name evenly, hoping it would relax her and make it easier to get her in the car. Instead her bony shoulders went back and her eyes went wide. Like he was the monster, not her.

She turned and ran away through the ankle-deep water. He tried to slosh after her as she disappeared around a corner, but his tennis knee wasn't having it. He doubled back to the Land Rover and went slowly after her, narrowly avoiding collision with a floating chunk of boardwalk and a woman pushing a surfboard with two pet carriers strapped to it.

He was on a side street, not far from the beach, the rain still loud and heavy as wreckage falling on his roof. Even with the handcuff chain, the girl had somehow managed to make it across a lawn and onto the front porch of the only house on the street that had lights. The sight of her frail, sopping figure under the bulb caused a wild churning panic to take hold of him. If she made it inside, it would all be over. Everything they'd constructed since that night behind the football field. The dream of the lives they'd had. All wiped out and swept away, leaving the hideous foundation exposed.

Plunger watched her ring the bell and hug herself as she waited for a response. His own sense of powerlessness at this moment made him want to throw up all over the steering wheel. If he ran up and tried to grab her, her scream would open the door or bring neighbors running from the watery shadows.

All he could do was cut his headlights and wait, with the engine idling. He saw her lift one bare foot and then the other. Even from twenty yards' distance, he could see how dark and wrinkled the soles were from walking in the street. She was pregnant. Why hadn't Joey told him? The water was getting deep again, lapping against the sides of his vehicle. This was it. They were done for. No one would turn away a woman carrying a baby in the middle of a hurricane.

She sank into a squat. Whatever pity he'd felt for her turned inward. Why had he been put in this position? Why was it *his job* to clean up this mess after so many years? Hadn't he paid up already? Didn't he have a right to go on and live his own life, give or take a few lapses of his own? Why was he being forced to go back to where he'd been?

In an instant, the girl on the porch became the monster again. A bitch, really. Who wouldn't stop running her mouth, so someone had to stop it for her.

She stood up and leaned against the door, lips moving, trying to make her problem into the problem of whoever was inside. Then she looked over her shoulder, knowing he was out in the street, waiting for her, even with his lights off. His engine heaved and grumbled, restless from all this idling. She put a hand against the door, like she was starting to plead. The engine revved, as he accidentally touched the gas pedal. She looked back at him, turned to the door, said something else, threw her head back in despair, and darted back out into the street, trying to stay ahead of him in the blackening rain.

48

Even during apple season, with trees along the highway turning umber and crimson and Kendrick popping on the speakers, Lourdes hated driving upstate. Nothing against nature. But the smell of gas fumes made her carsick as she remembered the endless bus trips with Izzy and her mother to see Papi in the prison, where he was just beginning his twenty-five-to-life bid for killing another dealer. If shame and bad memories weren't enough to keep her guts constantly agitated, a general sense of paranoia would do the rest.

No one else on the task force wanted to make the three-hour-plus drive because (A) there and back was the better part of a day tour; (B) most of them had already reached their overtime caps; (C) it seemed like a long shot that anything would come of visiting either address; and (D) the Chief of D's had just laid the lumber to her, so anyone with a lick of sense was keeping their distance.

The first stop was a large, bright yellow house in Saratoga Springs on what looked like a horse farm, near the National Museum of Racing. It had tall hedges, a Western-style fence and gate, a corral in back, a dog kennel big enough for a family in Sunset Park, and a garden that was twice as big as the one Delaney Patterson had been tending in the Bronx, with a watering system elaborate enough that it could have kept Papi and his fellow inmates hydrated all day long.

There was a security system with a camera by the gate, but Lourdes happened to catch the lady of the house easing a white Lexus SUV out of the two-car garage.

"Excuse me." She came up to the driver's side. "Are you Beth Carter?"

She'd gone in blind, with no ID photo on file, just a common name, a birth date, and a forwarding address from a forwarding address, thoughtfully provided to the NYPD by the U.S. Postal Service.

"Who are you?" the woman at the wheel said. "What do you want?"

She was a blonde and a little horse-faced, Lourdes thought. The darkness of her sunglasses emphasized the whiteness of her teeth. A lady in her sixties who'd had some pretty good work done, cosmetically speaking, and took some care with her body.

"We were hoping you could assist us with an investigation." Lourdes showed her badge. "I promise it won't take long."

"I was married to a police officer," Beth Carter said, removing any doubt that Lourdes had the right woman. "I know what a cop's promise is worth."

"We wouldn't be bothering you if it wasn't for an important case—"

"Is this about the chief?" Beth Carter interrupted her.

"Not necessarily." Lourdes tried the soft sell. "We're just looking at some things that happened on Long Island—"

"I'm not interested." Beth Carter cut in again, refusing to let Lourdes get into a rhythm.

"Excuse me?"

"I said, I'm not interested in speaking to you. And if you had a warrant, you would have shown it to me already. I haven't lived on Long Island for a long time and I don't talk about Joseph Tolliver."

Lourdes consciously ducked her head low, so she appeared to be looking up, asking for help woman to woman. "Can I ask why not?"

"No, you can't." Beth Carter reached for her gearshift. "You're on my property, in my driveway. I expect you gone by the time I get back. If you're not, I'll call the police on you."

The second stop was even more of a long shot. A ramshackle farmhouse just outside the town of Colonie, with a fire-damaged roof, a small patchy lawn, and unsupervised chickens wandering around like recently paroled prisoners who didn't know what to do with their freedom.

The woman Lourdes was talking to was decidedly more welcoming. Although Shauna Martinez lived only a little over half an hour away from

Beth Carter and was at least twenty-five years younger, she looked like someone from another, harder country. A weather-beaten face, thatchy, home-cut hair, and a body thick from bad diet and hard farmwork.

"I have to be honest," she told Lourdes in a husky voice, turning her squint toward the sun. "I never really understood what my mother was up to."

She looked about as likely a Martinez as Lourdes would have been a Kelly or an O'Connor. All the Spanish must have been on the father's side. Another jailbird, according to Lourdes's preliminary research: like her own papi.

"She never mentioned this Long Island case to you?" Lourdes asked.

"Oh, she talked about it all the time." Shauna let out a raspy laugh. "But if you ask me, was anybody listening? I'd have to say no."

"What'd she say about it?"

"To be honest, I don't remember much." Shauna wagged and turned her face to the afternoon sun. "I was twelve, thirteen, fourteen years old while most of this was going on. I didn't want my mother to solve Watergate. I wanted her to be my mom and take me to the mall, help me buy makeup. But that's not what I got from her."

"That must've been really hard." Lourdes gave her a sympathetic nod, even though she was impatient to get down to business here.

"She wasn't what you'd call a real girly girl." Shauna waved dismissively. "Even when she loosened up, she was more into playing ball with my brothers. I'd have to say she was driven. Especially since she was surrounded by men who she felt she had to prove herself to. In fact, there's something about you that reminds me of her."

"Is there?"

Lourdes forced a smile.

"Not that I'm saying you're not feminine or a good mother or anything." Shauna patted the air apologetically. "I hope you don't take that the wrong way."

"Of course not." Lourdes wrinkled her nose at the smell of hay and goat shit from the animal pen beside the house.

"It's just a certain fixed look in your eye."

"Anyway, we were talking about Long Island," Lourdes prompted.

"Yeah, she was obsessed with that case. Every night after dinner, she'd disappear upstairs with her files. And every morning, I'd come down for school with my brothers, and she'd be at the kitchen table with her coffee and folders. To tell you the truth, I think it's part of what drove her and my father apart. Because she was spending all this time reading police records and looking at these disgusting crime scene photos. And it was left to him to make us lunch for school and help us with our homework. Which he had no business doing, let me tell you. He was a mechanic, not a scholar. And then, after they got divorced, he was just a mess. But instead of stopping and asking what she was doing, she just got deeper into the case. Like the work was sustaining her as much as her family. I guess you think that sounds harsh, right?"

"It is what it is," Lourdes said: the police officer's koan. "If you don't mind my asking, how long after she passed was it before your father got locked up?"

"Not long." Shauna glanced over, momentarily distracted by the desultory braying of the goats. "The police zeroed in on my father right away. He'd been fighting with my mom about alimony and child support. He left all these stupid threatening messages on her voicemail, and they buried him at the trial."

"He got found guilty?" Lourdes said. "He didn't take a plea?"

"On his deathbed, he swore to me that he didn't do it. And it's only now that I believe him." Shauna shook her head. "For twenty years, I wouldn't go see him. Tore our whole family apart. Or whatever was left of it. Me and my brothers turned on each other, fighting over what was left. That's how it is with family, sometimes. Right? The less there is to share, the more you fight over it."

Lourdes nodded and watched the goats nudging each other with their horns to get at a tin can in a corner of the pen. She realized now that the original trouble with Izzy had started when she was just a kid, soon after their father got himself locked up. Before she'd just been the adoring little sister, shyly asking to borrow Lourdes's hairbrush and happy to snuggle whenever Lourdes decided to be generous and lie next to her, reading Goosebumps until they both fell asleep.

"So sorry to keep coming back to these cases, but I know your mother wrote one report for the state investigations commission and she was

working on another one later," Lourdes said. "As far as you know, did
that second investigation end when she died?"

"Yes, as far as I know." Shauna nodded. "It's not like any of her kids
were going to pick up the trail. I work at a Walmart when I'm not trying
to keep the house from falling down. And one of my brothers just works
on his motorcycle in Arizona and I don't know what the other is doing in
New Mexico, but I'm sure it's not police work."

"So that's it. All that work she put in and there's nothing left behind?"

No way to prove that Tolliver might have ruined yet another set of
lives, even though Lourdes sensed he was part of this. She should have
known it would be a waste of time, trying to retrace another cop's foot-
steps. Even another female cop. Twenty-one years since Leslie's murder.
People forget. Time is a beast. It devours everything.

"Well." Shauna sighed. "I wouldn't say 'nothing.'"

Ten minutes later, they were in an attic crawl space, the smell of cedar
heavy in the air, yellow foamy insulation hanging down in clumps, a Ha-
vahart trap big enough for a raccoon by Lourdes's feet, and a few stray
shoe boxes lined up against a wall.

"I don't know why I still keep these." Shauna aimed a flashlight beam.
"I've thrown out most of my mother's files and the fire a few years ago
got most of the others."

"Still looks like a fair amount of material," Lourdes said. "Are these
her files and notebooks?"

"Oh my God, it filled the whole attic. You didn't use to be able to
move up here. You're not getting the picture—when I say my mother was
obsessive, I mean she was a pack rat. She never threw anything away.
These days, I think we'd call her a 'hoarder.' In fact, I'm starting to worry
I may have inherited it from her. I'd hate to have you see what I've done
in the basement."

"So you don't mind if I have a look at these?" Lourdes said, trying to
contain the growing excitement that had turned Mitchell off the other
day.

"Knock yourself out." Shauna shrugged. "You'd be doing me a favor
if you hauled some of it away. Just leave any photos of her that you might
find. I don't have that many."

"Thank you," Lourdes said, gripping the daughter's wrist a little too urgently. "I promise I'll do right by her."

"Make yourself at home." Shauna handed her the flashlight. "I'll make us a late lunch."

The daughter left the attic, slowly descending the rickety stairs, as Lourdes directed the flashlight at the remnants of the archive, crooked stacks of loose-lidded boxes that reminded her of the charts she'd set up in Mitchell's spare room. Make yourself at home, Shauna had said. *I already am home,* Lourdes thought.

49

Joey had his head in his hands for an uncomfortably long time.

At least it was uncomfortable if you were alone in the garage with him and the silence had been going for three minutes and counting.

"Help me understand what happened here," he said.

It was maybe an hour before dawn. Outside, most of the water had receded back into the bay and the ocean, leaving sand dunes in the streets and the beach strewn with kitchen appliances. Soon, people would return and begin the hideous business of looking at where they used to live and figuring out what it would take to get back to the way things were.

"I'm serious." Joey finally raised his head. "Explain to me how we got in this position."

Plunger looked over at the girl in the rowboat, half-covered in a plastic tarp, gravel spilling out of her mouth.

"All I told you was find her, bring her back to the house," Joey said.

Plunger laced his hands behind his neck, elbows out like bat wings. His joints were aching and his clothes still felt cold and damp from being out in the flooded streets.

"I don't know what to tell you, J. I did the best I could with circumstances. *You weren't there.* I was."

"I wasn't there because I had a thousand fucking jobs to do at once, keeping people in my community safe." Joey raised a finger. "You had one job. *One.*"

"I know . . ." Plunger rubbed his long white hands together, wondering if the chill would ever leave his bones.

"Jesus." Joey rubbed a corner of his eye. "If you just left her facedown in the street, like she'd drowned, no one would've questioned it . . ."

"Got it . . ."

"Instead she's got these rocks stuffed down her throat that we'll never get out? What were you thinking?"

"I said, I *know*. What do you want me to do, J?"

"*Again*. How could it have happened again?"

Plunger got up and made himself go over to look at her. It wasn't necessarily true that she could have passed as a regular drowning victim. Her face was too bruised and abraded from the struggle after he'd finally caught up to her in the neighbor's gravel driveway. Her clothes were torn from his thrashing around in the water with her. His right index finger was cut and throbbing from one of the many times she'd bitten him.

"I was just trying to control her when she started screaming her head off and I was afraid someone was coming out of the house. So I grabbed whatever was around me to shut her up."

"*Twice*." Joey's voice rang out. "How could it happen twice? They say history never repeats."

"I don't know, J. I panicked. I guess maybe I even flashed back."

"What the fuck are you talking about, you flashed back? Where do you think you were? Vietnam?"

"Feels that way sometimes," Plunger mumbled.

"What was that?"

Plunger bit his lip, still trying to sort through it all himself. At the moment, everything was blended together and mixed up in his mind, like it was all going on simultaneously. What happened with Kim and what happened with the one last night. Girls with red open mouths screaming bloody murder. J said they had to shut her up that night behind the football field. Especially since Plunger had already hit her over the head with a rock, and she didn't go down. She was yelling that she was going to tell everyone everything. It would have brought the whole shit house crashing down on all of them. A hand over her mouth couldn't keep her quiet. She sank her teeth into Plunger's palm and drew blood. And even Joey strangling her didn't stop the noise. So Plunger had panicked and grabbed a handful of grass. She looked so shocked when he shoved it in her mouth that she didn't have time to close her teeth. She'd started thrashing and fighting him, so he grabbed another handful of twigs and leaves and pushed them inside. By then, Joey was on top of her, holding her down, as they both went into a frenzy, shoveling more and more. Stop her up to shut her up. When she tried to clamp her jaws shut, Joey pried them open. Always was a strong bastard.

And the truth was, Plunger had gotten sort of turned on doing it. They both had, though they never talked about it. But man, it was a powerful feeling. That look in her eyes when she knew they were going to keep jamming things in until she couldn't breathe. Nothing had ever gotten him off like that since. Thirty-five years.

"I want to ask you something," said J, taking a deep breath like he was having a hard time with this. "And I want you to tell me the truth."

"What?"

"Did you do it on purpose?"

"No, J. I told you. I saw her. Then she ran away from the house screaming and I went after her, trying to get her to calm down and be quiet. Then what happened . . . happened. She wouldn't stop fighting me. I'm sorry."

"I'm saying, did you do it this way deliberately?" J was pointing at the girl's mouth. "With the stones. So people would know."

"What are you asking?" Plunger bunched up his fists close to his chest, his voice geeky with outrage.

"You did it on purpose. Didn't you? So people would remember Kim and you could point the finger at me and say I did both of them."

"J, what are you talking about? That's nuts."

Joey pulled a Glock 17 from his waistband and aimed it at Plunger's head. "Then tell me why you did it."

"I don't know, J. It was an accident."

Joey pulled back the slide and took a step, so the barrel was less than a foot from Plunger's face. "Tell me the truth. You did it because you're jealous."

"Joey, no. I wasn't trying to fuck it up."

"But you did fuck it up. Like you were trying to get us both caught. And it's not the first time."

"What are you talking about?"

"Brittany Forster. You sick fuck. Fifteen-year-old with a missing sister. I know you called her up, pretending to be me."

"*Brittany Forster?* Seriously? After all this time? You're calling me out about that after what you did to the sister?"

"You don't talk about what I did—okay?" Joey yelled, both hands on the grip, neck veins popping. "Let's talk about what you've been doing. Those last couple girls they found near the highway? Miriam in Jones Beach? Yelina in the wildlife refuge? I didn't have anything to do with those. In fact, I haven't done any of them since two thousand fucking six."

"You think it was me, J?"

"Yeah, I fucking think it was you, trying to get free rides on my ticket. You almost blew up both of us, because you're a fucking freak. I should do *you* right now."

"Dude, you're wrong."

"Then who else could it have been." J looked at the girl in the rowboat. "You did this one, didn't you?"

"Just put the gun down. We're talking here."

"Were you trying to punish me, for treating you like the bitch you are? Is this your way of getting even?"

"I said I'm sorry, J." Plunger put a hand in front of his face, trying not to cry. "I don't know why it happened again."

"Is that supposed to *reassure* me?"

They were close enough that he could see Joey's knuckle turn white as it tightened around the trigger.

"Dude, don't kill me," Plunger begged him. "Seriously. We've been friends forever. You know I'll help you make this right."

Joey was still holding the gun steady and looking at him in that insane, implacable way, like nothing you could possibly say would get through to him. Right on the edge of doing it. Plunger could almost smell the discharge from the gun and the odor of his own blood, like his death had already occurred.

"You don't want to be dealing with two bodies on your own," Plunger said. "Remember the insulin girl? Remember Albany? You're better off with me than without me."

"I must be getting soft." Joey nicked him on the tip of the nose with the muzzle. "Because I really should get rid of you right now."

"Please, man. I'll owe you for life. More than I already do."

Reluctantly, J stuck the gun back in his waistband and Plunger saw that the chief looked almost as badly shaken as he was.

"You need to get your shit on a leash, pronto," he said. "This isn't the first time you've crossed the line."

"*I* crossed the line? Joey, what about what you do?"

"I said, you do *not* get to talk about what I do." Joey shoved him. "You're the sick one here. What I do isn't like that, and hasn't been for a long time. I keep my dog on a leash and under the porch. In fact, it's none of your concern what I do."

"Until you make it my concern. How long is it going to be like this?"

"Forever, bro. You know it's true. We're in it together. It's always been this way and it's always going to be this way. And don't pretend you never got anything out of it yourself."

They both stopped talking. There were pings and drips on the tin roof of the garage, as if the rain was about to start up again. Then sounds of leaking and seeping. Plunger realized it was just more water draining away outside, offering a clearer view of the wreckage left by the storm.

Joey looked at the girl again, as the smell of garage mildew began to mix with the odors of body secretions, drawing flies. An unfamiliar look of melancholy had crossed his face.

"I didn't want to lose this one," he mumbled.

"What's that?"

"Never mind." Joey shook the mood off, moving his mustache around as if trying to remember how it fit with the rest of his face. "We have to deal with this mess now."

"What's 'we'? I'm done."

"You're done when I say you're done. And you're never going to be done, as long as there's no statute of limitations on murder. Remember you were the one who hit Kim first, because she was gonna tell your daddy what you did and what you really are."

"It's different now, J. I've got a life."

Joey grabbed him by the throat and squeezed it lightly. "Pull yourself together. Okay? This isn't just about you, or me. We're servants of a community that's been in a natural disaster. People are depending on us. So we're going to make this problem go away, like it never happened. And then we're going to go back to being who the people need us to be, to come back from this."

"Who they *need us to be*?" Plunger pulled away and touched the side of his neck. "Joey, if anybody finds out about this, we're dead. You and me. And we're gonna take a lot of other people down with us."

"Then we better make sure no one finds out. Right?"

Joey turned back to the boat, knelt down and folded the tarp over the girl with a kind of fastidious tenderness.

He wouldn't burn this one. He'd seen what happened when the fire department came too quickly with Angela Spinelli. And he wouldn't dump her in the Pine Barrens or leave her in a car like he did with some of the others. He'd make sure that she remained more or less intact. And then he would put her some place deep where no one would ever find her, but he would always know where she was. And maybe come visit some time. It would be his secret and sacred place. Not just another trophy, but a memoriam, to show why he was more than the Gacys and Zodiacs of the world. He could be human. If he wanted to be.

"Fucking storm," he said softly. "Help me clean this up. I need to call my insurance company and see how much coverage I have."

50

"So why'd you have a handicap bar in your basement, chief?"

A week after her visit with the Martinez daughter, Lourdes was at a state police facility in Riverhead, watching from behind the one-way glass as B.B. and Jason Tierney from the Nassau County police interviewed Joseph Tolliver. An attorney had just arrived to represent the chief: Brendan O'Mara, former assistant district attorney from Suffolk County, now counsel to the police supervisors' union.

"You want to run that by me again, Detective Borrelli?" Tolliver frowned, creating ridges up to the crown of his stubbly scalp.

Lourdes was beyond ballistic when she was told B.B. was going to be in on this interrogation. But what could she do? There was no proof that he'd told the Suffolk people about her background before she got pulled over. And as Chief Pritzker pointed out in a blistering text to Lourdes, B.B. was almost as familiar with the details of the case as she was. Just the same, she no longer trusted Borrelli and as she watched him slide a folder across the table to Tolliver and his attorney, she had a queasy draining sensation in the pit of her stomach, like she was about to see state secrets given away to a mortal enemy.

"Chief, you filed a claim with the Allstate insurance company for a flood at a home you inherited from your father in Rockaway, Queens," B.B. said.

"And you know that how?" the lawyer interrupted.

"We'll get to that." B.B. reached across to open the file and turned several pages. "Look here. It says the claims adjustor inspected the basement and found holes, which you said were there for a handicap bar you'd put in because your father was having trouble walking toward the end of his life."

"Yeah." Tolliver tugged at the side of his mustache. "My father developed ALS before he died. You're going to make that a crime?"

"Definitely not." B.B. said. "But the thing is, no steps to the basement. No elevator. No chairlift. And no additional handicap bar near the bathroom. Doesn't that seem a little odd?"

"Only if you're looking to make it seem bad." Tolliver uncrossed his arms, a man with nothing to hide. "Obviously I took the stairs out after my father died because I was in the process of renovating and converting the whole house into a rental before the storm hit. I applied to change the certificate of occupancy as soon as I got the settlement from the insurance company."

"But you took the stairs out *before* the hurricane caused the flood?" Tierney asked, a little too much buttonhook in the question for Lourdes's taste.

"Yeah, you got me." Tolliver raised his hands. "Guilty of starting the work without a C of O. That certainly justifies all the time and expense you and Detective Robles have wasted on investigating me and my department."

"Okay, but you had a fully plumbed bathroom in a basement without stairs?" B.B. affected confusion.

"Wait a second." Brendan O'Mara put an arm in front of Tolliver to prevent him from answering. "You still haven't told us where all of this is coming from. By what conceivable method did you even access this information about the insurance settlement?"

"We just got a subpoena to look at the chief's financial records." Tierney handed the lawyer the document. "It's all right there for your reading pleasure, counselor."

"Hang on." Brendan shook his head. "We got this quashed. You have no probable cause to get into any of this."

He was a milky-looking man in his fifties with streaks of gray and a softening chin that gave him a vague resemblance to pictures Lourdes had seen of his father, Philip. Even in his gray attorney suit and red power tie, there was something a little boyish and self-conscious about him. Like he still had to remind himself to shake hands firmly and look people straight in the eye.

"Actually, we do have probable cause." B.B. leaned forward quickly and clasped his hands, his polished rings shining under the fluorescent lights. "You're talking about the old subpoena. We refiled and got a new one based on information we just developed. Read it and weep."

While Brendan donned a pair of half glasses, B.B. threw a look at the one-way. Lourdes had to admit Borrelli was doing a good job here. If he kept this up, she might have to start trusting him again. A little. Maybe he'd just slipped up earlier with Tolliver because he was trying to get his kid a job and didn't realize the full monstrosity of the situation they were facing yet.

Now Tolliver followed B.B.'s glance and gave a slow baleful headshake as if he could see Lourdes on the other side of the glass.

"You should all be ashamed." Brendan set the subpoena aside. "The chief is one of the finest, most upstanding law enforcement officials I've ever known and you're using these flimsy excuses to dig through his service record and personal information to try to find dirt. And you men call yourselves professionals?"

Tolliver mumbled something that sounded suspiciously like "The men aren't the problem."

"What's that, chief?" B.B. asked.

"Leave it alone, J." Brendan put his arm out again. "I'm seriously beginning to question the purpose of this interview. If you had enough to make an arrest, you would have done it already."

Bogdan, the FBI agent on the task force, had finally arrived in the observation area. He gave Lourdes a nod and she knocked on the door of the interview room before she entered, holding a file.

"Counselor, can we get a word with you outside?" she asked.

"I think we better." Brendan stood up. "This little discussion has gone way beyond the parameters of what we agreed to."

"We hear you." She put the file in front of her mouth. "We'll just be a minute, chief."

"No discussion while I'm gone." Brendan threw a glance around the room. "My client doesn't answer questions if I'm not here."

Lourdes turned to lead the way out, just as she saw a flicker of a know-ing smile on the chief's face. Like he'd figured all along that she had to be behind all of this.

"Just over here, counselor." Bogdan was standing by an open door across the hall. "We ordered a coffee for you. We know it's been a long day already."

Brendan had brought his briefcase with him. He was the type who would have carried an official-looking bag just like this even in grade school. The DA's kid. Not just a former prosecutor himself, but the son of Kenny Makris's predecessor Philip O'Mara. The pieces were beginning to fit together.

Brendan entered and looked around the barren little room, with three chairs and one table, and then took the seat closest to the door. Not an alpha dog, but a beta. He hadn't earned the gray at his temples by wis-dom or gravitas but by worrying about what others were going to do.

"So how long you known the chief?" Lourdes asked casually, as if it was a throwaway question.

"Why does that matter?" Brendan peered inside the coffee bag but didn't reach in.

"Because when you work with people, sometimes you develop a social relationship." She shrugged. "Look at me and Agent Bogdan. This weekend we're going to a Balkan music festival together."

Bogdan just stared at her, nonplussed, monobrow pasted into place, not quite going with the riff, but not blowing it up either.

"So I'm guessing you have a social relationship with the chief that extends outside of work," she said. "I know you guys come from the same town. Right? Did you know him before?"

The information that Joey Tolliver and Brendan O'Mara had gone to school together in Shiloh came straight from one of Leslie Martinez's files. Just a dashed-off note on a torn-off piece of paper with a question mark on it, stuck between the pages of more official-looking documents. Lourdes had almost missed it that day at Shauna's house. And an even more cryptic entry below it: "Why no Ninja Turtle for Brendan? Where was he?!?" Leslie Martinez had sensed there was a lead here but had al-most certainly died not knowing what it could be. So a very good ques-tion had remained suspended for twenty-one years. Until right this second.

"How is that even remotely relevant?" Brendan looked back and forth between them, trying to read the room. "Where are you going with this, detective?"

"Have you ever been to the chief's house or his father's place in Rockaway?" Bogdan broke in.

"Of course not." The lawyer huffed. "What kind of stupid question is that?"

"So you weren't there in Rockaway, on the night of Hurricane Sandy?" Bogdan said.

"What the . . ." Brendan's voice cracked as he looked around, like someone just realizing he was ticklish. "Why would I be driving around in the middle of a hurricane?"

"*Exactly.*" Lourdes nodded. "You'd have to be nuts to be out on a night like that. Or have no choice."

"What is this conversation really about?" Brendan pushed back in his chair.

"You'd remember if you were out in the middle of a storm like that?" Bogdan said, ignoring the question. "Wouldn't you?"

"Okay, that's enough." Brendan stood. "I don't know what you people think you're up to, but I won't allow it. I'm the attorney of record here and if you're trying to do some kind of end run to interrogate me instead of my client, it's not going to fly."

"Sit down, Mr. O'Mara," Lourdes said.

"I don't think you're in any position to be giving *me* orders, detective." Brendan threw back shoulders that didn't quite fill out his jacket.

"Mr. O'Mara, you're aware that Agent Bogdan works for the FBI." She made a point of barely looking at him as she spoke, as if he was unworthy of her full attention. "And I'm sure you're also aware that lying to a federal agent is a crime. You could not only lose your law license, you could go to prison for five years."

"You don't have to explain the law to me." Brendan raised his voice. "I know just what's at stake here."

"Do you?" Bogdan asked, taking the folder that Lourdes handed him.

The agent opened the file and laid out the two photos, both night-time shots with 10/29/12 date stamps and both clearly showing the rear license plate of Brendan's Land Rover as it went through the tolls toward Rockaway.

"You would have thought the cameras wouldn't be working because all the street lights were out." Lourdes turned to Bogdan, as if this was just a matter that would only concern them. "But I guess the generator must have kicked on for the toll plaza. Because these pictures are clear enough."

Brendan stood stiffly, holding on to the back of his chair, his face turning the color of a crushed cigarette.

"This must be some sort of mistake," he said.

Lourdes took her time, walking around the table, sitting down across from him, crossing her legs, looking up, and breezily letting him know he was screwed.

"There's no mistake," she said, taking the second document from Bogdan and laying it down in front of him. "We also know you got a traffic ticket outside Albany on the day an investigator named Leslie Jesperson got shot to death there."

"I need to speak to an attorney of my own," Brendan said, no longer just ruddy complected but something very close to purple.

"That's certainly your right." Lourdes pushed the photocopy of the ticket at him. "But if I were you, I wouldn't want to tip the chief off that your interests may start to diverge. Just tell him that he needs a real defense attorney at this point, not just a union lawyer."

"I can't believe this is happening." Brendan seemed to be having trouble breathing. "A traffic ticket doesn't prove anything."

"Here's what we're going to do," Lourdes said—no need to get into the full crushing argument yet. "We're going to talk a little longer. Then we're going to go back in that room and you're going to act like everything's fine. You're going to assure the chief that it's all under control, and the change of attorneys is for his own good. He's going to go to his office and you're going to go back to yours. And then we're going to meet up again and have a much more real conversation about your friend."

"You can't use me against him." Brendan shook. "I'm his lawyer. There's attorney-client privilege . . ."

"Yeah, fuck that," Lourdes said, done playing nice. "That privilege doesn't apply here. We know you guys went to high school together and you've known each other all your life. We're talking about acts *before* you were his lawyer. And you'll find a reason to get yourself recused, so none of your ongoing discussions will be privileged."

"But you don't understand what you're asking me to do." Brendan had started to tremble. "I might lose my license . . ."

"We're a long way past that exit, counselor."

She tried to shrug off his concern, but something about seeing a grown man not just scared, but palpably unnerved, like a child on the verge of tears, made her unlock her hands and sit up straight.

"We better get back," she told Bogdan. "If we're gone too long, he'll start to think something is up."

51

Only a handful of people still remembered when the place was called the Brazen Fox. Not that many more recalled closing time at Cheers Too or even the TGI Fridays for that matter. Now the location was a Chipotle—naturally—with what looked to Joey like at least a half dozen illegals behind the counter, veggie options, and "responsibly raised meat" on the menu, and those tall tables with the high chairs that made you feel like you were dangling and off-balance while you were eating.

He was near the back with Kenny Makris and Plunger. Buzzing and sweating in his chief's uniform, blue shirt sticking to his back, jaw sore from grinding his teeth.

"No one's cutting anybody's lifeline." Kenny paused from fussing with his rice and beans. "But I'm not going to lie either. The senator is concerned about where this is going."

"Tell Steve Snyder that I have done *nothing wrong*," Joey said, for maybe the third time since they'd sat down. "This fuckin' little dago bitch Robles is just looking to get another white man's scalp on her belt and she thinks mine's worth more because I happen to be a chief."

"A lot riding on this, Joey." Mr. DA looked down into his bowl—three decades in public life and the aging altar boy still had trouble meeting your eye. "The president's coming out next week for a big speech and Steve promised him a solid backdrop of blue uniforms and smiling faces. Something breaks right before he arrives, it's not going to be good for any of us."

"What's going to break?" Joey stooped his shoulders. "More rumors? Kenny, I can't catch every piece of trash in the wind. All I can do is pick it up after it's landed and put it in the garbage where it belongs."

"What's your sense of things, Brendan?" The DA looked over at Plunger. "How close is the task force to making an arrest?"

"Why the hell you asking him?" Joey lowered the burrito he'd been trying to hold together. "Last time I checked, I was still chief of the police department."

Again, they fell into that little pocket of quiet while everyone else in the restaurant was still talking. Like they were waiting for a noisy train to pass overhead.

"My office just got hit with four more subpoenas for cases you were involved in as a uniform officer." Kenny leaned across the table. "Obviously, someone is talking to them, a lot, and giving them information that supports probable cause. Brendan is as likely as you are to hear who that is through back channels."

"I got nothing for you." Plunger showed empty hands.

Joey stared at him for an extra beat. Still uneasy with him since Robles had called him into the other room and Plunger had come back looking like an Eagle Scout with a hard-on and saying that this was beyond what he should be handling as a union lawyer, and Joey should reach out to a more seasoned criminal defense attorney to handle these overly aggressive inquiries.

"Kenny, can't you see what this is?" Joey dropped the burrito in a heap. "It's politics, pure and simple. These fucking libs from the city want to expand their failed policies, so we'll be overrun with rampant crime, illegal immigrants, and street drugs like they are. That's why they put a fat little Hispanic female with no intelligence or real experience on this so-called task force and let her boss around a bunch of dickless wonders who ought to know better. Don't tell me you're falling for this too."

It made him a little crazy, the way neither of them looked at him or said anything after he was done talking. What was he, a pariah?

The sweat on the back of his shirt turned cold and the roof of his mouth felt dry. He'd started getting high again on and off, after the hurricane disaster with the girl a few years ago, but this was the most consistently he'd been using in years. Mostly weed to take the edge off, but cocaine was slipping back into the mix as well. It heightened his situational awareness and helped him stay alert to the threat of potential enemies in the vicinity, but at times it gave him sensory overload to the point of distorting reality.

He noticed how the court officers at the next table turned their backs as they carried their bags away. From the kitchen, the sounds of stainless steel utensils banging on counters and cooks calling out to each other in Spanish made him clench his fists and press his fingernails into his palms.

He turned and watched as Plunger kept unfolding and refolding his fajitas, trying to keep all the elements together. He didn't like how long Brendan had been alone with Robles and that one-browed yak from the FBI. And he didn't like the way Brendan had started recommending expensive private lawyers he should use, instead of handling this as a union matter.

In practical terms, there should have been nothing to worry about. Plunger couldn't implicate Joey in any of the other murders without the risk of Joey turning around and ratting him out for Kim and the more recent girl.

On the other hand, people under pressure in a criminal investigation didn't always think practically. If they'd gotten in trouble because they'd panicked in the first place, they might do it again. They might be induced to act against their own best interests. They might start talking when they should have kept their mouths shut. They might turn on their allies. They might come apart and spill like the flour roll coming apart in Plunger's hands.

Not for the first time, he thought about slapping a GPS on Brendan's car and hacking his cell phone, to see who he was talking to. But as he watched rice and onions ooze out between his friend's fingers, he realized that might not be enough. Other people could be spilling as well.

He needed to get ahold of the situation and put Robles in her place. As soon as this meeting was over, he was going to call his own man Ramirez and see how he was doing with the sister situation.

"J, take it easy," Plunger said. "People are starting to give us the stink eye."

Joey dabbed his mustache with a paper napkin. "All I'm saying is there's nothing to any of this." He addressed Kenny in a more modulated voice. "We've been over it. The girl who washed ashore in Rockaway was an escort who got mixed up with the gangs. The rocks in her throat were a message to someone else to stop snitching. She was probably murdered in Queens and NYPD is playing a numbers game by trying to keep it off their ledgers."

"Then what about all these others?" Kenny said. "They've asked the office about cases going to the 1980s. It's not all a numbers game. Is it?"

"For Chrissake, open your eyes." Joey crumpled the napkin in disgust. "Nassau *might* have had a serial back then dumping bodies on our side of the line, to fool the Keystone Kops over there. But if you subtract Rockaway, it's obvious that he hasn't been active in years. He's either dead, locked up for something else, or retired."

"*Retired?*" Kenny shot him a withering glance. "I didn't know serial killers retired. Do they get a pension?"

"You know what I'm saying." Joey didn't bother trying to ingratiate himself with a smile. "They stole this case from Nassau and now they've got nothing. So they're grasping at straws, trying to make it look like they have something."

"Maybe not." Kenny took off his glasses and rubbed them with his tie; no wonder he'd never run statewide. "Sounds like they've got multiple sources. They already had your time sheets and entries from logbooks of over thirty years ago. They're deep into this."

"Oh, now we're really off in the ozone." Joey shoved his plate away. "What do you want me to say about that, Kenny? You know who I am."

"Do I?"

Kenny had his chin down as he spoke the words. Like he was talking to himself.

"Of course you do," Joey said. "I put you where you are."

He shouldn't have even had to say it out loud. To either of them. Not after he'd kept Brendan off the hook for what happened to Kim Bird Dog that night. Not after he'd started dropping hints to Kenny that he might have seen the son of then–district attorney Philip O'Mara in the vicinity of the football field at the time of the murder, but might be able to conveniently forget that minor detail, information that allowed Kenny to have a frank conversation with his boss behind closed doors, which in turn led to Philip O'Mara's surprise decision not to run in the next election cycle. Clearing the way for Kenny to run for DA himself.

"And I put *you* where *you* are," Kenny reminded him. "And right now I am telling you that you are getting much too close to the flame. I need it put out, *stat*, before the whole house burns down."

"What do you want me to do, Kenny? Polygraph everyone in my department to find out who the leakers are? Let's be honest. I might be better off polygraphing everyone at *your* office. What do you think of that?"

Kenny's face pruned up like a wet fingerprint.

"Just shut this down." Kenny wiped his hands. "I don't need to know the who or the how. Just keep it away from me. It's gone too far already."

"What about loyalty, Kenny?" Joey looked up. "What about all I've done for you?"

"We settled our accounts when you got appointed chief. Now clean up this mess before it gets on anyone else." The DA started to turn toward the glass doors and then stopped to turn back. "Oh, and a word to the wise? I wouldn't try to put this lunch on your expense account, if I were you."

52

NOVEMBER
2017

The cell phone on the night table started ringing right after Lourdes finally fell asleep. The clock said 11:37 as she fumbled to pick it up and croaked hello.

"Hey, baby. What you wearing?"

The voice was a white man trying to sound black, almost like he was channeling Jay-Z or the dude who did the cook's voice on *South Park*.

"I don't know, chief." Lourdes switched the cell phone to her left hand and turned on the recording app. "What are *you* wearing?"

He laughed, a little more at ease than she would have liked.

It was a couple of days since they'd had Tolliver in the interview room and pulled his lawyer out for a secret-squirrel side deal. Since then, Lourdes had been going at the case full tilt, 24/7, ratcheting up the pressure on Brendan O'Mara to officially sign a cooperation agreement committing him to testify, working with the federal prosecutors to justify more subpoenas, and trying to pinpoint where "Joey," as he was known, would have been assigned when various women disappeared over the years.

The pieces were forming but not quite coming together yet. Brendan had hired his own lawyer, slowing down the process several steps. Kenneth Makris was trying to get the newer subpoenas quashed. And even cops who'd long since left the job were reluctant to talk about Tolliver in any real detail.

"Let me tell you something," a retired detective named Mullins had informed Tierney and Bogdan. "Most cops out here are honest but no

one's going to talk to you willingly, because Joey's got something on everyone. Shit, man, you ever get in his house, you'll probably find a closetful
of J. Edgar Hoover's dresses in the attic."

Most of the officers they spoke to had either been kept far enough
away not to know anything about Tolliver or sounded like they were still
working for him, asking more questions than they answered. It was more
like investigating a mob boss or a military dictator in a separate country,
someone with the means to control and intimidate not just regular witnesses but officers of the law. Which meant right now that the case was
not so much at a standstill but at a dangerous standoff.

"So is this really you, Chief Tolliver, or are you just some lackey doing
the dirty work for him?"

She got up and closed the bedroom door so as to not wake Mitchell,
who was already dealing with this more than he was dealing with his own
assigned cases and getting pushed up against the edge of his own consid-
erable tolerance.

"I'm your special friend, my lady," the voice said, with a hint of digi-
tization as if it was being run through some mechanism to disguise it.
"The only one who understands you."

"Riiight."

She settled back down on the couch, wearing Izzy's baggy old Derek
Jeter hoodie and wool socks. Stacks of files and notebooks covered the
coffee table in front of her.

"Your sister says hi, by the way," he said.

"Does she?" She reached for a pad and a ballpoint pen to start taking
notes.

"Izzy, right? Short for Ysabel. Dizzy Miss Izzy. I like that."

"Do you now."

Head games. She wondered if any of the men on the task force were
getting nasty calls like this at home. Or if this was just some personal
hang-up Tolliver had about her.

"Yo, your girl be cray-cray," he said. "Like I see why you all don't
wanna have kids of your own. Seeing how her and your moms turned out."

She pulled down the hem of her sweatshirt, feeling a shiver of expo-
sure. As if he could somehow see her in the living room, through the window of their fifth-floor walk-up.

"Wow, I'm *so* impressed," she said in a bland white-girl voice. "You got all this inside information about me from reading a Missing Persons alert that only went out to, like, every police department in the tristate area. You must be some kind of Master Sleuth."

He laughed again. "Yeah, baby. Just tell yourself that's all it is. Ain't nothin' but a ho thang."

"What is?" She put down the pen for a second and reached for her wineglass.

"That's all your sister is. *A ho.* Which is why they locked her up on Long Island. And it's all your mami is. And deep down, you know it's all you really are."

"Uh. That hurts, stud."

She realized her grip was too tight, threatening to pop the head off the stem.

"Hey, chief." She swallowed the dregs. "Seriously now—this is me speaking to you from the heart. Is this how you worked when you were a street cop? Because if I could have got away with shit this lame, I would have moved on to your department years ago. Your standards must be low."

"Trash talk." He gave a kind of happy mellow sigh. "Now that's what I like."

She put the glass down and reached for the pen again. He was right. What was getting accomplished here? Maybe he was just probing her for weaknesses, to see where she was with the case, when she should have been turning the screws on him. Or maybe he was trying to see what it would take to intimidate her.

"You sound tired, baby." There was crackling around his voice, like he'd moved to a different location.

She wondered where he was calling from. His home? An office? A safe house his department used for witnesses? The subpoenas had given them a partial list of properties he owned but it would take a while to get the full picture.

"I am tired," she said. "I'm tired of this case and I'm tired of this conversation. Why don't you tell me something interesting for once."

He let out a lower, more feral little chuckle. "Oh, that's good," he said. "I like to be teased. Your sister's a prickteaser. Did you know that?"

"Yeah, that's classy. How would I know that? And how would you know it?"

"You still don't believe she's here with me?"

"Put her on. Why don't you?"

There was a muffled female voice in the background. A little theatrical, Lourdes tried to tell herself.

"She's tied up right now," he said. "Maybe I'll let her talk to you in a little while."

"You're boring me, chief. This is some lame-ass internet porn shit you're playing in the background. If you bored the ladies you killed this much, they must have been glad when you finally put them out of their misery."

"Girl, you so hard," he said. "Why you so bad?"

Something about his cadence reminded her of Izzy. She told herself it was just a generic imitation of a typical ghetto girl, meant to unnerve her.

"Whatever it takes, chief. Whatever it takes."

"Why you keep calling me 'chief'? Would you like me to be in charge? I bet you would. I bet I could make you call me 'daddy.' "

"That's so pathetic. If I wasn't about to lock you up for these murders, I'd nail you for harassment."

"Aii, *mami*. Lourdes be picking on me again."

Her knees came up under her chin. Where did he get the exact words her sister would have used?

"Nice try," she said. "You been watching the *telenovelas* on Univision in your office?"

"You know, Izzy told me why you wanted to be a cop."

Something low, guttural, and overly intimate in his voice stopped her this time. As if the connection had suddenly become clearer and he was talking to her from the next room.

"Yo, why don't you shut the fuck up about things you don't know?" she said.

"Izzy told me the whole story." She could almost feel his rancid breath in her ear. "That was some fucked up shit."

"I will fuck you up and make you cry if you mention her name again."

Mitchell had come out of the bedroom, awakened by her raised voice. She realized her throat was raw and a hot tear was rolling down her cheek.

The hand holding the cell phone was getting clammy and unsteady against the side of her face.

"It was the night they locked Papi up, right?" He'd started laughing again and going heavier with his hood voice. "They was all them po-po in the house with they guns and shit."

"I don't know where you're going with this, chief." She turned her back on Mitchell, who was beckoning for her to put the phone down. "Or where you're getting it, but—"

"And Papi be down on the floor with the cop's foot on his neck and he be all mad and shit, talking Spanish and English. And then he be like, 'We gotta do this in front of *mi familia*, hombre? Why you gotta humiliate me in front of my daughters?'"

Every word, exactly as it was. An invasion so vivid and visceral that it felt like he was on the couch beside her, with a sweaty hand down her shirt.

"And Izzy, she be losing it, yo." He'd started to giggle. "Because she, like, really believed in your daddy. She idolized him. She thought he was some kind of hero to the people in the neighborhood who looked up to him. She didn't know he was just a scumbag drug dealer, who kept selling even after your brother died from an overdose. His own son, in an urn on the mantle. But now here he be, down on the rug, begging the po-po not to shame him in front of his wife and kids. And you know what I think?"

"I don't give a fuck what you think." Her voice broke.

"I think Izzy started to lose her fucking mind that night, from seeing her daddy like the dog he was. Your mami too . . ."

"Fuck you, Tolliver. I'ma kill you."

This was mental terrorism. Somehow he'd bypassed her defensive fortifications and gotten in her head.

"But *you*, L. Ro., you was being all strong and shit. Not falling apart like your moms and sister. 'Cause you had *the heart* to go against your own blood. You weren't going to be like them. You weren't going to fall apart and cry like a fuckin' bitch. You was ready to crawl right into that big white policeman's lap, do whatever you had to do to survive, because he was the one with the big fucking gun and his foot on your daddy's neck. You would've licked that whole fucking barrel in front of Papi if that officer told you to, because that's the kind of girl you were. And still are."

"You don't know shit about me." She was on her feet and shouting, not caring that Mitchell looked terrified. "Next time I see you, I'ma fuck you up . . ."

"And that's when the officer asked you, 'What do you want to be when you grow up, little girl?' And like a good compliant little bitch, you said, 'I want to be a police officer.'" He wasn't laughing anymore. "Now you know that was so long ago that the officer who said that is probably dead and gone. And so Izzy's the only other person who could have heard what you said that night. And if I know it, she must have told me. *Willingly.* So why don't you just think about that a little before you go back to your squad all fired up about kicking anyone's ass? Maybe you want to take a step back and put that shit in perspective. Sleep on it, muchacha. I'll see you in my dreams."

The line went dead. She looked down and saw that the recording app had paused three seconds into the conversation, losing the rest. She'd either accidentally hit the pause button or he'd found a way to turn it off remotely. She threw the phone down at the sofa cushions. Then just this once, she let Mitchell sit down beside her and stretch out his skinny pale arms, so she could collapse against him.

53

Joey rolled up his Escalade window, not liking how the two Arab women in ghostlike headscarves were staring as they walked past him on the sidewalk.

It was almost midnight in Lourdes Robles's Brooklyn neighborhood. The light in her fifth-floor window was still on. Probably crying to her boyfriend about what she'd just heard. Maybe fixing herself a drink. It'd taken a while, but he'd gotten to her with the phone call. Maybe rattling her enough to get sloppy and make a mistake.

An NYPD blue-and-white sector car cruised past him, and he lowered the binoculars he'd been looking through. Then a couple of dog-walkers looked through his window. He hadn't expected there to be this many people on the street. In the districts where his own officers normally patrolled, it was mainly prostitutes and pushers out at this hour. But here came the pub-crawlers, bike riders, families doing their wash at all-night Laundromats, and pain-in-the-ass bystanders of some hard-to-determine ethnicity hanging out on their stoops, talking idly. Any idea he'd had about grabbing Robles up as she was coming out of her building was on hold now. Too many eyes on.

He ground his teeth and sniffed through his nose, wishing he'd brought something to take the edge off. Maybe a couple of Lorazepam, just to calm himself. He'd tried going back on the tranquilizers a few years back but had started to worry they had been making him fuzzy. Maybe he needed to go back on them to balance off the excessive amount of coke he'd been doing the last few days. The newer blow heightened his awareness, which was a definite plus, but had its downside in terms of sleep deprivation and making judgment calls, so those were factors to consider.

Once the sector car passed, he raised the binoculars again. She was at the window, looking down at the street. "I'ma kill you," she'd said. After she knew he had her sister. This woman was an existential threat to his world he realized. An asteroid about to crash into his planet. She was the one driving this. She'd grabbed hold of the Rockaway case and steered it out to Long Island. She'd connected all the bodies along Sunrise Highway. She'd tracked down these lying whores and then wouldn't take the hint when his officers pulled her over on the highway. And she'd had the gall, the fucking *cojones*, to confront him publicly and make this a personal issue.

He had half a mind to pull his Glock and fire a round up at her right now. But from the distance, all he'd probably do was bounce a bullet off her building and get himself on a street camera driving away in a panic. He had to get a grip, slow it down, think more strategically. Scientists talked about asteroid belts. Systems in space. They had to be disrupted to change the gravitational field and isolate the problem.

Bright white light began to fill the interior of his vehicle. For a second, he thought the combination of drugs and adrenaline was giving him a coronary event. Jesus, don't let me die in this city. Suburban police chief found alone and dead in his car. Parked in Brooklyn for no explicable reason.

No.

He would not allow that. He was still in charge of his own fate. It was his story, not hers. He'd eliminate the existential threat, but he'd do it *intelligently*. The way he always did. Not by trying to shoot an asteroid with a handgun. But by understanding the system around it, first.

He realized the light flooding his vehicle was from the police car coming around the corner again, to see why he was still parked here. He lowered the binoculars just as he saw Robles move away from her window. Then he gave the officers in the sector car a friendly wave, started his engine, and began the long drive back out toward his home base, going precisely two miles under the speed limit.

Before Plunger even came downstairs the next morning, he could sense there was something different in the house. A presence that wasn't supposed to be there. He walked in to the kitchen and found Joey sitting in what would usually be the head of the family's chair at the table, talking to his wife and children.

"Good morning, sleepyhead." J raised the coffee mug that Brendan Jr. had made in ceramics class. "How were your dreams?"

The kids were dressed for school. Cathy was in her purple workout clothes. The clock on the microwave said quarter to eight. Everything appeared regular. Except J was here. Which meant dreamtime was over now.

The illusion that he could be someone else. That he could live a normal life, and put the rest of it in separate compartments. The night behind the football field, the mistakes he'd made with those women when he thought he could get away with the same things Joey had gotten away with all these years, and the disaster during the hurricane. Those were the stark realities of his life. All these other episodes—the marriage, the kids, the house—they were illusions. Dreams that were bound to fade. Now Joey was sitting before him and staring at him, like no time at all had passed between the moment when he'd realized Kim was no longer moving and this very second some forty years later.

"I know one of your cars is in the shop and you're shorthanded," Joey said with a smile that dropped Plunger's organs into an acid bath. "I figured I'd stop by, see if there was anything I could do to help out."

"We're good." Plunger tried to match the grin. "We're covered."

"Joey was saying he could give the kids a ride on his way to work," Cathy said, cheerful and oblivious. "And then you can give me a ride to that early spin class I wanted to get to."

She was so checked out sometimes that Plunger wondered if both kids were on the spectrum because of her genes. Other times, though, he admitted to himself that something must have always been off on his end. Otherwise, how would he have let Joey take over so much of his life?

"Or the other way around." Joey put the mug down. "I can give Brendan a ride to his office, and Cathy can drop the kids before the class. That way you don't have to do everything at once."

It was over now. Joey was going to take him somewhere and kill him. And if Plunger refused to go for the ride, Joey would come back to the house later and kill all of them. And make it look like Plunger had gone crazy and murdered the wife and kids before taking his own life. Either way, it was done.

"It would take a load off my mind," Cathy said, as the kids nodded.

"You sure?" Plunger looked at J.

"Hey." Joey shrugged. "It's what I do."

54

This time the phone started vibrating much later in the night, disrupting Lourdes's REM cycle, like someone had patched the call straight into her unconscious state. She'd been standing on Rockaway Beach with Sullivan, helplessly watching a baby float by in the water, when she heard the buzzing. Then she forced her eyes open in the dark and felt around for the phone on the night table, croaking, "Hello?" in a voice that sounded like a coffin lid opening in some old vampire movie.

"Lourdes?"

She looked around in the pitch black of the bedroom, trying to get oriented. The red numbers 3:33 hung suspended, like the digital clock was in outer space instead of just on Mitchell's side of the bed. Outside the window, the lights of the Verrazano-Narrows Bridge glowed softly and a few lonely drivers headed off toward Staten Island.

"Ysabel? *Eres tu?*"

Lourdes sat up on the edge of the bed, putting her bare feet on the cold floor, still trying to figure out if this was real. She'd been about to cry out in the dream as she saw the baby drift away and her heart crumbled as she realized she wasn't enough of a swimmer to go after it.

"*Sí, soy yo.*"

Lourdes fumbled to put on the night-light, still not entirely convinced she was awake. She and Izzy rarely spoke Spanish to each other, even when they were kids, because Papi always wanted them to talk like regular Americans. It was Mami, more high-strung and prone to outbursts, who sometimes let fly in the mother tongue.

"*Dónde estás*, Izzy?" she demanded. "Where the fuck are you?"

"Uh, I don't know, Lourdy," her sister said in her more familiar, spacey way. "They got me checking into this place, Kings Park Psychiatric. But it seems kinda sketchy."

"Wait—*what?*"

Mitchell was stirring, little muscles moving in his pale freckled back. This was really happening. It was 3:34 in the morning, her feet were on the floor, there was traffic on the bridge, and her sister, who'd been missing for nine months now, was on the phone, calling from a blocked number.

"Izzy, who are you with?" Lourdes asked.

There was no answer—just what sounded like a long intake of breath on the other end, too long for a normal human being to sustain.

"Are you still there, *mi hermana?* I'ma come get you."

Lourdes was on her feet, looking for her pants on the floor, her shirt on the chair, and her gun in the closet.

"Izzy, *qué pasa?* Are you okay?"

But the silence just continued, as if it would never stop. As if it had never really stopped and she had just imagined this fiercely desired reunion with her sibling.

"Don't be that girl." Mitchell was awake and blinking at her.

"What girl?"

"The girl who gets in trouble trying to save the day on her own."

The little sister was actually bigger and slower-moving than Robles, Joey had noticed. Walking with a beleaguered waddle with her hands clasped to her big belly. Dimmed and confused either by medication, street drugs, or some combination that made her seem like she was trying to walk around underwater with the oxygen tank strapped to her front. No wonder she hadn't tried to run when Ramirez and the little off-duty team he'd put together found her the other night, sleeping with other homeless people beneath an underpass near Huntington Station. She could barely put one foot in front of the other.

Under the sodium vapor lights of Kings Park, he watched Charlie Maslow Jr. take the throwaway phone from her and then put a hand on top of her head as he pushed her into the back of the squad car. A side of him still thought maybe he should just take full custody and get rid of her, making sure no one would ever find her again. But her current condition reminded him directly of Renee and he knew he wouldn't be able to abide killing a woman in this state.

"She still looks pretty wack." He turned to Ramirez.

"Yeah, she's been living rough for a while," Ramirez said, looking at the abandoned psych hospital shrouded in mist at the edge of the state park. "She could use three hots and a cot for a few more days."

"Put her in the system under the street alias she was using," Joey said. "Then let's get her into the special housing unit. Have them put her in the bing."

"Sir? The *bing?* Solitary? Under what charge?"

"Officer Ramirez, I shouldn't have to spell this out." Joey tried to shame him with a look. "That woman is a known prostitute. We're going to say she assaulted several officers in the course of resisting arrest. She's obviously off her meds and is a danger to herself as well as others. Is that clear enough for you now?"

"Yes, sir, but I'm still worried about getting in trouble."

"Your chief has given you an order," Joey said. "Worry about your family and how you're going to feed that nephew of yours if he's not getting deported."

"Yes, sir."

Joey stood in the parking lot and watched Ramirez trudge off to the squad car. And then waited for the red taillights to glide away and disappear in the night.

Don't be that girl. She wanted to smack Mitchell when he said it. Like she was going to act like some bubble-brain chick detective in a TV show or a movie, rushing out to the location on her own and getting grabbed up by the bad guy. Fuck that. Despite the fact that her pulse was triple-timing and she was having trouble catching her breath, she tried to be calm and deliberate about what she needed to do.

She called the other members of the task force one at a time to tell them about the call, even leaving a message for B.B. She didn't even blow her top when Danny Kovalevski admonished her for not recording the call, like that was something he would have thought of if he'd been woken up from a dead sleep, under the most stressful conditions imaginable.

Instead she took a deep breath and asked him if it was possible for the
Nassau County police's Emergency Service Unit to head out to Kings Park
and start the search for her sister without alerting Joseph Tolliver's subordinates in Suffolk County, where the hospital in the park was located. And
she didn't squawk or fall into name-calling when Danny said it would be
tricky but he'd see what he could do.

Then she made a cup of coffee and called her aunt Soledad to tell her
what was going on. By six in the morning, the sun was starting to rise
and Mitchell sat with her awhile, quietly holding her hand to try to keep
her cool. At 6:26, Danny called her back and explained the situation out
on the Island. The Kings Parks Psychiatric Center, where Izzy said she
was being checked in, had been closed since 1996, when most of its pa-
tients had been transferred to Pilgrim Psychiatric Center in Brentwood.
The facility itself was actually a series of buildings, most of which had
been demolished. A couple of structures remained standing, including a
forbidding, ivy-covered, thirteen-story hospital that was officially the jurisdiction of the Park Police and would be dangerous and time-consuming
to search because of structural and lighting issues. In the meantime, a
couple of ESU teams from Nassau had quietly encroached on Suffolk's
territory and conducted grid searches across the state park where the hospital once stood. They had found no sign of Ysabel so far.

"You sure you didn't just imagine her calling?" Danny asked. "So far,
there's no cell phone pings from the area in the time frame you gave us.
And you know you been a little on edge lately . . ."

She hung up abruptly and called Sullivan.

Joey sat in his Jeep, just outside Kings Park near the Nissequouge River,
monitoring transmissions from the state police and the Nassau County
cops. Of course, those sons of bitches were going to try to keep him out
of the loop and prevent him from knowing what was going on. But with
all the communication systems that had been set up to handle cross-
jurisdictional issues and car chases that went across county lines, there
was no way they could shut him down completely.

"I think she made it all up," a sergeant from Nassau was saying on
channel 3 of his radio band. "The woman's a goddamn pain in the ass, at
the best of times. But now I think she's gone off the deep end."

"You hear she's threatening to come out with a team and conduct her own search?" a lieutenant from the local state police barracks responded.

"Hey, it's a free country," the Nassau sergeant said. "Or at least it was last time I looked. As long as it's on her budget, not ours, she can go to hell and back as far as I'm concerned."

Of course, she wasn't going to be *that girl*, traipsing around an abandoned state mental hospital by herself. Instead she waited until eight in the morning and had Mitchell walk her to the Camry, which was parked on Fourth Avenue with Sullivan's "Erin Go Bragh" sticker on the back window. Then she drove out to Kings Park with a plan, arranging to meet Tierney, Bogdan, and whoever else they could muster in the parking lot off St. Johnland Road to do their own search.

Just as she turned off the Sunken Meadow Parkway, she decided to call Sullivan again from the car, having rejected his earlier offer to meet up ahead of time. But the Camry he'd given her was so old that it didn't even have a Bluetooth system in the dashboard and she had to dial the number by hand and put it on speakerphone, all the while aware that she was back on Tolliver's turf and his officers could use any excuse to pull her over again.

"Yeah, I'm on my way," Sullivan said before she could even ask if he wanted to join the posse. "Did you really think you could leave me out of it?"

Naturally she was driving out to see for herself. Ms. Bossy Bitch couldn't trust the men to do the job right without her. But that was exactly what he wanted when he had the sister call her. To get her knocked off her pins and emotional enough to start making bad decisions. He'd hoped she might even be worked up enough to jump in her car and look around for herself. But no, she had to go and call the cavalry. So she wasn't *that* brave or foolhardy.

It was all right, though. He was prepared for this possibility as well. He picked up the radio from the compartment between the seats and keyed into the Nassau police band.

"Guys, this is Sergeant Kovalevski. There's been a change in the tac plan."

It was almost eleven o'clock in the morning by the time Lourdes reached the south end parking lot. Most of the clouds had cleared, leaving a brilliant blue sky overhead. Though Thanksgiving was just a few weeks away, the temperature was in the fifties and there were still people biking through the state park. The grounds were still green and when she turned off the engine, she could hear birds singing through the car windows. Everything was so idyllic that for a few seconds she could almost imagine taking a weekend stroll here with Mitchell and a baby carriage. Until she looked across the lawn and saw the giant, graffiti-covered, red-brick edifice of the abandoned psych hospital, surrounded by a chain-link fence, and remembered with a falling heart that she was here to look for her lost sister.

There was one other car in the lot, a white Jeep with New York plates, but no sign of the other cops. She adjusted her mirrors, to see behind her, trying to figure out what was going on. Tierney and Gallagher had said they were already waiting in the lot when she got off the parkway exit. B.B. and Danny had texted that they were close. And Sullivan was coming from nearby, at the Commack Motor Inn. But something jagged quivered inside her, like a broken tuning fork. She pulled in behind the Jeep and took out her phone, cursing the fact that she wasn't on the radio system out here with the Nassau cops and had to make a call instead. She tapped Tierney's number and checked both side mirrors, making sure no one was coming up behind her.

"Yo, what the fuck?" she said. "Where you guys at?"

"We're in the lot, waiting for you, detective," Tierney replied, a little phlegmatically. "We've been here twenty minutes. Where are *you*?"

"I'm in the lot, by the hospital. I don't see you."

She turned the mirror again and a poultry-legged hiker in shorts with matted hair and an overloaded backpack waved to her before disappearing into a thicket.

"Kovalevski changed the meetup," Tierney said. "We're just down the road at Nissequouge Park lot. Didn't you get that message? It went out on the radio."

"I'm not *on the radio*, dawg." She began looking around more nervously and turned her engine back on. "I'm talking to you on the phone."

She heard a blast of static and anxious male voices on Tierney's end of the line.

"What's going on?" she said. "Talk to me."

"Uh, bad news," said Tierney after a second. "We just checked. Kovalevski says he didn't put anything out on the radio."

She abruptly threw the phone down to put the car in reverse and when she looked up, Tolliver was pointing a gun at her.

"Put your window down and move over," he said. "Or else you're dead and so is your sister."

After 9/11, he'd spent a week of vacation time taking an anti-terrorism seminar taught by a former Navy SEAL in Quantico. So he was pleased with his own speed and efficiency in getting the door open, Tasering her liberally, rear cuffing her, and wedging her faceup between the front and back seats of her car. Then he relieved her of her gun and tossed her cell phone on the pavement, just to be sure no one could track them.

"Let's get something straight." He got behind the wheel and started the engine. "If I wanted you dead, you'd already be dead. Understand?"

"Yes."

"Second thing." He put the car in drive and steered the Camry out of the lot. "I'm not exactly sure how this is going to go. You've put me under a lot of stress with this investigation and I haven't been able to take care of myself or think things through the way I should. So I'm not totally in my right mind. Do you understand that's what you've done to me?"

Binging on coke like it was 1984 and sleeping maybe an hour and a half a night wouldn't do much to clarify anybody's thinking. He was proud he'd done as much as he had, getting the sister into custody and Robles herself hog-tied in the back of the vehicle.

"Yes, I understand," she said in a dutiful voice undergirded by an insolence that he'd make her pay for later.

"So there's a few different ways this can go," he said, putting on the right-hand turn signal as he left the lot, so as not to attract undue attention. "But here's the main takeaway. If I don't get what I want during this ride, it doesn't end well for you."

"Okay."

They had left the state park and were driving along some winding Long Island back road now. She looked up at the windows and saw sky, treetops, sun, birds, and just the occasional street sign. The same view a baby in a runaway carriage would have. Because that was as much control as she had at the moment.

She raised her head enough to look at him in the rearview with his baseball cap, wig, and shades. The other guys on the team wouldn't necessarily recognize him and, except for Sullivan, they probably wouldn't recognize this car either.

"You've been talking to someone about me for your case," he said evenly. "And I want to know who it is."

"Are you putting me on?" She squirmed, her arms pinned painfully beneath her weight.

"No, I'm not putting you on," he said. "Someone's cooperating and I want to know who it is."

"And I would tell you that . . . *why?*"

He pulled up at a stoplight, casually reached back, and zapped her with 50,000 watts again. This time he kept the Taser on her thigh for a good fifteen seconds, so that her bone structure became a system of conduction, her nerve circuitry was in flames, and her whole body shook.

"Here's the deal," he said, putting both hands back on the wheel again. "Your horizons need to change. If you keep lying to me, I will kill you and then I will kill your sister."

"Oh fuck," she groaned, trying to recover. "You're probably gonna kill us anyway so what's the difference?"

"But you can't be sure," he said. "Right? There's just a tiny chance I won't."

"If you say so, chief."

"I like that," he said. "I like it when you call me chief. Makes me not want to hurt you as much. So let's just make it simple. Is it Kenny or my ex-wife, Beth, talking to you?"

He was speaking to her in the kind of quiet, reasonable voice that she used when speaking to skells. The voice she learned from Sullivan, which more often than not worked to persuade criminals that walking to the edge of the abyss and looking down unflinchingly at the reflection of their own worst deeds below was the only way to salvation. She wondered why he didn't mention Brendan O'Mara possibly cooperating.

"What are you, high, chief?" She struggled and cringed as he hit a bump in the road, pulling her joints from their sockets. "Look, you already know the task force guys are out looking for me." She tried to turn it around. "Why don't you make it easy on yourself and pull over now?"

"Nice try." He began to press down on the accelerator a little. "Detective Robles, let me remind you that you are in my jurisdiction now. If something were to happen to you—if, say, your body were to be found dumped in the Long Island Pine Barrens? It would be investigators that I promoted personally processing the crime scene and handling your body. Coroners I play golf with would be cutting you open for the autopsy. If I want to make it look like you killed yourself with your own gun, I could do that."

"Nobody's gonna buy that," she said, trying to talk sense to him. "What about all the burns on my body now?"

"With your family's history of mental illness, that's not a problem." The engine was starting to grumble as he pushed it. "You just made a crazy call reporting that your sister was wandering around in some state park, where there was no sign of her. So it'll look like you've gone off the rails. My friends at the ME's office will say your marks are self-inflicted cigarette burns. Your other injuries they may just conveniently overlook. And everybody will just say you killed yourself because you couldn't stand the humiliation from going after me and failing."

Her conscious mind told her that this was just intimidation, but each bump on the road was registering as a body blow, with her spine and kidneys getting the worst of it.

"Just remember, everybody has a breaking point," he said. "And we're gonna find out what yours is. I'll take you somewhere, make you feel things no woman's ever felt. You'll be begging for the end by the time I'm done."

She realized Sullivan would be wondering what happened to her on the phone. Maybe there was a chance he called this in. Or just as important, that the LoJack subscription he'd tried to convince her to renew on this twelve-year-old car hadn't run out yet, meaning there might be a chance of someone tracking them.

"You want me to tell you who's ratting so you can go and kill them?" she asked.

"Innocent people could get hurt otherwise," Tolliver said. "And that'll be on you."

"Seriously? On *me*?"

Another pothole jolted her spine and threatened to pop both her shoulders out of their sockets. Her arms had almost gone dead from being pinned under her weight.

It was hard to tell how crazy he was right now. The man had literally been getting away with murder for forty years. This manic edge could be a sign of desperation or just the state he regularly worked himself into when he was about to kill someone.

"Save yourself the agony," he said. "Who's been talking to you?"

"Leslie Martinez." She grimaced against the g-force as he kept pushing the speed.

When she opened her eyes, she was looking up at racing clouds that had now entered the blue sky. Cirrus, cumulus, stratus. The clouds she'd learned about in middle school science. "Take On Me" was on the radio. One of the first songs she remembered. The clouds began to thin from winding sheets to diaphanous shreds. This was it. This was what people meant by life flashing before your eyes. Death was in the vicinity and they were rapidly closing in.

"Ho-kay, lady," Tolliver said, mocking her in a cab driver's Puerto Rican accent, foot all the way down on the gas pedal now.

They must have gone to a section of the highway without stoplights. The Toyota engine was shrieking and the chassis was shuddering beneath her. He began swerving wildly. She rolled back and forth on the floor mats that she hadn't gotten around to cleaning for a while. Gum wrappers, empty plastic bottles, and brown paper bags confronted her. The smell of old food and his aftershave turned her stomach. He was giving her a rough ride. Used to torture unbuckled suspects without laying a hand on them. Her joints were tearing and her vertebrae were coming apart. Her eyeballs turning to jelly from all the shaking and her guts in a seasick uproar.

"Look," she yelled out. "I know you didn't do it all alone. Instead of asking who's talking to me, you should be telling me who else was involved on your end."

"Why? You gonna help me mitigate, Robles?"

"I'm just asking."

They suddenly pulled off the road and went into what felt like a parking lot.

"Where are we?" she said.

"We're right outside the DA's office. It's not that far from Kings Park."

"What?" She strained trying to sit up and see if he was telling the truth. "What are we doing here?"

"You're right," he said coolly, slowly cruising around the lot. "I didn't do it alone. Brendan, his father Phil, Kenny, Steve Snyder, my ex. They were all in on it in some way. All the upstanding citizens who got better houses, lower taxes, and fewer people like you next to them. Actually, Brendan killed some of those girls, without me. Maybe just to see what it was like. That's how sick he was. So what I want to know is, which of them turned on me first?"

"Why?" she asked, realizing that the last bump before they turned into the lot had jarred her so much that her cuffed wrists were just slightly below the curve of her ass.

"Because I'm going to kill whoever betrayed me and bring the whole shit house crashing down if I have to," he said, still driving around the lot carefully. "You say the word and I will go into that building, and I will kill Kenny Makris. Because I'm the one who put him where he is. And then I will kill my ex-wife. And then, who knows?"

"You really want to do all that?"

She squirmed, trying to loosen her shoulders and give herself a little more slack to try to get the cuffs down past the rest of that big old butt she was usually so proud of.

"Damn right," he said. "All the fine, responsible folks who got where they are because of me doing their dirty work. Well, it's time to fucking pay up."

This was good that he was talking to her this much, she told herself. He was maybe beginning to see her more as a human being, and less as an object he needed to be rid of. She curled in a little more, the cuffs slipping down over her ass and almost touching her thighs.

"Sure that's the play?" she asked, trying to keep him preoccupied.

"I wouldn't knock it if I was you," he said. "If I go in and kill Kenny, maybe you'll have a chance to be found before I come back. There's like two dozen police cars parked around here. On the other hand, if you let me go in and kill someone for something he didn't do, that'll be your fault."

"Now you're getting too deep on me, chief." She gasped, trying to fold herself up like a jackknife and get the cuffs down to the backs of her knees. "I think you should just give it up."

"Someone's going to die today, Robles," he said with a sort of inarguable finality. "The question is do you want to join them or do you want to give yourself a fighting chance? I know what I'd do if I were you. Kenny Makris? My ex? These are bad people. If you tag one of them so that you or your sister gets to survive, what's the difference? All I'm doing is asking you to tell me who stuck the knife in my back."

He was right. None of these people were the salt of the earth. But she didn't want any of their blood on her hands.

"So why did you do it?" she said, as she brought up her shoulders and started to raise her legs.

"Why did I do *what?*" He adjusted his rearview, trying to see what she was doing as he kept driving.

"Why did you kill all those girls?" she asked.

"I *didn't.* I just told you."

"Oh, come on," she said, as she rolled back on her shoulders and aimed her toes at the ceiling. "You keep asking me to tell you something. Now I'm asking you."

"Oh what, are we in a relationship now, Robles?"

"Wouldn't you want to know if you were me?" The cuffs were nearly down to her heels now, less than two inches from clearing the soles of her shoes.

"Maybe they couldn't be what somebody wanted them to be. Or what they pretended to be . . ." He started to turn around. "Hey, what the fuck are you doing?"

All at once, her shoes were off and the cuffs were in front of her. He reached back blindly, trying to subdue her with one hand while keeping the other on the steering wheel. She got up on her knees, reached over the seat back, and got him around the neck with the handcuff links. He braced, stretched, and bucked, trying to get his fingers under the links.

His foot hit the accelerator and they careened into a guardrail. Lourdes fell back, as she heard the crash of metal on metal and felt her shoulders getting yanked from their sockets.

The airbag deployed and exploded, filling the air with whitish powder and tiny sharp particles. Tolliver was pinned against his seat, hands limp at his sides as if his head hitting the steering wheel had knocked him unconscious.

The car horn sounded. Soon cops would be emptying from the DA's office and the nearby police building. Somehow she still had the cuffs around Tolliver's neck as he remained slumped behind the airbag. Fifteen to twenty seconds compression to render a man unconscious. More than a minute you start thinking about brain damage.

"Robles," Sullivan was approaching from the driver's side.

She realized that he must have tracked her from the LoJack in the car. She ignored him and leaned back, cuffs against Tolliver's windpipe, bracing her feet against the back of his seat for leverage.

"Robles, stop." Sully was at the window now. "He's out."

She pulled with all her weight, until her legs were fully extended and her arms were shaking. Choking the life out of him the way he'd choked all the women.

"Robles, let go." Sullivan was reaching in, trying to stop her. "He's not conscious. This isn't the way."

Sirens were wailing, other cops were coming. They'd be here within seconds. But she pulled back and held on as long as she could. The fat girl staying on her horse. Holding the reins like she was riding Lucky Day to the finish line at Aqueduct and bringing all that beautiful dinero home to mami.

55

It made it slightly easier to deal with the pain when the doctors told her that the cervical herniation they kept mentioning had nothing to do with her actual cervix. She was less pleased when she heard it might require surgery. She also had a concussion, a herniated disc in her lower back, a dislocated right shoulder, a fractured collarbone, numerous cuts and bruises, and a strained Achilles tendon. But once the morphine drip kicked in, it was all good.

Until her sister was shown in.

"Oh shit. You're pregnant? Are you fucking kidding me?"

Lourdes winced as she tried to prop herself up on the pillows and piece the world back together. The East River was outside her window. There was a clip on her finger connected to a heart monitor that had just started beeping. She could hear Mitchell and Soledad talking to nurses out in the hall. Right before the door shut, she caught a glimpse of Sullivan looking even more grim and purposeful than usual. She realized she'd been at the hospital nearly twenty-four hours and had been unconscious for most of them.

"Be happy for me, *mi hermana*," Izzy said. "It's what I always wanted."

The borrowed clothes would have looked tight on her even if she hadn't been carrying a child. Ysabel was back to her shut-in weight, maybe even a little heavier. Her skin looked rough and patchy from months on the street, doing whatever she had to do to survive. Her eyes looked tiny and wayward, which meant it was back to the drawing board in terms of a treatment plan with prescribed medication. But when she put her hands over her big belly, her smile lit up the room.

"*Lo siento.* I'm sorry I ran away, Lourdy. I knew you'd be mad."

"I'm not mad," Lourdes said hoarsely, her mouth desert-dry. "I'm glad you're all right. I love you. That's why I spent so much time looking for you. Now tell me, who the fuck is the daddy?"

"You wouldn't know him."

"Try me."

"He's not in the picture."

Izzy was doing that semi-autistic staring at the floor number. The way she did when she'd broken something. Or was about to break it.

"What does that mean 'not in the picture'?" Lourdes asked, struggling to focus.

"He's not around anymore," Izzy mumbled.

"Whaddaya telling me? Like he left or he's dead?"

"The latter."

"*What?*" Lourdes grimaced, trying to tuck pillows behind her so she could sit up. "What happened to him?"

"I don't want to get into it now." Izzy shook her head. "Something happened in New Jersey while I was with him. The police were looking into it. That's part of the reason I ran away."

"Oh my God."

Lourdes sighed with druggy exhaustion and felt her eyes rolling back in her head, imagining all kinds of terrible scenarios. Like her sister telling some Lothario she was carrying his baby and then clobbering him with a tire-iron when he said he wouldn't stick around. Which would explain her sudden disappearance.

"I know what you're thinking, and it wasn't like that," Izzy said. "I'll tell you about it another time. Right now, you just need to rest and get better."

"Shit . . ." Lourdes sank back on the bed, temporarily overwhelmed. "Just tell me this much. What're you gonna do about the baby?"

"I'm keeping it. Of course. Almost nine months. I'm not getting rid of it or giving it up for adoption."

"And who do you think is gonna help you raise it?"

Without a word, her sister took Lourdes's hand, which was blackened and taped up from the IV needle, and put it on her stomach.

"Feel anything?"

Lourdes pressed gently, eyes practically rolling back in her head.

Her aunt Soledad, who had a crazy sister of her own, had once told her, "Be careful what you wish for; you might get it." Which had never made sense to Lourdes, given where people like themselves came from. But now it did.

"Yeah, it's beautiful, Izzy." She nodded. "Kind of like a miracle."

Exactly. A miracle. The kind that made you feel like crying and laughing at the same time. After all the back-and-forth and agonizing about whether to have a baby, and her bipolar sister shows up with the fait accompli. And now somebody was going to have to deal with the thing.

"Hey, Iz," she said wearily. "I'm super-happy for you. And we got a lot to talk about. But can you give me a little time here?"

"Sure." Her sister gave her a beatific smile that made Lourdes feel like curling into a fetal position of her own. "I'll go wait out in the hall. But I know there's an old guy who's been waiting to talk to you."

"Okay."

Izzy opened the door and Sullivan gave Izzy a long, appraising look as she slid out past him.

"Jaysus," he said, placing a vase of flowers on the radiator. "Like you don't have enough on your plate?"

"Tell me about it."

His hand rested on one of the rails surrounding the bed.

"How you doing?" he asked.

"It's going to be a while until I get back to yoga." She covered his paw with the hand that had the pulse clip on it. "But I'm not retiring."

"You sure? You go out on three-quarters disability for a line-of-duty injury."

"And do what? Stay at home all the time, helping my sister raise her baby? I'm not ready for that yet, boss."

Sullivan frowned. There was no other word to describe what was happening to his face. It was something that could only occur in white men of a certain generation. Not just an expression of disapproval, but the look of someone witnessing the collapse of a whole value system, a crumpling of a map that would need to be carefully straightened and smoothed again.

He took his hands back, went over to close the door, and then returned to sit in a chair beside the bed.

"We have something else to discuss," he said quietly.

"Sully, before we get into anything, I need to talk to the doctors about these drugs they're giving me . . ."

"*No.*" He silenced her with a Mount Rushmore look. "This can't wait. I need to get something straight with you right now."

"Okay." She pressed her palms into her bedsheets, backing up.

"Joseph Tolliver was a bad man and we both know it."

"Right." She felt a tingling down her left leg, a sign that her pain was starting to wake up.

"He killed at least seven or eight women over the course of forty years. He had a major police department, a raft of local politicians, and God knows how many regular citizens terrorized and under his control so he could get away with almost anything."

There was a growing sting in her right shoulder, where the doctors had popped the joint back into its socket while she bellowed like a gored ox.

"And now that he's dead and people aren't scared of him, we're probably going to find out even worse things he did," Sullivan said, in that methodical brick-by-brick voice he used to wall in suspects. "The state attorney general is opening a countywide corruption investigation into what's been going on all this time. Brendan O'Mara has gone missing and Kenny Makris just announced he's retiring to spend more time with his family—which means he's expecting to be indicted any day now. All the rats are leaping from the sinking ship."

"So what's the problem, Sully?" She thrust her jaw out, defying both him and the pain as it tempted her to reach for the morphine again.

"We both know what you did, Robles."

"What did I do?" She kept her chin up.

"We both know he was out cold. You didn't need to keep choking him."

"Says you."

"There's a right way and a wrong way," he said.

"And the right way would've been to turn him over to the system that's been protecting and supporting him for forty years? So they can cut him a break and turn him loose to keep doing it again? No thank you, amigo. I like my way."

"What I saw there in that car wasn't police work."

"Don't even try that, Sully. He was a goddamn serial killer that nobody was stopping and everyone was helping. You're seriously going to blow me in for making sure he was over and out?"

"I was on the job in the old days, when they threw the book out the window and did whatever the hell they wanted sometimes. Hung people out windows by their ankles. Strangled them in the back of squad cars. Beat their heads in with the Manhattan Yellow Pages. And I didn't like it. Because it was like the department that Tolliver ran. Above the law. And people like you were usually the victims." He clasped his hands in front of him and leaned forward. "The attorney general's office is interviewing me later today," he said softly.

She looked up at the heart monitor, to see if the rate had gone up. "What are you going to say?"

"I don't know. All the years I was on the job, I did a lot of things I question now, but I never lied under oath."

"Come on—"

"*No.*" For the first time ever, he was truly angry at her. "Everybody thinks cops have to lie sometimes, but that was where I drew the line. That's how I was brought up. That's who I am. And that's who I intend to be when I go to see my wife and son again. You're asking me to change that."

She shook her head. "I couldn't have let him get away with it again."

"I expect better from you." His voice stopped her like a slap in the face.

"You just told me it was like that in the old days . . ."

"That's not good enough," he raised his voice. "Don't you get it? You're supposed to be *better than me.*"

She looked down. "You don't think they'd let me slide?"

"Not if I tell the truth, they won't."

"Sully . . ."

"But if I lie for you, and say you choked him out during an active struggle? With my record and reputation?" He shook his head. "They'll believe me."

"So what're you gonna do?"

"I don't know." He sucked in his lips. "You were my partner. I have to stand by you. But it doesn't sit right with me. Not at all. Especially not when I have stage 3 prostate cancer and I'm thinking about the life I lived. You can laugh, but a part of me still thinks a lie like that can keep a man out of the place where my wife and son are waiting."

"Sully, I don't know what to say." She put her hands over her face, trying not to cry. "This isn't how I wanted it to end up."

He got up without looking at her and wiped his hands on his pants. "Don't say anything. Just remember, if I do this for you, we're even now."

She sniffed, forcing out a laugh. "If you do it, we'll be more than even."

"All right then." He ambled toward the door. "Enough said. For now."

"I fucking love you, Kevin Sullivan," she blurted out. "If that baby is a boy, he's getting your name."

People in the hall were staring as he opened the door.

"Christ." Sullivan hurried out, ears bright pink as he passed Mitchell. "Look after her, will you? I think your girl's gone mad."

ACKNOWLEDGMENTS

I would first like to thank my agent Richard Pine and my editor Kelley Ragland for their continuing support and enthusiasm.

Honor and dangerous duty pay is due to Marisa Silver, Elizabeth Keyishian, David Denby, and Peg Tyre for reading early drafts and offering their thoughtful comments.

I also want to acknowledge Jesse Kornbluth. Although the book you have in front of you is a piece of fiction, the seed for it was planted many years ago by Jesse's excellent nonfiction work. I should note that the epigraph comes from the song "Neat, Neat, Neat," lyrics by Brian James.

Much appreciation to Dr. Jonathan Hayes, who was there when I needed his sage counsel at the beginning and the end of this process.

I was further aided and abetted by the following accomplices:

Peter Fiorillo, Tania Lopez, Reed Farrel Coleman, Tim Hardiman, Kevin Fox, Sophie Hagen, Lonnie Soury, Maggie Callan, Matthew Perez, Richard Firstman, Michael Quartararo, Thomas Maier, Bruce Barket, Hector DeJean, Paul Hochman, Robert Trotta, Andrew Martin, Joseph Brosnan, Rob Mooney (him again!), Jim Nuciforo, Frank MacKay, Paul Gianelli, and Rob Maitra.

Michael Parmelee

Peter Blauner is an Edgar-winning, *New York Times* bestselling author of seven other novels, including *Slow Motion Riot* and *The Intruder*. He has written for such TV shows as *Law & Order: SVU* and *Blue Bloods*. A former journalist and lifelong New Yorker, his previous book, *Proving Ground*, was also published by Minotaur Books.

20 YEARS OF KILLER READING

MINOTAUR BOOKS